DARK MEMORIES

A NOVEL

OTHER BOOKS AND AUDIO BOOKS
BY JEFFREY S. SAVAGE
Cutting Edge
Into the Fire

SHANDRA COVINGTON MYSTERIES
House of Secrets
Dead on Arrival
A Time to Die

UNDER THE NAME J. SCOTT SAVAGE
Water Keep
Land Keep

DARK
MEMORIES

A NOVEL

JEFFREY S. SAVAGE

Covenant Communications, Inc.

To Kirk Shaw, without whom you would probably not be reading this book. Blame him if it keeps you up too late shivering in the dark.

ACKNOWLEDGMENTS

I WROTE THIS BOOK JUST over ten years ago. Back then, I fully expected that it would see the world (if it did) through a national publisher. Covenant and the other LDS publishers published a lot of genres, but horror wasn't high on that list.

Don't get me wrong, this isn't a blood-and-guts slasher novel. It's more like the scary movies I watched growing up, before everything frightening started turning to blood and guts—when the most terrifying parts of the story took place in your head. But trust me on this: It is scary. The agent I was signed with at the time told me, "I was up until two in the morning with your book. I finished it at eleven. I just couldn't fall asleep until two."

But a funny thing happened on the way to publication. *Dark Memories* didn't get published by a New York house. But a good friend and my editor at Covenant, Kirk Shaw, asked to read it. He loved that it was both terrifying and had a strong redemptive message. And get this— he thought Covenant might want to publish it. Crazy, right? But the craziest thing is that he was right.

It was a long haul, with lots of work. But the amazing people at Covenant believed in the story, and we worked together to bring it to pass. This is a work I am proud of for many reasons. I love the story. I love Cal, the small-town police chief. I love taking a lot of things straight from the little town I live in. (Not the murders, thank goodness!) But most of all, I love the people at Covenant and those in my writing circle and my family who made this book what it is.

So thanks, everyone at Covenant! Thanks, Women of Wednesday Night. Thanks, family. And thanks to those of you readers willing to risk a few hours of lost sleep by giving this story a try. When I write, it is always you I am thinking of.

CHAPTER 1

Twin Forks, Colorado—1977

"WHAT DO YOU MEAN YOU can't find the children?" Paul Andreason pressed his fingers to his temples, wishing for the thousandth time that day he was back in his office signing report cards instead of traipsing after thirty-three second-graders at this abysmally hot class picnic.

"Not *all* of them. Only six." Sheila Bell, a nineteen-year-old teacher's assistant with bushy hair the color of shredded carrots, had a whining, nasally voice that vibrated in Paul's brain like a sour chord.

"I see," he said, glaring into her wide green eyes. If she'd been paying attention to the children instead of pining over the imminent return of her college boyfriend, they would be in the bus and on their way back to the school right now. "That will certainly be of great comfort to their parents when we show up at the school without them, won't it?"

Sheila blinked. "N-no," she stammered. "I'll go look again."

"Yes, you do that." Paul pulled a damp handkerchief from his pocket and mopped at his sweating face.

"No, wait." He called her back and crooked a knobby index finger at the dirty yellow school bus. Its ancient springs shed rust and groaned wearily as the rambunctious children inside bounced about. "You stay with them. I'll find the others."

"Yes, Pastor Andreason."

"*Mister*," Paul grumbled.

"Sorry?" Sheila cocked her head, glancing back toward the bus where a boy with grass stains on both of his elbows hung halfway out the window.

"Never mind." He waved her back to the bus, and she hurried away, pushing the miscreant back through the window just before he could have fallen.

Sheila was a goodhearted girl, if perhaps a little flighty. Paul had spent the entire year trying to explain to her that although he taught a small congregation on Sunday, at school she was to address him as Vice Principal Andreason—or, at the least, *Mr.* Andreason. She'd nod her head and then immediately forget.

"They can't have gone far," he said to himself as he began picking his way through the trampled stalks of waist-high grass. He'd done a count of the bobbing little heads less than an hour earlier, and all the children had been present.

Paul—or Pastor Andreason, as he was known to the roughly six hundred Methodists who made up most of the population of Twin Forks—was a man of integrity. It was his responsibility to see that every last child returned home safely, and he would sooner forget to put on his pants in the morning than neglect his responsibilities for even a moment.

If only it weren't for the blasted sun. It beat down on his balding head like the Inferno itself, giving him a real whopper of a headache. It was the kind of pain that started at the base of his neck and worked its way inexorably forward until it felt like a pair of blunt fingertips trying to jab his eyeballs from their sockets.

Reaching a grove of white-jacketed aspens, he ducked gratefully into the shade and surveyed the narrow stream that gurgled through their midst. During spring runoff, this little brook turned into a raging torrent that could easily carry off a child—or even a full-grown man, for that matter. But now it was scarcely deep enough for the children to wet their feet up to their ankles.

Still, it lifted a weight from his heart to assure himself that they weren't there. He'd seen a drowned child once before—back in the summer of '66 when the Petrie boys capsized their rowboat out in Charity Lake during a fast-moving thunderstorm.

Little Stevie Petrie—now a freshman in college—had managed to hang on to the side of the boat until help could reach him. But eight-year-old David had been washed away by the powerful waves that kicked up quickly in the shallow lake. Three days later, when Paul and the other searchers had discovered the boy's body, his face was a bloated purplish-white mask, and the suckers had been at his nose and fingers.

Paul had no desire to see anything like that again as long as he lived.

Cupping his hands to his mouth, he shouted out the names of the boy and girl who were undoubtedly the ringleaders of the missing group. "Ezra! . . . Amanda!"

He waited for an answer, relishing the cool of the shady spot until it was obvious he would have to return to the blazing heat. Pulling the now-soggy handkerchief from his back pocket, he mopped his red face and trudged up toward the old mining road.

He should have been back at the elementary school preparing year-end teacher evaluations and double-checking the inventory counts before the books and supplies were locked away for the summer. He'd even harbored the secret hope that he could slip out an hour or two early and get a head start to the Castlewood cabin where he and Barbara spent every summer. But that flame of hope had been cruelly extinguished when Betsy Trotwood phoned in sick this morning.

"A terrible head cold," she'd said, hacking several times into the phone for emphasis. "I guess I won't be able to make the end-of-school picnic."

After twenty years in the education system, working his way up from timid first-year instructor to vice principal, Paul could tell a phony cough from the real thing every time. But he couldn't exactly call a fifty-two-year-old teacher on the carpet the way he would one of his pupils—even if he knew for a fact that her cold was no more real than her peroxide-blond hair color.

So instead of making an early exit from his office, he found himself searching for six wayward children on the hottest June day he could remember. It galled him to think that Betsy's no-account husband, Phil, was probably already unpacking his fishing tackle at *their* cabin. But neither the oppressive heat nor thoughts of Phil Trotwood snagging the biggest trout would keep Paul from doing his job.

He paused at the thick iron chain that closed off access to the old Seven Stars Mine. Could the children have headed up there despite repeated warnings to stay in the park?

It was exactly the kind of adventure Ezra would find exciting—but Paul would be flabbergasted if little Frankie Zoeller had gone along with such a plan. Benjamin, Theresa, and Olivia—he could see them tagging behind Ezra and Amanda, who were always getting into one scrape or another. But Frankie was a quiet little fellow who scarcely said *boo*. And he certainly wasn't part of Ezra's crowd.

Paul cupped his hands to his mouth again. "Ezra! Amanda! Benjamin! . . . Frankie!" No answer. Wearily, he raised first one leg and then the other over the chain. He was too old for these kinds of shenanigans.

The road leading to the old mine entrance—overgrown with grass and thistle—was a steep one, and before long his legs were trembling.

Sweat soaked through the back of his shirt and left long dark ovals beneath his armpits. Ordinarily Paul eschewed using the paddle that hung on his office wall, leaving the children's discipline up to their parents—he knew that Ezra's father had no compunctions about cutting off a limber tree limb and using it on his wayward son. But this afternoon, Paul decided, he might make an exception.

The thought that the children might actually have gone *into* the mine had never crossed the vice principal's mind. The Seven Stars was boarded up—had been for years. The school would never have approved this spot for their picnics if that wasn't the case.

The closed gold mine had a rather spotted history. And although Paul knew most of the stories were bunk—fodder for late-night campfires—this much was true: people *had* died in the Seven Stars, and the labyrinthine shafts wound miles into the mountainside. Its crumbling interior was no place for children.

Just as he thought he couldn't take another step, Paul reached the top of the road, his heart hammering. What little gray hair he had left lay plastered against his scalp in a dripping cap. Out of temper and out of breath, he raised his hands for another shout. His fingers stopped just short of his mouth and hung there.

No. No, it wasn't possible. Paul took a shuffling step forward, hesitated, began to take another step, and faltered. His tired blue eyes stared at the mine entrance, unwilling or unable to comprehend what he saw there.

The boards that covered the opening—sturdy two-by-six beams, held in place by long carriage bolts—had been ripped away in several places. Their broken edges stood out like teeth in the stark afternoon sun. And behind them, the mineshaft beckoned, dark as sin.

Paul's paralysis broke in a wave of desperate terror. Forgetting his pain, his weariness, his anger, he raced across the road and over the dusty field to the mine entrance. He was a religious man, and as he ran his mind reached out to his God. *Please,* he mouthed. *Please don't let them be in there. Please, I'll do anything, if only—*

He skidded to a stop, his legs nearly collapsing beneath him. For the first time that day he didn't feel the heat. His body seemed encased in a sheath of frigid, mind-numbing ice as he stared down at the footprints. Looking terribly small and fragile, they clustered around the opening to the Seven Stars mine—and then disappeared into the blackness.

* * *

Long after his wife had fallen asleep, Paul slipped from beneath the blankets. Crouching on the hard wooden floor, he prayed until the joints in his knees became swollen and stiff.

For five days, every able man and woman for one hundred miles around had helped in the search effort. Five long days in which the weight of haunted eyes seemed to linger on Paul wherever he went. Although they never said it to his face, he could hear them asking questions behind his back. *How could he let this happen? Why wasn't he watching them? How can he ever face those poor children's parents?*

"It's not my fault," he told anyone who would listen, wringing his long pale hands together. "I was watching them as closely as any loving parent."

"Not my fault," he told Harvey, the constable, who organized search parties consisting of dozens of men—their hands and faces red and rough from long days spent working their fields. "I was watching them."

"*Not . . . my . . . fault.*" Each evening as the sun, shimmering blood-red, dropped behind the hills to the west, he whispered it over and over to his God.

But as one twenty-four-hour period after another passed with the little ones still missing, doubts began to surface in his mind. Perhaps it *was* his fault. Was it possible that he had allowed his own petty needs to come before the well-being of the children? His confident assurances turned into questions and, finally, pleas.

When he wasn't helping with the search, he was kneeling at the side of his bed begging for mercy on the souls of the lost children. And on his own soul.

Finally, just when all seemed lost, word came that the children had been rescued, and he wept with joy. It was a miracle. But then he learned one was still missing and the news sank into the pit of his stomach like a cold, black stone.

He found he could no longer sleep for more than an hour or two a night. At his wife's urging, he tried the pills his doctor had prescribed. They were supposed to give him rest, but what good were pills against the guilt eating him up inside? Each night he tossed and turned, finally ending up back down on the floor at the side of his bed.

When at last it became obvious to everyone that the boy couldn't possibly be found alive, the search was called off—the entrance to the mine blasted closed.

And Paul began to hear voices.

The childish cries of the five who were found, but especially of the one who was still trapped inside, haunted his nights. He imagined he could hear the little boy calling out to him, begging for rescue from his pitch-black grave.

Now, more than two weeks since the search had been called off, he knelt, praying into the wee hours of the morning. Everything was quiet and the darkness wrapped around him like a death shroud when he thought he could just make out the sound of a child's weeping carried on the still, cool air.

In a trance, he rose to his feet and stepped to the window. There, standing halfway across the front lawn—midway between the house and the driveway—was the boy. The figure wavered in and out of focus so that Paul could actually read the license plate of his Buick station wagon through the child's body, but there was no question of who it was.

Slowly, the boy raised his hands as if in supplication. His eyes, dark emeralds against pale white skin, met Paul's. The suffering Paul saw there, the utter loss, struck him with such unspeakable guilt that he welcomed the hammer-blow of pain that struck his chest. His fingers clamped onto the windowsill, releasing their grip only when his legs collapsed under him.

Hearing the fall, his wife leaped from bed, but it was already too late. Her husband's fifty-seven-year-old heart had stopped beating. The expression on his face, a mixture of horror and relief, was something she would never forget.

CHAPTER 2

Twin Forks, Colorado—2011

WITH A GASP, MANDY OSGOOD woke to absolute darkness. She felt like she was suffocating. She reached out for the switch on her nightstand lamp, twisting it viciously enough to raise blood blisters on the tips of her fingers. The master bedroom at the end of the double-wide trailer remained pitch black.

Fighting off panic, she slapped at the chipped surface of the little wooden table, knocking over a glass of water and sending a plastic bottle of Tylenol PM tumbling before her hands closed around the alarm clock. Its display—the brightest she'd been able to find—was dark.

With one sweat-damp palm, she traced the cord back to where it plugged into the wall. It hadn't come loose from the outlet like it sometimes did, but it was just as dead as the light she always left on when she went to bed.

The power was out. It had happened before—power lines were always breaking under the fierce mountain winds that gusted from the mouth of the canyon—and despite her dread, she'd managed to survive. Only tonight . . . tonight felt different.

For one thing, there was the silence. If a storm had knocked down the power lines, why couldn't she hear wind whistling through the gaps in the trailer's metal siding? That always happened when the gusts came.

Sitting up in bed, clutching the cotton sheet to her chin like a talisman against the night, she couldn't hear a thing. Not even the mind-numbing *reek, reek, reek,* of the crickets, which, along with the mice, seemed to be the only other things capable of surviving out on this crappy little half-acre of land she and Eddie had purchased the year before. It felt as if she were no longer in the trailer at all, but in a dark, dank cave.

That's when she remembered the dream. All the air escaped from her lungs in what should have been a scream, but she only managed to reach a reedy little whimper. *The dream.* She'd been having the dream for the first time since . . . at least since her miscarriage, and that had been back in '98. She'd hoped it was gone forever, but now she could remember it all too clearly.

In her nightmare, she is seven and cold, and it's soooo dark. Her fear has finally abated, but only because an eternity of endless terror has drained her of the strength to feel anything. She isn't alone, but she might as well be. Her cries for help, and those of the other children, have given way to soft sobs, until even that becomes too taxing, and the silence is broken only by an occasional hoarse moan or a whispered, "Mommy?"

Lying on the hard dirt, her thumb planted firmly against the roof of her mouth, she listens to the sniffled breathing of someone off to her left and tries not to imagine the walls closing in on her. She tries to think about something nice instead, like her family.

So far, this is not dream at all, but memory—merely a replaying of a terrible experience she has never quite been able to erase from her mind. There were five of them. Had been six until . . . but no. She wouldn't think about that. She couldn't!

She'd been curled up into a hard little ball, trying to remember what her mommy's face looked like, when the men with the lights finally arrived. The men had lifted her into their arms, though she was barely conscious enough to realize it, and carried her to safety.

But in the dream, the men with the lights never arrive. She is lying on the ground—a sharp piece of rock is cutting into the small of her back, but she is too tired to move—when she hears the voice—*his* voice—calling her name.

"Ama-a-a-a-n-n-n-n-d-d-d-a." The plaintive, singsong cry echoes off the mine's walls.

She wants to get to her feet and bolt into the darkness like a terrified rabbit. There are things in the darkness—things much worse than the tracks and abandoned pieces of equipment that trip the children up and gash at their feet and legs—things that brush silently past them, touching their faces before disappearing again. But she would rather risk those other things than face *him.*

Because she knows that he isn't coming to rescue her. He is coming to drag her deeper into the darkness.

"Ama-a-a-a-n-n-n-n-d-d-d-a."

She hears his voice again, and the air grows even colder against her skin. She can no longer hear the others. They are hiding too, covering their mouths with dirt-crusted hands like she is, because they all know what he wants. He hates them. He blames them for . . . for . . . what happened.

From only a few feet away comes a sound, the *snick* of a child's shoe kicking up a pebble, and she knows that in a moment she will feel his icy fingers clutching at her throat. And when she does, the walls will close in. They will wrap their dank, crumbling arms around her, crushing the last breath of air from her body, and she will spend eternity here in the dark. Sharing *his* fate, sharing *his*—

"Ama-a-a-a-n-n-n-n-d-d-d-a."

Mandy jerked. She must have drifted off again. She'd been doing that a lot lately—seeing things and hearing things that couldn't be. *Heebie-jeebies*, Eddie called them—drug flashbacks from her halcyon days. She didn't tell him that she'd never really been much of a drug user, not even in her wild teenage years.

It was easier to blame it on the lasting effects of the couple of joints she'd experimented with than to face the very real possibility that she was losing her mind. People who started hallucinating and hearing imaginary voices usually ended up stalking celebrities—or believing that their imaginary visitors were real. Either course led to a tightly strapped white coat in a padded room.

The thing to do was steel herself, get out of bed and walk across the room to the bureau. There was a flashlight in the top drawer—actually three flashlights. She would turn on all three and keep them on until Eddie got home from his shift.

If she moved quickly, she wouldn't have time to think about dead children waiting for her in the dark. The walls wouldn't begin closing in on her like they always did when the lights were turned out.

She started to rise from bed, the soles of her feet just beginning to brush against the nub of the bedroom carpet, when she heard the noise in the hallway.

Swish, swish, like the whisper of a silk blouse being pulled from its hanger. Almost too soft to hear—but not quite.

"Eddie? Eddie, is that you?"

Nothing but the sound of her own pounding heart for almost a minute. Nearly enough time to convince herself that she hadn't heard anything at all.

And then there it was again.

Swish, swish. Was it the sound of the field mice that were forever finding new ways to get up into the trailer?

Or the wispy sound of a child's footsteps?

"Who's there?" She pulled back into bed, knees tucked up against her chest, the sheet pulled almost to her eyes.

"I have a gun." She tried to sound intimidating. But even to herself, her voice sounded empty of any real threat. She waited, wanting to jump from the bed and race across the room, but unable to even move.

Another almost interminable silence, then the stealthy creak that she recognized as the sound of the bedroom door swinging open.

"Oh God, please help me." She couldn't remember praying since she was a little girl, and the only words that came to mind now were the lyrics to a Sunday School song.

"Jesus, loves me. This I know. For . . ." The sound of her voice was so much like her seven-year-old self that she immediately stopped.

From the corner of the room came something that might have been just the water heater gurgling but sounded too much like a soft chuckle.

"Don't . . . don't hurt me," Mandy whimpered. She could feel the walls beginning to close in, could hear moisture dripping from the ceiling somewhere in the distance.

Another sound, this time clearly the titter of a child's voice, and her terror bloomed full and overpowering. She couldn't stand it any longer—couldn't bear to spend another second in darkness. Hallucination or not, she had to get away.

The dresser with the flashlights was less than ten steps from the bed. Fueled by mind-numbing fear, she managed to roll off the mattress, her knees wobbly and barely able to hold her up. She took three tentative steps and paused. The room suddenly felt far too big. Was she even moving in the right direction? In the pitch black it was impossible to tell.

She shuffled forward another two steps and froze, suddenly sure that someone was standing only inches away in the darkness. Waiting silently for her to step into his grasp. Pressing her hands to her mouth, she stood trembling in the middle of the room, the words repeating mantra-like over and over in her head. "Jesus loves me. This I know. Jesus loves me. This I —"

"Ama-a-a-a-n-n-n-n-d-d-d-a."

The voice that whispered to her from the blackness was as quiet as a falling leaf, gentle as a lover's touch. At its sound, all rational thought left her mind. Hands outstretched, she fled—no longer caring in what direction she was moving, knowing only that she had to escape. Her thigh collided with something hard, and a hot burst of pain exploded down her right leg.

Her hand dropped to a smooth surface littered with bottles and pieces of cosmetic jewelry—the dresser. She found the top drawer and yanked it open, peeling back a nail but not even feeling it. Fumbling around inside, she finally found the barrel of a flashlight. Nerveless fingers pressed at the button, missed, and pressed again. A ray of light cut wildly through the darkness as she spun around.

The tight beam revealed nothing—only an empty bedroom in a cheap mobile home. It had been just another hallucination. Collapsing against the dresser, she allowed the light to waver slightly down and to the left.

From the darkness the face of a child appeared, skin slick and pallid, black hair damp and matted.

The flashlight dropped from her sweaty hand, its light snapping out as it hit the floor—and the walls closed in on Mandy for good.

CHAPTER 3

CAL HUNT ESCAPED SLEEP GRADUALLY, like a deep-sea diver trailing bubbles of poisonous nitrogen as he rises from the dark abyss. He'd been dreaming that some frightening creature was chasing him—something black and chitinous, with sharp claws and a poison-dripping stinger. As he reached the point where sleep and waking merge—the strange gray land where fantasy fades and reality has not yet taken hold—he turned, terrified of what stalked him but unable to keep from looking, and he saw . . . nothing.

And *that* was most frightening of all.

He jerked awake, his chest tight, and the words *nothing's there, nothing's there, nothing's there,* trembling on his lips. Instinctively he reached for the warmth of his wife's shoulder. It wasn't until he touched the cold sheets, flat and still tucked beneath her half of the king-size mattress, that his hand remembered that with which his mind had slowly been coming to grips. Kat was gone.

Rubbing the tips of his fingers gently across her pillow, he tried to imagine that he could still feel the slight indentation where her lovely head had rested. It was only wishful thinking. He had buried his face in the goose-down pillow so many times in the months following her death, inhaling Kat's fragrance—trying in some small way to bring her back— that even *that* was lost to him now. The cotton pillowcase and feather-stuffed sack beneath it smelled only of his own salty tears.

Intellectually he understood that the woman he had loved for more than twenty years was now buried beneath the well-manicured sod in the Garden of Hope Cemetery. But at times like tonight, discovering her absence all over again, the pain was as fresh as it had been on the snowy morning he'd dropped the first clump of frozen dirt onto her casket.

Why did he keep doing this—forcing himself to relive the pain of his wife's loss, like a big, dumb bull too stupid to remember the shock of the electric fence? *Wonder what Kat's making for dinner tonight.* Zap— she's dead. *Maybe I'll see what's new over at the video store; Kat loves those stupid romantic comedies.* Zap. *Kat'll be so excited to see the first of her bulbs pushing up through the snow. Or the beautiful sunset. Or hear her favorite song on the radio.* Zap. Zap. Zap.

He couldn't hold on to her. He could feel his wife's essence fading around him like a wilting flower. And yet he couldn't seem to let go of her completely either, no matter how hard he tried.

In the distance, the forlorn sound of a train whistle echoed down from the mouth of the canyon. Without looking at the clock, Cal knew that it was exactly 3:05 A.M. Hadn't someone called this time *the dark night of the soul?* He wondered what the engineer with the meticulous pocket watch would think if he knew that he had become one of Cal's closest friends in the six months following Kat's death.

But it wasn't the train that had awakened him, or the memories of his wife. Without turning on the light, he rose from the bed and stepped into the walk-in closet. Avoiding the half-full boxes that he'd never quite been able to finish packing her clothes into, he lifted the blue terrycloth bathrobe from the back of the door and shrugged it on.

Taking his cell phone from the top of the dresser, he auto-dialed the first number stored in its memory. The luminescent screen glowed ghostlike against the side of his face as he descended the stairs.

"Twin Forks Police Department, is this an emergency?" the voice on the other end of the line asked, as though she couldn't see his number on the caller identification screen in front of her.

Cal played along. "Don't know, Lindy. You tell me."

"Hi, Chief." Lindy Barnes, twenty-two and fresh out of college, had been soloing at the county dispatch desk for only a few weeks and was still eagerly trying to make a good impression.

"Anything going on?" Cal asked. For a brief second an image popped into his head, a dark, enclosed space pressing in on him—something he'd been dreaming about?—and he was sure Lindy was about to give him bad news.

But her answer was business as usual. "Oh, you know, couple of complaints about barking dogs. Rudy Hawkins had too much to drink again and backed his car into one of the pumps at the Texaco."

As quickly as it had appeared, the claustrophobic image was gone, but the feeling behind it remained.

"Any damage?" Cal asked. He opened the front door, hoping against hope that the newspaper might be there. Kat was always giving him a hard time about hanging onto his subscription when everything was available online. But he liked the way the newsprint crinkled in his hands while he sipped his morning coffee.

The only thing on the porch was a neon-pink Frisbee one of the neighborhood kids must have misplaced. He picked it up and set it on the brick wall next to the rosebushes where its owner would be able to spot it.

Half-heartedly he glanced up and down the driveway, but the paper was nowhere in sight. If he missed anything about L.A.—and truth be told, there wasn't much—it was having a newspaper that always beat him to the porch in the morning.

That and watching the Dodgers play a night game. He and Kat had gone as often as they could—him eating three or four hot dogs and her wearing her mitt through the entire game, hoping to catch a foul ball.

He really ought to buy a couple of first-base tickets. He could surprise her with them for her—Zap.

". . . would blame him."

Belatedly Cal realized that he'd missed what Lindy had just said. "Sorry, I was wool gathering."

"You know if you'd get enough sleep, you wouldn't start to doze off during phone calls," Lindy chided. Before Cal could think up a snappy comeback, she continued filling him in. "I was just saying that Mr. Hawkins's car is so banged up that another dent or two won't make the least bit of difference. The only damage to the pump was a little scratch on the side. The kid who works nights got himself into a lather worrying that his boss would blame him. But I think Greg's got him calmed down."

"Greg's good at that." Greg Luke had been assigned to the graveyard shift since before Cal moved to Twin Forks. The officers were supposed to take turns, with the rookies bearing the brunt of the duty. But Greg liked working nights. He was good at dealing with the wackos who seemed to come out only when everyone else was asleep.

"Is something up?" Lindy asked, her voice betraying a trifle too much curiosity.

"Nope. Just thought I'd check in. Talk to you later." He thumbed the *end* button on his phone before Lindy could ask anything else. Someone at the station must have clued her in to what they called *the Chief's hunches*. Cal had heard the guys discussing it when they didn't think he could hear them. They thought he had some kind of premonitions. He'd even heard one of the guys calling it "Cal's spider sense."

The truth of the matter was much simpler. After twenty-seven years wearing the blue, including twelve working some of the nastiest sections of Los Angeles, you just started to become more attuned to your senses than most people. It's what kept you alive.

Cal opened the door to go inside the house and Buster, a Persian with a perpetually quizzical expression on his flat gray face, came running around the corner from the kitchen into the entryway. He skidded to a stop when he saw that it was only Cal and fixed him with an accusing glare. He'd been doing that ever since Kat died. *Maybe I'm not the only one getting zapped,* Cal thought.

"Sorry, pal," he said, scratching the cat under his chin until he started to purr.

Walking up the stairs, he considered going back to bed. But he couldn't shake the feeling that something was wrong. He might as well go ahead and get dressed. He wanted to feel the weight of his gun at his hip. If it proved to be a false alarm—and if the lazy kid who delivered the papers hadn't come by—he could catch up on the Ulysses S. Grant biography he'd been slogging through and enjoy a leisurely cup of coffee.

He never made it to the coffee. He was just pulling on his belt when the phone rang again, the electronic trill driving into his heart like an icicle.

"Chief," Lindy's voice trembled on the other end of the line. "We have a problem."

CHAPTER 4

CAL HAD READ SOMEWHERE THAT every city, from the smallest burg to the most sprawling metropolis, was a living creature. He took most so-called "words of wisdom" with a healthy dose of skepticism, but in this case he thought the author had been right on target.

As a rookie cop, and later as a homicide detective in Los Angeles, he'd always felt like he was living in the shadow of some great hungry beast with sharp teeth and watchful eyes. Here in Twin Forks, the feeling was far less pronounced. Driving south on Pine Street, the center of the oldest section of town, it was easy to imagine that the city was, if not completely asleep, then at least dozing at this time of the morning.

In another half hour or so, the fast food places would fire up their grills, preparing Egg McMuffins and Croissan'wiches for the benefit of the morning commuters. Later on, shops with names like Krissy's Cuts'n'Curls, The Book Nook, and First Tack and Hardware would open their doors for business.

Tonight all the young studs would be out, cruising up and down the street in their jacked-up pickups shouting insults at each other and acting like complete fools as they vied for the attention of the ladies.

But for now, the only signs of life were the brightly illuminated windows of the Texaco station that stayed open "24 hours to serve you" and the smell of frying donuts coming from Dan's Bakery.

It would be easy to take the city for granted at this early hour—to turn your back on it. But in his experience, you were better off keeping things in front of you where you could see them. Because even the tamest creature, if neglected long enough, could bite.

Like many towns, Twin Forks had started off as a rough grid that became topsy-turvy the more it grew. Pine Street ran north–south, intersected by Center Street, which ran east–west. The four corners at the intersection of Pine and Center housed the library, city offices, the police department, and—not surprisingly—a chapel. Although there were a sprinkling of Baptists, Catholics, Jews, Mormons, and atheists, Twin Forks was still mostly made up of the Methodists who had founded it in the late 1800s.

He wasn't a religious man himself, but to each their own. For the first few years after he and Kat had moved here, he felt like some kind of project—constantly being invited to this church dinner or that ice-cream social, until he began to wonder if he'd been put on some kind of church extra credit list. Convert the new chief of police and earn a get-into-heaven-free pass. But eventually they seemed to realize he was too set in his ways to change.

Now they only bothered him when they tried to convince him Kat was still alive somewhere—waiting for him in a glorious afterlife. He wouldn't put up with that. Refused to listen, even if it meant being rude.

At Plum Street, he turned west. Businesses were replaced by older homes, which in turn were replaced by subdivisions, most of them built in the last five to ten years. At last the houses disappeared altogether as he drove past mile after mile of open fields. A low marsh-smelling fog had blown in off the lake, and the rows of early waist-high corn and ground-hugging strawberries played hide-and-go-seek in the shifting curtains of mist.

The address Lindy had given him for the Osgoods was five or six miles out of town. That usually meant a farmer or someone raising horses. But Eddie and Mandy Osgood were no farmers.

Up until about a year ago, they'd rented an apartment over by the fairgrounds. He knew this because they'd been a regular on the domestic disturbance route. At least once a month the two of them got into a row that escalated to the point where a neighbor would phone in a complaint.

Several times punches had been thrown, and on at least one occasion, a kitchen chair had been heaved completely through the front window. Eddie had spent a night or two in jail, but as often as not, he had gotten the worst of the deal, ending up with a broken nose or a blackened eye.

Mandy was a brawler, and she had a nasty temper. But apparently they had moved—or, more likely, been evicted—from their apartment sometime over the last year. It seemed that the new location had done nothing to quell their fights, however. And this time there had been no neighbors to call the police.

Although this was the first murder he'd had to deal with as the police chief of Twin Forks, Cal had seen plenty with the LAPD. Husband on wife, wife on husband, boyfriend on girlfriend, brother on sister, child on parent—he'd pretty much seen it all. And he thought he'd become immune to it.

But now, slowing his cruiser as he neared the address, studying the numbers on the occasional mailbox, the thought of Eddie killing his wife made Cal furious. It made him want to take the punk and slam him against the wall over and over. He wanted to look him in the eye and shout, "Do you have any idea what you've done? What your life is going to be like without her?"

It took all his force of will to loosen his hands on the steering wheel to a normal level and steady his breathing. He looked out the car window. Out here, the day was well underway. Nearly every house in sight had its lights on, and he could already see several tractors trundling slowly across the fields.

A little farther ahead, he could just make out a double-wide trailer. Parked off to one side was what looked like a late seventies utility pickup. Even from this distance, Cal could tell that it had seen better days. Behind it on the narrow dirt drive were two black-and-whites—those would be Greg and Andy—and an ambulance. The red lights on top of the ambulance were dark, and the two EMTs were leaning against the side of the vehicle. Not a good sign for Mandy.

Pulling onto the dirt shoulder a few feet off the side of the road, Cal grimaced at the line of cars in the driveway. On the extremely unlikely chance that Mandy had been killed by someone other than her husband, any tire tracks the perp might have left would've been obliterated by the string of vehicles that had pulled into the drive.

It probably wouldn't matter this time. He felt confident that the killer was sitting in the trailer right now, smelling of too many beers and crying his eyes out.

After radioing in his location, Cal took the heavy black flashlight from under the front seat and left the car. Crossing the weedy patch of dirt that served as a front lawn, he studied the trailer.

It was a newer model, but already the aluminum around the front door showed several dents. Near the back, a small satellite dish hung at a drunken angle, wires dangling loosely from one end. Along each side of the cement-block steps that led to the front door, two white painted tires held what looked like some kind of pansies. Not exactly Martha Stewart, but at least someone had been trying. He didn't imagine it had been Eddie.

As he neared the line of police tape, Cal stopped and turned. He had the unmistakable feeling that someone was watching him. Letting the beam of his light play across the field on the far side of the road, he searched for any sign of movement. Nothing out there. And yet—

"You still want us to hang around, Cal?" At the sound of the EMT's voice, Cal jumped, the hand holding his flashlight rising as he spun around.

"Easy there, Chief." Steve Hammonds, a volunteer who managed the grocery store during the day, fell back a step.

"Geez, Steve, you scared the bejabbers out of me." Cal lowered the flashlight, wondering what had gotten into him. He wasn't prone to nerves.

"Sorry. Guess I just crept up on you."

"Yeah, I guess." Cal gave a final glance across the road. He had the distinct impression that he'd missed something, and it itched at him like a burr.

"Mind if we head on back? That lady isn't going anywhere."

"No, that's okay, Steve. Go on home," Cal said. He could already see the lights of the medical examiner's car coming up the road.

CHAPTER 5

"So what do you make of it?" Cal squatted on his haunches, hands resting on his knees. He spun the gold wedding band on his finger around and around as he studied the room.

"Domestic dispute got out of hand," Andy Kurbowsky said. Andy, a rookie, had been the second officer to arrive. He'd finished sealing off the crime scene while Greg questioned the husband.

Cal looked around the room. "Awfully neat for a knock-down drag-out. Lamp's on the floor, a few things tossed off the nightstand. But that's about it. And the body looks like she's posing for a mortuary ad."

"So hubby sobers up a little after he does the deed. Maybe he's trying to make it look like an accident. I don't know." Andy and Cal watched as the medical examiner, LaVernius Black, studied Mandy's body. Greg had transported Eddie back to the station for further questioning.

Cal checked Andy to see how he was holding up. The kid had already handled a few scrape-and-bag cases out on Highway 83. Compared to those, this was a cakewalk. But you never really got used to seeing a dead body.

Andy looked fine, but Cal knew that the rookie's theory had several holes. This scene didn't have the feel of a fight gone too far. It seemed too clean for that—too *planned*. And there was something missing, something Cal was sure he would have spotted right away if he hadn't been out of homicide for fifteen years.

"Come take a look at this." LaVernius waved the two officers over as he returned his medical instruments to his bag. Cal approached the bed with Andy at his shoulder.

Mandy Osgood was lying on top of a brightly flowered comforter. The bed itself was made up and looked as though it had not been slept in. She was a trim woman, full-figured in some ways but narrow through the thighs and hips. Cal remembered her as being a heavy makeup user, big on dark eyeliner and bright lipstick. But now her face was clean. It was easy to make out the bluish tint to her skin and the dark purple hue of her lips.

Her wavy red hair had been braided back into two pigtails that rested on each of her shoulders. She was dressed in a dark tartan skirt, white blouse, and a pair of black leather shoes with silver buckles that Cal remembered as Mary Janes. The outfit and lack of makeup made her look about ten. Her hands had been arranged carefully across her chest.

LaVernius looked down at Mandy's body. "Something very strange is going on here."

"Tell me something I can't see for myself," Cal said, twisting his ring harder than ever.

"Right, well the posing of the victim and the outfit are clear enough." The ME, a small man with thinning gray hair, rubbed one hand up the side of his cheek and shook his head. "But it's the less obvious signs that distress me even more."

"Like?"

"For one thing, this was no domestic dispute."

"How do you know?" Cal asked, thinking that the words *domestic dispute* sounded far too clinical for their meaning.

"There are no other lesions or contusions on the body. No skin under her nails. If the two of them had been going at it, as you say they have in the past, you'd see something—scratches, scrapes, bruises. But there are no self-defense marks of any kind." That synced with Cal's observations. He had stopped briefly to meet Eddie on the way in—careful to control his emotions—and the man didn't appear to have so much as a scratch on him.

"So he never gave her a chance to hit back," Cal said. "He probably killed her while she was sleeping. Just proves what a coward he is. What else have you got?"

LaVernius lifted the blouse and pointed to a dark purple bruise in the middle of Mandy's stomach. "Blunt force trauma to the abdomen indicates that the first blow was probably a punch or a kick. I suspect it knocked the air from her."

"That fits with the theory. The husband's been abusive for years," Cal said, clearly impatient. He wanted the first homicide in Twin Forks since he took office to be wrapped up quickly.

"The husband's not your killer." The ME pulled Mandy's blouse back down.

"What? How could you possibly know that?" Cal glared at LaVernius as if he could make him retract his words by sheer force of will. But the little man deflected his stare.

"After the killer hit her, he strangled her." He held back Mandy's hair so that Cal and Andy could clearly see the finger marks on each side of her neck.

"Small hands," Andy murmured before looking away, his face as white as cottage cheese.

"Correct. The bruises are clear. Her husband could never have made these marks." The medical examiner placed one of his hands alongside Mandy's neck for comparison. His hands were small, his fingers narrow, but the bruises were smaller still.

"So what are you saying?" Cal asked. "A woman did this?"

"A woman, a very small man, a youth. Could've been a midget for all I know."

"A *midget*?" Cal shook his head, fuming.

LaVernius shrugged. "I'm just telling you what I see. But here's the part where things really start to get wonky."

"There's more?" Cal took a step closer. The feeling he'd experienced that morning, a sense of things closing in, was stronger than ever.

"The only other marks I could find on her that look recent are these." LaVernius turned Mandy's body a little to reveal the back of her leg and thigh. "See these abrasions?"

"Rug burn," Cal said.

"Right. And these blue fibers? Carpet. Somebody moved the body— dragged it across the floor."

"Dragged it where?"

"My guess would be the bathroom."

"Why would—" Cal started to ask. But suddenly he understood. It was the smell, the first thing you noticed in any murder scene. When a person died, their bowels almost always evacuated. It was a smell every homicide cop associated with death. It was what had been missing.

"If you look around, I think you'll find soiled underclothes, because they're not here." LaVernius waved a hand over Mandy's lifeless body. "No makeup on her face, not a speck of dirt beneath her nails, even a faintly minty smell I'd peg as toothpaste."

"After she was killed someone dragged her body—probably into the bathroom—cleaned her up, changed her into this outfit, and placed her back on the bed. The killer posed her body just as you see it, for us to find."

The three men were silent as they all digested the information. Andy looked like he was fighting to keep from throwing up.

"And still, that's not the strangest thing."

Cal waited, knowing that he didn't want to hear whatever was coming.

"Unless your victim has been experiencing some strange weight fluctuations, these are not her clothes." LaVernius tugged on the waistband of the dark skirt, and it gave under the pressure of his finger, revealing nearly two inches between it and the dead woman's hip.

"Look here. The skirt is far too big, but the buttons on the blouse are straining to the limit. I haven't checked the shoes yet, but I think we'll find that they are also the wrong size." He waved both hands in the air as if trying to clear away a haze. "I believe that whoever murdered this woman brought along an outfit to dress her in."

The ME wiped a sweat-damp palm down the leg of his pants, and beads of perspiration dotted his receding hairline. His eyes looked a trifle too wide to Cal, slightly glazed. "Don't know who your killer is, Chief. But you're definitely dealing with a very disturbed individual."

CHAPTER 6

"A MIDGET WITH A TASTE for schoolgirls," Cal muttered as he swung his cruiser into the station parking lot. In L.A. it would barely have made the evening news. But here? He didn't believe it for a minute. No way the husband was clean on this one. If he didn't do it himself, he knew who did. And Cal would see Eddie's hide nailed to a wall before he let the creep get away with this.

Careful not to let his steaming Styrofoam cup of coffee fall from its holder, he pulled into his reserved space. He'd stopped off at Dan's as he always did on his way into the office in the morning. There was a perfectly good coffee machine inside the station, but Cal had learned from sad experience that expecting one of his officers to make a decent cup of coffee was akin to asking a blind man to choose your outfit.

The Twin Forks police department was a squat brick building, hunkering down against the fierce canyon winds. Nobody's idea of an architectural wonder, it had served its purpose well for the last twenty years, and Cal suspected it would continue to do so for at least another twenty. The main entrance was around front, but all the officers used the back door.

As Cal entered the building, he could hear a familiar voice braying at Michelle Calloway, who was manning the front desk. Dickey Jordan had been coming down to the station at least once a week since the city council voted to drill two new wells near his farm. Cal grimaced and hurried down the hallway.

"Chief Hunt," Dickey bellowed, his face even redder than normal. "You gotta help me out here."

"Not now, Dickey, I don't have time for this." Cal headed for the stairwell.

"But they're stealing my water," Dickey groaned. "You're the law, Cal. You gotta do something about this. See, it all started in June of last year when the council approved that dagnammed irrigation system. Even then I told them it would never—"

"Michelle, see what you can do to help Mr. Jordan."

Michelle shot Cal a look of desperation, but before she or Dickey could respond, Cal disappeared down the stairs.

The station house was divided into two levels. The main floor was primarily administrative. Composed of the lobby, several offices—including Cal's—a few cubicles, and an area known as the bullpen that was designed for taking reports and filling out forms, it was all that the general public normally saw.

Downstairs were four holding cells—two on each side of a cement walkway—the dispatcher's desk, and two interrogation rooms. The cells hadn't actually been in use since the county jail opened more than a decade earlier, but Cal found that suspects were far more likely to be cooperative after passing by the bleak-looking cubes. Three of the four cells were empty, used occasionally for storage and such. The fourth was rigged with an AV system hooked to the hidden cameras in both of the interrogation rooms.

Checking the monitor, he saw that Greg and Andy had begun questioning Eddie Osgood while Cal was wrapping things up at the crime scene.

Eddie had the wiry kind of muscles that you see on a lot of men with small frames. He looked almost scrawny, but Cal had no doubt he was stronger than he looked. His red hair had been buzz-cut fairly recently and was just growing back out, making him look a little like a toilet brush.

It was his eyes that Cal studied. They were bloodshot, which, along with his runny nose, gave the impression that he'd been crying. But they were also cunning, the eyes of a ferret.

Exiting the cell, Cal approached the closed door of the interrogation room and gave it a quick rap. Greg came out and closed the door behind him.

"So what's his story?" Cal asked.

"He's innocent, of course." Greg grinned. He had unruly hair and a hangdog face with a long nose and dozy eyes that naturally lulled people to sleep. He was lanky but not as tall as Cal. And where Cal was barrel-chested, Greg was nearly scarecrow thin. His looks often fooled people into thinking he wasn't all that bright, but Cal knew that he had a sharp mind.

"Aren't they all?"

"Yeah, well, he claims that he was at work until three A.M. down at the bottling plant in Castle Rock." Greg glanced at his notes. "That would put him at the trailer more than an hour and a half after the ME pinpoints the victim's time of death. They work on a time card system down at the plant, so his story should be easy enough to check out."

"Unless he talked one of his buddies into punching his card. I'm going to walk him through his story again," Cal said, taking Greg's folder. "You've got a couple more hours until the end of your shift. Why don't you start questioning some of the neighbors? The area's remote, but there are some early risers out there. Maybe one of them spotted something."

As Greg left, Cal entered the interrogation room and extended his hand to Eddie. "Mr. Osgood, Chief Hunt. How are you doing?"

Eddie took Cal's hand, his grip cool and damp. "I'm pretty wiped, man. Can I go home now?"

Cal sat beside the square cigarette-burned table, across from where Eddie remained slumped in his plastic chair, and nodded sympathetically. "Soon. I just have a couple of questions to ask first. Can I get you anything? Coffee? Soda?"

"I could use some coffee." Eddie swiped at his nose with his right hand, and Cal unconsciously scrubbed his own hand across the leg of his uniform.

"Andy, would you get Mr. Osgood a cup of coffee?" Cal waited for Andy to leave the room before fixing Eddie's eyes with his own.

"This must be trying for you, Eddie. Do you mind if I call you Eddie?"

"Whatever." Eddie shrugged "This whole thing's got me really pretty stressed."

"Uh-huh." Cal pretended to read through the folder before looking up. "And yet I can't help noticing that you and the late Mrs. Osgood didn't always get along so well."

Eddie dropped his gaze and began to skate his palms across the top of the table. "Doesn't mean I didn't love her. We just both got wicked bad tempers, you know?"

"I understand," Cal commiserated. "Is that what happened? Did you come home from work early and find her with another man maybe?

Or the house was a mess? You lost your temper and punched her in the stomach and then without thinking, you strangled her?"

"No!" Eddie shouted. His fingers clenched into tight fists, turning his knuckles white.

"You felt bad about what you'd done," Cal continued in the same understanding tone. "So you went into the closet to find something nice for her to wear—something decent. You cleaned her up and laid her on the bed, because you loved her. Is that about how it happened?"

"No. No way. Look, I told your partner, I never touched her. I never even seen those clothes before, and I sure didn't do her hair up like some farmer's daughter. Mandy would've had a cow if she ever seen her hair like that. I never touched her."

Cal leaned closer, flexing and then relaxing his big fists on the table. "But you know who did."

"Nah. I got no idea, man. Don't you think I'd tell you?" Eddie was crying again. He looked around the bare walls of the room, then down at his hands. "Where's my coffee?"

"I'm sure it'll be here any minute." Cal glanced over at the clock with the hidden video camera, knowing perfectly well Andy was watching the monitor, waiting for his signal.

"Let me tell you something," Cal said, fixing Eddie's eyes with a glare until the other man finally returned his gaze. "We're going to stay here as long as we need to. And you're not leaving until you tell me everything that happened. So why don't you go over your story again, without leaving anything out. Nice and slow so we're clear. Then I'll check on that coffee for you."

Eddie shook his head. "Man," he sighed tiredly. But he was resigned to the fact that he wasn't leaving until he told his story at least once more.

"I got off work at three o'clock sharp. You can check that. I came straight home 'cause I was bushed. They been working our butts off down at the plant trying to make up for the hundred guys they laid off last month.

"Anyways, when I get back to the trailer, I see that the power's out again. Friggin' power takes a crapper all the time out there, but Mandy's got to have a place in the country." Eddie looked up as if finally realizing that his wife really was gone. His mouth opened and closed silently, and a tear dripped from his left eye.

"Take your time," Cal said. If Eddie was going to crack, this would be it. He slipped a Polaroid of the dead woman from the case file and slid it across the table. Eddie stared at it morbidly for a moment before pushing it away.

"Mandy's scared to death of the dark, and I knew she was probably throwing a hissy. You'd think she'd want to live in the city being a'scared like that, but she don't like small places neither. Comes from this time she got lost in a mine."

Cal felt an inexplicable wave of something like *déjà vu* wash over him, but he ignored the feeling, not wanting to interrupt the flow of Eddie's story. "Go on," he encouraged. As Eddie continued, Cal jotted *Scared of dark enclosed spaces* on his pad and circled it.

"I go around back to fire up the gennie," Eddie said, folding his arms across his chest and cupping his elbows. "It was Mandy's idea to get one. Danged expensive, but it's pretty cool. When the power goes out and everybody else is sitting around in the dark picking their noses, we're watching TV and eating popcorn."

"Nice."

"Only when I get there I see that the power ain't out, after all. The fuse box door's hanging open and somebody'd thrown all the switches. That's when I started getting freaked. I just about got back in my truck right then and there and hauled butt back to town. But I had to check on Mandy first."

"You're a prince," Cal said. Eddie wiped his nose again and nodded, taking Cal's words as a compliment.

"So once I reset the fuses, I went back to my truck and got out a tire iron. I mean I was thinking it was probably just some of the local kids screwing around, but I figured it might have been a burglar or something, so why take chances?"

"And you didn't see anyone or hear anything?" Despite his wishes, Cal found himself believing Eddie's story. It sounded neither rehearsed nor made up. Either Eddie was telling the truth or he was a very accomplished liar. And Cal didn't think he was smart enough to be that good a liar.

"Not until I got to the bedroom and seen Mandy all dressed up like one of them Catholic schoolgirls. I figured she was sleepin'. But then I see how she ain't moving. When I got closer, I could see that her face was all blue and she wasn't breathing. Man, that's when I just lost it completely. I called you guys and booked out of there. I didn't even go back in until the cops showed up."

"And that's everything you saw?" Cal asked, watching Eddie's eyes.

Eddie nodded. "Yeah, that's it."

Cal looked at his notes. "You said something about a mine?"

"Uh-huh. Back when Mandy was a little girl, she and some other kids disappeared into an old mine. They were lost for like five days. People just about give 'em up for dead. But then the rescuers found 'em. I guess it freaked her out pretty bad."

Eddie picked at something under his thumbnail. Without looking up, he muttered, "Mandy was right."

Cal leaned forward. "Right about what?"

"About that trailer, man." Eddie's eyes narrowed as he ran his tongue across his upper lip. "Said it was spooked or something. She's been telling me she wants to sell that place, even though we just bought it end of last year."

"Spooked?"

"You know, like ghosts and stuff. I always figured she was full of crap. But this morning, I don't know. I got this feeling like someone was watching me."

Cal felt goose bumps race up his back. "Did you see anyone?"

"No. But it felt like that *Poltergeist* movie. You know, the one where the kid gets pulled under his bed by that freaky clown?"

"And who do you think it was?" Cal asked. "Who was watching you?"

Eddie seemed embarrassed. He drummed his fingers on the table without looking up.

"Tell me who it was and I'll go check on that coffee for you."

"Don't care 'bout no coffee, man. I just wanna get outta here."

Cal waited, perched on the edge of his seat.

"Okay, fine." Eddie rubbed his face with both hands. "Mandy said there was a ghost in the trailer."

Cal dropped back into his seat. It was a con, after all. Well, it wouldn't be the first time he'd been fooled by a born liar. This guy was already angling for a diminished capacity plea. He nodded toward the camera, signaling Andy to bring in the coffee.

Cal stood just as Andy came through the door with a red-and-white-striped cup. He set it on the table, but Eddie seemed to have lost his thirst. He looked from Andy to Cal, wiping his mouth with the back of his hand again.

"She said it was the spirit of some kid come back to haunt her. But when I was in that room and I seen her all laid out like that, dint feel like no kid . . .

"It felt like the devil was in there with me."

CHAPTER 7

"Greg, you go home and get some shuteye. You all handled this real well. Andy, I want you to take these fingerprints down to BCI this afternoon. Let's see if the Osgoods have had any interesting visitors. And stop by the local thrift shops. See if anybody was in shopping for clothes that match the vic's."

Andy nodded, taking the folder from Cal.

"Mandy's body will be autopsied today," Cal continued as the men rose from their chairs, "but Doc Black says it looks like a pretty clear case of strangulation. We also have forensics checking the clothing she was wearing at the time of the murder, as well as the clothes she was dressed in, and fibers from the bathtub.

"Oh, and one other thing. I don't want any of you talking to the press about this. They're covering the murder, of course. But right now most of them believe it was a domestic. They don't know anything about the condition of the victim's body, and I'd like to keep it that way as long as we can."

The men gathered their notes, and Andy left the office, but Greg lingered behind. Cal waited for him to speak, and when he just continued to stand there with that faintly sleepy look on his face, Cal asked with some irritation, "Was there something you needed, Detective?"

Greg poked a finger into his ear, twisted it around a little as if searching for diamonds, and asked, "You sleeping okay, Chief?"

"Fine," Cal growled. "Is there anything else?"

"It's just that—if you don't mind my saying—you look like *you're* the one who's been up all night." Greg raised the right side of his mouth in a sympathetic half grin.

Cal dropped back into his chair. There was no point in lying to Greg—the man was practically a human lie detector. "Okay, so maybe I didn't sleep so well. What's your point?"

Greg pulled his finger out of his ear and studied it before dropping his hand back to his side—apparently no diamonds this time. "You still think about her a lot, don't you?"

Cal sighed. The man was far too perceptive. It wouldn't do to let himself forget that. "There's no point in thinking about her," he said. "She's dead and buried, and that's that. What I need to do is get this case solved. And what you need to do is get home and get some sleep. You don't look any too perky yourself."

Cal knew where Greg was going with this, but he wasn't about to rehash the discussion they'd had more than once. As a devout Methodist, Greg believed in life after death. He'd tried explaining to Cal that only Kat's body was dead, that her spirit still lived on. But Cal wasn't buying that.

He'd seen plenty of people die. There was nothing special about it. One minute they were a living breathing being capable of love and laughter, pity and pain, and the next minute they were meat, capable of nothing but stinking and drawing flies.

"So you're over it, then?" Greg turned toward the door as if getting ready to leave.

"Yeah," Cal said, keeping his gaze glued to his desk. "I'm over it."

Greg opened the door, paused for a moment, and then looked back over his shoulder. "Maybe I should set you up with some women I know. I imagine they'd think you're quite a catch."

Cal laughed despite himself. Greg was way too good at this sort of thing, and they both knew it. He waved at the door. "Get out before I throw you out."

Once Greg was gone, Cal stared contemplatively out the window. He took a paperclip from the holder on his desk and began to twist the metal into different shapes—a triangle, a square, bunny rabbit ears. He wished Greg hadn't brought up Kat. He didn't have time to think about her right now. There were too many other things going on. Things he didn't even dare discuss with his officers.

The pieces didn't fit together right. He wanted to pin this on the husband, but he had the sinking feeling he wouldn't be able to. True, Eddie had a history of violence, and the trailer and Mandy's small checking account were as good a motive as any. But nothing else fit. The clothes, the handprints, the preparation of the body—those didn't match the profile of a greedy husband.

It was bad enough to have a man murder his wife in your jurisdiction. But as far as Cal was aware, there was no such thing as a perfect town.

It was the other possibility that frightened him. Because if the husband didn't do it, that meant there was one very sick puppy loose on the streets of Twin Forks.

And the chances were that he wasn't done killing.

CHAPTER 8

"DAD—HEY, DAD! CAN WE go for a ride in your truck?"

Ezra Rucker studiously ignored his four-year-old son, Sam, hoping that if he kept his eyes on the television, the kid would find someone else to pester.

"Can we, Dad, huh?" Sam leaned his head between his father and the screen.

"Hey, look out." Ezra pushed the kid to one side. The announcers were going crazy over a no-look pass Andre Miller had just thrown to Danilo Gallinari, a pass Gallinari had missed completely. "Go pester your mom."

The kid wandered right back in front of the screen. "Didja know that all cars gots alterbators? That's what puts 'lectricity in the battery."

"Get out of the way of the TV." Ezra shoved his son's head to one side. The refs had just whistled Harrington for a foul, and Ezra wanted to see the replay. He was sure that big galoot, Pau Gasol, had flopped again.

"You hurt me," Sam wailed, rubbing his head and starting to cry.

Great. He'd barely touched the kid, and now Tamara would come running into the room any minute acting like the whole thing was *his* fault. He turned off the set and stumped out the front door.

Behind him, he could hear Sam shouting. "Sorry, Daddy. I'm sorry! Take me with you, huh? C'mon, lemme go?"

Fat chance. The kid was a bigger pest than his brother, Joshua. Although Ezra would have thought that was impossible until Sam had been born. That was the thing about kids, they came into the world with a squall and as they got older the only thing that changed was the volume of their wailing.

His truck was parked in the gravel driveway in front of the house. Placing both hands on the top of the cab, he laid his head against the cool glass and closed his eyes tightly. What was wrong with him? He was acting more and more like his own father every day. That was something he'd sworn to himself he'd never do.

His father had been a tyrant. A pious saint in church, he could quote his Bible with the best of them. But once he got home and took off his suit and tie, he was anything but saintly. All of the Rucker children—boys and girls alike—knew the sting of their father's thick black belt. They knew what it felt like to go to bed without supper, your legs and back so sore you had to sleep on your stomach.

Ezra had never seen his father hit his mother, but he'd seen him scream at her—hurling obscenities and insults alike, until she was reduced to a sobbing heap. He'd sworn that he would never be like his father, and look at him now.

Well he'd gotten the first part right. He hadn't been to church in more than six months, much to Tamara's dismay. He knew people were talking. Tamara had been to see the pastor twice, once with Ezra and once without him. Was she thinking divorce? He wouldn't be surprised. Heaven knew she deserved better than him.

Ezra had tried to pull himself together. But things just seemed to be slipping from his control lately. Like his job. He'd spent years building up a successful painting business and in only a few months he'd destroyed it to the point where people wouldn't even trust him to paint a doghouse. Somehow he always seemed to get his appointments wrong, or buy the wrong paint, or completely forget that he'd even scheduled a job for that day.

Thing was, it had all fallen apart in the last few months. Right about the time he took the kids on that trip to Glenwood caverns, when he'd flashed back to—but no. This couldn't be tied to what happened all those years ago—in the mine. It couldn't be. The kid was dead and gone. Any thoughts to the contrary were just another sign of the way things were going screwy. He was losing his mind, along with his marriage and his job.

And Mandy? Now there—there was something that really *could* drive you crazy. He'd heard rumors around town—stories that made his blood turn to ice. Because if they were true—if he wasn't the only one seeing things, then . . .

Inside the driver's door, under the front seat, was a small brown bottle. He slipped it out with a furtive glance back toward the house and unscrewed the cap. The smell was strong—almost medicinal. He paused. Was this really what he wanted to do? Tamara had an idea he'd started drinking again. He told her it was only cough syrup she smelled on his breath.

But if he had a drink now, he wouldn't stop at one. Something moved out in the trees and he spun around, hiding the bottle behind his back. "Who's that? Who's out there?"

There was no answer.

"That one of you Gately kids? Cause if it is, and I catch you, I'm gonna wail on your little butt."

Slowly an image appeared in his mind. A little boy with dark, slicked-back hair and thick glasses. And eyes that seemed to look right through you.

Almost of its own volition the bottle rose to his lips. Grimacing as the whisky burned its way down the back of his throat, he took a second swallow, and a third. Little by little the image of the boy faded.

Probably just one of the nosy neighbors. "Mind your own business!" he shouted, waving the bottle in the direction from which the noise had come. All at once the yard began to spin, and he barely had time to leave the truck before throwing up. Guess he wasn't much of a drinker after all.

Wiping his mouth on the back of his sleeve, he capped the bottle. He was leaning into the truck to slip it back under the seat when movement near the trees caught his eye.

He jerked up, staring into the trees, but whatever he'd seen was gone. *Go on home and tell your folks how Ezra Rucker puked in his yard,* he thought. *Maybe they can put it in the church bulletin.* Where was his dog, anyway?

"Prince! Here, boy," he called, surprised that the mutt wasn't already slobbering all over his leg. That crazy dog was always jumping up on anyone who came into the yard. It cracked Ezra up to see Prince knock the kids sprawling. He called again. No response. More than likely he'd smelled some dog in heat and had taken off.

Ezra headed around to the back of the house, in the general direction of the trees, tucking the bottle into the waistband of his pants. His house was small, and although he was a house painter by trade, the peeling wood siding had faded to the point where it was impossible to tell what color it had originally been. But it stood on nearly three and a half acres of land, and it was his opinion that one day this was going to be prime real estate.

He kept telling himself that he ought to grow something out here. Maybe strawberries like his old man had done. But over time the aspens at the back of the lot—trash trees, his father called them—had spread their roots, sending up saplings everywhere. And now the place looked like a darned forest. You could actually get lost in your own backyard.

Stopping at the edge of the grass, he tried to peer into the darkness. For a second he thought he could just make out a pair of coal-black eyes staring back at him, and his heart took a leap. Suddenly it wasn't his woods he was standing in front of at all, but a dark, cold cave. He pulled the bottle from his pants, took a long swig, and it was just his yard again. Still, he wished the dog would show up.

At the back of the house was a cord and a half of solid ash. He'd taken it in trade for painting a couple of bedrooms. Not exactly the payment terms he preferred but he'd put down only one coat of the cheapest flat white he could find. And at least the IRS couldn't ding him for this. So he guessed it had worked out okay.

Every time he felt his temper starting to heat up, he came out here and started splitting logs. He found it relaxing to watch the razor-sharp blade of his ax ripping into the heart of a big chunk of wood. The repetition of the actions helped burn away his anger. *Lift, swing, thunk. Lift, swing, thunk.*

It was coming up on nine o'clock, and even though it was late May, the evening air had a bite to it. It had been cloudy all afternoon, and a slight mist hung in the air, as though the sky couldn't make up its mind whether it wanted to rain. Ezra thought about going back into the house to get a jacket then decided against it. He'd work up a sweat pretty quickly chopping logs.

A few years before, he had run an extension cord out to the backyard. Stringing it to an old four-by-four, he'd hooked up a bare light bulb with a chain to turn it on and off. But now as he tugged on the chain, the light refused to turn on. He stretched up to jiggle it. No dice. He'd told Tamara a thousand times it didn't pay to buy the cheap bulbs. Did she listen to him? Apparently not.

Again he considered going into the house. He thought there was a package of sixty-watt bulbs under the kitchen sink. But then he'd probably have to listen to Tamara complain about how dinner was getting cold. It would be a hassle.

He could do without the light. It wasn't like he was scared of the dark. The only things Ezra Rucker was afraid of were death and taxes. And so far he had done a pretty good job of avoiding both. He just preferred to see what he was doing. A guy could lose a toe chopping wood in the dark.

The thing was, although he would never admit it out loud, he *had* been feeling a little uneasy lately. Since he read about Mandy's death the day before, he'd been struggling with a bad case of the jim-jams. Not that he and Mandy had been close. He wasn't even aware that it was her until he saw the picture in the paper. They'd hung around sometimes as kids, but he'd lost track of her after her second marriage.

It wasn't her death that rattled him as much as the memories it brought back. The whole mine thing. He thought he'd gotten over that a long time ago. His father had certainly seen to it that he didn't linger over the past. Two days after he was rescued, he'd been out on the back forty doing his chores.

Then he'd seen Mandy's picture, and it all came rushing back like a river of foul-tasting water. All day yesterday and today he'd been spooking himself. He knew he couldn't be seeing the things he thought he was. But knowing it was all in his head only made things worse.

He picked up a log and balanced it on the stump he used as a chopping block. Spitting into his palm, he picked up the ax. *Lift, swing, thunk.* The wood split neatly in two. He set one of the halves back on the block. *Lift, swing*—Something rustled in the trees, and he just missed bringing the ax down on his foot. Staring into the darkness, he swept a cold sheen of perspiration from his forehead with his arm.

"Prince? That you, boy?"

No answering bark.

The wind, he thought.

He lifted the ax above his shoulder and brought it down. Crack. The ax head narrowly caught the edge of the log, sending it careening into the darkness. Suddenly the night seemed far too quiet. Holding the ax crosswise in front of him with both hands, he took a step toward the trees.

"Somebody out there?"

The splintered piece of wood was lying only a few feet from the edge of the trees. He picked it up and tossed it into the darkness. There was a faint crackling sound as it settled into the brush but nothing more.

He took another step toward the trees before thinking better of it. Probably just a raccoon. The dumb dog would scare it off once he found his way home. Returning to the stump, Ezra swung the ax and buried it halfway to the handle. He didn't need this aggravation. He'd just go in and catch the end of the basketball game.

Heading to the house, he stopped to study the sky. It looked like it might rain in earnest after all. He'd better put the ax away in the garage so it wouldn't rust.

Taking two long strides back toward the stump, he was reaching down for the handle when he realized the ax was no longer there.

"What the . . . ?" He stared stupidly down at the battle-scarred circle of wood before sensing movement off to his left. He pivoted quickly—he'd been a pretty good athlete back in school—but not quickly enough.

He had just enough time to see the blade of the ax, shimmering silver in the moonlight as it rose toward the sky. The last thing he heard was the front door swinging open and his son calling, "Dad, time for dinner."

Lift, swing, thunk.

The night closed in on Ezra for good.

CHAPTER 9

CAL STOOD IN THE GRAVEL driveway, staring woodenly at the front of the Rucker house. The dull clapboard bungalow was the same shade of gray as the turgid clouds dripping steadily overhead, lending sky and ground alike a leaden hue. Maybe it was just his imagination, but already the empty windows and dark interior seemed to radiate a sense of isolation, as though the entire structure had drawn in on itself.

"You heading back to the station?" Greg asked, hands tucked into the pockets of his yellow slicker.

Cal shook his head. Both men hunched against the rain, shoulders bowed this early morning as if drawn down by the weight of what they'd seen. Dressed in dark pants and matching raincoats with TFPD stenciled on the back, they looked like overgrown school boys who had missed their bus.

"No." Cal wiped a thick hand across his face and rubbed his bloodshot eyes. "Apparently I'm a glutton for punishment. I'm gonna take another look around and see if this mess makes any more sense in the light of day."

Both men turned, almost painfully, toward the spot where Ezra's body had been discovered. The night's steady drizzle had done nothing to wash away the long rust-colored stain—if anything, the rain had made it bigger. Tire tracks in the thick grass showed where the body had been wheeled away from the scene on a stretcher.

"You really think it's the same guy?" Greg asked.

"Don't know." Cal shrugged, his knuckles cracking audibly as he clenched and unclenched his fists. "You like the idea of two murderous freaks running loose in our town?"

Both men stood silent.

"What's the relationship, though—between Ezra and Mandy?"

Again Cal shrugged. His broad shoulders cascaded water down the yellow fabric of his coat in tight little rivulets. He sighed, long and deep, as if the sound had come all the way up from the soles of his feet. "There's got to be one," he said at last. "And we have to find it soon."

Cal studied the lingering bystanders still watching from just outside the crime scene tape. The press had shown up in force this time, leaving Cal with no illusions about keeping this thing under wraps. Most of the reporters had gone back to file their stories. The few who remained were being kept at a distance by Andy and Sheldon Heathcliff, a part-time officer who had been approved by the city council just this year.

"You want me to stick around?" Greg asked. "I don't mind." The detective's features betrayed his words. His droopy eyes—sleepy looking under the best of circumstances—appeared to be staying open only by sheer force of will. Neither of the men had gotten much rest over the last forty-eight hours.

The same could be said for everyone in their little department. Two murders in as many days had them all on full alert.

"Go home and get some rest," Cal said. "If this keeps up, you're going to need it."

Greg opened his mouth, as if he wanted to say something else, and then closed it abruptly. He crossed the driveway, ducked beneath the bright yellow tape, and headed to his car. The onlookers gathered at the edge of the street parted as he walked past them.

Turning back to the yard, Cal was again struck by the profusion of greenery. Twin Forks was mostly arid. But here, in the swampy flats backing up to Twin Forks Creek, plant life seemed to thrive in an almost predatory fashion.

He walked to the backyard, out of sight from the onlookers, and stopped halfway between the sagging stoop and the woodpile. Although Ezra's body was long gone, the taste of violence hung in the air like a dank miasma.

Squatting, taking in a ground-level view of the scene, he tried to see through the eyes of the killer. What did he want? How did he feel? What was he thinking?

If there was one thing Cal's years in homicide had taught him, it was that the best way to catch a killer was to become a killer. They called it *profiling* now, and the people who did it had formal degrees and fancy software, but cops had been doing it long before computers came along.

He replayed the night's events in his mind—some of the information coming from the victim's wife, some from the forensics guy, and some just based on intuition.

Ezra Rucker walks out his front door. It's about nine o'clock and overcast. Too dark to be out chopping wood, but he is in a foul mood. And lately, when Ezra's temper flares, he usually strikes out at someone or something.

He heads out to the truck and stops for a drink of whiskey. The bottle was still tucked into his pants when they found his body. According to what little his distraught wife is able to tell them before she breaks down completely is this has become a fairly common occurrence over the last few months.

Does he notice that his dog is missing? He certainly wouldn't have remained out in the dark if he knew his seventy-five-pound German shepherd was lying dead less than a hundred yards away, poisoned by hamburger laced with antifreeze.

After taking a couple of slugs from the bottle, Ezra walks around to the woodpile. He tries to turn on the light. He reaches up and fiddles with the bulb when it won't turn on. The bulb had been wiped clean, and Ezra's fresh prints were clear as a bell.

But the light is not going to come on no matter how long he works at it. It won't come on because the same person who poisoned the dog also unscrewed the light bulb and stuck a folded-up piece of fast food napkin between the base of the bulb and the socket.

Cal stood and moved from his spot, twisting his ring as he approached the area where Ezra was found. The grass was still matted where the body had lain. A few feet away, a sparrow lay dead on the lawn—its body stiff and damp. Cal nudged it with the toe of his boot before turning to examine the rest of the yard.

Did Ezra notice the torn sod where his chopping block had been moved? In the light of day, the marks showing that his soon-to-be killer dragged the stump to use as a stepping stool while he disabled the light are obvious. But in the dark, Ezra may not have seen them or noticed how the killer replaced the stump just a little off the circle of dead brown grass where it had been before.

Something happens after Ezra has been in the yard only a few minutes—something that causes him to stop chopping.

Cal walked to the edge of the thick stand of trees. Even in the light of day, the woods were a maze of shadows. At night they would have been impenetrable. He imagined Ezra standing in the yard, staring into the darkness.

Does Ezra hear someone moving around in the woods? A rustle of leaves or the crack of a branch? Or maybe he just senses a presence there. It must have been something like that, because they recovered half of the log Ezra had been splitting from several feet into the trees.

This is where things get a little unclear. Somehow, Ezra loses the ax. There are no abrasions on his palms to indicate that it was wrestled away from him. Perhaps he is heading into the house. But for some reason he turns back. Does the killer call out to him?

The wound is to the front of the skull. Just off center, as though he was turning toward, or away from, his attacker. It is deep enough to kill, but not as deep as you'd expect from an ax that sharp. The lack of force used and the angle of impact suggest the attacker was smaller than his victim, making the size of the attacker a possible match with the Osgood case.

Now things happen quickly. Shortly after the fatal blow is struck, the victim's son comes outside looking for his father. It must be after the attack, because the boy doesn't see anything. But not too long after, because by the time the boy's mother hears her son's screams and finds him standing frozen with shock in the backyard, Ezra is still bleeding out.

In the period between when Ezra is struck and when his son finds him, the killer is busy. He isn't content with murdering his victim. He wants to leave a message. This stage-setting matches the Osgood case as well. He dips one of the victim's own paint brushes—presumably taken from Ezra's truck earlier—in the fresh blood, and while Ezra's heart is still pumping, draws a rudimentary pair of glasses on the man's face.

After painting his victim's face, possibly while Sam is wandering around the front of the house calling his father's name, the killer returns to the pool of spreading blood and again soaks the brush. He may be spotted at any moment, and yet he risks being seen to paint two words on the side of the truck. He probably needs to make at least two trips back for more blood to complete his broadly stroked message.

The two words don't mean anything to Cal or the other officers on the scene. Did they mean anything to the victim? Or the victim's family? The message obviously means something to the killer.

The words splashed in gore on the side of the truck—right next to *Rucker's Painting*—are *FROG EYES*. A reference to the glasses he'd drawn on Ezra's face? A nickname of some kind?

Cal closed his eyes, pressing his fingers to his temples as he tried to put the pieces together. But he couldn't seem to get into the mind of this killer. The pattern was all wrong.

On the one hand, there was an incredible amount of planning involved—the light bulb, the dog, choosing a hiding spot near Ezra's chopping block. And yet the murder itself seemed almost spur of the moment—instead of bringing his own weapon, the killer uses an ax that Ezra just happens to have with him.

And the timing of the whole thing—how could the killer possibly know that Ezra would come out to chop wood on this particular night? It wasn't cold enough to actually *need* the wood. And the forecast called for rain. Sure, the killer might have known that Ezra chopped wood when he was angry, but was that enough to take the risk of poisoning the dog and fixing the light bulb?

Again Cal sighed. This kind of thing wasn't supposed to go down in a town like Twin Forks. That was half the reason he'd taken this job. Twelve years ago, back when he and Kat still thought they'd be able to have kids, they decided to move someplace safe. Someplace where drive-by shootings weren't a nightly occurrence. A place where kids sold lemonade instead of crack on the street corners.

It hadn't worked out any better for Kat than it had for Ezra and Mandy. All three were just as dead as if they'd been gunned down by gangbangers or dope heads, and all three deaths were just as senseless.

There was nothing else to see out here. They'd swept the woods the night before with the county forensics guy, but the only thing they'd found was a spot where the murderer *might* have waited for his victim. The neighbors apparently used the woods behind the Rucker house as a shortcut, and the ground was covered with hundreds of different footprints.

Cal approached the back of the house. He reached into his pocket for the key Mrs. Rucker had provided and then stopped to look back at the trees. The sky had darkened even more, casting everything in a sickly greenish tint. Branches swayed and shifted like grasping hands, although Cal hadn't felt a breeze.

Was there someone there? For a moment he thought he saw something just beyond the edge of the woods—a furtive streak of movement flickering in the shadows. He took a step forward, and it was gone. The trees were just trees again. Whatever breeze had rocked them abated, and he could see that there was no one there.

He considered exploring further anyway, but he still had to go through the house and then get out to meet with Mrs. Rucker. She and the children were staying with her parents for the time being. If he was going to speak with her in less than an hour, he had to get a move on. Checking the knob, he found that he didn't need the key after all. It was unlocked.

The back stoop opened into a cozy kitchen. The linoleum was peeling in a couple of the corners, and the dinette set looked like it had come straight out of the early seventies, but the feeling was one of warmth.

Half a dozen cookies stood sentry on a sheet of waxed paper, six grease spots attesting to the demise of their comrades. Herbs grew in little clay pots on the windowsill, and a slew of school papers with red stars and smiley faces were attached to the front of the refrigerator with fruit-shaped magnets.

Cal stopped to look at a crayon drawing—the work of the youngest Rucker boy, he assumed. Crude brown lines formed a small house, complete with windows, a door, and a squiggly black curl of smoke coming from the chimney. Beside the house stood a stick family. The mother was only discernable as a woman by her red triangle dress. The big brother's arms were raised to either side of his body, flexing upside-down U muscles.

But it was the father that captured Cal's attention. He was wearing a pair of scribbled blue pants and a red shirt. In one hand he held a paintbrush. His other hand rested on the head of the smallest figure—a boy. The boy looked up at his father with a wide, red smile, his blue eyes filled with an expression that even drawn by the unsteady hand of a four-year-old could not be mistaken for anything less than adoration.

Cal turned away. He noted that the table was set for dinner. A casserole that would never be eaten sat cold in a Pyrex pan. Butter congealed in a bowl of corn. Two large plates—one chipped—were set across from a pair of smaller red and blue plastic plates. All four glasses—two large glasses and two small cups that looked like they'd been saved from a Happy Meal—were filled with milk.

It looked like a setting for a play or a fairy tale. Any minute Goldilocks would slip stealthily in the door to try the porridge. Only in this story, Papa Bear was never coming home. Cal's stomach burned with a tight, hard ache, and he moved quickly on.

Past the kitchen was a pint-sized living room. Most of one wall was taken up by a large, cheap-looking entertainment center—the kind you bought at Kmart and spent half the day assembling. But it was the family photographs on the other wall that caught Cal's attention.

On one side were pictures of the kids. Joshua holding up a large rainbow trout. Sam and Joshua on a kiddy roller coaster. There were baby pictures of both the boys and school photos of Joshua. On the other side were pictures of Tamara, Ezra, and several people Cal assumed to be relatives.

In one, a young Tamara was wearing a long white dress. Another showed Ezra as a boy. He was standing beside a grim-looking man in patched overalls that must be his father. Here were Tamara and Ezra on their wedding day, standing on the steps of the chapel. Tamara barely looked old enough to drive, and Ezra didn't look much older.

Cal stepped around the coffee table to take a closer look at the pictures, and his shoe caught the edge of something tucked beneath the base of the couch. He leaned over and picked up a brown leather book with the word *Memories* stenciled in gold on the front cover. Flipping through the pages, he saw that it was a scrapbook.

Certificates, news clippings, and photographs had been carefully centered on pages of colored cardstock, surrounded by fancy borders— Ezra's graduation certificate, his senior class picture, and their wedding announcement.

A piece of paper slipped from the book, and Cal snatched it deftly in midair. It was a folded newspaper clipping, the paper creased and the newsprint smeared from repeated handling. He turned it over and was somehow not surprised to find himself looking at the local paper's story of Mandy's murder.

Cal looked through the rest of the book, stopping on a faded class picture. It was obviously from the late sixties or early seventies—the boys in button-down shirts had slicked-back hair, most of it cut short and parted on the side; the girls wore sundresses or skirts and blouses.

The text under the picture read, *Mrs. Trotwood's Second-Grade Class.* Thirty or more children were lined up in front of a grove of trees.

The young boy in the center was obviously Ezra. He wore a devil-may-care grin, and from the surprised expression of the boy to his right, it looked like Ezra had just goosed him.

It was the girl on Ezra's left that caught Cal's attention. She was taller than most of the boys, trim, with wavy red hair. Ezra had his arm slung companionably around her shoulders.

Cal's pulse raced. This might be the connection he'd been looking for. He gently removed the photograph from the black studio corners holding it to the page. It was impossible to tell for sure, but he'd be willing to bet a week's worth of lunches that the girl standing next to Ezra was Mandy Osgood. Back then it would have been Amanda Porter.

CHAPTER 10

CAL WORKED HIS WAY OUT of the neighborhood of small, older homes. Fat drops of rain splashed against the windshield, remaining just long enough to diffuse the landscape into a kaleidoscope of colors before the wipers swept them away. Despite the rain, the yards and street were awash with children.

As the patrol car passed by them, some of the boys and girls stopped their play long enough to wave. A few of the older ones made faces or turned away. Most just continued with what they were doing. Cal knew they'd all heard by now what had happened at the Rucker house.

As he approached the corner, he noticed a solitary boy dressed in a white short-sleeved shirt and long blue pants. The boy sat solemnly on the wet concrete watching the cruiser approach, his eyes partially obscured behind thick, black glasses. His dark hair was plastered to his head. Kid must be soaked, Cal thought. But if the boy was uncomfortable, he gave no sign of it—almost as if he was unaware of the weather at all.

Something about the boy pulled at Cal's heartstrings. Maybe it was the expression of resigned loneliness. He looked like the kind of kid who never got picked to play kickball or asked to be anyone's partner in the science project. That was emphasized by the way he sat all by himself, not even standing hopefully near the other children, waiting to be invited to join their play.

Cal slowed the cruiser to a stop as he passed by. He was late for his appointment with Tamara Rucker, but another minute or two wouldn't hurt. He always kept a stash of Hershey bars in his glove box along with a box of gold Honorary Deputy badges.

As he reached for the box, the sun broke through the clouds, shedding a golden light on the glistening street and temporarily casting a blinding glare. When he looked up, the boy was gone. Cal checked his rearview mirror for a glimpse of the kid, but by the time his eyes adjusted to the bright light, the boy had disappeared.

CHAPTER 11

"I'm sorry, Chief—" Tamara Rucker struggled to remember Cal's name. "Chief—"

"Hunt. But call me Cal."

Tamara pulled another tissue from the box on the chrome-and-glass coffee table in front of her and wiped her nose. She was a mousy-looking woman with light-brown hair that clung to the sides of her face as though she were trying to hide behind it. Cal knew from the pictures he had seen at the house that she was an attractive woman. But now, with deep purple crescents standing out against the pale skin under her bloodshot eyes, her thin nostrils red and raw, she simply looked haggard.

She blew her nose and took a deep breath, trying to steady herself. "I just don't understand who . . . why anyone would . . . would want to . . . to . . ." She buried her face in her hands, breaking into fresh sobs.

"Take all the time you need," Cal said, reaching across the table to pat her shoulder. Somewhere nearby he heard the sound of footsteps. He hoped the Rucker children were being kept out of earshot. "It's all right."

"No," she said, wiping furiously at her nose. "It's *not* all right. It's never going to be all right again. My husband's dead!"

Cal said nothing. He knew the feeling all too well—the realization that things were never going to be the same. No matter how hard you tried, you could never make it right again. Biting the inside of his lip, he waited for her anger to run its course.

When at last her tears had slowed, Cal leaned toward her, hands resting on his knees. "Mrs. Rucker, I know this is hard," he said, his tone soothing. "I just need to ask a few questions, and then I'll let you get back to your family. Can you think of anyone who might have wanted to harm your husband? Anyone he might have argued with lately? Someone at work, or church maybe?"

Cal placed a small digital recorder on the center of the table and pressed the record button. Tamara glanced quickly at the device then averted her gaze. Cal noticed her sideways glance toward the living room door. She had asked her parents to leave the room when Cal arrived. Now, dropping her voice, she said, "Ezra doesn't . . . didn't go to church much anymore." She took another tissue.

"The last few months have been very difficult for my husband and me," she said, unconsciously referring to Ezra as if he were still alive.

"How so?"

Again Tamara's gaze drifted toward the door, and Cal realized she suspected one or both of her parents were listening from the other side. Rubbing her hands up and down her arms as if she was cold, she asked, "Are you married?"

Cal gave his head a quick shake. "No." Then, noticing Tamara glance down at his ring, he added, "My wife passed away."

"Oh. I'm sorry." Tamara seemed to relax a little, perhaps seeing Cal for the first time as not just a cop but as another person capable of feeling pain too. She brushed at her eyes. "How long?"

"Six months," he said, uncomfortable with the turn the conversation was taking.

She nodded. "Then I guess you can understand some of what I'm going through."

He could—all too well.

Keeping her voice low, she leaned toward Cal. "My parents never argue. At least not that *I've* ever seen. And they go to church every Sunday—even when they're so sick they probably shouldn't. They never wanted me to marry Ezra in the first place. So when the business started going downhill and Ezra began taking it out on everyone around him— and quit going to church—they were the first ones to say I told you so."

She studied Cal, as if deciding just how much information she could trust him with. "Did you and your wife ever argue?" she asked, her voice small and pleading, like a little girl's.

"Sure," Cal said. "I think every couple does at one time or another." He thought about the things he and Kat had fought over—paying bills, whose turn it was to clean out the litter box, what kind of furniture to put in the basement. Things that seemed so trivial now. And yet he'd give everything he had to hear her complain again about his lamentable penchant for big leather recliners. He'd grant every one of her wishes, no matter how trivial, and grin like a school kid the whole time.

"My husband's had his problems," Tamara said. "He's had a difficult time controlling his temper lately. He's gotten into fights. He's . . . hit the boys. Not hard, but . . ." She took a deep breath and hurried on.

"He wasn't always that way. His father was abusive. When we married, Ezra swore he would never be that kind of man. He was the sweetest, most caring person you could imagine. He opened the door for me all the time. We read the Bible together."

She paused for a moment, seemingly lost in thoughts of a happier time, before the reality of the moment crashed back down on her.

"I'm sorry," she said, "I was just realizing when things started to change. It was after we took Joshua and Sam to the caves right before the end of school."

Cal started. What was it about caves that rang a bell? "What caves were those?" he asked.

"The Glenwood caverns. You know, the ones where they take you on a tour and then turn out all the lights? It was a church activity."

Tamara's words sent an arrow of cold air shooting down Cal's spine. Hadn't Eddie Osgood said something about a cave as well? It hadn't been Glenwood, but there was something. He just couldn't quite remember what.

"I should never have let him go," Tamara continued, her words rushed. "I knew the whole cave thing still bothered him. He swore he was over it, but how could it be? I mean, do you ever really get over a trauma like that?"

"The cave thing?" Cal gripped his knees, the knuckles on his big fists turning white with the pressure.

"A long time ago," Tamara smiled sadly, "back when Ezra was a little boy, he and some other kids got lost in an old gold mine. Everyone had just about given up hope when they were found."

That was it! Eddie Osgood said that Mandy had been lost in a cave as well. It had to be the same one. That tied in with the class picture. What were the odds of both murder victims being lost in the same mine incident? It couldn't be a coincidence. But what did it mean?

"What is it?" Tamara asked, noticing Cal's stunned expression.

"Nothing, just a thought. Go on." He tried to pay attention to what she was saying, but his mind was racing. This was the first solid connection between the two victims.

"When Ezra brought up the Glenwood trip, I didn't think it was a good idea. I thought maybe it would bring back all his childhood trauma again. That can happen, you know."

Cal nodded, still wondering how an event that occurred nearly thirty years earlier could have any relevance on the two murders but knowing that it somehow did.

"Ezra just laughed off my worries," Tamara said. "He said he was over all that. He thought it would be fun for the boys to go on the trip. They were both so excited, and Ezra didn't want to disappoint them. That's the kind of dad he was." A fragile smile appeared and just as quickly vanished.

It was obvious Tamara would spend many hours replaying the good times to sustain her through the bad ones. That was also something with which Cal could commiserate.

"When we reached the mouth of the cave, Ezra started to feel sick to his stomach. I suggested maybe we should come back another time, but he insisted we go on. We hadn't been inside for more than a few minutes when he started to look bad. He was having a hard time standing up, and he said he felt like he couldn't breathe.

"I wanted to get him out, but then they did the part where they turn out all the lights, and I felt him collapse against me. It was like he was having some kind of seizure." Tamara pulled two more tissues from the box. The pile on the coffee table had grown to a small white mountain.

"When we got home I wanted him to go to the doctor but he refused. He said he'd probably just eaten some bad eggs that morning. And for a few days he seemed all right."

"But then?" Cal asked.

Tamara shook her head. "At first it was just a lot of bad dreams. He'd never admit it, of course. But I could hear him moaning in his sleep. He wasn't sleeping well at all, and he couldn't seem to concentrate on anything for more than a few minutes. I tried to make him see someone—a doctor, a counselor, or even the pastor."

"Did he go?"

She looked up at the ceiling, tears streaming down her cheeks. "No. And things kept getting worse. He started losing his painting jobs. And he started drinking, although he wouldn't admit that either. I'd hear him talking to himself, muttering things about mines and spirits. He kept repeating some name. Freddie, Francis, Frankie . . . something like that.

"He started disappearing for hours at a time. At first I thought . . . I thought maybe he was having an affair. He wasn't, though. Ezra may have been many things, but he was never unfaithful."

Cal shifted in his chair, a million thoughts racing through his head. "I'll need the names of any of his friends. The people he worked with. Anyone he might have upset."

Tamara nodded, pressing the tissue to her mouth. She squeezed her eyes closed, and two long, slow tears dripped down her cheeks.

When she seemed to have regained a measure of control, Cal said, "Just two more questions. Do the words *Frog Eyes* mean anything to you?"

Tamara shook her head. "Should they?" Apparently she hadn't seen the truck. That was probably for the best.

"I'm not sure," Cal said. That raised an interesting dilemma. Ezra's killer had obviously gone to a lot of trouble to leave behind a message. Mandy's appearance also seemed to be a message of some kind. Yet neither the police nor the victims' spouses had any idea what either of the messages meant. If the killer was the same person in both cases—and Cal felt certain that it was—for whom was he or she leaving the messages?

"Last question," he said. "Did your husband ever mention a woman named Mandy Osgood?"

Ezra's widow looked up sharply. "Why do you ask?"

Cal showed her the class photograph and the news story. He pointed to the girl standing to Ezra's left in the photo. "I think this girl may be the same woman who was murdered two days ago."

Tamara nodded. "That would make sense. He kept rereading the newspaper story about her and mumbling to himself. He wouldn't tell me anything when I asked, but I think he might have mentioned her name before." She studied the picture again.

"If I didn't know better," she said, "I'd have sworn he felt guilty."

CHAPTER 12

"You mind if I keep this for a while?" Cal asked, holding out the photograph. He had finished his questions for the time being, and he and Tamara were standing on the porch. He noticed Tamara's mother peer surreptitiously through the curtains at the front of the house.

"No. Not at all." Tamara tried to smile but couldn't quite manage it. "Do you think it will help?"

"You never can tell."

The boys had stayed out of sight with their grandparents the whole time Cal had been speaking with their mother. Now Sam, the younger of the two, peeked around his mother's legs.

"Is that your police car?" he asked shyly.

Cal nodded. "Would you like to see it?"

Sam looked up at his mother, who gave her okay before he said, "Yeah, sure."

"Come on," Cal said. "I'll give you the grand tour." He led the boy over to the cruiser and slid him onto the front seat.

"Candy bar?" Cal offered, opening the glove box.

The little boy shook his head. "Nah. I'm not supposed to eat sweets before lunch."

"That's good advice. How 'bout a badge, then?"

Sam nodded. As Cal pinned on the badge, the little boy looked over the array of equipment. "Does your car got an alterbator?" he asked.

"I'm pretty sure it does," Cal said. He expected the boy to ask about the shotgun locked to the dash or to want to turn on the siren. Kids always went for that kind of stuff. Instead Sam looked up at him with wide, solemn eyes.

"Do you know where my dad is?"

The boy's voice, soft and without guile, went straight to Cal's heart. Cal shook his head.

"My mom says he's in heaven with the angels."

"I see." Cal wondered what it was like to have that kind of faith.

"Think you'll catch the bad guy? The one who kilt my dad?"

The question slammed Cal in the gut. Sucking in his breath, he nodded. "Yeah. I do."

Sam seemed to think about that. He gave Cal the same studied look his mother had, and for a minute Cal thought the boy was going to tell him something—something important. But the moment passed, if it had ever been there at all. Sam gave a quick bob of his head.

"Good," he said, before jumping from the car and running back to his mother.

CHAPTER 13

CAL TOOK THE LIBRARY STAIRS two at a time, noticing the way the mothers at the playground whispered to each other as they watched him pass. Word was out, and it wouldn't be long before he started getting calls from concerned citizens, questions in the grocery store. Right now no one seemed to have tied the two murders together. But if there was another one . . .

He couldn't help thinking, as he watched the children climbing up the jungle gym and shooting down the slide, that if he didn't find the killer quickly, one of their parents might be next. Swinging open the glass door, he slipped into the dim cool of the library.

"You finished with Ulysses S. Grant yet?" Clara Bell was a tiny woman with a tall coif of perfectly arranged white hair that always reminded Cal of a dried flower arrangement. Every time he looked at her he felt surprised she didn't just topple over.

"He just won Vicksburg," Cal said.

Clara had been Twin Forks head librarian for as long as anyone could remember. She had broken her hip two years earlier when she slipped on an icy patch of sidewalk down by the post office, and now she always seemed to cant slightly to starboard. But she'd been back at the library as soon as they released her from the hospital and hadn't missed a day since.

"Don't forget, it's due back next week," she ordered, as stern as any general.

"Wouldn't dream of it." Cal was careful not to crack a smile. Clara considered the library books her children, and she was vigilant in seeing to their safe return.

With that bit of business taken care of, her face softened a little, and she moved toward the counter, her limp hardly noticeable as she took each careful step. "We sure do miss your wife around here, Cal. She was a gem."

"She was that," Cal agreed. Kat had volunteered two days a week at the library, taking on any duty from shelving books to fundraising. She'd loved books and had slowly won Cal over to loving them as well.

"So what can I help you find today?" Clara leaned halfway across the countertop and gave Cal a conspiratorial wink. "I have the new Stephen King," she whispered. "I keep it back here. Away from the children so I don't corrupt 'em. And away from the goodie-two-shoes so they don't accuse *me* of being corrupt."

"No thanks." Cal chuckled. Clara knew perfectly well that he stuck to nonfiction.

"Well you can't blame a soul for trying. I'll get you into a novel one of these days."

"You just might. But actually I'm here today doing a little research."

"Are you?" she asked, an unexpected glint in her eye.

"I was wondering where I might be able to find some information on an accident that happened quite a few years ago."

Clara nodded. "The Seven Stars."

"What?" Cal asked, half suspecting that the impish librarian was trying to sell him on another novel.

"The Seven Stars," Clara repeated. "The last great gold mine in Colorado. Those poor little children who got lost back in '77. I'm surprised it's taken you this long to come looking."

Cal was dumbfounded. "How could you . . . I mean how did you know what I was looking for?"

"Isn't it obvious?" Clara lifted the partition and maneuvered her way around to Cal's side of the counter.

"Listen, if someone's been leaking police infor—"

"Nonsense." Clara managed to command authority without raising her voice above a whisper, in the way of all good librarians. "No one's been leaking anything. Six children got lost in a mine back when Jimmy Carter was in office. It was quite a tragedy. When I heard that two of the five survivors were murdered within days of each other, it only made sense that you'd come nosing around."

"Wait, did you say *six* children?" Cal hurried to keep up with the librarian who was able to move rather quickly when she wanted to.

"Yes, yes. Six were lost. But only five were found." When they reached the microfilm readers, Clara pointed toward one of the chairs and ordered

Cal to wait. He took a seat. Clara headed into the restricted area in the back of the library.

"What happened to the sixth?" he called after her.

"The Seven Stars," she said before disappearing around the corner.

What did she mean by that?

As Cal waited for Clara to return, he pulled out the class portrait again and studied the two children standing near the center of the picture. A muscular boy with a mischievous grin, his shirt sleeves hiked up to reveal a clearly discernable farmer's tan, and a raw-boned, red-haired girl with flyaway hair. He thought he could make out the gap where she'd recently lost a baby tooth.

Not long after this photo was taken, they would both disappear into something called the Seven Stars mine with four other children. Would their expressions ever be so carefree again? They both seemed to have suffered lasting emotional scars from the incident. Not surprising, considering that they couldn't have been any older than—he mentally counted off the years—seven or eight?

And if Clara was right, one of the other children—one of Mandy and Ezra's schoolmates—had never been found. Which of the faces—trapped forever beneath Cal's finger in the two-dimensional images of their youth—belonged to the other three survivors? Had they been emotionally scarred as well? Maybe scarred enough to kill?

Before he could reach any sort of conclusion, Clara was back with a spool of film. She deftly fed the spool into the reader. "Not bad for an old biddy with arthritis, eh?" she said, switching on the machine. As Cal watched, issue after issue of the *Douglas County Sentinel* flew by. About halfway through the reel, she slowed the reader, and there was the headline.

"Six Children Disappear from School Picnic."

Cal scanned the article then moved forward to the next issue.

"Children Feared Lost in Closed Gold Mine. County Mobilizes."

As he moved from story to story, the tragedy became clear, and Cal started taking notes. In the summer of 1977, six children had slipped away from a school picnic and entered a boarded-up gold mine. Two of the names were all too familiar—Amanda Porter and Ezra Rucker. But he'd never heard of the others. Benjamin Meyers, Theresa Truman, Olivia Godwin, and Frankie Zoeller.

Cal studied the pictures beside the newspaper article. One of the boys looked strangely familiar. "Which one is this?" he asked, placing his finger next to the youngster whose dark eyes, distorted and enlarged behind thick lenses, projected a sense of isolation

Clara leaned over Cal's shoulder. "That's Frankie," she whispered, her eyes solemn. "He was the poor lad they never found."

"Zoeller," Cal said, trying the name on his tongue. He couldn't place the name, and yet something about that face . . . Then he had it—the boy on the sidewalk, the one he'd seen sitting out in the rain. It had to be a coincidence, of course. Even if he had somehow survived, the Zoeller boy would be older than forty by now. Still, the resemblance was startling.

Cal looked up at Clara. "What about the other children? Couldn't they tell the searchers where—"

"No, not a thing." Clara shook her head so that her tall coif swayed perilously back and forth. "When the rescuers got them out, the children wouldn't or couldn't say anything at all about what happened to little Frankie."

Cal scanned to the article headlined, "Five Children Found Alive! One Still Missing," and read through the story.

The children had been lost nearly five days. Most of the rescuers had given up hope until they found an engineer who knew the mine top to bottom. It was the engineer who had pinpointed the children's location. Fortunately, the mine had been bored below the water table, so dehydration wasn't a problem. But the temperature deep inside the mine was only fifty-three degrees. Some felt that the cold had actually kept the children alive all that time by slowing their metabolism.

He scrolled through several more "Search Continues" headlines and then at last saw, "Search Over. Boy Presumed Dead. Mine Entrance Blasted."

Beneath the headline was the picture of a woman who looked like she was in her mid-twenties. She had collapsed on the ground outside the mine, and a group of men was trying to revive her.

Cal looked up at Clara, who had been reading along with him over his shoulder. "Frankie's mother?"

Clara nodded.

"Other than Ezra and Mandy, do any of the others still live in the area?" he asked.

The librarian ran one hand across her bony chin. "I know the Meyers family is still here, but I believe their boy moved away some years ago. About the Trumans, I don't know. Seems to me Theresa may have married a fellow in Denver, but I couldn't be sure. And of course there are the Godwins. You know them."

"Wait a minute." Cal stopped taking notes. "You mean *the* Godwins? The ones with that huge estate up in the canyon?"

"The very same," Clara agreed.

Cal began twisting his ring against the callused skin beneath it. "What about Frankie's mother?"

"Esther Zoeller? Sure, sure. Esther's still right where she's always been. That poor woman swore she'd never leave until her boy was found, and she kept her word." Clara gave Cal a questioning look. "You think she has something to do with this?"

Cal looked up from the viewer. "Should I?"

Clara shrugged, her expression unreadable. "Don't know if you should or not," she said cryptically. "You're the policeman. But folks say she blamed the others—especially Mandy and Ezra—for luring her boy into the mine. Don't imagine she's ever forgiven them, or forgotten what they did."

Cal added the note to his file. "Could she be right?" he asked.

Again Clara shrugged. Cal thought she knew more than she was telling but he also knew the woman could keep her mouth shut when it suited her. She'd tell him only when she was good and ready.

"Is there some way to make copies of these articles?" Cal asked, gathering up his files.

"All it takes is a little loose change," Clara said, all business again.

As Cal began to rewind the machine, a thought occurred to him. "Wouldn't they have sealed the mine after they closed it?"

"'Course," Clara said, her eyes darkening as she studied him intelligently.

"But then how . . ." Cal's words faded away as he noticed the odd, slightly twisted smile on the old woman's face.

"Places like that have a way of reopening," she whispered. "Been pulling that trick since long before you or I were around."

Cal shook his head, confused. He had no idea what Clara was talking about.

Clara laid a wrinkled hand on his shoulder. "You know, if you're going to be looking into the Seven Stars, you might want to take that Stephen King novel with you after all. Maybe it'll help you in your research."

"How's that?" he asked.

"I'd've thought a smart fellow like you would have figured that out by now," she said, a trace of disappointment in her voice. "The Seven Stars is haunted."

CHAPTER 14

CAL STRETCHED HIS LEGS OUT beneath the coffee table, swallowing the last of his beer and pressing his back against the couch cushions. He set the bottle onto the table, next to the remains of his ham sandwich.

Sunday used to be the day when he and Kat went all out, cooking up a big meal. A typical Sunday afternoon repast included leg of lamb in Marsala wine sauce, baby red potatoes with garlic, creamed onions, sliced carrots with brown sugar. Sometimes they invited another couple from the neighborhood, but often it was just the two of them.

His stomach rumbled at the memory. Nowadays he either went out or made something quick and easy—a sandwich or a frozen dinner. Kat would have complained vigorously at the thought of TV dinners defiling her kitchen, but making a big meal for one person seemed pointless.

You could *invite someone over,* a voice whispered in his ear—a voice that sounded a lot like Kat when she'd reprimand him over some little thing in an amused sort of way.

He *should* invite someone to the house. The Hickens maybe or the Horns. He hadn't had anyone over since . . . well, for a long time. It just seemed like too much effort. And yet that wasn't the real reason he hadn't invited anyone to the house, any more than it was the real reason he hadn't cooked a decent meal since Kat's death.

It was just too painful. Using the knife she always sliced the carrots with—remembering how she always gave him heck if he used the paring knife to slice the meat or the butcher knife to pit avocadoes. Remembering how she always made sure he used a wooden spoon with her good Teflon pans. Hearing in his mind the snatches of show tunes she sang as she moved from one pot to another.

No. It was easier this way. Eating tasteless food from throwaway containers and letting the past stay where it belonged. Buster rubbed against Cal's leg before jumping onto the table. He mewed as he sniffed delicately at the remains of Cal's sandwich. Cal pulled out a sliver of ham, and the cat immediately snapped it up.

"Guess you're not real discerning either, huh?" Cal asked.

Buster sniffed in disgust and leaped lightly down to the floor.

Cal slid the plate and bottle to one side of the table. He'd been watching the Reds beat the tar out of his Dodgers, hoping to take his mind off the murders for a couple of hours—Sunday being a day of rest and all. But his thoughts kept creeping back to the images of the children.

The case file lay at his feet. He lifted it to the table and spread out the pictures he had carefully clipped from one of the photocopied newspaper articles. Six children, three boys and three girls. He slid the girls to the left side of the table, matching names to faces.

Amanda Porter was the oldest of the three. He knew from his records that she was an only child. Her father had been killed in a farm accident when she was two, and her mother had never remarried. Mrs. Porter had subsequently died of breast cancer in her mid-fifties.

Amanda had married at seventeen, divorced, and remarried at nineteen. That marriage had lasted the longest of her three—nearly eight years. She'd gone through several relationships since then, culminating in her marriage to Eddie four years ago. He set Amanda's photo off to one side and moved on to the next.

Theresa Truman was a studious-looking girl with straight dark hair that hung down to her shoulders. Serious eyes were hidden behind a pair of thick-framed glasses. According to the article, she was a little younger than Amanda. Cal had checked for a phone number for the Trumans without luck.

The last girl, Olivia Godwin, was the smallest girl in her class. With her waist-length blond hair and upturned nose, she looked like a little elf. Cal wondered whether her family had been as wealthy back then as they were now.

Moving on to the boys, he glanced briefly at Ezra Rucker. Checking out the yearbooks he'd obtained from the school, Cal found three more Rucker boys, Adam, Josiah, and Samuel. Each had Ezra's broad shoulders and good looks. Cal was a little disappointed that the boy wasn't wearing glasses, hoping that glasses might somehow tie into the marks the killer had left on Ezra's face.

Ben Meyers was the boy standing to Ezra's right, the one with a surprised expression on his face. He had the fine, almost feminine features some boys possess at that age. Long, sooty eyelashes stood out against his pale skin. Cal suspected that he'd been a lady-killer as a teen.

The youngest of the six, Frankie Zoeller, had the eyeglasses Cal had been hoping to see on Ezra. His black hair was cut in what Cal thought of as a bowl cut, forming an even line from forehead to ears, as though someone had placed a cereal bowl on top of his head and gone at him with the clippers. He wore a bemused, dreamy expression.

He was smaller even than Olivia, his arms and neck pencil thin. Had the other kids picked on him? Cal thought they had. The kid had the look of a perpetual victim. He was an only child, and Cal couldn't even imagine what it must have been like for the boy's mother when the search was finally called off.

He swept the pictures and articles into a neat stack. He would take them to the office and study them more on Monday, gathering additional information on each of the children. But it was nearly four o'clock, and he had a trip to make before Sunday afternoon became Sunday evening.

As he lifted the stack to tuck it back into the case folder, Amanda's picture caught his eye. Something about the photograph seemed so familiar. Same red hair, not as thick as it would become. Same eyes. Freckles that would fade with time. The headshot cut off just below the collar of her—

Cal shot up from the couch, hurried to the kitchen, and began to search Kat's desk. Rifling through the top drawer, he failed to find what he was looking for and moved down to the next. Thumb tacks, paper clips, sticky-notes, envelopes. Not there. He opened the third drawer. Kat would know exactly where it was. She had a system that Cal had never quite been able to figure out. Finally, he found what he was looking for beneath the address book.

Snatching up the black-handled magnifying glass, he went back to the table. Under magnification, he could just make out the lacy-white collar of Amanda's blouse. He switched to the class photo, and a long, slow whistle escaped his lips.

"Son of a gun," he whispered.

Same blouse—probably her Sunday best—and same dark skirt. And at the bottom edge of the picture, just visible . . . Yes. There they were, the black Mary Janes with the silver buckles.

Not the same ones of course—the outfit of a girl seven or eight would never fit a grown woman. But the similarity was eerily accurate. That the killer had either studied this picture or worked from a very acute memory was undeniable. As Cal examined the photograph in greater detail, something else caught his eye. It was in the back left corner, nearly out of sight behind the last row of children.

He could just discern a line of picnic tables. Each of them was spread with a checkered tablecloth. On one of the tables was what looked like a large wicker basket, and next to that was a plastic thermos. As the reality of what he was seeing dawned on him, goose bumps broke out all along Cal's forearms.

This picture hadn't been taken months before the children became lost in the mine, as he had assumed. Not even a week before. He was looking at a photograph shot that very day—at the end-of-school picnic.

CHAPTER 15

SUNDAY AFTERNOON IN TWIN FORKS was one of the quietest times of the week. Most of the city's occupants were either still in church or at home eating large Sunday dinners. Many of the businesses up and down Pine Street were closed, and as he drove slowly past one of the city's many churches, Cal could hear the words to "Amazing Grace" drifting through the open windows.

Before Kat's death, he had enjoyed the sight of families filing into church. Although he didn't share their faith, the knowledge of their beliefs provided him a certain level of peace. If it helped people to believe that an omnipotent being watched over them, then why not?

But now the thought of their convictions bothered him. Why should they take comfort in the death of those they loved when he was left with only images of his wife's coffin being lowered into the ground and memories that crumbled to dust even as he tried to hang on to them? Despite the afternoon's heat, he rolled up the window.

Merging onto Highway 83, he increased his speed. Although the last snow had fallen the first week in April, the mountain peaks still wore their powdery caps. It would be another month or two before the white stuff disappeared completely.

Once he reached the canyon, the mountain air became cool and redolent with the smell of pine. Moving over to the right lane, he rolled his window down and slowed to savor the fragrance. A pair of binoculars and a map were on the front seat beside him, although he was pretty sure he could find the spot he was looking for.

Six or seven miles up the canyon, he began looking for the turnoff. He was expecting something small, but he still nearly missed the narrow road. As he pulled sharply off to the side of the highway, his tires spit up a wake of gravel. Watching the rearview mirror for traffic, he backed far enough to check out the lane.

He examined his map. The road he was looking for was only a tiny blue squiggle, impossible to match up with his current location. Craning his neck out the window, he looked for some kind of identification. It looked as if there might have been a sign at one time. But if so, it had been torn down long ago—the only remnant, a bullet-riddled post, was weatherworn a splintery gray. Dropping the transmission into drive, he started up the road. After several yards, he crossed over a cattle barrier, his tires rumbling on the steel grate.

The winter runoff had been rough on the winding switchbacks that worked their way slowly up the side of the valley, and Cal kept his speed to less than ten miles an hour, wary of bottoming out his car. At the top of the rise the ruts disappeared, but the improvement was short lived. As the road wound down a narrow pass, it deteriorated from gravel to dirt and finally to only a pair of ruts that drew the bottom of his car perilously close to the center of the road.

Pine trees began to crowd against the sides of his cruiser, brushing the fenders and doors as he drove past, and an alarming thought ran through his mind. What if he was on the wrong road? What if the surface kept deteriorating until he lost traction completely? Here in the lee of the steep, rocky cliffs, the temperature had plummeted. Patches of snow were still visible between some of the trees, and Cal had visions of trying to hike out with only a light jacket as protection from the frigid wind.

Just when he'd about decided that he'd taken the wrong turnoff, he passed between a narrow opening in the rock walls that had been blasted with dynamite, and the road ended in a circular parking area. At one end of the lot was a long wooden rail for tying off horses—and, much to his amazement, he found four other vehicles parked there. He pulled up next to a dusty pickup with a horse trailer hooked to the back, opened the door, and stretched his legs.

Taking the binoculars, he locked the car and set out to explore. Past a couple of four-wheel drives with bike racks on the top, he stopped to stare at what had to be the picnic tables from the school photo.

This *was* the place, then. How had they ever managed to get all those kids up here? School bus maybe? If so, either the roads had been better back then or the school buses had been tougher.

As he approached the tables, he could see that they were covered with decades of graffiti—some of it drawn on with ballpoint pens or markers, but most of it carved into the wood. He studied the initials, wondering whether E.R. or A.P. might be hidden somewhere among the hieroglyphs.

Facing the clearing, he tried to imagine the voices of thirty-three young children—he had counted them from the picture—celebrating the conclusion of another school year. Boys trying to put frogs down girls' backs. The girls running and giggling.

According to the newspaper, they were supervised that day by a female teacher's assistant and by their vice principal, a man named Paul Andreason. How difficult must it have been to keep track of more than thirty kids, all struck with an incurable case of spring fever?

He got the feeling that Andreason might have blamed himself from the way all of his quotes in the newspaper articles began with how closely he had been watching the children. It occurred to Cal that in a place like this it would have been impossible for even the best teacher to keep track of every kid for every minute.

The trail continued up the hillside. Cal followed it, noting the tracks of mountain bike tires and horse hooves. Beside the trail, a creek ran down the side of the mountain. Someone had propped a pipe into the creek bed, sending a continual stream of crystal-clear water into a horse trough that stood next to the dirt path. He stopped and cupped his hands under the flow. The water was so cold it actually seemed to stop his heart for a minute as he let it trickle down his throat.

As the wind began to pick up, he hurried his pace. The drive had taken longer than he anticipated, and the sun was rapidly disappearing over the western ridges. What had this area looked like back when the mine was open? Were the remains of tents and cabins buried somewhere beneath the brush?

Nearly a quarter of a mile from the tables, he stepped off the trail to let a group of bikers go by. He wanted to ask them if they knew where the entrance to the mine might be, but they raced past him—hunched against the cold—before he could get the words out of his mouth. After continuing five more minutes, he stopped and turned. Based on what he'd read, the old entrance couldn't be this far from the picnic area.

Backtracking along the trail, he studied the hillside through his binoculars. Halfway to the tables, he saw what he was looking for. The ridge above him showed a curved depression twenty or thirty feet wide. He began to climb the side of the hill, his feet slipping and sliding on the loose rock. Another ten feet and he realized he was standing on top of an old landslide.

He remembered that they had dynamited the entrance to the mine closed, and it was obvious that the opening was still sealed off. Part of him was relieved. An open mine was an invitation to trouble, as the citizens of Twin Forks had learned. He shoved his hands into his pockets, shivering at the icy breeze as the sun disappeared behind him. Another part of him pictured the dreamy-eyed boy with the funny haircut.

He had been sealed behind tons of rock and soil. His body would never be recovered. His mother would never visit his grave and lay flowers on his headstone. Somewhere in those pitch-black tunnels lay the remains of a boy not much older than Sam Rucker, and those remains were never coming out.

From farther up the canyon, the wail of a lone coyote echoed into the night. Cal waited to see if there would be an answer, but there was only silence. He had been raised a city boy, and the isolation of the mountains made him edgy.

Movement above him caught his eye, and he looked up just in time to see a black funnel rise into the twilight sky. A single dark shape separated itself from the cloud and dropped down to snatch something from the air with a high-pitched screech. Bats. He'd never seen so many at once.

He looked up at the hill of rock and dirt, remembering the librarian's words, and a shiver that had nothing to do with the cold washed across his body. He certainly wasn't religious, but he firmly believed that actions left their own residue—a kind of psychic stench that remained long after the people who left them were gone.

Something evil had taken place here. He could sense it with every nerve in his body.

CHAPTER 16

"HELP ME."

Cal was standing on the trail again, at a point just below the landslide where the entrance to the Seven Stars had been blasted closed. It was night, and although the moon was nearly full, it shone with a corrupt green light that did little to illuminate the landscape beneath it. Instead, its sickly glow distorted the trees and rocks into strange, indecipherable shapes. At the sound of the voice, Cal whirled around, searching the side of the hill.

"Help me." The voice came again, high-pitched and childlike, although strangely muted.

"Please! Help me. I'm trapped." It floated down to him from the impermeable darkness above.

He tried to climb the slope but found it nearly impossible to gain a foothold. Before, it had been tricky climbing—loose rocks and shale that slipped treacherously beneath his feet. Now the ground itself seemed to be actively fighting against him. With every step he took forward, the soil slid out from beneath his feet, forcing him back to where he'd started.

"Won't someone help me?"

Not real, he thought. *Has to be a dream.* And yet the plaintive desperation in the voice pulled him inexorably toward it. Charging at the side of the hill, Cal scrabbled with hands and feet, managing to gain a couple of yards before the rocky earth began to slip from beneath him.

In the disjointed shadows above, he thought he could see a wrist-thick root sticking up from the earth. He lunged forward and just managed to reach it. For a split second, as his fingers closed around the root, he thought that it wasn't a root he had grabbed at all, but rather something alive. The surface beneath his fingers seemed to pulse with an unnatural heat, like the flesh of some huge beast submerged beneath the mountain.

"Is anyone there?" The child sounded closer now.

Cal pulled himself forward, releasing the root with a sense of revulsion, and scrambled another few feet to where he could just make out something small and pale moving ever so slightly in the darkness. Reaching it, he froze in horror. The fingers of a child's hand protruded from the soil.

"Won't you please get me out?" the voice called. Now he understood why the words had sounded so strange. They were coming from underground.

"Not possible," he muttered. Still, he instantly began to scrape away the rocks and dirt. Pulling away handfuls of earth, he revealed a small, pink palm and a bony wrist.

"Ohhh, help me." The voice was filled with a greater intensity. He thought that part of it was due to the dirt he was clearing away, but there was something else—a sense of urgency. Suddenly the ground started to tremble beneath his hands and knees.

"Get me out!" Something was coming! In Cal's mind he pictured a huge mouth filled with hundreds of razor-sharp teeth.

The hand waved desperately, fingers opening and closing. Only now it was no longer a child's hand. For a moment he could only stare at the slender, white fingers stretching toward him—the one next to the pinky still wearing the gold wedding band he had once slipped over it.

"Kat," he screamed. The trembling of the earth changed to a roar, the pounding of something giant beyond belief racing toward him. The ground cracked and crumbled under his feet.

"Kat," he screamed again, reaching down to grip the small fingers in his own much bigger hands. The stony soil had ripped at his fingertips as he dug, and now they left bloody prints on the pale white flesh beneath them. With all his strength he pulled.

For a moment nothing happened, and then he felt movement. The ground gave an inch, then two, revealing a slender forearm, its light blond hairs flecked with dirt.

"Help me!" Kat's voice cried. The entire mountainside seemed to be coming down now. Boulders the size of refrigerators bounced past, but Cal paid them no notice. His attention was focused on Kat.

Leveraging his knees against the sides of the hole, he gave an enormous tug. The muscles in his neck bulged with the effort, but he was getting her. Dirt spilled away as first his wife's elbow and then the smooth white curve of her shoulder came into view.

"Hang on," he shouted. Another pull and he could see the line of her neck, her chin.

"I've got you." Kat's face had nearly emerged from beneath the crazily bouncing earth when he felt something pull against him. As quickly as his wife's chin and neck had appeared, they now slipped back beneath the surface.

"No!" Climbing to his feet, Cal bowed his body. With every ounce of strength he had, he strained at his wife's arm, leaving bright red fingerprints in her flesh. "No, I won't let her go. You can't take her!"

He nearly had her. Though his eyes were shut tight with effort, he could feel her sliding toward him—knew that if he looked, he would see the face that meant more to him than anything in the world.

And then something stronger than any force he had ever felt jerked him to the ground. With a gasp he landed hard on his shoulder, and Kat's hand was ripped from his grasp.

He opened his eyes in time to see all of the gains he had made disappear. Now, once again, only his wife's fingers showed above the dark earth. He dove forward meaning to take her hand, but instead her fingers closed around his wrist like steel talons.

"Wha—" he grunted before his hand was pulled down. With horror, he watched his arm disappear up to the elbow in the earth, dragging his body forward.

"No," he moaned, trying to pull away. But already the hole had swallowed him from fingertip to shoulder.

Terrified, he watched the earth begin to dilate as it sucked him in, and he realized that it had been the mouth of the beast all along.

Cal jerked awake. Sweat covered his body, and he was panting as if he'd just finished a marathon. He tried rolling over but knew he was done sleeping for the night.

CHAPTER 17

RAINY DAYS AND MONDAYS. WHOEVER *penned those lyrics hit the nail on the head,* Cal thought. He stared through his office window at the dismal weather outside. Lightning flashes seemed determined to rip the gray sky in two, while heavy rain slashed diagonally against the glass.

It had been a lousy morning. He had awakened feeling groggy and hung over from the vivid dream he'd had. Ordinarily he couldn't remember his dreams. And even when he could, they were about everyday kinds of things—mowing the lawn, filling out paperwork, gassing up the car. Kat claimed he had no imagination, which was why he couldn't enjoy novels. She might have been right.

But *this* dream. Even thinking about it now under the bright neon lights of his office brought goose flesh to Cal's arms. He could still see every second of it in his mind as clearly as if it had actually happened. Undoubtedly a shrink would tell him it was some kind of subconscious communication from his ego, alter ego, or id—whatever the latest jargon was.

He didn't need a shrink to translate the message, though. It had been all too obvious. He'd done everything he could to make sure that Kat would always be safe. Moved to a Norman Rockwell town. Installed the best alarm system. Made sure she had access to a handgun and knew how to use it.

None of it had made a bit of difference. She'd died anyway from something as simple as a slip from a ladder.

Now the same thing was happening to his town. People were dying, and he didn't know why or how to stop it. He'd sworn to protect the people of Twin Forks, and already he'd broken his promise twice. The worst part was, unless he could get a handle on things quickly, it would, more likely than not, happen again.

With those uplifting thoughts on his mind, he'd arrived at the office to find Dee Dee Cornwall, the mayor of Twin Forks, waiting for him. Dee Dee was four-feet-six-inches of constant motion. She said what she thought and didn't pull any punches.

"Tell me what you've been holding back from the press," she'd said as soon as they'd entered his office.

"There really isn't a lot to tell," he said. "Certain clues the killers may have left at the scene, exact nature of death, that sort of thing." The mayor was his boss, and as such, she could demand any information she wanted, but that wasn't ordinarily her style. She respected his experience and let him do his job.

For his part, Cal had a natural distrust of giving out too much information to anyone who didn't wear the blue, though he tried to keep the mayor in the loop when he could. He hoped she wasn't going to change all that.

"You said 'killers.' Does that mean these murders aren't the work of the same person?" The mayor studied him with keen interest.

Cal shrugged. "Right now it's just a guess. I'll tell you as soon as I know anything."

Dee Dee stared at him hard as if weighing his words. "I've been getting calls," she said.

He nodded. He'd been getting them too. Twin Forks was a small town, and word got around. If a husband killed his wife, people would talk about it over dinner. They would shake their heads and ask each other what kind of crazy world they were living in. But it wouldn't spoil their appetites. It was an isolated incident that had no real impact on their lives, unless they knew the victim or killer personally.

But if word began to spread that a killer was loose in their community— if their own families might be at risk—that was another matter. Parents would start keeping their children home from school. Doors would be locked, and strangers would be eyed with suspicion and fear. Most of all, action would be demanded.

The phone calls coming in now were a sporadic few, really more curiosity than anything else. But Cal and Dee Dee both knew that in a small town, curiosity is only a stone's throw away from fear. And fear is next-door neighbor to panic. They had to get this thing put to bed before that panic could take hold.

"I'll keep you posted," he said.

Dee Dee stood and reached across the desk to shake Cal's hand. "You've done a good job here," she said. "Get this solved. *Soon.*"

Now sitting alone in his office, sipping cold coffee from a Styrofoam cup, he hoped there wouldn't be a need for Dee Dee to make another visit.

The phone on the desk buzzed, and the yellow light went on.

"You ready for an update?" Greg asked.

"Yeah." Cal dropped the rest of his coffee into the trash. "Come on in."

A few seconds later, Cal's door swung open and Detective Luke strolled in with his usual languor. He popped the last bite of a bagel into his mouth, licked his fingertips, and took a seat. Cal could never look at the man without picturing a redbone hound stretching out in front of a fire.

"So tell me what you've been able to learn," Cal said, the fingers of his right hand going to his wedding band.

"Well, first off," Greg said, extending a single long finger, "Eddie Osgood appears to have a pretty solid alibi for the time Ezra Rucker was killed. Friday night Eddie was in his trailer drinking with three of his buddies."

"Drowning his sorrows, no doubt."

"No doubt," Greg chuckled. "I'm not saying that he couldn't 'a talked his friends into lying for him. But it'd be a stretch to tie him to the Rucker murder."

Cal agreed. It had been a slim chance at best. But now they were left with no suspects at all.

"Second," Greg held up another finger, as though flashing a peace sign. "I checked with the ME's office. The autopsies turned up *nada*. Our killer is either very careful or very lucky. No hair or fibers that don't match the victims or their families, and no skin under the victims' nails.

"We already knew that the clothes the Osgood woman was dressed in weren't her own, but it looks like they could have come from any one of fifty thrift stores between here and Denver."

"Okay, don't worry about that for now," Cal said, taking Greg's notes and adding them to the folder. They didn't have the manpower to do that kind of research anyway. "What about the other three names I gave you?"

Greg pulled a mangled notebook from his pocket and flipped it open to the page he was looking for. "Benjamin Meyers. Married with a boy and a girl. Lives in up in Centennial but comes down to visit his folks at least a couple of times a month. No criminal record. Did a hitch with the National Guard. I've been trying to reach him since yesterday with no success."

After Cal had copied the information, Greg turned to the next page. "Next on our hit parade is Theresa Truman, now Theresa Obrey. You really hit the jackpot with this one."

"How's that?" Cal asked, leaning forward over his desk.

"Theresa's bio reads like one of those Mothers of the Year—gourmet cook, mother of four, black belt in karate. Up until her last baby, she even had her own cooking show."

"A regular angel."

"And her husband's got connections at the capital."

"I see," Cal said, not entirely sure that he did. "Is that a problem?"

"Shouldn't be, but I'd tread carefully all the same. They're both pretty well plugged into state politics."

Cal noted the information. "How'd you manage to get so much on her?" he asked.

"She and my sister were roommates in college." Greg smiled knowingly.

"Small world," Cal muttered.

"No, big world," Greg said. "Small town."

"You talk to her?"

"No. Left two messages with her husband, but she won't return our calls."

"That's strange," Cal said. "You told him it was urgent? That there was a possibility his wife might be in danger?"

Greg nodded, rolling his eyes. "Got the feeling neither of them has much use for small-town police."

"Humph." Cal flipped through his file. "What about the Godwin woman?"

"Mother and father are Howard and Grace Godwin. Her brother, Spencer, is kind of a local big shot. Owns a bunch of car dealerships and investment properties."

Cal nodded. He'd heard the name.

"Her dad inherited a good bit of money. He turned it into a fortune when he founded Perfect Write."

"The word processing program?"

"Yep. He sold the company before Microsoft took over the market. Built that big mansion in the mouth of the canyon."

"What about her?" Cal asked with a grimace. "Is she too good for our little department too?"

Greg grinned. "Didn't actually speak to the woman herself. But the butler says you can come by this afternoon."

"The butler, huh? This should be fun. I'll swing by their place after I meet with Esther Zoeller." Cal started to get up, but Greg waved him back to his seat and lowered his voice as though he were telling secrets in the back of the classroom.

"One other thing. Olivia was married to that guy who used to anchor for Channel Five."

"So?" Cal asked, tiring of the detective's dramatics.

"They divorced after only three years. It was a pretty big deal. Apparently when Olivia was a little girl, her mom was sent to the mental hospital in Greenwood. She died a few years later, and the scuttlebutt is that Olivia may have experienced the same kind of mental breakdown as her mother."

CHAPTER 18

ZIRBES . . . ZMITRAVICH . . . ZOBEL, CHARLES . . . ZOBEL, Lance. Cal ran a thick finger down the column of names in the phonebook, stopping on Zoeller, E. Since there was only one Zoeller in the book, he assumed that the E stood for Esther. As he dialed the number, he tried to picture the woman.

Older. Living alone, or had she remarried? Losing her only son must have taken a lot out of her but he imagined her as kindly, all the same.

"Hello." Cal's image of Esther was shattered by the voice on the other end of the line. Cal didn't know how a single word could convey animosity, suspicion, and impatience—but Esther Zoeller somehow managed that and more.

"Ms. Zoeller?" Cal asked, wondering if phoning the woman in advance had been a mistake.

"Who's asking?" Before Cal could answer, Esther was on him like a pit bull. "This better not be that glass cump'ny again. I told you, I don't drive no car, so I don't need no windshield repair. If it's you, I'm calling the police. This is harassment."

"Ms. Zoeller, this is Chief Hunt with the Twin Forks Police Department." There was a slight gasp, and the line went so quiet that Cal could hear the actors on what sounded like a soap opera coming from a TV somewhere in the background. He gave the woman a moment to recover. No one really liked to get an unexpected call from the police but that often worked to his advantage.

"I wonder if I might be able to drop by and speak with you."

"'Bout what?" The animosity was gone for the moment but the suspicion was still there, stronger than ever.

"I'd like to speak with you in person." The address listed in the phone book was only a few minutes away.

"I got nuthin' to say."

"How can you be sure when you don't even know what I want to talk to you about?"

"I got nuthin' to say 'bout nuthin'." Cal's mental picture had gone from the kindly old grandmother on "The Waltons" to Granny on "The Beverly Hillbillies."

"It will only take a few minutes," he tried, and when that drew no response, he went to his ace in the hole. "I'd like to talk to you about your son, Frankie."

The volatile reaction he'd expected never came. Esther gave a faint sigh. Cal couldn't tell whether it was sadness or just resignation.

"I got no car."

"That's all right. I can be out to your house in ten minutes."

"I need to straighten up first."

"Why don't we make it half an hour, then?"

"Fine." Esther's voice was so soft that he could barely make out what she said. And then the line went dead.

CHAPTER 19

BEN MEYERS HAD A LOT on his mind. Memories were returning—memories he thought he had put to rest years earlier. Rain plastered his hair to his scalp, and gusts of wind snapped the fabric of his jacket back and forth like a flag. Still, he continued up the steep terrain of the mountainside behind his house, ignoring the involuntary shudders that coursed through his body.

Things had changed. He wasn't sure how or why, but he felt it with every nerve ending. A phrase came to mind that his father had used. "The wheel has turned." *A wheel*, that's what it felt like. A great wheel in some unimaginably immense piece of machinery had slipped forward a cog, shifting the course of events with its movement.

As he stepped around a chokecherry bush, a fist-sized rock slipped out of the mud and he nearly fell. Catching his balance, he watched the chunk of granite spin and bounce its way into the canyon below. That was too close. Although he was only a few miles from his house—he could actually look down into his backyard from where he stood—the terrain up here was pretty rugged. If he didn't pay more attention to what he was doing, he could end up breaking a leg or worse.

But that was just the problem. He couldn't seem to concentrate on anything but the past. The present had taken on a filmy, insubstantial quality as if it was only a memory, while events from thirty years earlier grew more real by the day. He tried to pay attention to where he was walking, but his mind was filled with images of children.

Seeing Amanda's—Mandy's, he corrected himself—picture on the news had been a nasty shock. After all this time he was surprised that he recognized her. But even before the anchorwoman mentioned Twin Forks, he'd seen the face and heard the word *murder*, and his stomach had contracted like a hot fist. Then two days later, it was Ezra Rucker. The force of *that* had been like a physical blow, sending him reeling across the room.

He thought he'd gotten over the past. Heaven knows he had the therapy bills to prove he'd tried. Turned out all he'd done was push the memories down into his subconscious like great poison-filled balloons. And now that the balloons were all rising back to the surface—their noxious gas filling his brain as they popped—he thought there was a very good chance he would go crazy.

That was, of course, assuming he hadn't already crossed that threshold. People who thought dead children were visiting them probably fell into the category of *crazy*—or at least very close to it.

He'd tried calling Theresa Obrey, sure that she'd seen the same news reports he had—hoping they might get together and talk about the things neither of them could ever share with their own families. What a mistake that had been. She'd flown off the handle as soon as she realized who it was and why he was calling.

She claimed she had no memory of what had happened in the mine. Who knows, maybe she was telling the truth. But wasn't she worried about what had happened to Amanda and Ezra? She'd said he was imagining things. Didn't she recognize that the odds were slim to none of the two deaths happening within forty-eight hours of each other?

Ahead of him the ridge of rock he'd been following dropped away into a narrow crevice, twenty or thirty feet deep. He'd left the trail half a mile back to escape the company of other hikers and mountain bikers. Still he found himself glancing over his shoulder every few minutes, sure that unseen eyes were watching him. Lately he'd found himself looking over his shoulder a lot.

Eyeing the space between where he stood and the other side of the crevice, he estimated the distance to be a little more than six feet. Scaling the rock face and climbing up the other side was out of the question. Even with his climbing gear, it would have been dicey in this weather. It looked like a lot of loose shale, the kind of stuff that dropped out from under your hands and feet without warning.

He could backtrack, but that would mean losing thirty to forty-five minutes, and he'd promised LuAnn that he'd be back to the house in time to take the kids to the library.

Moving as close to the edge as he dared, he studied the ground on the other side. The surface looked solid enough—it wouldn't slip out from under his feet or break away under his weight. That was an important factor, considering that if he fell back over the edge, it was pretty much a straight drop to the sharp rocks below.

He backed up several feet, mentally counting the number of running steps it would take to reach the edge, and took another two steps. Bracing one hand on a scrubby little spruce, he took a couple of deep breaths, checked his footing, and mentally counted down. *Three, two, one.* Pushing off on the tree, while at the same time shooting his right leg forward, he sprinted toward the opening.

One minute he was standing on solid ground, and the next minute he was looking down into the mouth of the ravine. Arms flailing at the air, legs straining, he stretched for the extra distance that would carry him to the other side. For a brief instant he thought he might not make it—he had chickened out at the last second, jumping a half-foot earlier than he needed to—and the thought almost brought a sense of relief. But he cleared the distance with a hand's width to spare.

Stumbling to keep his balance, slipping on the wet rock, he grabbed onto a small outcropping and skidded to a stop. Taking a risk like that usually pumped him up. The physical challenge, the flirtation with disaster, usually poured adrenaline through his veins and got his heart pounding. But none of that happened now. Instead, a dull gray sense of despair stole over him. He wasn't cheating fate at all, only postponing it.

He found himself staring at the rocks below with a dread fascination. Dropping over the edge would be so easy. They would rule it an accident. And it would be—nearly. Just a little slip. Hikers died every year from falls like this. A second or two of terror, a brief instant of pain, and it would all be over.

Except that he couldn't. The thought of LuAnn getting the news, of the kids growing up without a father, pushed him back from the edge. That and the fear of eternal damnation. He'd been raised with the understanding that a sane man who takes his own life has committed a grave sin. And at least for now he was trying to hold onto his sanity.

It hadn't taken the police long to connect him to Ezra and Amanda. There were plenty of people in town who would remember the mine. It only made sense that they would track down the other survivors. So far he'd been able to avoid their calls, erasing the answering machine messages before LuAnn could hear them. But he knew they'd be showing up at his door any day now.

He could picture his wife finding a pair of officers at their house. "Mrs. Meyers, we'd like to ask your husband a few questions." At that point he might wish that he'd taken the plunge, after all. Better that than having the world find out what really happened to that poor little boy. For the first time in his life he thought he really understood the phrase *Darned if you do and darned if you don't.*

A cold breeze brushed across the nape of Ben's neck, and he realized he'd been standing on the edge of the ravine longer than he thought. If he didn't return to the trail soon, he'd never make it to the house before dark. Scanning the side of the mountain, he spotted a ledge fifteen feet above him. He thought he remembered seeing it on a previous hike. If he could climb up to it, he'd be only a short walk from the trail.

The first five feet of the climb were easy; there were several rock outcroppings to grab on to. The next ten were going to be tricky. The rocky slope was loose and dangerous. Halfway up was a scraggly little Douglas fir that had somehow managed to take root in the barren mountainside. He wasn't sure if it would bear his weight but it was the only thing to hold on to.

Digging his boots into the slippery surface, he lunged upward and clutched the thin trunk. It bent beneath the weight of his body but the roots held. Then, just as he was about to pull himself up, the rock he had been standing on slipped out from under him. Without warning he found himself suspended on the side of the mountain with only his tenuous one-handed grip preventing a fall.

His heart pounding, he managed to swing his other hand up to grab the tree. Suddenly the idea of falling to his death held no appeal. He glanced down and realized there was no way to climb back without the possibility of going over the edge. Getting up to the ledge was his only chance. If he could just get high enough to wrap his leg around the tree, it would be within reach.

Grappling for purchase with both of his knees, he managed to gain six inches, then twelve. Before he could go any farther, he felt the trunk of the little tree shift beneath his weight. A cloud of dust and rock fell onto his face as he watched several roots slip from a small crack in the rock. He shifted his left hand from the tree to the crack. It was barely wide enough to squeeze his fingers into.

The tree was slowly pulling away from the side of the mountain. He could almost hear it groaning as it tore from the earth. Looking up to the ledge, he thought he saw a flash of movement.

"Hey," he shouted, his voice bouncing off the side of the cliff. "Hey, is anybody there? I need help!"

He waited, listening intently. There was no answer. He was sure someone was up there, just out of sight. "Help me! I'm going to fall."

Again no answer, though he thought he heard the sound of something moving around. Could it be an animal? He had no time to consider. The tree had pulled almost completely out now. He could see the last roots slipping from their hold. Putting as much weight as he dared onto the hand he had wedged into the crack, he released the tree and thrust his right hand up toward the ledge.

Convinced it was out of reach, he almost didn't manage to hang on when his hand caught the edge. His fingers began to slip, nearly losing their grip entirely before they dug in and caught. He held his breath, waiting to see whether he would slip any farther, but his grip was solid. Now all he had to do was—

A hand dropped over the top of his. There *was* someone.

"You, up there!" He called out, unable to raise his head to look up. "I need help."

For a moment there was nothing, and then a soft, high-pitched giggle floated down from the ledge above him.

It was a kid. That's why he hadn't answered. But a kid wouldn't be up here alone. "Get your mom or dad. Quick, I need someone to pull me up." Ben could feel his fingers slipping. He wasn't sure how much longer he could hold on.

The child's fingers remained on Ben's hand, cool and smooth, almost petting his scraped skin. Why wasn't the kid getting someone? "Help!" Ben screamed. "I need help, please."

"Humpty Dumpty sat on the wall." It was the child's singsong voice. He recognized it immediately, though he hadn't heard it since he was a boy. Fear swelled in his chest. He had to get up now.

He released his hold on the crack, putting all his weight on the ledge. But as he let go of the crack, the child's fingers suddenly began to pull, prying his hand away from the rock. Reaching wildly up with his left hand, Ben swung for the ledge.

"Humpty Dumpty had a great fall."

"Help, I'm falling!" he screamed. Something hard smashed down on his fingers, and he lost his grip completely.

The side of the cliff was a blur. A spine of rock ripped at his cheek, and his head banged against the wall with a sickening blow. His left leg connected with the ridge on which he had been standing only a few minutes earlier, and he heard a snap like the sound of a tree branch cracking before he cartwheeled over the edge.

He didn't know how long he slid, only that the entire side of the mountain seemed to be coming down with him. Spinning sideways, completely losing control, he saw that the shelf of rock he was tumbling down ended a few feet below. Beyond it lay only the bruised purple of the stormy sky.

Just before he went over, his legs collided with something hard and unyielding, sending bright shards of pain shooting up his hips and back. His body jackknifed around, and he found himself looking at a hoary old pine, its trunk leaning out over the abyss. Without thinking, he wrapped his arms around it. His legs dangled out over the abyss. For the moment, at least, his body had stopped sliding.

Arms wrapped in a death-grip around the rough bark, he ducked his head. An avalanche of rocks and debris roared down from above, and the earth closed in on Ben.

CHAPTER 20

ESTHER ZOELLER LIVED IN A tidy brick home in an older section of Twin Forks. Cal estimated that the house was at least as old as its resident. At some point, the exterior had been painted a canary yellow but over the years most of the paint had worn away, leaving the bricks with a stippled appearance that seemed to suit the structure.

As Cal pulled up next to the curb, the rain stopped falling, and a single ray of golden sunlight broke through the clouds. A gray-and-black-striped cat stuck its head curiously out from under the partially opened garage door and gave him a quick once-over. Apparently deciding that the big man in the dark-blue uniform warranted no further attention, the tabby turned, nose in the air, and disappeared into the flower garden at the side of the house.

Walking up to the door, Cal noticed the manicured rose bushes along the front of the house and the freshly mowed lawn. He wondered whether Esther hired a neighborhood kid to tend to the yard or managed it herself. As he approached the front porch, he heard the television click off and the sound of muted footsteps coming toward the door. He rapped on the faded wood, and the door swung halfway open at the first knock.

"You're late." The interior of the house was dark, and Cal could make out only the woman's silhouette. He checked his watch, noting that it was almost exactly thirty minutes since he had spoken to Esther on the phone.

"Sorry about that, Ms. Zoeller," he said with a straight face. "Traffic was a bear."

Esther gave a choked cough that could possibly have been mistaken for a laugh and shuffled back a few steps, pulling the door open with her. "Well, come in, then," she said. "And knock off that *Ms.* crap. It's either Esther or Mrs. Zoeller. I don't go in for any of that feminist twaddle."

Cal stepped from the sunlight into the gloomy interior, expecting the sharp odor of cat urine. It had been his experience that elderly people who lived alone with their cats tended to become immune to the smell of their feline friends. But if Esther kept her cat in the house, she'd done a good job of cleaning up after it. The only scent was the mildly pleasant combination of old furniture and a lilac sachet that reminded him of his grandmother.

"Close the door," Esther called as she walked back down the hallway, her house slippers whispering against the floral-patterned carpet with each deliberate step. "I've got a touch of glaucoma so the bright light hurts my eyes."

Shutting the door, Cal followed her through the hallway and into a small living room. The cramped space was further crowded by several shelf units and assorted end tables, each loaded down with a variety of knickknacks and porcelain figurines. Cal crossed the room and stopped before a heavy console television that he assumed Esther had been watching before he arrived. He picked up an ornate silver frame with a picture of a young boy dressed in a shirt and tie.

"Frankie?"

Esther eased herself into an overstuffed chair. "Took that picture in Denver when he 'as only four years old. Talked about that trip for years." Esther's words carried the familiarity of constant repetition. Cal suspected that she gave the same response to everyone who asked about the photograph. He set the frame back down onto the television and lowered his bulk gingerly onto a fragile-looking loveseat.

"Handsome boy."

Esther seemed to choke again and shook her head. "He was a pasty-faced little carp, just like his daddy. Couldn't see naught without those Mason-jar glasses of his." She pulled an embroidered handkerchief from the pocket of her bulky sweater and gave her cheeks a quick pat. "But he had a good heart, that one. Couldn't say the same for the man that fathered him."

"Is Mr. Zoeller still alive?" Cal asked.

"Mr. Zoeller. Hah! Frankie's daddy was a shifty-eyed little good-for-nothing that left town before Frankie was even born. Good riddance, I say." As if realizing that she'd said more than she had intended, Esther pressed the handkerchief back into her pocket and clamped her mouth shut.

Taking her cue, Cal changed the subject. "Nice house you have here."

"My father built it in 1945. Daddy wasn't much of a farmer, Mama always said, but he was good at building things." Esther stared at the television as if watching a program only she could see.

"It must get lonely here all by yourself."

Esther looked up from the television, her eyes studying Cal's in the room's dim light. He sensed a canny intelligence hidden behind the woman's coarse speech and frumpy looks. If he was going to get any useful information from her, he would have to come by it cautiously.

"I get along. I have my gardens and my cats."

Cal nodded.

"Up until a few months ago I was a housekeeper." Esther stood and took a feather duster from behind the television. She went to one of the shelves and began dusting the figurines there, even though it didn't look like they needed it. "But that didn't work out."

"Why was that?" Cal asked, but Esther only shook her head and grunted.

"You said you wanted to talk to me about my boy." The firm set of her jaw and the way her lips pressed together until they nearly disappeared told Cal that if he didn't get down to business soon, he was going to find himself out on the front porch.

"Tell me about Frankie," he said. The digital recorder was in his front shirt pocket, but somehow he knew that the woman would clam up the minute he pulled it out.

"He was murdered." Esther's voice was low and grim. She moved from the figurines to the photograph of her son.

"I thought it was an accident."

"T'weren't no accident."

Cal waited for her to elaborate, but she continued to dust the silver frame.

"The paper said your son wandered off during a school picnic."

"Lies," Esther spat, working the duster furiously across the top of the television. "All lies. That's what *they* wanted everyone to think."

"*They?*" Cal asked.

"All of 'em. They *all* wanted to cover it up. But mostly it was the families of those little brats who killed my boy."

Cal sucked in his breath. He didn't know what he had expected from the visit, but it hadn't been this. The papers made no mention of a murder, and Clara had only slightly alluded to it. He wondered briefly if Esther Zoeller was mad.

"Why don't you tell me about it?"

"What's to tell?" Esther set the duster back behind the television and began moving around the room, going from shelf to shelf, straightening the figurines.

"For starters, what makes you think your son was murdered?"

"Don't think. I *know*." She pulled the collar of her sweater up as though the stuffy room had suddenly grown chilly. "My son never would've wandered off into no cave. He was scared of the dark, and he didn't like small spaces. It was that little short-pants tramp that talked him into it."

Cal's tongue felt bolted against the roof of his mouth as he tried to speak. "Amanda?"

"That's the one. Amanda Porter." The name twisted on Esther's purplish gray lips as though they were coated with some foul substance. "She talked my boy into that cave and then left him there to die."

"Why would she do that?" The idea of an eight-year-old girl murdering a schoolmate was ludicrous, but this woman obviously believed that's what happened.

"Because she was cruel. Her and that miserable little friend of hers. They tormented Frankie every single day." Esther nearly knocked over a pair of haloed angels before folding her arms across her chest. "I think I'd like a drink of water. Would you like a drink?" Before Cal could answer, Esther had disappeared into the kitchen. He could hear her turning on the tap and getting ice from the freezer.

When she returned, she seemed to have regained some of her composure. Cal took a sip from the glass she offered and asked, "Who was Amanda's friend?" although he figured he already knew the answer.

"Ezra Rucker. Miserable little excuse for a boy, that one. Frankie knew enough to keep his distance from him. But he couldn't see what a hellion that Porter girl was. I warned him about her, but he thought he *loved* her." She pronounced the word *loved* as though it were at least five or six syllables.

"They were always pulling pranks on my baby. The boy was merciless. Frankie used to come home with knots on his head the size of walnuts where that little Rucker brat had knuckled him." An image of Ezra Rucker's head split by an ax came into Cal's mind, and a shudder ran through his body. He didn't know what was going on here, but this was far more than coincidence.

"Frankie learned to keep away from that Ezra, but he'd go anywhere the Porter girl asked him to. Didn't seem to matter how many times she tricked him, he'd just keep going back. Like Lucy and Charlie Brown, he was always willing to trust her one more time. Until it finally killed him."

Cal tried to assimilate what he had just heard. It was a stretch, but farfetched or not, it sounded like a motive for murder. This woman obviously believed that her son had been led to his death by the two people who had just been violently killed themselves. But he couldn't imagine the hunched figure in front of him managing to strangle Mandy Osgood, and he certainly couldn't see her swinging Ezra Rucker's ax.

She could have hired someone to do the killing. She might have squirreled some money away over the years. But why wait all the years? It didn't make any sense.

"Do you have any proof that Amanda and Ezra were involved in your son's death?"

She stared at him silently for a moment before leaning forward, the ice in her water tinkling against the inside of the glass. Dropping her voice so that Cal had to lean forward to hear her, she whispered, "He told me."

"*He?*"

She glanced back over her shoulder at the window as though afraid someone might be eavesdropping. "My Frankie. He told me everything."

Cal snapped backward, the water in his glass sloshing over the side and down his hand. "Your son is alive?"

"Of course not, you fool," she said, rolling her eyes. "Haven't you been listening to a blamed thing I've said?"

Cal wiped the water from the back of his hand. "I must be missing something here. Are you saying that your son's *ghost* told you he was murdered?"

"Well, not in so many words." Esther's eyes narrowed with distrust, but she continued on. This was obviously something she'd been wanting to get off her chest. "It's not like he can actually speak, at least not in words that we mortals can understand. But he's come back to me many times, and a mother can read what's in her child's eyes—what's in his heart."

Ghosts again, Cal thought. Why was it that everyone involved with this case seemed to want to turn it into a *Twilight Zone* episode? Two people were dead, and the ranting of a disturbed woman wasn't getting him any closer to solving their murders.

"Mrs. Zoeller, can you think of any reason why someone might have wanted to hurt Ezra Rucker and Mandy Osgood?"

Esther gave him a haven't-you-listened-to-a-single-thing-I've-said look. She took a long, slow drink of water before speaking, but when she did, her voice was filled with venom.

"I can think of lots of reasons. That woman was a tramp. She slept with every warm body who asked her. And that Rucker fellow was no better. I hear he slapped around his wife 'n kids. And he was always out drinking and carousing. I'm not surprised at all that . . ." She paused, suddenly seeming unsure.

"You're not surprised that what?" Cal asked. She knew they were dead. That wasn't unexpected; it had been on the news and in the papers. But why was she refusing to acknowledge it?

"That someone might want to . . . to hurt them. That's all." She was stonewalling, but there was nothing he could do about it. A hunch suddenly struck him.

"Mrs. Zoeller, you said that Ezra Rucker picked on your son. Do you know if he called him names?"

"'Course he did. Frankie'd come home crying the way all those kids picked on him.'"

"All of the kids? Not just Ezra and Amanda?" Cal started to place his glass on the end table next to where he sat, and Esther was instantly on her feet with a coaster.

"They all took their turns. Those two were just the worst of the bunch."

"Do you remember any of the names they called him? Any in particular?"

Again she studied him from across the dark room. "I'm sure I don't."

He needed an angle, some way to break through the brick wall that this woman had erected around herself. For all her tough talk, Cal didn't get the impression that she was a murderer. But something didn't add up. If she was telling the truth, what was she so nervous about?

"Is there any more information you might be able to give me? Anything at all?"

"What kind of information?" He had set her on edge now, and her voice was wary.

"I don't know. Something else about his childhood. School papers? Maybe a scrapbook?"

"He kept a journal."

"A journal? But he was only seven when . . ." Cal's voice trailed off.

"Nearly eight, but he was smart as a whip. That's why the other kids picked on him. He wanted to be a writer when he grew up, and I got him a little book to write things in. They was mostly stories, about pirates and battles, things like that. I'd help him now and then, but mostly it was on his own." She tugged out the handkerchief again.

"Sometimes he'd write about school. It near broke my heart to read the things he wrote. I should'a kept him home. Should'a taught him myself. I'd've done a sight better job than that Betsy Trotwood. But I thought he'd toughen up there. I thought school'd be good for him."

"Do you still have the journal?"

Esther nodded and pushed herself up from the chair with a grunt. "In the garage."

Cal followed her from the living room and through the kitchen where something was simmering in a slow-cooker. The kitchen was spotless except for a box of Cocoa Puffs on the counter. When she saw Cal notice them, her face went red, and she quickly put them back in the pantry. Cal tried to hide his smile, amused at the old woman's guilty pleasure.

She pulled open a narrow door that had a real estate calendar tacked to the back and stepped into a garage as neat as the kitchen. A wide range of hand tools hung from a peg board.

Esther pointed at a set of shelves on the far side of the garage; Cal crossed the concrete floor and saw the box she had indicated. It was on the top shelf, a large square carton with a picture of an apple tree on the side. In neat dark letters near the top, the name "Frankie" was printed. It was heavier than he'd anticipated, and he nearly lost control of it as he pulled it from the shelf. Holding the box chest-high, he slipped in something on the floor as he carried it back and nearly dropped it.

"Careful," Esther snapped from the kitchen doorway.

"Sorry." He stepped into the kitchen and set the box on the table. Esther elbowed him away and carefully lifted the corners of the carton as though she were opening a holy relic. Cal guessed that maybe that's just what she *was* doing.

The contents seemed to be mostly papers—block lettering of the alphabet and pictures of stick figures standing in front of block houses with curls of smoke coming from their chimneys—but Esther handled each one with the utmost care. Soon tears were dripping unabated down her cheeks.

At last, she came to a small black book with gilt-edged pages. Cal estimated that it was maybe a hundred pages thick. Across the front in gold lettering was the word "Journal." She held it to her breast for a minute as though she would not be able to give it up before turning it over to Cal.

He opened it, immediately struck by the neatness of the printing and the quantity of it. Words filled each page from top to bottom with only the tiniest margin to each side. He read a few of the pages at random. As Esther had said, most of it was stories. The spelling was sporadic at best, but the writing itself was the kind of thing he would have expected from a ten- or eleven-year-old. One page in particular caught his attention. As he read the first paragraph, a sick ball formed in the center of his stomach.

Ezra stole my glasses again today. I thawt he wood brake them but he only threw them. The other kids started throwing them to. Amanda did to, but I no she was only doing it to show off for Ezra. She likes him. Then the teacher came out. Ezra gave me bak my glasses. But he called me frog eyes. The other kids herd him and now they all call me frog eyes. I hate Ezra Rucker.

Cal turned to see that Esther had been reading over his shoulder. The anger that had been smoldering in her eyes had banked into a fire.

"Can you prove it?" she asked, placing one trembling hand on his shoulder. "Can you prove what those children did to my Frankie?"

Cal closed the book. "Mrs. Zoeller, Amanda Porter and Ezra Rucker are dead. They were murdered. Why not just leave the past alone?"

Esther didn't blink an eye. "What about those other kids? They were there too. They're just as guilty."

"Did it ever occur to you that maybe it *was* an accident? That maybe it was just a bunch of children who made a mistake?"

"No!" Esther shouted, snatching the book from Cal's hands. "No, they killed my baby!"

"You can't know that," Cal said.

Esther stared at him, cheeks bright red, eyes seeming to nearly burst. Spit flew from her lower lip as she breathed in and out. Her gaze dropped to the kitchen floor, and she pointed to Cal's feet. "Look what you've done," she shouted. "Look what you've left on my clean floor."

Cal followed her trembling finger and saw black footprints leading from the garage to where he was standing. Whatever he'd slipped in on the garage floor was now tracked across the kitchen linoleum. He bent to unlace his shoes, but Esther was already pushing at him. As small as she was, it was still everything Cal could do to keep the woman from tipping him over.

"Get out! Leave my house now. And don't you ever come back!"

CHAPTER 21

"THIS WAY."

Cal followed the butler, who had not bothered to identify himself, down a long hallway of some kind of dark wood parquet—walnut maybe, or mahogany. They passed a pair of partially open double doors, and Cal caught a glimpse of a dining room the size of a basketball court—no TV dinners in there. On the right was a library and beyond it was what looked like a music room.

So this was the famous Godwin Mansion. That was how it was referred to by the residents of Twin Forks—complete with capital *G* and capital *M*—although Cal had also heard it referred to as the Godwin Monstrosity and several other less charitable names. He estimated that, not including the outbuildings, the house was at least 40,000 square feet, and the estate was more than 150 acres.

"Olivia and her father live here alone?" he asked, trying to imagine how they found their way around without a map.

The butler turned. "Her brother visits often," he said, as if that explained the immensity of the mansion. Jeeves, as Cal had already come to think of him, had a long, narrow face with a nose that looked like someone had pinched it too hard when he was a child; on either side were watery gray eyes. All he was lacking was an English accent to fit right into a *Monty Python* sketch.

Just when Cal was beginning to wonder if the house went on forever, they came to a pair of white French doors. Jeeves stopped, opened one of the doors, and waved a pale hand. He lowered his voice before saying, "She'll be needing her medication soon."

Cal looked through the doorway to an immense screened-in gazebo. Thick exposed beams curved overhead to create a soaring cathedral-like archway. Seated toward the end of the gazebo, facing away from them, a woman in a calf-length, white cotton dress bent as she worked at something on a table in front of her. Her light blond hair was pulled into an intricate braid.

"What's wrong with her?" Cal asked. Then, realizing the insensitive nature of his words, he corrected himself. "I mean the medicine. What's it for?"

Jeeves looked at the woman silhouetted by the early afternoon sunlight and, without a trace of irony, said, "She's too good for this world."

"Miss Godwin, your visitor is here," Jeeves announced before disappearing down the dark hallway.

Cal walked into the room, realizing what a beautiful view it had on all three open sides. Rolling hills to the left were dappled with thick groves of aspen—their leaves rustling softly in the breeze. Straight ahead was a beautiful flower garden with hundreds of rose bushes surrounding ponds and waterfalls. Although the sky was now clear, the air was still redolent with the smell of rain and flowers.

It appeared as if the whole house had been designed with just this spot in mind. It was exactly the kind of place Kat would love. He'd have to see if he could bring her up here sometime to—*Zap*. There it was again, his loss catching him unaware, like a cold slap across the face.

He stopped a few feet behind Olivia, trying to pull himself together. She must have been aware of his presence but she didn't look up from her work. Peering over her shoulder, Cal saw that it was a sculpture.

He watched her draw a wooden knife across the grayish lump of clay in front of her, instantly creating the slight angle of a forehead. Feeling like a peeping Tom, he coughed into his hand.

"Chief Hunt," she said in a preoccupied monotone, her eyes still on the clay in front of her. Her nimble fingers plied the smooth surface, and a moment later a brow began to appear as if by magic.

Cal waited for her to look up or turn around. When she didn't, he said, "I wonder if I could ask you a few questions, Miss Godwin."

"Olivia." She gouged out a chunk of clay from the pile on the table and began to form an ear.

Somewhere in the distance the jangle of a bell carried across the still afternoon air. A cow mooed, and Cal felt inexplicably as if he'd been transported years into the past. The house, the woman, the scenery—none of it belonged in Twin Forks. It was all straight from an antebellum plantation years before the violence of the Civil War.

He glanced around—assuring himself that this was real and not some kind of strange daydream—and realized it was *he* that was out of place, not the other way around.

"What can I do for you, Chief Hunt?" Olivia set her knife aside and looked up, giving Cal a momentary glimpse of the deepest blue eyes he'd ever seen before quickly dropping her gaze.

Kat. I'm looking at Kat. The thought entered Cal's mind before he could push it way.

Where had *that* come from? The woman sitting in front of him looked nothing at all like his late wife. Kat had dark hair that she wore short with bangs. She was tall, with strong features and a quick smile.

Olivia was petite—almost fragile looking. Her face had the fine bone structure of a china doll. Her hair, so light it looked almost white in the sun's glow, was pulled back from her face and held with a turquoise and silver clasp.

With her elegant good looks and graceful body, she could have been an actress or a model. But she seemed almost painfully shy, unable to meet his eyes for only a second or two at a time.

Trying to shake off the strange feelings that had come over him, Cal pulled the recorder from his pocket and pressed the red button on its edge. "I just met with Esther Zoeller."

Olivia lifted the partially finished ear from the marble surface of the table, pressed it to the work in front of her, and made a slight adjustment. She worked with the economy of movement Cal had seen in surgeons, her hands sure and steady. And yet, at his words, her fingers trembled ever so slightly and a line appeared in the center of her forehead.

She paused in her work, eyes still cast down, and he realized that she was waiting for him to continue.

"Mrs. Zoeller seems to think that her son was coerced into entering the Seven Stars mine." Cal wasn't sure exactly why he was steering the conversation in this direction. He'd intended to ask Olivia what she knew about Ezra and Mandy. But he had a strong feeling that Olivia would react to his words, and he almost always played his hunches.

He set the recorder on the edge of the table. "She says Frankie was afraid of the dark, and he had claustrophobia."

"Did he," Olivia said, her words neither a question nor a statement.

"I was hoping you might be able to confirm that. It seems strange he would have gone into the mine under those conditions."

"I suppose we're all afraid of something." She pressed the bottom of the clay ear between her fingers, forming a lobe.

Cal leaned forward, resting his forearms on the edge of the table. "What are you afraid of?" he asked, pushing but having no idea of where he was going.

For a moment, he thought Olivia wasn't going to answer his question at all. She folded her hands in front of her, closing her eyes as if in prayer. When she *did* speak, her voice was so quiet that when Cal played the recorder back later that day, he found it hadn't picked up her response at all.

Her lips moved ever so slightly, and what he thought he heard her say was, "Myself."

CHAPTER 22

"Miss Olivia, your medicine." Jeeves walked into the room, startling them both.

Olivia blinked and wiped her fingers on a damp cloth. The butler handed her two light-blue pills—*Valium?*—along with two black and red capsules and a glass of water. She took the pills and swallowed them easily.

"Do you miss your wife?" she asked after Jeeves left with the water glass.

"I . . . I don't . . ." Cal stumbled for words, surprised by this sudden turn in the conversation.

"I only ask because you spend a great deal of time playing with your ring." She reached across the table to adjust Cal's uniform. As she pulled the corner of his collar back down into place, the cool of her fingers brushed against the warmth of his neck. "But your shirt looks like it was ironed by a man."

"She's dead," he said. "It'll be six months on Friday."

"I'm sorry," she said, returning to her work.

"So am I."

Cal watched her continue to work on the sculpture. It was almost eerie how the clay took shape under her fingers, flowing and molding from nothing into the rough curves and planes of a face. "She's in a better place now," she said.

"Is she?" He didn't know why he was allowing the discussion to turn so personal with this stranger—something he never did—but he found himself amazingly disarmed by her.

"Yes." Olivia looked up at him, her gaze slightly out of focus now—a sign of the drugs kicking in? "After this life we go somewhere wonderful—a place so beautiful you can't even imagine. If we're worthy in this life, we'll return to live with Him."

"Him?" Cal clasped his hands tightly together across his stomach.

"God. He is the sculptor, and we are His clay. But we must be clean to return." Olivia picked up the cloth and scrubbed violently at the back of her knuckles before laying it back on the table—an action Cal found telling.

"Umm hmm." Cal looked out over the garden. He couldn't tell this woman what he really thought. How could he tell her about the stench of a rotting corpse or the times he'd watched a gunshot victim take his last rattling breath? If God had been waiting with open arms, He gave no sign of it. There was no flash of spectral light, no choir of angelic voices.

He'd give anything to believe that Kat was playing a harp on some soft fluffy cloud or picking flowers in a celestial wonderland, but he knew exactly where his wife was. And he knew exactly what she would look like after six months underground. He'd seen the sloughed-off skin of a dead body—the flesh infested by worms and maggots.

"Maybe if you told me what you remember about that day. The day you and the other children went into the mine," he said, changing the subject.

Olivia went back to work on the sculpture, humming softly as she worked. She seemed to have completely forgotten he was there, and he was about to ask his question again when she turned to him and smiled.

"Do you like my new dress?" she asked. He stared at her, confused. Before he could respond, she continued with a girlish giggle.

"Mother bought it for me special. She said the blue brings out my eyes, and the yellow flower matches my hair."

Her eyes were now completely clouded over as she clasped her hands together in her lap. Was it just the drugs? "I was playing jump rope with Theresa, and I fell down in the grass. Father will be so angry when he sees the stain. He gets upset when we ruin the things Mother buys for us."

Cal stared, fascinated, into her unseeing eyes. Olivia looked down over the gardens and open pastureland beyond but Cal had the feeling she was seeing a different landscape entirely.

Olivia turned her head and nodded, as if at an invisible friend. "Theresa, do you want to go down by the creek and listen to Sheila read? It's probably cooler down there."

She listened for a moment, before giggling softly into her hand. "Okay, we'll stay and watch the boys." She turned back to Cal, although he realized by now that she wasn't seeing him at all. Cupping a hand to her mouth, she whispered, "Ezra's big, but Ben Meyers is cuter, don't you think?"

Cal nodded, afraid of breaking whatever spell she was under. But she didn't appear to see him at all.

"They're done playing." She pointed, and Cal found himself looking, even though he knew there was nothing but an empty hillside. An icy sweat broke out on his forehead. He could almost see young Ezra and Ben walking toward them, dress shirts off and tied around their waists, T-shirts matted with dirt and sweat.

Olivia leaned back in her chair, a coy smile touching the corners of her mouth. "Hello, Ezra. Ben."

In the moment of silence that followed, her eyes widened with the feigned look of fright that little girls pull off so easily. "Go in the mine? But it's haunted." Her voice deepened a little as she changed the focus of her gaze. "Are you going, Ben?" she asked.

She slapped a hand over her mouth, and her cheeks flamed red. "Amanda!" she whispered from behind her hand. "I do *not* like Ben. I never said anything of the kind." Although Olivia was forty-two, Cal was looking at the blushing face of an eight-year-old girl with a crush, and he swore he could hear children's laughter floating on the air.

"It *is* hot out here. But how will we see inside the mine?" She turned her head as though listening to someone next to her. "Amanda, where did you get candles? You and Ezra planned this whole thing, didn't you?"

He didn't know how, but somehow Cal could tell that Olivia and her friends were standing up from the picnic table and walking toward the mine. Although she never moved from her chair, a sense of motion seemed to sweep through her.

She leaned forward. "I don't want to climb in that hole. It looks dark, and there are spider webs." She shuddered, and Cal felt a cold breeze brush by his face, although he knew the air around them was warm and still. "I don't want to go in there. There's something inside. It's not just the spiders. It's . . . it's . . ."

Olivia stared straight ahead, her face a mask of abject terror. The color had drained from her cheeks, leaving them a pale gray nearly the same shade as her clay. Her lips trembled as her eyes grew wide. "Inside. It's . . . it's . . ." She pressed her hands to her face, her entire body shaking, and Cal realized that whatever was happening had gone too far.

He reached out to shake her, meaning to wake her from the trance—if that's what it was—but someone beat him to it.

"Olivia! Olivia!" A short man with the same light hair and fine features as Olivia came running into the room. He grabbed her by the shoulders, jerking her limp body back and forth.

"What's going on here?" He demanded of Cal. "What did you do to her?"

Cal raised his hands. "I didn't do anything. We were just talking, and—"

"Spencer, when did you get here?" Olivia looked dazedly up at her brother, as if emerging from a dream. "Stop that," she said, pulling his hands from her shoulders.

Standing protectively over his sister, Spencer glared at Cal. "Who gave you permission to interrogate her? If you've done anything to—"

"It's all right." Olivia squeezed her brother's hand. "Chief Hunt was telling me about a discussion he had with poor Mrs. Zoeller, and I guess I must have dozed off."

"*Zoeller.*" Spencer's grimace clearly expressed his distaste for the woman.

"I think I'm done with my questions for today anyway," Cal said, dropping the recorder back into his pocket with the polished grace of a slight-of-hand magician.

Olivia stood. "I think I'll lie down for a little while. Chief, it was very nice meeting you." She reached out to shake Cal's hand, her fingers slipping easily inside his, and again Cal thought of his wife. The connection between the two women floated at the edge of his brain, but he couldn't quite grasp it.

As he watched her gather up her tools, Cal tried to understand what he'd just witnessed. Some sort of drug-induced flashback to the day she and the other children disappeared? If so, what had she seen inside the mine? What had terrified her?

She lifted a damp cloth, and Cal realized for the first time that she had continued to work on the bust, even during her flashback. Just before she laid the cloth over it, Cal recognized the face she'd been working on.

It was Frankie Zoeller.

CHAPTER 23

"I WONDER IF I COULD speak with you for a minute?" Spencer took Cal's elbow and led him from the gazebo.

The two men walked down the long, dark hallway, stopping outside the library Cal had seen earlier. Spencer waved him inside.

Spencer Godwin had the same willowy build as his sister. His honey-blond hair was combed up and back from his prominent forehead. He entered the room and posed before one of the two floor-to-ceiling windows, his chin resting on the thumb and index finger of his left hand, his right hand cupping his left elbow. Cal thought that Spencer looked like a man who needed to be holding a pipe. "I'm terribly sorry about my outburst back there."

Cal shook his head. "You were just concerned about your sister."

Spencer nodded. "She isn't well."

"She seemed fine," Cal said, although that was patently false. He looked over the leather-bound volumes that lined the room's walls. There were several books he'd like to explore but he got the feeling that although they were dusted regularly, they didn't leave their shelves much.

Spencer moved around to stand in front of him. His voice dropped to a whisper as he glanced toward the door. "Chief Hunt, my sister is . . . *fragile*. She's had a very hard life."

"How so?" Cal again glanced around at the room. If *this* was a hard life, he wouldn't mind a little of it himself. The books alone were probably worth more than twice what he'd paid for his house.

Spencer stared sharply up at Cal. Although his eyes were the same shade of blue as Olivia's, they had none of her depth. It was like comparing a shopping mall fountain to the ocean. "You have no idea what she's been through. Our mother passed away when we were both children. She was in an . . . institution at the time.

"Our father has never recovered from the loss, and now the doctors think that Mother's illness might be hereditary. Olivia is on a strictly controlled diet, and she takes medication every day. Her doctor says that she must not be upset in any way. If anything were to happen to her, I don't think Father could bear it."

Cal placed a hand on the smaller man's shoulder. "Mr. Godwin, I have to tell you, I believe your sister might be in danger."

"What *kind* of danger?"

Spencer listened attentively as Cal explained about the two murders, stopping him occasionally with an astute question. He had heard about the deaths, and he knew both victims had been friends of his sister's, but apparently he'd never connected them with the children's disappearance into the Seven Stars.

"So this has something to do with the Zoeller boy?" he asked. "The one who was never found?"

"Why do you say that?"

Spencer waved one hand theatrically in the air. "I assume that's why you were taking to Olivia about Esther. Who else would want to come after the survivors? Frankie's mother blamed them for her son's death."

"You knew that?" Cal pulled out his recorder.

"You don't need that," Spencer said. "Of course I knew that Esther Zoeller blamed my sister and her friends. She told everyone who would listen. She actually came down to the school once and threatened them herself. She was deranged even then. I'd focus on her if I were you."

"I'd like to ask you some questions about that," Cal said, still holding out the recorder.

"I'd love to. But unfortunately that's impossible today." Spencer turned abruptly and walked to the door, "I'm late for an appointment. Maybe another time?"

"Do you live in Twin Forks?" Cal asked.

"*Me*? No," Godwin laughed. "I just came down to visit my father. I have a house in Vail and a place on the coast."

"Maybe I could speak with your father."

"I'm sorry. That isn't possible. His health is very poor. But call me anytime you'd like. I'll have Richard give you the numbers." Spencer stepped into the hallway, and the butler immediately appeared.

"Richard, please give the chief my card."

Cal paused in the doorway and turned. "Mr. Godwin, I'd like to place an officer outside the house. We're short-handed but I'd sleep better at night knowing I had one of my men up here."

Spencer appeared to consider the proposal for a moment. "That's a generous offer, and I certainly appreciate your concern. Let me look into this situation a little further, and I may take you up on it."

CHAPTER 24

THE SUN WAS A BLAZING crescent disappearing slowly into the purple mountains as Cal stepped to the front porch of his house and slotted the key into the lock. Flipping through the mail, he swung open the door and entered the dim hallway. As usual, Buster stood sentry just inside. The cat's wide blue eyes studied the doorway expectantly. When he realized that Cal was once again alone, Buster turned and slouched into the kitchen.

"Know the feeling," Cal said to the disappearing feline. For the first time since his wife's death, he was beginning to think seriously about selling the house. It wasn't a big place—too humble even to be the guest quarters of the monstrosity Olivia Godwin called home. But he found it unsettlingly large even so as he rattled aimlessly through its empty rooms.

He was torn between a longing to rid himself of the many painful memories held by the home he and Kat had shared for all these years and the fear of leaving it all behind.

He tossed the mail—two credit card applications and an ad—into the trash and noticed the voicemail icon on his phone was flashing. He set his phone on the counter and hit play then popped a frozen chicken dinner into the microwave as he listened. The first two messages were from reporters—he quickly erased those—but the third voice brought a smile to his lips.

"Chief Hunt, this is Clara Bell from the library. Your book is overdue." He could hear her frown of displeasure clearly over the machine's speaker. "The fine is seventeen cents per day. Not that we can't use the money, but other patrons are waiting."

He wondered exactly how long the line was for others waiting to read *The Complete Biography of Ulysses S. Grant.*

"I would be happy to renew it for you if you've been a little pokey in your reading, but you'll need to come right in. I know, I know, you're very busy these days, what with those horrible murders and all," she said, as though he'd just contradicted her. "But while you're here I might just have a little information that could help you. I'll see you soon."

A beep signaled the end of the message. He checked his watch. It was too late to go to the library tonight, but he'd stop by in the morning on his way to Ezra's funeral. It was probably just Clara's way of tricking him into bringing the book back, but right now he'd take any lead he could get.

He was opening the fridge—hoping he hadn't finished the last beer— when the final message began to play.

"Chief Hunt . . . Cal." Olivia Godwin's voice sounded slurred as if she'd just awoken—or was it the drugs? "I don't believe that I thanked you for coming by today. I know it's your job, but . . ."

The phone played silently for several seconds. Cal stood with the refrigerator halfway open, cool air bathing his face.

"Thank you for looking out for me."

The sound of the receiver hanging up was followed by a beep. Cal let the refrigerator door slip closed, forgetting what he'd been looking for. Leaning against the counter, he brought a suddenly damp hand to his forehead.

He knew why Olivia had made him think of Kat, and the knowledge twisted in his stomach like a greasy fist. It wasn't their looks. The two women's features were as different as summer and winter. And it wasn't their voices. In fact, it wasn't anything about the women at all.

It was about *him*.

Despite his best efforts he'd been unable to keep Kat safe. That knowledge wrapped around him in the middle of the night like a cold, wet sheet. *You failed,* a dark voice that he recognized as his own whispered. *When she needed you most you weren't there.* It was stupid. There was no way he could have anticipated a fall from a ladder.

And yet inside he knew that he should have. Somehow, some way, he should have prevented his wife's death. And the knowledge that he hadn't would haunt him forever.

Now he was experiencing the same icy dread over a woman he barely knew. She was in danger. He felt it coursing through his body like a raging fever. She was in mortal danger, and it was his responsibility to keep her safe. The recognition he'd felt today was the terror that he'd fail once again.

CHAPTER 25

THE SIGN IN THE FRONT window read *Closed*, but before Cal could reach the top of the library steps, Clara had unlocked the double glass doors and was waving him inside.

"Thought you might get here early," she chirped, taking the Grant biography from his hands. As they entered the building's dim interior, Clara looked through the book's pages. *Checking her baby for any damage*, Cal thought, and he was glad he hadn't spilled any coffee on it or folded a page corner. He had the impression that Clara would not be especially forgiving to any who returned books marked up or damaged.

"Have you finished reading it?" she asked, slipping behind the checkout counter. The computers were turned on but the overhead lights were still out and the building felt vaguely morgue-like with its dark, empty aisles.

"No, haven't had much time for reading lately," he admitted. "Why don't you just go ahead and reshelve it?" He considered mentioning the crowds of anxious people waiting for the book's timely return but thought better of it. Clara had said something about information on the phone, and he didn't want to chance riling her up.

"I'll just renew it for another two weeks. A body without a good book handy is a woeful body indeed." As Clara entered his information into the computer, Cal noticed how she painfully pecked out each of the keys. Her fingers were not moving with the same speed as when she'd been running the microfilm reader a few days earlier. Her arthritis must be acting up this morning.

"That'll be thirty-four cents," she said.

After handing her a dollar bill, he glanced at his watch. "I've got to get down to the church."

"Yes, the Rucker funeral." A small printer next to the computer spit out a receipt, and Clara tucked it neatly into the book's front cover. She handed it back to him, along with his change. "I'll be going myself, if the girls ever show up."

Cal smiled. The "girls" had to be in their late fifties. "You mentioned you had some information. About the murders?"

"Don't know if it has anything to do with the murders or not," Clara said, throwing a reproachful look in his direction. "It's not as if anyone keeps me up to date with the case."

Cal opened the book and pretended to read the receipt.

"Fine, fine, be that way. But I don't know how you expect me to help you when I don't even know what you need."

He checked his watch.

Clara finally turned and walked to the back counter, her limp more pronounced than he'd ever seen it. Watching her painful steps, he was tempted to throw her a bone or two when he caught her shooting a surreptitious glance in his direction. For a moment her limp disappeared completely.

Why, that old faker! Her arthritis wasn't acting up at all. She'd been trying to play on his sympathies to get him to open up.

Sensing that Cal was onto her act, Clara returned more quickly and slid a sheet of paper across the counter to him. It was a name, *Jeff "Two Bears" Clapton*, and an address in a small town about a hundred miles to the south.

Cal looked up quizzically. The name sounded familiar, but—

"The mining engineer," Clara helped him.

"The one who found the children." Cal remembered reading about him in one of the newspaper articles. "How did you track him down?"

Clara partially succeeded in suppressing a grin and began placing books onto a wheeled cart. "You'd better get going. Don't want you to be late for the funeral."

CHAPTER 26

"IN FIRST CORINTHIANS WE READ, 'Behold, I shew you a mystery; We shall not all sleep, but we shall all be changed. In a moment, in the twinkling of an eye, at the last trump: for the trumpet shall sound, and the dead shall be raised incorruptible, and we shall be changed.'"

Cal shifted uncomfortably in his folding metal chair at the words of the pastor who stood before the gathered congregation. The padded benches in the front of the chapel had filled with friends and family of the Ruckers before he and Greg arrived, forcing them to sit back in the overflow area.

Like most of the town's residents, the Ruckers were Methodists, and the service had a distinctly Christian flavor to it.

Cal glanced at Greg, who seemed caught up in the service, and then at the rest of the funeral attendees who filled the chapel. Most of the mourners were middle-aged or older, with an occasional smattering of families. Clean-cut men in dark suits and white shirts—many of them with leathery necks and sunburned ears, attesting to hours spent working in the fields—leaned forward in their seats, chins resting in their palms. Women fanned themselves with folded paper programs.

"Death is not an end, but rather a return to—" The words buzzed in Cal's head like an angry fly.

He rose from his seat, unable to listen to the sermon any longer. Startled, Greg began to rise as well, but Cal motioned for him to stay. Ignoring the heads that craned around to watch him, Cal stalked out into the foyer.

It was one thing to live in a religious community. But it was another thing entirely to watch a building full of otherwise intelligent people brainwashed into believing that death was beautiful—a gift-wrapped passport to heaven.

How comforting it must be to hide the brutal reality of the dead man inside the coffin at the front of the chapel behind a veil of pretty images and vague homilies. Would the people listening to the eulogy be as comfortable if they'd seen Ezra's skull split open with a blood-soaked ax?

Pacing up and down the hallway, he tried to clear his head, closing his mind to the pastor's words that carried clearly from the amplified speakers. He dropped onto an empty couch in the foyer and pressed his face into his hands, hoping to calm the pounding in his temples.

What good was faith when all it could do was pick up the pieces after the damage had been done? The faith of Ezra's family hadn't protected him from whatever was waiting in the woods behind his house. Esther's faith hadn't kept her son from disappearing into the mine.

Not that he blamed people for seeking comfort wherever they could find it. If it helped Tamara and the Rucker boys to imagine Ezra sitting on a cloud playing a harp, or whatever one was supposed to do in heaven, more power to them. But to imagine for a minute that a brutal murder was part of some divine plan was just wrong.

That was the problem with religion. It tried to find meaning where there was none. When Kat died, nearly every person in town tried to tell him that the accident had been God's will. "God works in mysterious ways." "No one knows His will." "She's with the angels."

Cal wanted to scream at all of them, "No! She's not with the angels. My wife is on a table in the basement of the mortuary having chemicals pumped into her body so she won't stink at the funeral. And if I could find someone to blame, I'd empty my pistol into their worthless body until the clip ran dry, and then I'd reload and start all over again."

It had been all he could do to make it through the funeral without hitting someone. And when he finally made it home—

"Are you all right?"

Cool fingers brushed against the back of Cal's neck, and he jerked backward.

Olivia Godwin sat beside him on the couch. He hadn't heard her approach. "I noticed you leave the service. This must be hard for you."

"I just . . ." He rubbed his brow. "Headache."

Olivia nodded. As if reading his mind, she said, "It's all right to miss her."

"No. It's not that. I was . . ." His words dried up as he looked into her blue eyes. Without the drugs, they were amazingly clear and deep, innocent while at the same time knowing.

He slumped against the back of the couch, a protracted sigh escaping his lips. "It's just hard sometimes."

"You want to go on," she said, rubbing her fingers across the edge of an embroidered handkerchief, "but you find yourself pulled back."

"Exactly," he said, amazed that anyone could understand so well how he felt.

"You wonder why you have the right to go on breathing, to smell freshly cut grass, to enjoy the sounds of children's laughter."

"Yes." Cal leaned toward Olivia. "I feel guilty for eating a good meal when she never will again. Every time I start to feel the least happiness it seems like a betrayal. I want to get on with my life but I don't know where to go."

Olivia pressed the handkerchief to her eyes, and Cal saw that she was crying. Realization washed over him. She understood his feelings so well because she'd had them herself. Over Frankie? Or Ezra and Amanda? He reached out and touched her cheek, her skin as soft as a child's.

"Olivia, if there's something you want to tell me—"

"There you are." Cal and Olivia both looked up with similarly guilty expressions on their faces as Spencer Godwin entered the foyer. He stopped short as he recognized Cal. "Chief Hunt."

Cal removed his hand from Olivia's face. "Mr. Godwin."

Spencer looked from Cal to Olivia, noting the tears on his sister's face. "The service is over. We need to leave."

People were filing from the chapel now. Cal and Olivia stood. Spencer took his sister's arms and led her to the door. Cal wondered if she'd look back before leaving. She didn't.

He followed the crowd into the parking lot. Waves of heat already rose off the baking asphalt. Olivia and Spencer Godwin got into a small red car and pulled quickly away.

Cal turned to watch the Rucker family file into a long dark limousine. Ezra's father, his face a mask of weather-wrinkled skin beneath a cap of grizzled hair, fixed a narrow-eyed grimace at Cal before ducking into the sedan. Sam Rucker, following his grandfather's gaze, saw Cal as well and gave him a two-fingered wave. He had the look of an abandoned pet found wandering along the side of a highway. Just before Sam disappeared into the limousine, Cal noticed the boy was wearing the gold plastic badge he'd accepted the day after his father died.

Think you'll catch the bad guy? The one who kilt my Dad?

Cal turned to head for his patrol car. Before he could take a step, though, he was intercepted by a familiar face.

"Chief Hunt, you done anything about my water?" Dickey Jordan gripped Cal's hand in his own and pumped it as though he were milking a cow. Cal had forgotten that the Jordans and the Ruckers shared nearby fields.

"Mr. Jordan, I really have to—" Cal looked around for Greg, but the detective was nowhere to be seen.

Ignoring Cal's distracted glance, Dickey plowed the same territory he and Cal had gone over a dozen times. "First my pond dried up. Then the pasture well. Now even the water at the house is turning brown. Ya gotta stop 'em."

"Look, Dickey, I'd really like to help you if I could. But you know as well as I do that the city council makes the rules. All I do is enforce them."

Dickey stared up at the postcard-clear mountains, rubbing his chin. "Tried to get me a lawyer to sue 'em, but he wanted too danged much money up front."

"Have you ever considered that maybe it's just the drought drying up your wells?" Cal suggested. "Might be time to think about hooking up to the city water." He wasn't even sure Dickey was listening anymore. The man's eyes had taken on a glazed faraway look, making him appear slightly crazed. It made Cal nervous.

"Thought you could arrest the whole city council. Put 'em behind bars and they'll think twice about stealin' my water. 'Specially that Calbert Neffinger. Wouldn't mind seeing his nasty carcass left behind bars forever." The old farmer nodded to himself, a smile cracking his dried lips.

Cal placed a hand on one of Dickey's wiry arms. "Maybe you ought to come by the office for a few minutes. Let's see if we can't come up with—"

"Chief!" Greg shouted from across the parking lot. Cal turned to see the detective running toward him, and his throat tightened with sudden dread.

"Cal." Greg's red face dripped with sweat. "You know that guy you wanted me to track down, Ben Meyers?"

"What about him?" Cal asked, icy fingers reaching into his chest. *Please don't let this be another murder*, he whispered to himself, already knowing it would be.

"He fell from a cliff last night."

The icy fingers wrapped around Cal's heart, freezing it. "Fell or was pushed?" Cal, forgetting the confused-looking Dickey Jordan, was already reaching for his car keys.

"Don't know," Greg said. "But he's alive. He's in the hospital, in critical condition."

"Which hospital?" Cal and Greg jogged toward the patrol car, never noticing the way Dickey's face tightened and his eyes narrowed as he stood alone in the baking sun.

CHAPTER 27

THEY TURNED THE PAGES OF news magazines, not seeing the words or images in front of them. They held paperback books between carefully steadied fingers, never turning the pages at all. At first glance, the half-dozen people seated at safe intervals around the waiting room all seemed occupied—the magazine readers, the woman with the mystery, the man sorting through the contents of his wallet, even the teenage girl, sleeping, spread out across three of the vinyl-upholstered chairs.

But he knew these people. He'd made their acquaintances far too intimately on the hellish night he'd spent waiting through Kat's surgery. At every squeak of a rubber-soled shoe on the highly polished tile, every *whoosh* of a door opening, every ring of the phone at the nurse's desk, their eyes left whatever they were doing and their faces hardened, awaiting the blow they all secretly anticipated.

The door swung open, and instantly everyone looked up.

"Chief Hunt?"

Their faces relaxed, spared for the moment.

Cal stood and shook the doctor's hand.

"I'm Dr. Simmons." He was a tall man with sharp features and intelligent gray eyes. But the green scrubs and the faintly alcoholic smell of disinfectant emanating from him brought back memories that balled Cal's stomach into a tight knot.

"Nice to meet you," Cal said, watching as the doctor's eyes took in his badge and uniform, stopping briefly at the pistol strapped to his waist before returning to meet his gaze. There was a hesitancy that was almost universal with doctors when a cop came to check one of their patients—a protectiveness.

"May I ask what your interest is in Mr. Meyers?"

"I'm investigating a pair of homicides." Cal spoke carefully, knowing that his words carried to every person in the room.

"And you think that Mr. Meyers might be the . . . ?"

"No." Cal motioned toward the door, and both men stepped from the waiting room and into the hallway beyond. As the door swung closed behind them, Cal could hear the beeps and buzzes of monitoring equipment coming from the patient rooms lining the corridor. Were those the last sounds Kat had heard? Would they be the last sounds Ben Meyers would hear? He hoped not. They were depressing—frightening—a heartless countdown to death.

"How bad is he?"

"It's a miracle he's alive at all." Dr. Simmons enumerated the extensive injuries Ben had sustained, starting with two broken ankles and finishing with a fractured skull and forty-nine stitches' worth of scalp lacerations. It took him almost five minutes to complete the catalog, and by the end Cal was wondering if it wouldn't have been easier to just list what was still intact.

He could feel the veins in his temples pounding. It was maddening to know that a brutal killer was moving easily from one victim to the next, leaving the police helpless to do anything but pick up the pieces behind him. "You're right, doctor. It *is* a miracle that Mr. Meyers is alive. Whoever pushed him from that cliff *was* trying to kill him. The killer succeeded with his first two victims."

"You must be mistaken." Dr. Simmons's eyes flashed shock. "He wasn't pushed. It was an accident."

"Are you sure?" Cal growled, already knowing the answer.

"Well, I—" the doctor began, but something in Cal's expression stopped him.

"Has anyone spoken to him?"

"No, but a hiker witnessed the fall. And the emergency medical personnel—"

Cal took out his notebook. "I'm going to need the names of all medical personnel who were on the scene and any witnesses. As soon as Mr. Meyers can communicate I want to be notified. I'll see what I can do about getting some security outside his door, but in the meantime, make sure that no one but immediate family gets in to see him."

"Yes, of course."

"And I'll need to speak with Mrs. Meyers as soon as possible. Let her know that I'll be in the lobby." Cal turned and walked through the door, not meeting the eyes that followed him as he moved quickly across the room to the elevator. The smells and sounds of the dying were pressing in on him like a lead-lined jacket, and he knew that if he didn't get some fresh air soon, he was going to lose it completely.

He jabbed the down button. After what felt like an eternity, the electronic chime sounded, and he stepped inside. As the doors slid closed, Cal felt an almost palpable sense of relief. Pressing his hands against his eyes, he tried taking deep, slow breaths. What was happening to him? He'd dealt with death and injury hundreds of times over his career—it was part of the job description—but it had never affected him like this before.

It would be easy to blame the feelings on Kat's death, and that was definitely part of it. Everywhere he turned, her memory was waiting for him, launching one surprise attack after another on his already-frayed nerves. But there was something more, something subtler. This whole case felt wrong. There was almost a sense of inevitability about the killings.

For one thing, the murders were happening too fast and too easily. Serial killers usually took more time, studied their victims. That's one reason why they were so hard to catch. Whoever was committing these murders was rushing from one victim to the next. He should have been making mistakes, leaving clues behind. And clues *were* being left, but they seemed staged and insubstantial, handfuls of mist.

For another thing, there were the victims themselves. Ezra had been obsessing over Amanda's death, and if Mandy's husband was to be believed, she had experienced some kind of premonition. It seemed unlikely that Olivia, Ben, or Theresa could possibly have been unaware of their classmates' deaths. And yet not one of them had come to the police for protection.

He'd been trying to reach Meyers for two days. The man wouldn't return the phone calls of the people who were trying to protect him, but he'd strolled along the edge of a sheer precipice as if he *wanted* to die. What was the secret they were all protecting? What could a bunch of seven- and eight-year-old kids have done that was so bad that they would rather face violent deaths than risk revealing the truth?

It didn't make any sense.

As he left the elevator and walked through the crowded lobby, he passed a woman in tailored slacks and an expensive blouse. Something about her face looked familiar. He paused, turning to watch her approach the reception desk.

He drifted closer, catching bits and pieces of her words over the other conversations taking place around him.

"I'm sorry," the woman at the desk was saying, shaking her head. "Mr. Meyers may only be visited by immediate family."

"But we're very close. Just like family." The woman's voice was professional but demanding. She was someone who was used to getting her way.

"I'm sorry."

"Let me speak to your supervisor."

Cal slipped over to an angle where he could see her face. The hair was still jet-black, but now short and styled. The glasses were gone—replaced by contacts or, more likely, laser surgery. But he knew who she was. She caught him watching her and turned quickly away.

Stepping next to her, he placed a hand on her elbow. "Theresa Obrey?"

"Who are you?" She asked, pulling her arm from him.

"Cal Hunt, Twin Forks PD." He offered her his card, but she refused to take it.

"I was just leaving." Waving her hand in the direction of the woman at the desk as though brushing off a bothersome insect, she turned from the desk.

Cal stayed by her side as she walked briskly toward the entrance. "Mrs. Obrey, are you aware that I've been trying to contact you for several days?"

Theresa continued across the lobby as though she hadn't heard him.

"I can bring you in for questioning."

She whirled on him like a tiger. "Just try it." Her voice was barely above a whisper, but it boiled with venom. "I know the governor personally, and I lunch with the attorney general at least once a month. You come within a hundred feet of me, and I'll see that badge of yours flushed down the toilet."

Cal stared at her, stunned. What was wrong with this woman? She was acting as if she were a suspect rather than a potential victim. "You do know that three of your friends are either dead or seriously injured?"

"I have no idea what you're talking about," she hissed—then, apparently realizing that he'd overheard her conversation at the front desk, pointed a manicured finger in the general direction of the receptionist. "Ben and I have stayed in some contact over the years. I was hoping to offer comfort to his wife."

Cal couldn't fathom her callousness. "I don't know what you're hiding, Mrs. Obrey, but you are in grave danger, and I'm trying to help you."

Theresa glared at him, pure hatred in her eyes, and carefully enunciated her words, biting off each syllable with perfect white teeth. "I am not hiding anything. I can take care of myself. And if you have anything else to say, you can tell it to my lawyer."

With that, she turned and pushed her way roughly past him and out through the double doors.

CHAPTER 28

CAL WAS HALFWAY BACK TO Twin Forks when he remembered the phone number Clara had given him that morning. LuAnn Meyers had been cooperative, but their conversation had proven as unproductive as the ones he'd had with the spouses of the other two victims. She promised to contact him when her husband regained consciousness.

The local police had been similarly unhelpful. With no evidence to the contrary, they were still viewing Ben's fall as an accident. They promised to send someone out to examine the scene but were unable to provide security for Ben's room. Cal understood—their department wasn't much bigger than his own, and resources were stretched thin. Still, the thought of Ben Meyers lying unconscious and unprotected in a dark hospital room filled him with dread.

He'd have Greg check out the canyon where Ben had fallen. Greg was a young guy and stood a better chance of returning in one piece than Cal did.

Cal pulled the slip of paper from his pocket, keeping an eye on the stop-and-go traffic in front of him. He read the name again—Jeff "Two Bears" Clapton. It sounded Indian. There were two Ute tribes in Colorado—the Mountain Ute Tribe and the Southern Ute Tribe. The mining engineer might be from one of them or he might not be from a local tribe at all. He typed the number into his cell phone and waited for the call to connect.

Partway through the third ring, he heard a click and some kind of background noise.

"Hello?" Cal said, wondering if he had a bad connection.

More of the background noise, then a rough voice shouted, "Be quiet!"

"Excuse me?"

"I said, be quiet, or you'll be sleeping under the stars tonight."

"Who is this?" Cal asked, hitting the brakes hard to avoid rear-ending a grandmother in a boat of an SUV. She glanced nervously back at his patrol car in her rearview mirror and moved into the right-hand lane.

Cal thought he heard a door slam, and then the gravelly voice was back on the line. "Sorry about that. Pepper has been in high spirits all day."

"Pepper?" He was still not sure he had the right connection.

"A sprightly little border collie. Sweet as molasses, but not too strong in the obedience department." The man on the other end of the line paused as if remembering something. "What'd you say your name was, by the way?"

"Actually I hadn't quite gotten to that part yet, but it's Cal Hunt."

"Cal Hunt. Good name." The man cleared his throat, choked a little, and finally gave in to a string of harsh coughs that Cal recognized from the heavy smokers he'd worked with in homicide.

"Gave up the coffin nails a little more than ten years ago," the man said, catching his breath, "but they don't seem to want to let go of me. Name's Two Bears, case you didn't know. What can I do for you, Cal?"

Cal smiled at the man's forthright nature. He explained who he was and how he had obtained Two Bears's phone number. "I'm interested in what you might know about the Seven Stars mine," he said. There was a long pause.

"Bad place, the Seven Stars. Very bad place." Two Bears's voice was subdued.

"You mean because of the children," Cal said, remembering Clara's comments about the mine being haunted.

"Nope. Always bad. Worked that mine back in '43, and it was bad then. Always been bad, far as I know."

"1943?" Cal mentally added up the years. That would make Two Bears—

"Eighty years old," Two Bears offered. "I was twelve. You want to stay away from that place. People and animals go in, sometimes they don't come back out."

Sometimes they don't come back out. The words crawled a slow, cold trail up the back of Cal's neck. "Well, at least we don't need to worry about that anymore," he said. "I went up there myself, and the entrance is completely sealed."

Two Bears laughed, a painful-sounding croak. "Bad places are hungry, Cal. You close one mouth, they open another."

"No, I checked myself. There isn't any—" Cal stopped, suddenly remembering the cloud of bats he'd seen rising into the night sky. Where had they come from?

"You felt it, didn't you?" Two Bears said. "If you went up there, you felt its hunger."

Inexplicably the patrol car seemed to grow too confining, the air stale. Cal cracked the driver's side window. He *had* felt something.

"Don't go into the mine." Two Bears's warning seemed to resonate over the phone line like the echo of a gong.

But Cal knew that was exactly where he *had* to go. It might be the only place where he could find the clues to what was happening in his town. "We've had a couple of murders up here."

"You think they have something to do with the Seven Stars?"

Cal told him about Mandy, Ezra, and Ben, and heard the old Indian suck in his breath.

"You're going in, then?" Two Bears asked.

"Yes," Cal said. "Will you come with me?" He wasn't sure how much help an eighty-year-old guide might be, but the thought of entering the mine alone raised goose bumps along his back and arms. "The city will pay you a consulting fee."

"When will you go?"

"Tomorrow." To wait any longer would put more lives at risk.

"I can't talk you out of it?"

"No."

"I'll come, then." The old Indian's voice trembled. "Pray, Cal, to whatever God you believe in, that these deaths have nothing to do with that terrible place."

"I don't believe in God," Cal said.

"Pray anyway."

CHAPTER 29

CAL WAS ALL RIGHT UNTIL he peered into the opening. Two Bears had called it a mouth, and that's exactly what it looked like—a gaping black maw, its throat descending deep into the side of the mountain.

"Still want to go in?" The corners of the old Indian's mouth rose slightly, creasing his dark, leathery skin and revealing a row of yellowed teeth. If it was meant to be a smile it came up severely lacking. Not that Cal could blame him. He didn't feel much like smiling himself.

"Just give me a minute." They had spent a good part of the morning searching for one of the airshafts that slanted up from the mine. Cal was exhausted but Two Bears didn't even seem to be breathing hard. The old man was short—no more than five feet tall—with thin, wiry limbs and skin like weathered strips of beef jerky. He looked his age but rather than breaking him down, the years seemed to have hardened him.

Although the opening was nearly as tall as Cal and wide enough for him to enter without any trouble, it had been overgrown with brush and debris. He wasn't sure how Two Bears had finally located it.

Taking off the hard hat the old man had provided, Cal wiped the sweat from his forehead with one hand and sat on a nearby log. Pepper, the Indian's border collie, immediately jumped onto Cal's lap, planting a muddy paw in his crotch and licking his face.

"Pepper, get down," Two Bears admonished the black-and-white dog, but it was obvious his mind was elsewhere. After a quick glance in her master's direction, Pepper continued trying to wash Cal's face.

The old Indian stared down into the airshaft, head cocked to one side as though listening to something. Kneeling, he took a pinch of the arid soil and raised it to his mouth. His grayish tongue darted out lizard-like to lick the dust between his fingers.

"Pah," he spat, shaking his head and wiping his hand on the side of his jeans.

"Why did you do that?" Cal asked, holding the dog at bay with one hand.

"Every mineral has its own flavor." Two Bears opened his pack and took out a long coil of knotted rope. "Gold tastes a little like nutmeg, copper tastes like blood. Once knew a fellow could taste a vein of silver near two miles away."

Convinced the old man was trying to pull one over on him, Cal rubbed his own fingers in the dirt and raised them to his mouth. "So what does *this* taste like?"

With a gleam in his faded brown eyes, Two Bears reached out with the toe of his boot and nudged a pile of deer scat, grinning as Cal immediately dropped his hand from his mouth. Then his eyes grew serious.

"The ground here is turned—corrupt—nothing good can come of it."

Cal didn't know about corrupt ground, but there was something about this place that set him on edge. In the light of day it was easier to shake off the sense of foreboding that he'd felt the last time he was up here, but once they left the light behind . . .

Two Bears pounded a spike into the ground and tied one end of the rope to it, looping the rest of the rope over his shoulder. He pulled on his pack and checked the light on his helmet. "You ready?"

Cal wasn't ready at all. East L.A. had been an armpit, but right now he'd have taken the worst section of the city over this in a heartbeat. "Yeah. Let's go."

"Follow me," Two Bears said. "It may be steep, so hold on tight to the rope." As he started into the opening, he glanced back at Cal, seeming to compare the breadth of Cal's shoulders to the entrance. "Don't get stuck," he said, a solemn expression on his wrinkled old face. "I want to be able to get out."

As promised, the airshaft was steep but not impassable. Cal kept an iron grip on the rope, moving only when he saw that Two Bears had safely passed through the next section. When they had gone twenty feet or so, Cal heard a high-pitched cry coming from the entrance. Looking back up at the circle of blue sky that already seemed impossibly small, he saw Pepper staring after them, her paws anxiously kicking down showers of dirt and pebbles.

"Come on, girl," Two Bears called. The dog yapped, took a step or two forward, then backed out again. "Come." At the old man's gravelly command, Pepper gave a forlorn howl, ducked her head, and scrambled down after them.

"I know how you feel," Cal muttered, taking a long last look at the azure disk of sky. The next time he turned around, it was gone.

CHAPTER 30

THEY WERE NEARLY TO THE bottom when the shaft began to narrow. "Ever hear about the guy whose left side was crushed during a cave-in?" Two Bears called back.

"Huh?" Cal studied the shaft wall. It looked like part of it had collapsed over time.

"Left side. Completely crushed. Ever hear about him?" Cal watched the smaller man slide through the close space, his light bobbing in the darkness before disappearing completely from sight. The dog followed Two Bears through the opening.

"No," Cal said. He wasn't sure this was exactly the conversation he wanted to be having at the moment. He reached up to rub his eyes, the light on his own helmet bouncing from floor to ceiling as he moved his head.

"He's all right now." Two Bears's voice echoed off the wall.

"What?" Cal stopped. Was the old man laughing?

"He's all right." Two Bears called from around the corner. He was definitely laughing. "Lost his left side, so he's *all right.*"

It was a joke. The old Indian was telling a joke. Cal couldn't believe it.

"Your turn now," Two Bears said.

Cal edged toward the narrow opening through which Two Bears had disappeared. So far he'd been able to walk, head slightly bowed, down the cramped tunnel, ducking only occasionally when the top of the passageway dropped a little. His shoulders had barely cleared the walls on either side, but now, as the earth closed in, he was forced to turn sideways to squeeze through the narrow space.

"I don't know if I can make it." He couldn't see Two Bears's light, and his own headlamp glowed weakly in the tight confines.

"You'll be fine. Take off your pack and tell me a joke."

Inhaling deeply, Cal removed his pack and began to edge sideways down the passage. "I don't know any jokes."

"Everyone knows a joke." Two Bears's voice seemed inexplicably far away. "And no knock-knocks."

Cal's headlamp shot awkwardly toward the ceiling and to his left, leaving him unable to see what was ahead. The air down here was considerably colder than it had been on the surface, and he found himself shivering despite the sweat that ran down his back and sides.

"I don't—" He was about to tell Two Bears that he really didn't know any jokes when he remembered a dumb story Greg had told him one night while they were on a stakeout.

"Okay," he said, feeling extremely stupid and scared to death all at the same time. "There's these three asparagus kids, right?"

"Asparagus?" Two Bears sounded a little closer.

"Yeah, asparagus. So they're screwing around by the railroad tracks. You know, trying to prove which is the bravest. The first one stands on the left rail as a train comes and jumps off just before the train gets there. Then the second one stands in the middle of the tracks. And he jumps off when the next train comes."

Cal's face brushed against the wall, smearing his cheek and lips with a foul, powdery soil. He spat, trying to get rid of the sour, mildewed taste in his mouth, but it didn't help.

"Go on," Two Bears called back.

"Well," Cal tried to draw in a deep breath but his chest wouldn't seem to expand, "the last kid really wants to impress the other two so he stands on the right track and just as the train gets there, he jumps over the left track. But the train clips him, and he goes flying down the side of the hill."

Three more sidling steps and he could feel the walls brushing against both his chest and back. "Two Bears," he called, his heart pounding.

There was no answer.

As he pushed farther into the passage, a sharp chunk of rock, embedded in the earth behind him, dug into his back. Twisting his shoulders, he attempted to readjust his position.

"They, uh, call the asparagus ambulance and these asparagus EMTs start CPR while they rush him to the asparagus hospital." Cal tried to concentrate on the story, struggling to keep himself from panicking. But he could feel his mind starting to waver.

"And this, uh, asparagus doctor rushes him into surgery, but . . ."

Dirt crumbled from the wall in front of him, falling into his eyes. He couldn't get his hand up to brush it out. The passage was too tight. He wasn't going to be able to make it through.

He tried to back out, but somehow he had managed to slide past the edge of the rock, and now it blocked his retreat. He was stuck.

"Two Bears, where are you?" he shouted. He tugged on the rope, but it seemed to be jammed as well. Two Bears couldn't have gone far. When he realized that Cal wasn't following him, he would come back. Closing his eyes, Cal took several long, slow breaths, but the cold, dank air felt heavy and lacking in oxygen.

He could feel his heart racing. He needed to relax. Getting excited would only make matters worse. Something brushed against the back of his neck, skittered across his skin, and dropped down the collar of his shirt. It felt like a thick, hairy spider; he slammed his head against the wall, and a shower of rocks and dirt cascaded onto him.

It was coming down. This part of the shaft had collapsed before, and now it was caving in completely. Panic raced through his body like a wildfire. He slammed his shoulders to the left and right, trying to break free. The walls no longer felt like dirt and rock at all but rather fingers clutching at him—holding him in place while they buried him alive.

He couldn't breathe. Hands pressed on his chest and back, keeping his lungs from expanding. A whisper of childish laughter blew across his ear. He stretched his hand out, reaching for any kind of purchase.

Something cold and clammy closed on his fingers, and he screamed.

CHAPTER 31

"YOU'RE ALL RIGHT."

Cal gasped, sucking the cold air into his burning lungs. He was standing on the floor of the mine, Two Bears gripping his hand firmly.

"Thought I was a goner. How'd you—"

He turned to look at the shaft, sure that it had caved in completely, and was shocked to see that other than a few rocks scattered across the floor it was unchanged. His backpack and rope lay abandoned on the ground.

"Heard you calling and thought maybe you were stuck," the old man said, his eyes darting toward the passage.

Realizing that he still held Two Bears's hand locked in a death grip, Cal unclasped his fingers and stepped warily to the opening. It was narrow, but nothing like the vice that had squeezed the air from his lungs only seconds earlier. Edging over to retrieve his pack, ready to bolt at the first sign of anything out of the ordinary, he crouched and hooked a shoulder strap with one hand. Slowly he stood.

"Guess maybe I caught myself on something," he said.

"Guess so," Two Bears agreed, but he didn't look any more convinced than Cal felt.

"I must have panicked. I thought that . . ." Cal stepped into the mineshaft, letting his words fade away. He was unsure of exactly what he had just experienced.

"It can happen."

"What can happen?" Cal glanced uneasily back toward the opening.

"Claustrophobia," Two Bears answered. "Mine fever. Seen fellows enter a shaft for the first time and just run headlong into the walls. Knock themselves clean out."

Cal had never had problems with closed spaces before, but whatever it was seemed to have passed.

"What happened?" Two Bears asked.

"Guess I just panicked, like you said."

"Not to you," said Two Bears, completely serious. "What happened to the asparagus? Did he live?"

"Yeah. But he was a vegetable."

The old man groaned.

Using the beam of his lamp, Cal began exploring his surroundings. They were standing in a squared-off passageway roughly seven feet tall by five feet wide. Every six feet or so along the tunnel the walls and ceiling were braced by wooden supports so black they almost looked like stone. "What was with the jokes?" he asked. "Some kind of trick to take my mind off the passage?"

Two Bears glanced uncomfortably at the shaft as though he wished he hadn't come down. "Protection."

"Huh?" Cal had been reaching toward one of the beams. He stopped and turned.

"Laughter—from in here," Two Bears patted a gnarled hand on his chest, "wards against evil."

Cal studied the Indian's face to see if he was pulling Cal's leg. The old man's expression was dead serious. Cal shook his head and snorted. He wouldn't have expected an engineer to fall for such superstitious nonsense. "So what's wrong with knock-knocks? Don't they keep the oogie-boogies away?"

"Nope, that's just me," Two Bears said, starting down the shaft. "They don't make me laugh."

"Baloney," Cal muttered under his breath. He reached up to run his hand across a nearby beam. It had a damp, oily feel to it. He pushed against it and the entire support groaned.

"Don't do that," Two Bears grabbed Cal's arm.

Cal pulled his hand quickly away, shooting the old man a questioning look.

"Most of this wood is at least seventy years old. You put too much pressure on it, and the whole place'll come down on our heads."

Cal stepped away from the beam, nearly tripping on something protruding from the floor of the shaft. Focusing his helmet light on the ground, he saw a pair of rusted metal rails running the length of the passage in both directions.

"More than three miles of track ran through here 'fore they shut 'er down."

"Wouldn't they have cleared this all out when they closed the mine?" Cal knelt next to Two Bears and rapped one of the rails with his knuckles, shedding scales of rust onto the rotted wood of the crosstie beneath it.

"Nope. World War II came along, and everybody left to go fight. Vein was nearly played out anyway, so he just up and closed her."

"He?" Cal asked, realizing that he had no idea who had actually owned the mine. "*Who* closed it?"

Two Bears gave him a sidelong look that Cal found impossible to read behind the bright glare of the man's lamp. "Figured you knew. Once his partner left, the mine was owned outright by Caleb Godwin."

The name should have surprised him, but somehow Cal found that it didn't. "That would be Olivia's . . ."

The old man nodded. "The girl's grandfather."

CHAPTER 32

"COME ON." TWO BEARS STARTED off down the shaft, Pepper at his heels. "I'll tell you what I can while we walk. Don't want to stay in here any longer than we have to."

Unable to argue with that, Cal shouldered his pack and followed Two Bears along the center of the rust-pocked tracks, stopping only occasionally to examine a battered pickaxe head or an old oil-burning lantern.

"First heard of this place as a boy. My father had been drinking and he was arguing with my mother. My two sisters and I shared a bed in the other room. We were supposed to be sleeping, but the walls were made of plywood and we couldn't help but hear them.

"I knew they were arguing about me. Two white men had come onto the reservation."

"From the mine?" Cal asked, trying to keep up with the old Indian's swift pace.

"That's right." Two Bears nodded, the light from his helmet bobbing up and down. "Caleb Godwin and his partner, a man named William Sheehy from California. They were offering cash for boys to work in a new mine they were opening." The old man's gravelly voice had a soothing, almost hypnotic effect. It was the voice of a storyteller.

"How much money?" Cal asked.

"Three dollars and seventy-five cents a day. This was back in the 1940s, when three dollars could feed a family for a week. The rest of the country was just recovering from what they called the Great Depression. For the Utes, like most tribes back then, it was just business as usual. We didn't have anything in the first place, so we didn't know we were doing without."

They came to a fork, the tracks continuing more or less in the direction they had been following while a narrower tunnel branched off to the left. Two Bears took the left without hesitation.

"I could tell that my mother wanted me to take the job. The money would mean a lot to the family. But my father didn't trust the men. And there was something else—something neither of them would name, only talked around. When he came into the room, I pretended to be sleeping. He wasn't fooled though.

"He took me by the arm, and we walked out the front door. My mother was sitting at the table crying. The night was cold, but my father's hand was warm on my arm. After a few minutes I realized where we were going. It was a ridge that looked out over the desert for miles. The elders gathered there to discuss things. I'd never been up—children weren't allowed."

They continued from shaft to shaft in silence, Two Bears apparently caught up in his memories. The silence was eerie, and after a few minutes, Cal couldn't stand it any longer.

"What did your father say?" he asked.

"When we reached the top of the ridge, he gathered dried grass and brush and lit a fire. He squatted across the flames from me and stared into my eyes. Even though I was only twelve, I'd been thinking of leaving the reservation for some time. I couldn't see any reason to stay— there wasn't anything there for me. I figured this was my chance. He must have seen that, because he didn't try to talk me out of going."

"He told me many things up on the hill that night," Two Bears continued. "Some I'll tell you, some were for my ears alone. I could smell the alcohol on his breath, but his eyes were steady, his voice was strong."

Mesmerized by the old man's story, Cal had been mindlessly following Two Bears through a maze of twisting passages. Some of them were big enough to drive a car through while others were not much larger than the airshaft by which they'd entered. He had quickly lost all sense of direction, but the old man moved unerringly from tunnel to tunnel. Still, it gave Cal an uneasy feeling to realize that if anything happened to his guide, he'd be hopelessly lost.

"He talked until the moon had dropped low in the sky and the mountains glowed pink. The fire had burned out, and my legs were stiff. At last he stood and took my face in his hands. He pointed west toward the mountains and asked me what I saw. At first I couldn't see anything— only the moonlit desert. Then I spotted a pair of silver eyes watching us from a distance."

"What was it?"

Two Bears studied a fork in the tunnel for a moment before turning right. "Coyote."

"A coyote?" Cal had been expecting something more sinister somehow.

"My father told me, 'You can learn more from following a coyote than you'll learn in the all the white man's cities combined.' At the time I didn't understand. But later I learned what he meant."

Two Bears stopped abruptly, and Cal nearly ran into his back. They were standing at the spot where another smaller tunnel converged with the one they had been following. The Indian nudged at something with the toe of his boot and it took Cal a second to realize he was looking at the remains of some small animal.

"Bat," Two Bears said. "They're the only animals that will come in here other than an occasional mouse or coon. The bigger animals all know better. Coyote, bear, mountain lion. All the big mammals stay away—except for the white man." He grinned at Cal. "No offense."

"None taken."

The old man took his helmet from his head, pulled a handkerchief from inside it, and wiped his face. "You still sure you want to do this?"

Cal nodded, although what he really wanted to do was turn tail and get out of this place as fast as he could.

"All right, then." Two Bears pulled a pair of rags from his pocket, offering one to Cal. "Hold this over your nose and mouth."

Ducking his head, Cal followed Two Bears into the shaft. He estimated that it was less than five feet high, and its walls seemed more ragged than the other passages they had seen. Immediately a strong ammonia-like scent assaulted his nose. Pressing the cloth to his face, trying to block the smell, he followed the tunnel for several hundred feet until it opened into a cave.

"What is that horrible stench?" Cal asked, his voice muffled by the rag.

Two Bears brushed the toe of his boot across the floor. Cal looked down, his lamp illuminating the white powdery ground. He knelt and ran his fingers across the dirt, brushing up something that felt almost like flour. It didn't look like dirt at all, more like some kind of droppings.

"Guano," Two Bears said.

Something fluttered above their heads and as Cal raised his head, his throat closed to the size of a pinhole. The entire top of the cave seemed to be moving in long black waves. It wasn't the ceiling of the cave he was looking at but rather thousands and thousands of bats hanging upside down. Their bodies pressed tightly together.

Pepper let out a long, low growl.

Cal tried to imagine the children—trapped in here for what must have felt like an eternity with no light of any kind—listening to the rustling and screeching of the nightmarish cloud roosting above them. His throat closed completely.

"Is this where . . . ?" he managed to gasp.

Two Bears shook his head and motioned toward another opening on the far side of the cave. Cal followed him through the opening, and immediately the smell became a little more bearable.

It was obvious now that they had left the Seven Stars itself and passed into a series of connected caves. Natural rock passages had replaced the rough-hewn walls of the mine. Two Bears stopped in a roughly oval opening and looked around, seeming to search his memory before nodding.

"Right here. Found the five of them curled up. So pale and still I thought they were dead at first."

"But how did you know?" Cal asked. "To come here, I mean."

Two Bears shrugged and ran one hand along the wall. "Knew they'd searched the mine proper already. Figured it had to be one of the older sections. I dug a lot of that last passage out myself."

"The caves were here before the mine was built?" This was news to Cal, as was seemingly everything about the Seven Stars.

"Sure it was," Two Bears said. "Godwin and Sheehy came into these caves searching for a legend. Rumors were going around about a secret Ute mine hidden up in the mountains somewhere."

"A gold mine?" The story just kept getting stranger and stranger.

"Gold, yeah. Few folks even claimed they'd seen it but that anyone who tried to get in would be killed by the Indian spirits guarding it."

"Was that true?" Cal asked.

Two Bears tilted his chin. "Ever hear of millionaires on the reservation?"

Cal shook his head. Stupid question.

"I'd never heard of such a mine, and neither had my father," Two Bears continued. "But if it did exist, this wasn't it."

"How do you know?"

"My people wouldn't come near these caves. They said the caves were cursed. Only the white man was stupid enough or greedy enough to ignore the bad feeling."

"So what kind of curse are we talking about here? Some kind of pharaoh's tomb thing?" Cal tried to grin, but his lips felt frozen. Beside him, the old man's face looked like stone.

"My father told me that the spirits who inhabited these caves were lost—wanderers who had no bodies of their own and hungered for the bodies of others, even animals if they could get them."

Cal remembered the feeling he'd had back in the airshaft, like fingers groping at him. Bumps of cold flesh formed along his arms.

"You don't believe that, do you? After all, you worked this mine and you're still here."

Two Bears knelt and rubbed his dog's head. His eyes wandered the cold gray walls. "My father called on the spirits to protect me. He said it would keep me safe. The others weren't so lucky."

"Others?" Cal rubbed his arms. The cold down here worked its way through your clothing and into your bones.

"Three of the boys I worked with disappeared in the first six months after the Seven Stars opened. More after that. The white men liked to hire us. We were small, and they could work us long hours. Pretty soon the others ran away. They knew it was death to stay here."

"So is that when they closed it down?"

"Sheehy wanted to," Two Bears said softly. "I think he felt the evil. But Godwin wouldn't hear of it. FDR'd raised the price of gold from twenty to thirty-three dollars an ounce, and Godwin was crazy with greed. Sheehy eventually left to seek his fortune back in California, and Godwin took full control.

"That's when I left too. Fellow told me about another mine here in Colorado. Thought I'd try my luck there."

"What happened to Godwin?" Cal asked, still amazed that he hadn't heard about any of this before.

"After a few years the vein started to play out. World War II came along, and everybody signed up to go fight. By then he'd made near a fortune, so he shut her down. Heard he chained the road and boarded the entrance so nobody else could get in."

"Until the picnic," Cal added.

"Until then."

Two Bears stared at the ground a long time before meeting Cal's eyes. "Something you need to see 'fore we leave. Don't imagine you'd believe me if you didn't see for yourself. I'll show it to you only once. I'm not coming back."

Cal looked into the man's eyes and saw an expression he didn't recognize there. It took him a moment to realize that it was fear.

CHAPTER 33

"WHAT IN THE WORLD?" CAL stared upward, his mouth hanging comically slack-jawed. He was aware that he probably looked like a hayseed fresh off the bus in New York City but he couldn't keep from staring. They'd been following a narrow passage for nearly ten minutes. He'd finally started to adjust to the close confines when the walls and ceiling seemed to disappear completely.

They stood on one side of a cavern so huge that the beams from their lamps couldn't reach the far wall. The ceiling—forty feet or more above their heads—hung with hundreds, even thousands, of stalactites. Below, stalagmites rose from the cave floor like towers of melting ice cream. Seeing the multicolored rock formations was like discovering some kind of underground cathedral.

"It's beautiful," he whispered. He walked to a still pool of water formed in a depression several feet below the floor of the cavern. The reflected beam from his light disappeared into its bottomless depths.

"My people called this the Hall of Lost Souls." The old man's voice quivered. He stood pressed against one wall, and Cal realized that the man was terrified.

"Lost souls?"

"Listen." The old Indian pressed a gnarled finger to his lips.

Cal waited, cocking his head. He was not sure what he was listening for. All he could hear was the sound of his own breathing and the lub-dub of his heart pounding in his ears. Then, faintly, he found he could just make out a soft moaning—the kind of sound he'd made as a kid by blowing across the mouth of a soda bottle.

"It's just the wind," Cal whispered.

Two Bears wet the tip of one finger with his mouth and held it up in the air. His message was clear—the air in the cavern was as still as a crypt.

Cal shrugged. There had to be other air shafts like the one they'd entered through, not to mention natural crevices reaching up to the surface. In an open space like this, the smallest sounds would be amplified.

Two Bears opened his mouth, as if to say something, then shut it again. He rubbed his jaw with one hand, eyes clamped closed, as though trying to make a difficult decision, before suddenly reaching up and turning out the lamp on his hard hat. He motioned for Cal to do the same.

Cal raised one hand to his helmet and then hesitated. What would turning out the lights prove? It was childish, like telling ghost stories around the embers of a dying fire. They were investigating a crime, not playing games.

The Indian waited, motionless. In the yellow glow of Cal's lamp, his weathered skin took on the appearance of the rock around them.

Under the weight of the old man's stare, Cal finally turned out his lamp. He gasped. The entire room glowed a ghostly iridescent green. He'd heard of things like this, some kind of microbes that created their own faint light, like the fish in the depths of the ocean. But the effect was disturbing nonetheless.

In the headlamps, the rock formations had looked fanciful—fairyland creations. But now, illuminated only by this sickly radiance, they seemed specter-like—misshapen bodies trying to heave themselves from the earth, clawed hands reaching down from the ceiling.

The moaning seemed louder in the dark, washing across the room in waves. Rolling down from the ceiling and echoing off the walls, the sound swelled from a low rush to something that sounded almost like a cry—an animal or a child in pain.

He could see why the Indians had called this the Hall of Lost Souls. Listening intently, he could almost convince himself that he actually heard voices. Intermingled with the moaning was a high-pitched wail that could have been a woman sobbing. Under that he could hear a deep rattling that sounded like demented laughter.

Somewhere in the dark, Pepper began to whimper softly. For the first time Cal noticed that the glow in the room seemed to pulse, ebbing and flowing with the sound. His eyes had adjusted to the darkness, and a cold chill ran down his shoulders as he noticed how much the rock formations resembled human faces. How had he failed to see that before?

Something brushed against his cheek and he spun around, sure that the old man was trying to scare him. Two Bears hadn't moved—he was just another stone formation in the pulsing light.

Help me . . .

A child's voice whispered in his ear. Cal turned, eyes searching the darkness for any sign of movement, but no one was there.

Not real. It was the wind—or those bats from the other room.

The moaning was much louder now: *Help . . .* and he could make out a voice. A child crying.

Lost . . . It was all in his head—or was it a woman screaming?

Need . . . Two Bears was playing some kind of joke on him. Messing with his mind. . . Or was it men laughing and howling as if they were mad?

Come . . . Not there.

Bone-chilling weeping.

Scared . . .

It was one voice at first, but many came from all around him now—young, old, desperate, gleeful. All one voice.

. . . Hunger . . . feed . . . want . . .

The air itself seemed to be imbued with light and sound, floating and swirling around his face. And the smell—a dank, meaty stench, like rotting flesh—assaulted his nostrils. He tried to reach for his lamp, but his arms felt weighted to his sides.

Not real. Not real. NOT!

Somewhere in the distance—from another chamber maybe, or another continent—he could barely make out the old Indian's voice. "Why did the chicken cross the road? To prove to the possum that it could be done. How many Coloradoans . . . does . . . it . . . take . . . to . . ."

A circlet of icy fingers dropped around Cal's neck.

All in my . . .

With Herculean effort, Cal managed to lift one arm halfway up but couldn't bring it any further. His entire body was frozen. The fingers around his neck tightened.

"Tell . . . me . . . a . . . joke." The words were glittering stars from another galaxy.

Cal tried to tell Two Bears that he didn't know any jokes but his tongue was lead in his mouth, his vocal cords frozen. His lungs refused to draw in air. He began to gray out.

Just before he lost consciousness, a white beam speared through the mist and a warm hand closed on his shoulder. He sensed the force in the room shrinking back from the light. The fingers released their grip on his throat, leaving a frosty chain of ice around his neck.

He fell forward. With a low grunt Two Bears managed to catch him. "Come," the old man commanded, and Cal stumbled after him.

CHAPTER 34

"WHAT . . . WHAT WAS . . ." CAL LEANED against the cold, hard earth of the shaft wall, trying not to vomit. His throat burned, and his temples were pounding. His thoughts seemed to be filtering through a thick gray haze, as if he'd been breathing carbon monoxide. Two Bears passed him a canteen. Cal swallowed, gagged, and swallowed again, wiping his mouth with the back of one clammy hand.

Cal was a hard-headed pragmatist. Kat used to say that if he died and met St. Peter at the pearly gates, he'd ask the angel for identification. She'd said it jokingly but they had both known it was pretty accurate. If he couldn't see it, touch it, or measure it, it didn't exist. He knew there had to be some rational explanation for what had just happened.

"Must have stumbled into some kind of underground gas pocket. Poisonous air or something." It had taken a while to affect him—that's why he hadn't noticed anything out of the ordinary until they turned out their lights.

Two Bears watched him, seemingly unaffected.

Cal shook his head. "You must have built up some kind of immunity working in this place for all those years. Maybe that's what happened to the kid, Frankie. Poisonous gases." That had to be it.

Except those voices—on the surface they'd sounded like children, calling for help. But he remembered thinking as he'd started to pass out that they weren't really children at all, only something pretending to be children. When those fingers had closed around his throat, he'd seen a momentary image of something foul beyond belief—something so black it was past color, cankerous, and ripe with disease. When he'd tried to inhale, he felt it sliding down his throat.

His stomach heaved, and he turned his head just in time to avoid puking on his boots.

"Easy, easy." Two Bears patted Cal's back.

"Thanks." Cal wiped his lips on the sleeve of his shirt, took another sip of water, and handed the canteen back. He found that he could stand now and that his thoughts weren't quite so muddled.

"Guess I really lost it back there."

Two Bears reached down to stroke Pepper, who was cowering against his leg. "Later. Not here."

Cal nodded. Never in his life had he wanted to stand under open sky so much. He watched Two Bears start down the passageway, spared a final backward glance toward the cavern, and hurried after the old man.

CHAPTER 35

DICKEY JORDAN WAS GOING SLOWLY crazy. He hadn't been sleeping well lately and his head throbbed, but it wasn't a lack of sleep that was muddling his thoughts. He'd seen his father go through this and his father before him. At first it was a simple forgetfulness—misplaced keys, a tool left to get rusty in the field. But as it progressed, he found it harder and harder to remember what he was doing, to control his temper.

The doctors had names for it, pills to take—just as they had in his father's time. But the truth was inevitable and as hard as unplowed earth. He had his good days and his bad but sooner or later he'd end up in the state nut house or slobbering on himself in one of those old folks homes. He'd thought today was going to be one of the good days, but now he wasn't so sure.

He pulled his tractor next to the barn and massaged his sunburned neck with permanently callused fingers. Tilting the bill of his cap against the slanting rays of the sun, he shut off the ignition. As the throaty rumble of the tractor's engine died away, the evening air was filled with chirps of frogs and insects. Out in the pasture the soft whinnying of horses announced the impending night as surely as any clock.

Dickey tossed a coil of barbed wire to the ground. Climbing down after it, he ran a hand over the John Deere's worn tires. He ought to have replaced them a month or more ago but with money the way it was, they'd have to do until harvest.

"Sad state when a fellow can't even 'fford to buy hisself a set a tires," he grumbled as he hoisted the wire and entered the darkened barn. Overhead, a few swallows darted among the rafters, chirping noisily at his appearance, but most had already settled in for the night. He hung the coil on a rusty nail, pulled a pair of pliers from his back pocket and dropped them into his toolbox.

"Mortenson's cows knock down that fence one more time and I'll send him a bill for parts and labor." He grinned, imagining the look on his neighbor's fat, red face when he saw a bill for an afternoon's work at twenty-five dollars an hour. He'd have a fit all right.

The truth was that, like a lot of things lately, Dickey couldn't remember for sure whether it was his neighbor's cows or his own horses that had knocked down the fence. Sylvester, a three-year-old stallion, was feeling his oats lately, and Dickey couldn't blame him for wanting to break out and explore the fillies down the road apiece. Why, back in his own teenage years, he'd been known to travel as far north as Fort Collins or south to Pueblo for a pretty face and a soft voice.

Drawing a handkerchief from his pocket, he trudged to the back of the barn where a red-painted spigot rose from the hay-strewn ground like an aged sentry. Yvette'd have his head if he came into the house 'thout rinsing off first. She said he left a pound-and-a-half of country dirt in the bathroom sink for her to clean up every time he washed there.

Holding the limp blue cloth under the bib, he turned the handle and waited for the rush of cold water the family well had been delivering for nearly a hundred years. But instead of a fresh stream, the spigot belched twice and groaned like an out-of-tune tuba before finally producing a dribble of rust-colored goo.

For a moment, Dickey could only stand there, faded eyes shocked with disbelief at what he was seeing. He wet his fingers with the muddy sludge. Holding it up to his nose, he inhaled the musky aroma of damp clay, and a soft moan escaped his lips.

As understanding came, all the color drained from his face except for two balls of crimson fire that glowed in his pallid cheeks. His hands balled into fists and dropped slowly to his sides, brown liquid oozing from between his knuckles.

"Thieves." The word, hissed through clenched teeth, was barely audible, but the expression on the farmer's drawn-back lips was clear. It was the expression a junkyard cur wears just before he lunges for the throat of a trespasser.

"Filthy thieves stole my water." Dickey's arms, lined with cords of wiry muscle, began to shake with helpless fury, and his throat produced a high-pitched wheezing as his chest heaved.

"I told 'em," he gasped. "Told 'em they was drawing all the water from my well. And now they've gone and ruin't it. Ruin't the well my grandfather dug."

His eyes, watery and bulging, drifted to the heavy pipe wrench hanging on the wall. His hands opened and closed. In his mind he could see himself taking that wrench to Calbert Neffinger's skull—could picture the pompous city councilman's head . . .

"Take that, Calbert," Dickey cawed, swinging his arm in the imaginary blow. "Take that, you thieving jackal."

For a moment the snarl on his lips turned to a victorious smile. It would be sweet, all right, to see that dirty bureaucrat get his comeuppance. Every member of the council deserved to suffer for taking what was not rightfully theirs. If there was any justice . . .

Slowly the image of Calbert Neffinger's terrified face faded away, and with it, Dickey's smile.

There wasn't going to be no justice. It was one dirt-poor farmer against the city. Used to be a fellow had a fighting chance of getting his wrongs put right. Nowadays with the U.N. and liberal judges running everything, the gov'ment didn't give a hoot what happened to the people who put food on the country's table. They wrapped you up so tight with red tape you didn't know whether you was coming or going.

Dickey wiped the back of his hand across his eyes and reached to shut off the faucet. He didn't know how he was going to scratch up enough money to drill his well another hundred feet. "Dagnabbed Neffinger," he muttered.

"Why don't you do something about it?"

Dickey jerked at the unexpected voice that came from behind him. He spun around, squinting into the darkness in the corner of the barn.

"Who's there?" he called out, his voice cracking. "Who said that?" He took a step forward and then stopped as something moved in the darkness. A shrill giggle floated on the chaff-filled air.

"Come out from there," Dickey said, his eyes narrowing. The voice had sounded like a child's, but the grandkids were gone for the day. He'd seen Margie driving them home a couple of hours back. And the laughter—that hadn't sounded like a child at all. It scarcely sounded human.

Something moved back by the harrow, its dark shape just visible as it slipped past a crack in the barn wall.

"That one of the Mortenson kids?" he asked uncertainly. "You shouldn't be playing back there. You'll cut yourself on the equipment."

The child's voice spoke again. "And the Lord said unto Moses, 'Behold, I will stand before thee there upon the rock in Horeb; and thou shalt smite the rock, and there shall come water out of it, that the people may drink.'" It sounded like a verse from the Old Testament.

Something squealed behind Dickey. He turned around, at first unable to find the source of the noise. It came again—the sound of metal on metal—and he caught a flash of movement. He rubbed his eyes, unable to believe what he was seeing. The spigot handle was turning—by itself. He watched the handle spin a full 360 degrees. Instead of piddling brown sludge, a full stream of clear water jetted from the bib.

"What in blue blazes . . . ?" Dickey walked to the pipe, his eyes locked on the water gushing out as clear and fast as he'd ever seen it. He reached out his hand, but before his fingers could touch the stream, the spigot spun shut so violently the handle snapped off and fell to the dirt floor, where it hissed in the puddled water.

"They stole your water."

Dickey's head swiveled around to look back into the darkness. He thought he could just make out a pair of eyes watching him. His mouth opened, closed, and opened again.

"Thou shalt not steal." Despite Dickey's unease, the voice—he had decided that it sounded like a young boy—had an almost hypnotic effect on him. He nodded dumbly.

"God gave you that water." The figure stepped closer to the light, and Dickey thought he had been right. It looked like the outline of a child. The golden light of the setting sun seemed to entwine itself above the child's head.

"Are . . . are you an angel?" Dickey asked. His voice felt thick, his throat raw.

But if the angel heard him, it didn't respond, instead pointing out toward Dickey's field. "The next thing you know, they'll be taking your livestock, and then your land." The angel spoke calmly and with confidence. It was the voice of reason, putting words to exactly what Dickey had been thinking. "Why, they're already driving you crazy, just like they did your father."

"No!" Dickey's hands clenched back into fists, his head pounding. "I won't let them!"

"How are you going to stop them?" The figure stepped closer, and Dickey could see that it was holding something in its arms—a small rectangular shape that looked familiar.

"I . . . I don't . . ." Dickey struggled to think. His mind felt mired in hot glue. His eyes drifted toward the pipe wrench. Again the giggle that sounded more animal than human floated toward him.

"That old wrench isn't going to help you, Dickey. If you want to stop the city from pumping away all your water, you'll have to fight fire with fire."

Dickey looked to the child. He had drifted back into the darkness, and now the sunlight no longer encircled him. In fact it seemed to disappear as it reached him, as if the strength had been sucked out of it. The object he had been carrying lay on the floor. Dickey recognized it. It was a metal box, closed with a heavy padlock. He knew that inside were half a dozen sticks of the dynamite that he used to blow up stumps and loosen large rocks in his field.

"They can't very well steal away your water without any pumps, now can they?" the voice asked. Dickey looked at the box, and then at the eyes shining out from the darkness. A wave of cold air blew across his body, and for a moment his eyes lost the dull glaze they'd taken on.

He wasn't really thinking about blowing up the city pumps, was he? They sent you to prison for that kind of thing. "They'd know it was me," he moaned. "I've talked to the chief of police."

"So you're just going to give up? Let them take everything you've worked so hard for?" The words made sense. He'd tried everything else to protect his water, and no one was willing to help him. Did he really have any other choice?

"Cal Hunt's the one who should have been protecting your rights." The angel's voice—it *was* an angel wasn't it?—soothed Dickey's frayed nerves. "If he'd been doing his job you wouldn't be in this fix, would you?"

Dickey's head wobbled slowly to the left and right, his face going slack. Cold sweat clung to his forehead and arms, but he didn't notice.

"He's been the one behind this all along. All the time you've been asking him for help he's been laughing at you behind your back. Do you really think someone like Calbert Neffinger would dare take your water without the chief of police giving him the thumbs-up?"

Dickey shook his head. From the back porch of the house, Margie was calling his name, but Dickey had ears only for the voice in the darkness.

"Don't you worry about Chief Hunt," the voice said. "We can take care of him."

The voice from the darkness told him what to do, and Dickey listened.

CHAPTER 36

"Gonna eat those beans?" Two Bears gestured toward Cal's plate with a salsa-soaked tortilla chip.

"No." Cal handed across his plate and watched as Two Bears scooped the refried beans and Mexican rice from it. He hadn't touched the beans and had barely tasted his enchilada. His appetite seemed to have left him, although he had gone through three glasses of dark beer—finally switching to Seven-Up when he felt the alcohol starting to go to his head. Two Bears had stuck to water.

They were sitting in the back of Dos Hermanas, a local restaurant nearly deserted at this time on a Wednesday night. Juanita and Elena Valiente had looked the other way as Cal and Two Bears sneaked Pepper under the table, even bringing over a plate of scraps the dog had instantly gobbled up as they wiped down the tables for the evening.

The trip out of the mine had been short and singularly uneventful. Apparently Two Bears knew a shortcut, because they hadn't passed back through the "Bat Cave," as Cal had dubbed it, on their way out.

The old Indian had been silent on the way into town, seemingly lost in his own thoughts. That was fine with Cal. The things he'd seen and heard seemed a little less real with every mile they put between them and the mine, and he wasn't sure he wanted to examine the events too closely.

Two Bears scooped a pile of refried beans onto a chip, added a forkful of Mexican rice, and washed it down with a swallow of ice water.

"Something you want to ask me?" he said, wiping his mouth with a paper napkin.

Cal thought for a minute. "What do *you* think happened to Frankie? Could he have run into that pocket of poisonous gas we found?"

"Lots of ways to die in a mine. Maybe he drowned."

"Drowned?"

"Underground springs in those caves run hundreds of feet deep. Or it could have been a cave-in. Some of those timbers were pretty rotted, even back then."

"Is that what you think happened to the boys you worked with? Cave-ins?" Cal took a long, slow drink of his soda, wishing for another beer.

Two Bears shook his head. "I hoped they'd run away—returned to the reservation maybe. But . . . I don't think they ever left the mine."

"Frankie's mother seems to think the other children may have done something to him. Did the children . . . say anything to you? Anything about what might have happened in there?"

Two Bears shrugged. "They didn't say anything to me. But . . ."

"But what?"

"Bad things happen in there. People act crazy."

"Crazy how?" Cal remembered his only-too-recent brush with craziness at the Seven Stars.

"Saw two men kill each other over a dipper of water once. One fellow took a pick to the other un's chest. And the second managed to drive a chisel through the first un's neck."

"They both died?" Cal said, wondering how many deaths had happened in the Seven Stars.

"Um-hum." Two Bears toyed with the last of his beans for a moment before laying down his fork and sliding his plate away. His dark eyes studied the Formica tabletop. "But that's not the question you've paid me to answer."

"I didn't bring you here to answer anything," Cal said. "I hired you to show me the mine."

"You didn't need an eighty-year-old man for that. You could've found the entrance on your own." Two Bears rested his bronzed arms on the table, hands clasped together.

"Eventually, I guess."

"What are you afraid of?" Two Bears asked.

"I don't know what you're talking about." Cal's eyes broke away from the old man's gaze as he thought about the feelings he'd had going down into the mine. Was it fear? Yes, he had to admit it was.

"Is it your wife?"

The question seemed to come from out of the blue, catching Cal unaware like a swift uppercut to the jaw. He brought a fist down hard on the table, rattling the silverware and shocking Pepper into a surprised *Arf*. "What does this have to do with my wife? I've got two dead bodies and a third body that's on the verge. The only thing I'm afraid of is another innocent victim being murdered before I can find the killer. If you can help me, fine. If not, quit playing games."

Two Bears seemed unperturbed. He leaned back in his chair, belching softly into his hand. "Fellow I knew got hold of some especially powerful whiskey. Not much more than glorified wood alcohol. Decided he was invincible. Stood out in the middle of the highway, kind of like your asparagus friend. Only when an eighteen-wheeler came barreling down the road, he didn't jump. Wanna guess which one of them came out on top?"

"What does that have to do with—"

The old Indian held up one hand, palm facing Cal. The wrinkles in his cheeks deepened. His eyes bored into Cal's. "Those caverns are a dark place. Not just physically but spiritually—full of hate and evil. And something else—something not of this world."

Cal set his glass on the table, his hand trembling. "You don't really believe in all that nonsense, do you? Ghosts or vengeful spirits?" he said, unable to believe he was even asking the question.

"Yes, I do."

"Fine. Believe what you want." Cal placed both hands flat on the table. "It's probably some cultural thing anyway. Indian mysticism or whatever."

Cal expected Two Bears to be insulted—maybe even hoped for it as a way to end this conversation. He was disappointed. The old man only grinned a knowing smile. "Believe the Christian Bible makes reference to them as well."

"What?" Cal had gone to a few years of Sunday School as a kid. He remembered hearing stories about things like Moses parting the sea and Christ turning water to wine—both had seemed equally unbelievable as far as he was concerned, even back then. But the only spirit he remembered was the Holy Spirit.

"Read your New Testament." Two Bears seemed amused. "Christ himself commanded a whole pack of evil spirits to depart some poor chump who lived down in the tombs. Whole pack of 'em entered into a bunch of pigs. Jumped right off a cliff. Guess they didn't like being pigs."

"Tell you what," Cal said, twisting his wedding band so hard his finger had started to bleed, "you happen to run into Christ wandering around the streets of Twin Forks, you ask Him to take care of this whole business.

But in the meantime, us mortals are just gonna have to stick to the evidence. And I'm sorry, but the evidence tells me I'm looking for a cold-blooded serial killer."

Two Bears shifted forward in his seat, eyes set, face hard. "You seem like a good man," he said. "So I'm going to tell you. You're standing in the middle of the road and a big old logging truck is coming straight for you. Even a coyote knows enough to get out of the way when the truck comes. But you're just going to stand in the middle of the road with your eyes screwed closed."

Cal started to protest, but Two Bears waved a weathered hand. He stood, pulling his wallet from the back pocket of his jeans. "You can see the headlights. You can feel the eyes of the beast. But for some reason you're too scared to admit it.

"Don't know why you're afraid to admit what you've seen with your own eyes. I think it might be your wife. You know she's dead, but I think you might be afraid to find out she's going on with her life . . . Then you'd have to go on with yours too. But if you don't move soon, you're going to get flattened."

Two Bears pulled a handful of bills from his wallet. The conversation was over.

"It's on the city," Cal said, standing. He felt a little woozy, as if he'd had more than the three beers, after all.

"'Preciate that." Two Bears tucked the wallet back into his pants. "I believe I'll be going now."

"You could stay at the house," Cal offered. "Get a fresh start in the morning."

"No." Two Bears shook his head, his face looking tired and gray. "I don't think I want to stay in this town any longer than I have to. And I won't be coming back."

Cal shook the old man's hand and watched as Two Bears and Pepper walked out the door and got into the rusty white pickup. The truck's rear lights blazed first red and then white as it backed out into the street. He watched the truck disappear into the night with something that felt a little like envy.

CHAPTER 37

CAL SAT PARKED IN HIS driveway, staring blankly out the windshield of his patrol car. He looked up at the dark, empty house, trying to will himself to get out of the car and go in. Normally by this time of year the garden areas along the front walk and under the windows were blazing with color.

Kat had always seen to the choosing and planting of the year's flowers, enlisting Cal's help only to haul the nursery flats and heavy bags of fertilizer from the car. As soon as she felt reasonably sure that the last of the late winter snowstorms had passed, she went into action.

But this year the spring planting season had somehow managed to come and go without his notice. The flowerbeds, lit by the overhead fluorescence of a streetlight, were choked with hawkweed and thick tangles of grass. With its long bay windows dark and streaky, the house had the abandoned look of a bank repossession. It seemed to loom over him like a great cold vault, and he knew that to go inside in his current state of mind was only inviting trouble.

He thought about the old Indian's words. *I think you might be afraid to find out she's going on with her life . . . Then you'd have to go on with yours too.* And the words of the little Rucker boy. *My mom says he's in heaven with the angels.*

How *could* you go on when you know how the story ends? Zip, zilch, nada. Eventually everyone ends up feeding the flowers. What was the point of that?

He dropped the car into reverse and pulled out of the driveway, intending to go back to the station. Instead, he took a right at the light and drove up the gradual hill that passed Twin Forks Junior High. Bright yellow sodium lamps—their glow attracting hundreds of fluttering moths—illuminated the group of old men that came out every night to circle the track. In the past, their turtle-like shuffling had been a source of amusement to him, but tonight he found himself envying their sense of purpose.

He didn't know that he'd had a destination in mind all along until he pulled up to the tall wrought-iron gate of the cemetery. He idled in front of the entrance, unsure why he was there. He didn't go to cemeteries unless he absolutely had to. They were all overpriced monuments to man's mortality, which he was reminded of often enough just doing his job. Kat wasn't here any more than she was back at the house.

And yet he found himself driving through the gate, passing row after row of weather-worn headstones until he was parked next to Kat's. It stood out from the others around it, its surface still shiny and new, its lettering readable even in the dim moonlight. There was a flowerpot next to the grave. The flowers looked like African violets, Kat's favorite. Someone had remembered her garden, after all.

Almost without realizing what he was doing, he slipped from the car and walked across the grass, kneeling on the sod that now hid the spot where his wife's body had been lowered into the ground. The recent rain had left the soil in the pot damp, and the flowers were doing fine. He imagined that the beginning of summer would dry them out quickly though and someone would haul away their shriveled husks.

If Kat were still alive, she would take them home and water them. Probably find a nice sunny spot to transplant them. She took special care with plants. But Kat wasn't here anymore, and suddenly the thought of her absence made him angrier than he could ever remember being in his life.

Getting to his feet, he turned and started toward the car, then spun back, his hands balled in rage.

"Why did you have to die? We had plans. We were going to go to Scotland; you always wanted to feel peat squish between your toes. We were going to get a little place up on the coast and listen to the waves crash at night. We were going to make love in the Grand Canyon under the stars, remember? That was less than a day's drive, and we never even got *there*. We promised each other that we'd never leave. *You* promised. And now you're gone."

The roar of his words echoed across the manicured lawn and carefully placed trees. They would carry to anyone else who might be in the cemetery. But he was beyond caring what anyone else might think. His entire body shook as he dropped to the ground and pressed his forehead against the cool stone of the marker, the pain washing over him like sheets of ice-cold water.

"It's just a little bump. Look, it's almost stopped bleeding," she'd said when he tried to make her go see a doctor. She wouldn't even take the ice pack he offered, more embarrassed than she was hurt by her slip from the ladder. Two hours later she'd collapsed to the ground, and by the next morning she was dead. Everything they'd built together, everything they'd planned, torn apart by a tiny clot of blood. How was he supposed to go on for the next forty years alone?

Pounding the grass until his fingers were stained green, he wept tears that he thought had dried up months earlier, his broad shoulders jerking convulsively with each new gust. He'd never been mad at Kat in his life. They'd had arguments, of course, just as he'd told Tamara Rucker. But they'd always been about little things—gotten over quickly. For the life of him he couldn't remember ever being really mad at his wife, and now that she was dead he was so angry he wanted to shake her.

He knelt there on the grass sobbing until his rage faded, leaving him drained and feeling more alone than he'd ever been in his life. He traced her name on the tombstone with a thick, callused finger.

He just wanted to touch her, to talk to her. He'd give everything he had to hear the soft sound of her laughter again. "I miss you so bad, Babe." The tears were drying up now, but his face felt hot and stretched, like a poorly fitted mask. He started to wipe at his cheeks before noticing the grass stains on his fist. Kat would have seen the joke in that right away.

You finally have a green thumb, Cal. He could hear her voice as if she was right beside him, could hear that wonderful laughter rolling off down the hillside.

"If you could just tell me," he whispered. "If I knew you were some kind of spirit or ghost or just part of the cosmos—if I knew you were happy—I could find a way to go on." Although his voice was now scarcely audible, he glanced around self-consciously for the first time. "Do . . . do they . . . have gardens wherever you are?"

He listened for a moment, halfway expecting to hear Kat's voice coming up from the ground or floating on the still night air. The only sound was the engine of a car driving by on the street next to the cemetery.

He stood and brushed the blades of freshly cut grass from his uniform. He'd have to take it to the cleaner to get the stains out of the knees. Bending back down, he picked up the flowers. Maybe it wasn't too late to replace the weeds, after all. He carried the pot back to the car and placed it carefully on the floor next to his briefcase so it wouldn't slide around.

He never noticed the figure that slipped silently back into the trees— the boy with the strangely cut hair and deep-set eyes. Cal started up the car and turned on the headlights, their beams stabbing twin circles through the darkness. But by then the boy had disappeared from view.

CHAPTER 38

CAL RESTED UNEASILY. HE WATCHED the moonlight shifting through the curtains as they danced on currents of air gusting through his bedroom windows. The Mexican food lay heavy in his stomach while thoughts lay heavy in his mind.

The wind had picked up, blowing a rain gutter he'd been meaning to tighten down back and forth against the side of the house in a steady rhythm. He thought about leaving his bed to close the window but decided it wasn't worth the effort.

Eventually he drifted off to sleep on memories of children's cries.

Sometime later that night, Cal woke with a start. He sat up and looked around, rubbing the sleep from his eyes and wondering what had awakened him. The bedroom door was closed. The wind must have banged it shut. He started to pull back the blankets, meaning to get up and shut the window, but stopped, frozen in place.

Someone was in the room.

He could just make out a figure silhouetted against the bedroom curtains. It was standing motionless next to the window, watching him. The figure stepped away from the window. Cal's heart pounded. Slowly he sat up and began to reach for the top drawer of the nightstand where he kept his gun.

The curtains blew inward, and Cal's hand stopped moving. He knew the face reflected in the moonlight. It was the boy he'd seen sitting on the sidewalk across from the Rucker home—the boy who looked so much like Frankie Zoeller.

Only this couldn't be real. It had to be a dream, because the moonlight wasn't just illuminating the boy's face, it was shining right through it. The boy made no movement but somehow drifted closer. Cal pulled away, the back of his skull cracking against the headboard.

He knew he had to be sleeping. In the morning he would hardly remember this at all. But right now it felt unlike any dream he'd ever had. The pain in the back of his head, the chill of the wind blowing across his bare chest, the tape where the little boy's glasses had been mended all seemed far too real.

The boy floated to the foot of the bed, and terror raced through Cal's veins. He felt frozen by his own inability to believe what he was seeing—incapable of moving a muscle or saying anything.

Cal stared at the figure standing before him. He made out the dark stains of sweat and dirt on the boy's white dress shirt, his dark canvas high-tops with the laces untied and dragging as little boys' shoelaces always seemed to do. Everything was so real—even the pale strip of skin above the boy's ears showing where his hair had been cut. The details were so vivid, yet he could see right through them to his open closet door.

Ray . . . The sound blew across Cal's face as though carried on an icy breeze. Suddenly the temperature in the room seemed to drop twenty degrees. Cal jerked away and then leaned forward.

Ah . . .

Had the boy been trying to speak? Trying to tell him something?

Ray . . . *Ahd* . . .

He *was* trying to say something. Cal could see his lips moving, his face screwed up with effort. Icy bumps of flesh broke out all across Cal's body.

He leaned toward the boy. It was like putting his face into a freezer. The moisture in his nostrils cracked, and his eyelids stuck to his eyes.

"What do you want?" he asked, his voice trembling. "Why are you here?" He didn't care if this was a dream or not. He had to know—had to understand what this was all about.

Across from him the small figure closed his eyes tightly as if trying to concentrate. His brow furrowed, and his fists clenched. All at once, every ounce of energy in the room seemed to be sucked toward the center of the boy's being. Cal felt the strength sap from his limbs. And then, as if they had physical force, the words battered him backwards.

Grays Gahd!

The figure instantly winked from existence.

Grays Gahd, what did that mean? *Gray's God?* Who or what was Gray's God? But had he said *Grays* or was he trying perhaps to say something else? *Grace* maybe?

Grace of God, Cal thought; that's what the boy had been trying to say. *Grace of God.*

CHAPTER 39

BEN MEYERS LOOKED LIKE A man who had taken the full force of a hand grenade. It was almost impossible to make out the man behind the bandages and tubes. His head was locked in place by a series of clamps that forced him to look straight up at the ceiling. The only hints that the lump beneath the blankets was a living, breathing human being were the screens of the equipment monitoring his vital signs and his dark green eyes.

Cal stepped to the edge of the bed, trying to hold at bay the overwhelming sense of hopelessness brought on by the sights and smells around him. He touched the back of Ben's hand. It was cold, almost like touching a corpse. He looked at LuAnn, who was sitting beside her husband's bed and watching him with great care.

"Can he hear me?"

She nodded. "He can hear you, and most of the time he can respond. But he gets tired quickly."

He leaned over the bed. "Ben, I'm Cal Hunt. I'm the chief of the Twin Forks Police Department. Do you understand?"

The green eyes blinked, and from the swollen lips came a soft, "Yes."

"Good." Cal studied the mass of casts and bandages. It was amazing the man was even alive. He knew his questions would have to be brief and to the point.

"Did you see who pushed you from the cliff?"

Ben's eyes closed. "Fell," he whispered.

Thinking Ben had misunderstood, Cal tried again. "I know that you fell, Ben, and this must be difficult for you. But try to remember. Was there someone there? Was it a man or a woman? Think hard."

Ben's eyes cut toward LuAnn, who looked away, and then back to Cal. "No . . . one . . . there." Silence except for the slow inhale and exhale of breath. "Alone . . . accident."

Cal shook his head. "Are you sure you didn't see or hear anything?"

A blink, then another. Cal could read pain in Ben's eyes. No surprise there—it took a heroic act of courage just to stay awake long enough to speak. The need for painkillers had to be overwhelming. But there was something else in those eyes. Fear? What was this man scared of?

"No," Ben whispered and shut his eyes.

"I'm sorry," LuAnn said, her face drawn and pale.

"It's all right." Cal stepped away from the bed, trying to hide his disappointment. It would have been too much to hope for a solid ID. But to strike out completely again was nearly unbearable. "Maybe he'll remember something later."

LuAnn leaned over her husband, as though checking to make sure he was asleep, before tilting her head toward the door. "Outside," she mouthed.

Cal followed her through the door.

Once in the hallway, she glanced into her husband's room and toward the nurses' station. Other than a candy striper collecting food trays, they were alone. Wrapping both arms across her chest, cupping her elbows, she leaned toward Cal and said, "I think he's lying."

Cal stiffened. "What makes you say that?"

She checked her husband again. "I went down to the cafeteria. Just for a minute. To get a soda. When I came back, there was a woman in his room."

"Who?" Cal asked, but he thought he already knew, and the idea made the back of his neck burn.

"That supposed *friend* of his. That Obrey woman."

Dropping his voice, he stepped between LuAnn and the door to her husband's room. "What was she doing?"

LuAnn's eyes glared. "As soon as she saw me, she tried to play all nice. She'd brought a big bouquet of flowers and a card."

"But?" Cal asked.

"She didn't know I'd been watching her from outside the door. I saw her threatening him. She wasn't shouting, but she might as well have been. It was in her voice."

"What did she say?"

"She told him that if he said anything, he'd be sorry."

CHAPTER 40

THE GIRL IN THE PINK slacks and smock leaned over the cart of used food trays, pretending to count them. This whole thing was so cool, like one of those *CSI Miami* episodes. The cop glanced in her direction once, and she quickly looked down at the cart, feeling her heart go into overdrive. But when she looked up, he was just leaving and Mrs. Myers had gone back into her husband's room.

She pushed the cart to one side of the hall and stopped by the nurses' station. "I'm gonna go catch a quick smoke break." The duty nurse on the phone nodded.

Hurrying through the waiting room, she looked quickly around to make sure no one was watching her before slipping into a small alcove, where a bank of three pay phones were located across from the doors to the men's and women's restrooms.

She was taking a big risk, and she didn't want to lose her job or end up in jail. But the benefits were worth it. She fingered the gold locket hanging around her neck. The guy at the pawn shop had offered her a hundred bucks for it, and he was a crook. That meant it had to be worth at least four.

And there was more where this one came from.

She pulled the slip of paper from her pocket, dropped a couple of coins into the phone, and dialed the number.

"Mrs. Obrey, I've got some more information for you."

She waited as the woman on the line went somewhere private.

"Yeah, I'm all alone. No one can hear me. I'm using one of the pay phones like you said."

She glanced around, lowering her voice. "You told me to call you if I heard anything. Well I did. That cop you were asking about came by.

He was in Mr. Meyers's room for a while, and then he came out really upset."

She listened for a minute and shook her head. "No, I don't think he learned anything from Mr. Meyers. But the wife told him you came by."

She nodded. "Okay, I'll call you if I hear anything else." She clasped the pendant. It felt heavy and solid in her hand. "That cop said this was about some kind of murder investigation. That makes me nervous. I think I should get something more for helping you."

She smiled at what she heard and hung up the phone. Earrings might go nicely too. People with secrets could be very generous.

* * *

The men's room door had been cracked open half an inch. Now it swung open all the way as Cal stepped out. He took out his notebook and jotted down the number of the pay phone the candy striper had called out on. Using the next phone over, he dialed the main department number and asked for Greg.

"I'm down at the hospital. I've got the number for a pay phone here, and I want you to pull the LUDS on it as soon as possible." He read off the number with a grim smile. "Call me back as soon as you get the list of outgoing numbers. I think we might have a suspect."

CHAPTER 41

"Detective Lyon." The voice on the other end of the line sounded slightly bored. Cal could commiserate. For most cops, pulling desk duty was the worst part of the job.

"Hello, Detective, this is Chief Hunt of the Twin Forks PD." Cal rolled his chair back and put his feet up on the desk. He couldn't help smiling a little at what he was about to do. The Obreys might have political clout, but cops had been finding ways around politics since dinosaurs roamed the earth.

"What can I do for you, Chief?" Detective Lyon asked, his voice perking up a little.

"I wonder if you could do me a favor?" Cal said. "I'd really rather that this didn't go all the way to the top, though, if you know what I mean."

Cal gave the detective a brief description of his case, sticking only to the relevant points—two murders and one possible attempted murder. He explained that he would appreciate it if the Denver PD could keep an eye on Theresa Obrey.

At the mention of the Obrey name, Detective Lyon let out a long, slow whistle. "I can understand why you'd want to keep this low profile," he said. "You looking at her as a possible for your perp, or another victim?"

"I'm not quite sure at this point," Cal admitted.

"I'll see what I can do for you," the detective said. It was common practice for departments to cooperate, but Cal knew that his problems would have to take a backseat to whatever else the detective was working on.

There was a knock at the door, and Cal looked up to see Dee Dee Cornwall peeking in. He waved her to a chair.

"I appreciate that," he said, dropping his feet back to the floor. "And I'll let you know if the case starts to spill over into your jurisdiction."

"Do that," Detective Lyons said and hung up the phone.

As he hung up the phone, Cal noticed how haggard the mayor looked. Stress lines creased her forehead, and dark bags underscored her eyes. He didn't imagine that he looked much better himself. He wondered if she'd been getting any more sleep than he had.

"I didn't happen to hear you mention the Obrey name, did I?" Dee Dee asked.

"You were eavesdropping."

"Caught me," she said, unapologetically. "You think you could pick on somebody a little less high profile for awhile? I got a call from the governor himself yesterday."

"I don't know what's wrong with these people." Cal frowned. "I'm trying to protect them, and they act like suspects. I've never met a group that was so hard to get through to."

"Are you saying she's not a suspect?"

Cal rubbed a hand across his chin. "I wouldn't go *that* far."

"Um-hum." Dee Dee frowned. "And speaking of people who are hard to get through to, I couldn't reach you yesterday."

"I was checking out some leads," he said, trying to skirt the subject. But she wasn't going to let him off the hook on this one.

"Someone said that they saw you and another man driving up into the canyon." He wondered how much she knew, but he didn't have to wonder long. Her next words made it clear that she knew everything.

"You wouldn't have been heading to the old mine?"

"Seems like everyone but me knows about it," he sighed, leaning back in his chair and interlacing his fingers behind his head. "Who's your snitch?"

She grinned, her eyes regaining some of their old glow. "Didn't anybody ever teach you not to reveal the identity of a good source?" She pulled her chair up to the edge of the desk, her smile fading as quickly as it had come.

"You really think this has something to do with the Seven Stars?" she asked.

He considered everything he'd seen—or thought he'd seen—over the last few days and nodded. "It's looking that way."

Dee Dee shook her head, lines creasing her brow. "You're stirring up a lot of old tensions with this, Cal."

"Tensions? What kind of tensions?" He leaned forward.

"The Seven Stars carries a lot of history with it," she said. "I was in sixth grade and home with the flu the day it happened. My mother came into my room that night and told me. I remember how she cried and held me for what seemed like forever. She just kept repeating, 'It could have been any one of you kids. It could have been any one of you.'" The mayor wiped at the corner of her eye with one finger and stared out the window.

"There was a lot of acrimony flying around. And the longer the search went on, the worse it got. People are like that. They always want someone to lay the blame on. Of course Esther Zoeller blamed the other children, and more than a few people agreed with her. The Rucker kids were a bunch of bullies, and Amanda was trouble even then. But I think most people wanted to lay it at the feet of Paul Andreason. They thought he wasn't paying close enough attention to the kids that day."

Cal shook his head. "It's wild country up there. It would be impossible for one man to keep an eye on that many children the whole time."

"That was the other thing," Dee Dee said. "When Paul's heart gave out a few days after the children were found—all except for Frankie, of course—his wife lashed out at Clara's girl."

"Clara?"

"Clara Bell, at the library. Margaret blamed it all on Clara's daughter, Sheila, who was working as a teacher's assistant. She was supposed to be helping watch the children. But Paul claimed she'd spent the whole day missing her boyfriend."

Cal opened his folder and flipped through the newspaper articles. "I didn't see any mention of a teacher's assistant."

"No, you wouldn't have. Clara's husband was the newspaper editor back then." Dee Dee smiled a hard, tight grin. "I told you it was a small town. Everybody's fingers end up sticking into everybody else's pies."

"But I was down at the library. Why wouldn't Clara have mentioned it?"

"You'd have to ask her," Dee said briskly, and then changed the subject. "So how do these murders tie into something that happened so long ago?"

Cal rubbed his hand up one cheek. He felt like he was swimming in an unfamiliar and treacherous ocean. Just because he couldn't see the undercurrents, that didn't make them any less real. He had a strong suspicion that there were sharks in this water and blood. Lots of blood.

"That's just it," he said. "I think they're related. I just don't know how."

"Why didn't you tell me all this last time we talked?" she asked.

He shook his head. "It sounded so farfetched. I didn't think you'd believe it. I didn't believe it myself."

Dee Dee studied him with intelligent brown eyes. He could see in those eyes a little of the drive that had made her Twin Forks mayor. "You know," she said, "when you first applied for the chief position, there were a lot of people who questioned your ability to do the job. Not that you weren't qualified, but you were from the city. Everyone wondered if you could adapt to a small town."

"A small *Christian* town," Cal said, considering where she might be going with this.

"That too. Well, you proved them wrong."

Cal smiled, a little surprised. He thought she'd been leading up to firing him.

But she wasn't finished. As she stood, her eyes hardened. "You've done a good job here, and Twin Forks is the better for it. But you still don't really understand the small-town mentality, Cal. You could live here another twenty years and you'd still be an outsider—a move-in."

Yes, he knew that phrase.

"Keep me in the loop," she said. "I'll help you where I can."

"I will."

She started to the door but turned back. "How long are these attacks going to go on, do you think?"

"No more than a few days," he answered.

"So sure?"

It was his turn for the hard, flat smile. "Any longer than that and there won't be anyone left to kill."

CHAPTER 42

CAL LOOKED FOR A PLACE to set down the glass of sparkling water the butler had given him. There were several tables—all solid wood—but no coasters. He'd just have to hold it until the butler returned. He was standing in a waiting room of sorts just off the front entrance of the Godwin home.

Spencer had refused a second meeting at first, citing a packed schedule. But his calendar had opened quickly enough when Cal suggested how it might look to the citizens of Twin Forks if they were to find out that one of their own was refusing to cooperate in a murder investigation. Especially one in which his own sister was a potential victim.

Cal approached one of the dark-paneled walls, studying the portraits hanging several feet above his head. It appeared to be a rogues' gallery—although he was quite sure they didn't refer to themselves quite that way—of the Godwin men, starting with Spencer and moving progressively back in time to what had to be his great-great-grandfather.

The first two paintings, those of Spencer and his father, Henry, appeared to have been done by different artists, while the earlier works were all done by the same hand. Presumably Caleb Godwin had commissioned them when he had come into his fortune. Hanging directly beneath each man's image was a portrait of his wife.

Henry Godwin was a spare-looking man; long, gray sideburns framed a narrow, pensive face. Dark eyes stared querulously forward as though he were wondering if he had overpaid the artist doing the painting. He had Caleb Godwin's narrow patrician nose and weak chin, but both men seemed capable of giving orders and being obeyed.

Spencer, on the other hand, had inherited his looks from his mother, Grace. They both had the same upturned noses, the same high cheekbones. They were the same features he shared with his sister. Cal thought that Olivia looked very much like her mother at her age. The artist had captured the timeless depth of her mother's eyes, intelligent but somehow sad too.

Cal had suggested meeting at the mansion again in the hope that he might get another chance to question Olivia—and her father, if possible. So far, though, neither of them had appeared.

"Chief." Spencer entered the room at a brisk, business-like pace.

Cal shifted his glass from his right hand to his left, unobtrusively pressing the record button on the digital recorder in his shirt pocket before accepting Spencer's handshake. He nodded toward the portraits.

"Just noticing how much you and your sister look like your mother."

"Do you think so?" Spencer shot a fleeting glance at the painting. "Most people tell me I look like my father." He turned for another quick, almost painful glance before looking away. "Neither of us really remembers our mother very well. She left when we were young."

Left. That was an interesting way to put it. But then, that's probably how it had seemed to the two of them at the time. "Wasn't that shortly after Olivia disappeared into your grandfather's mine?"

Spencer blinked. "It was actually several months prior to that."

Cal held out his glass. "Is there somewhere I can put this?"

"Richard." At Spencer's call, the butler appeared as if by magic and took Cal's glass.

"Why don't we take a walk? It's a nice day out, and I could use some fresh air."

Cal nodded and followed Spencer into the hallway and out the front door. A large driveway paved with river rock led down a gentle slope. Cal's boxy cruiser looked out of place among the bevy of sleek foreign automobiles. They followed a narrow flagstone path around the side of the house and into an English garden.

"So tell me," Spencer said, taking a seat on a curved stone bench beside a small pond, "what is so pressing that you had to speak with me today?"

Cal watched a fat koi rise slowly to the surface of the pond, where it snapped at something floating on the water. "Why didn't you tell me the last time I was here that your family owns the Seven Stars?"

"Is that all?" A strange mix of emotions seemed to wash across Spencer's face. Relief, but something else as well, something deeper. What question had he been expecting?

"I assumed you knew," Spencer said. "It's not like it's some kind of secret. Property deeds are a matter of public record, you know. Besides, we don't own it anymore. My father deeded the land to the city after the mine was blasted closed. I think it's some kind of park now. Go up there yourself if you want to see."

"I've been there," Cal said, and again something unreadable crossed Spencer's eyes. "I was interested to learn that your sister and her friends weren't the first people to disappear in the Seven Stars."

Spencer's jaw tightened, and a slow red burn rose up his neck. "That's a lie. People started those rumors because they were jealous of our money."

"What rumors would those be?" Cal asked. He could almost see Spencer force his anger down. In its place, a crafty smile edged up the corners of his lips.

"You like to play games, don't you, Chief?"

"Games, Mr. Godwin?"

"Like bringing that crazy old Indian up here to fill you full of ghost stories."

Now it was Cal's turn to be surprised. The muscles in his stomach tightened. Was Godwin having him followed?

"What Indian?"

Spencer laughed, a titter that Cal would have expected to come from a little girl. He spat into the pond and watched as a fish snapped the spittle off the surface. "He's an old drunk. Tells people fairy tales to earn a free meal or two. Tell me, Cal, did you buy him dinner in exchange for a couple of *ve-wy sca-wy sto-wies*?"

Cal could feel his headache coming back. He balled his fists at his sides, willing himself to stay calm. Godwin was just trying to bait him, attempting to change the subject. "That's not much of a way to talk about the man who saved your sister's life."

"Is that what he told you, that he saved her? That's bull." Color rose in Spencer's cheeks, and Cal knew he'd hit a sensitive spot. "Everyone helped search for those kids. He just happened to be in the right place at the right time. He probably staggered there on accident."

"I assume that you and your father helped in the search?"

"Yes."

"But you didn't find them?"

"I told you that Indian was lucky. We would have found them eventually without his help." Spencer turned and began to walk deeper into the garden, passing rows and rows of daffodils and tulips, now starting to wilt from the heat. Cal followed. There was more to this story, but he had no idea what it was.

"Did Olivia ever talk about what happened to Frankie?"

"No." Spencer broke a branch from a weeping cherry tree and began stripping the leaves from it. "None of them could remember what happened."

"Did she ever talk about seeing anything strange in the mine? Anything that might have scared her?"

"I told you, none of them could remember anything. They nearly died. It traumatized them all, okay?" Spencer continued to pull the leaves from the branch, his hands green with their juices.

"What about you?" Cal asked. "Did you see anything strange in the Seven Stars?"

Spencer spun around, slashing out with the branch, cutting the blossom from the top of a lily. "You didn't come here to ask about ghost stories, Chief Hunt. I've got to get back to my office, so tell me what you want, or leave."

"Who killed Mandy Osgood and Ezra Rucker?" Cal stood toe to toe with Spencer, their faces only inches apart. "Who killed them and why?"

"I have no idea," Spencer growled.

Cal studied his eyes, trying to read the darkness he saw in them. "What aren't you telling me?"

For a fraction of a second something appeared, like a koi rising to the top of the pond, and he thought that Spencer was about to reveal whatever he'd been hiding—then it disappeared, replaced by cold calculation.

"I have to go." Spencer dropped the denuded branch and stalked toward the house.

"I'd like to speak with your father," Cal said, hurrying to keep up.

"He's gone."

"I can slap obstruction of justice on him just as easily as I could on you."

"Save your breath," Spencer said, not bothering to look back. "He's gone to a clinic. You want to talk to him, charter a plane to Palm Springs."

"Fine, then I'd like to talk to Olivia."

"I told you," Spencer said. "She can't be disturbed." They'd reached the driveway. Spencer pointed stiffly at Cal's car. "I've helped you as much as I can. Now please leave. Don't come back unless it's to tell me you've found the killer."

CHAPTER 43

CAL STOPPED AT THE GATE and watched as it slowly trundled open on its metal track. Once again he'd come up empty. Spencer was hiding something. So what else was new? Everyone involved in this case seemed to have some secret. Right now, all he could say for sure was that the man was scared.

And wasn't that natural? His mother was dead, his father was ill, and his sister was in danger. Anyone in that situation would be a little bonkers. And yet you'd think he'd be more anxious to help find the killer. But then, you'd think Theresa Obrey and Ben Meyers would be just as anxious.

The gate stopped at the end of its track with a smooth whir, and Cal let his foot off the brake. As he began to pull forward, he caught a flash of movement from the corner of his eye and turned to see someone standing near a small grove of trees. It was Olivia. She waved him over and stepped behind the foliage.

Leaving the car idling, he opened the door and looked up toward the house. Spencer was nowhere in sight. What was going on here? This had a very strange feel to it. Still, he found himself intrigued by the prospect of seeing Olivia again.

He walked into the trees. She was standing beside a tall aspen. She was dressed in blue jeans and a white man's shirt with the sleeves rolled up.

"Spencer doesn't want me to talk to you." She grinned like a child who has just sneaked out of bed, blues eyes gleaming.

"He's your brother, not your guard," Cal said. "You don't have to do what he says."

Olivia shrugged, glancing wistfully toward the house. "What have you found out?" she asked, turning back to him.

Cal rested his hands on his gun belt. Was she a victim, or was she hiding information from him like her brother? "For one thing, I found out that your grandfather owned the Seven Stars."

Olivia's head jerked backward as if he'd just slapped her. Her cheeks darkened. "You . . . you didn't . . ."

"What? Go into the mine?" He took a step toward her, and she stumbled away. "Yes, I did."

"You shouldn't have done that," she whispered, eyes wide.

"Why not?" He took another step forward, but she held up one hand as if warding off a blow. "What are you hiding?"

A breeze picked up, tugging at the front of her shirt and blowing her hair back off her shoulders. "You're in danger."

"Danger? What kind of danger?" He held out his hand toward her. "You can tell me."

"No." She shook her head, her long hair swinging back and forth. "No, you should not have gone in there." She turned and, as if she were one with the wind, disappeared back into the trees.

"What kind of danger?" he shouted. But he was calling to empty space.

She was gone.

CHAPTER 44

CAL WAS HALFWAY TO THE station when the radio squawked. "15-J-1, this is dispatch. Do you copy?"

He keyed the microphone. "This is 15-J-1."

"Cal." It was Lindy. "We've got a report of an explosion at irrigation pumps three and four."

Cal grimaced. "Please repeat. Did you say *explosion?*" Pumps three and four were the city wells Dickey Jordan had been complaining about.

"Affirmative. The man who phoned in the report said both pumps were blown to smithereens."

"Roger." It had been a long day, and it looked like it was only going to be getting longer. "Is Greg at the station?"

"Affirmative."

"Tell him I'll be by in a couple of minutes to get him. And call somebody over at the water department."

"Roger." The radio clicked off.

"What did you do, Dickey?" he mumbled. "What did you do?"

CHAPTER 45

CAL LIFTED A SHARD OF twisted metal from the side of the road and sniffed it before dropping it into an evidence bag. The sharp odor of cordite on the warm iron was unmistakable. Greg had taped off the area, but a large crowd had gathered anyway. Cal heard someone mutter something about al Qaeda.

Under the current political climate, the first thought that came into people's minds when they heard the word *bomb* was terrorism. He couldn't say he blamed them, but personally he felt confident that Twin Forks, Colorado, was not high on any terrorist hit lists.

On the other hand, wasn't this also a terrorist attack of sorts? He suspected that the person responsible for this mess had never traveled farther east than the agriculture convention in Des Moines. But he couldn't discount the seriousness of the offense just because the explosives had come from the stash of a local farmer instead of some Middle Eastern armory.

"I guess we'd better go pay Dickey a visit," Cal said, closing the evidence bag and peeling the latex gloves from his hands.

"Yup, we probably should," Greg drawled. "Poor old guy's really stepped in it this time." The two men watched the city maintenance crew begin to work on removing the mutilated remains of the pumps for another minute or two before returning to their patrol car. "He's just lucky no one was injured or he'd be looking at a lot more serious charges."

As Cal started the engine and headed east, he radioed in their location. They drove in silence for several miles, both men lost in their own thoughts.

"Any idea where he might have gotten hold of the explosives?" Cal asked.

"Most farmers around here keep a few sticks stored away for blowing up stumps or big chunks of rock in their field. Nasty stuff for the most part. Usually twenty or thirty years old and sweating like crazy." Greg rolled down his window and laid his head back against the seat.

"Surprised they don't blow their hands off," Cal said.

"Sometimes they do."

They stopped at an intersection. This wasn't a visit Cal was looking forward to, and he was in no hurry to get there. Dickey Jordan was a blowhard and a pain in the keister more often than not. But he was also a hard-working farmer, a husband, and a father.

Was it his fault that the city had arbitrarily decided to drop their wells into the same underground watershed that fed his home and crops? Cal hoped that a way could be found to see that Dickey paid for his mistake without putting him in jail, but he wasn't sure that would happen.

The light changed, and Cal began to pull out when a silver pickup truck with rusty side panels blew through the intersection. Cal hit the brakes, narrowly avoiding a collision.

"Crazy drivers," Greg said.

As Cal glared at the back of the truck, wishing he had time to pull it over, a woman in the passenger's seat shot a quick look in his direction before turning away. It was Esther Zoeller.

Probably out with a neighbor doing their grocery shopping. "She ought to pick someone who drives a little more carefully," he muttered. "Or they'll both end up dead."

A mile and a half outside of town, they stopped next to a green metal mailbox with the name *Jordan* hand-painted on the side. Cal thought the mailbox might once have looked like a tractor, but it had been smashed so many times by kids driving by with baseball bats—a popular activity out here—that now its original shape was all but unrecognizable.

It was nearly seven, and the sun was low in the western sky. If he remembered right, Dickey's children were all married. He thought that maybe Dickey's wife—was her name Marilynn? Maggie?—tended the grandkids in the afternoon. He didn't want to embarrass the man in front of his family, if he could help it.

"Okay, let's take this nice and easy," he said, smiling at his own words. He didn't think Greg had ever rushed anything in his life. As they drove slowly up the dirt road, twin plumes of red dust rose from the tires of the cruiser, and Cal registered the fact that if Dickey was watching, he'd have plenty of notice that someone was coming.

They rounded a bend, passing a pair of arthritic-looking walnut trees, and the white clapboard house came into view. He was not surprised at all to see that Dickey himself was sitting in an old wooden rocker out front on the porch. The farmer's eyes were hidden by the shadow of a cap pulled low on his forehead, but his leathery neck turned jerkily as he tracked their approach.

"You wait in the car while I try to talk to him. If it looks like we're going to have any trouble with him, get on the radio and call for backup. But whatever you do, don't spook him. He's apt to be pretty edgy right about now."

Cal casually swung open the driver's side door and stepped from of the car.

"Pretty warm today," he called out, stretching his arms. He hoped that his words and actions came across as relaxed and non-confrontational to the man on the porch, but inside, Cal's heart was pounding. There was something wrong here—something about the way Dickey's head twitched back and forth like a bantam rooster, snapping from Cal to the car, out toward his pasture, and then back to Cal again.

"Mind if I come up there and join you? Sure could use a glass of water." Cal took two steps toward the house and stopped, noticing for the first time how quiet everything seemed. The swing set around the side of the house was empty, and he couldn't hear the sound of kids' voices coming from inside the house.

Suddenly his throat was dust-dry and he really did wish for a glass of water. Again the old man's head darted toward his fields. Cal risked a quick glance out past the white fence, without ever losing track of Dickey. Something was wrong there too. The horses. There should have been ten or so horses feeding on the lush green grass, but the pasture seemed as lifeless as the house.

"Mr. Jordan, is everything okay?" Cal dropped his hand toward the butt of his revolver as the old man leaned forward in his chair. This was all wrong. Cal's body screamed danger from every nerve ending. He wished he was back in the relative safety of the cruiser. If only he could see the man's eyes . . .

Take off that cap, he willed silently.

"You sold me out." Dickey's voice, unnaturally loud in the still evening air, cracked.

At least they were talking. That was a good sign.

"I'm not sure what you mean, Dickey." He took another step forward.

"I thought you 'as my friend. But you're with them."

"I *am* your friend." Cal heard the crackle of the radio behind him and held out his hand, motioning for Greg to stay put.

Dickey heard the radio too. He leaned forward in his rocker, squinting toward the cruiser. "Who you got in that car with you? It's one of them, ain't it?"

"That's just Detective Luke. You remember him, don't you?" Obviously Dickey had cracked, but things could still come out all right.

"Where's your wife?" Cal asked. "Maybe she could bring us out some lemonade. Don't you think that would taste good right now?"

Dickey glanced uncertainly back toward the house. "She ain't here. I sent her and the kids up t' her mother's place. Didn't want her to see this."

"See what?" Cal took another step forward. He had a very bad feeling about this. Olivia's words came back to him. *You're in danger.* She couldn't have known about this. Could she?

He was lifting one foot, not entirely sure whether he planned on stepping forward or away, when Dickey leaned back in his rocker. For a split second, as Dickey's hand rose from the arm of his rocker, Cal thought that the farmer was going to take his cap off, after all. But then the old man's hand whipped snake-like behind his chair and Cal had just enough time to register the flash of metal.

"Don't move," Dickey screamed, his voice high and hoarse. He was holding a double barrel shotgun, both hammers cocked.

"Put down the gun," Cal shouted, hands still in the air. Behind him he could hear Greg on the radio.

"You're with 'em." The old farmer seemed almost to be crying, and the barrel of his shotgun dropped a little.

"No. I want to help you," Cal said, trying to calm Dickey down, but he could see that he was losing him.

"No. I seen it all last night. Seen it in a vision. A angel come an' warned me 'bout you," Dickey shrieked. The barrel of his shotgun came back up, and his finger went to the trigger.

Instinctively Cal dropped to the ground, his hand reaching for his pistol. Before he could get to his weapon, Dickey fired the first barrel. A rush of hot air blew past Cal's cheek, and an invisible hand clawed at the left sleeve of his uniform.

To his right, he heard Greg shout something unintelligible. The car's door swung open with a squeal, and for the only time since the farmhouse had come into view, Cal let Dickey Jordan out of his sight. Greg was climbing from the car, obviously unable to believe what he was seeing.

"Get down," Cal started to shout, waving his partner back into the car.

His words were cut off by the roar of a second blast from Dickey's shotgun. This time the heat burned down Cal's head and neck, fire tore through the back of his skull, and everything went black.

CHAPTER 46

THERESA OBREY WAS IN A blue rage. You couldn't tell it from the expression on her face, which was as icily cold as a department store mannequin. She'd had years and years of practice at keeping her emotions from showing. But you'd have to be deaf to miss the grinding of her molars, which, even from the next room over, sounded like shards of crushed glass slowly being pulverized beneath some tremendous weight.

Pulling the sheer, white drapes back an inch or two from the window, she watched the patrol car drive slowly past her front yard with grim intensity. It was the fourth time in the last ninety minutes. If she was a swearing woman, she'd be using words her husband had never even heard of. But she didn't allow that kind of language in her house. So instead, she stared silently at the disappearing cruiser, driving her lacquered nails into the palms of her hands and biting the insides of her cheeks until she tasted blood.

This was all the fault of that jerkwater cop. No doubt he'd asked the local blue boys to keep an eye on her. Not that they'd admit it, of course. "Just the standard patrol, ma'am," one of the arrogant little pups, fresh from the academy, had said when she demanded to know why she was being subjected to police harassment.

Yeah, right. Standard patrol if you happened to live in a slum. But not when you lived in one of the most exclusive sections of the city. Why weren't the cops out on the west side of town clubbing the heads of all the gangbangers that lived over there?

Well, she would deal with the police. She had connections, and they'd back off or heads would roll. It was Meyers who worried her—him and his frumpy little wife. He'd promised that he wouldn't say anything. But how long would that promise last? Hunt had been there twice already, and he would keep going back until Ben cracked. Either that or his wife would manage to weasel his weak-sauce story out of him.

Either way, it amounted to the same thing. Once his story got out, the press would be all over it like maggots on road kill. It didn't matter that it was a bunch of lies held together with the false memories of a man trying to deal with a terrible tragedy from more than thirty years ago. The *Post* reporters always had their nails out for anything bad having to do with state politicians and their families.

Something like this would ruin her family. Her husband's reputation would be tarnished. Her children would be teased and ridiculed at school. And she didn't know how they could ever go back to church and face their friends again.

She'd never told anyone about Ben's crazy stories, not even her husband. If word of this ever got out, he would wonder why she'd held it back from him. Of course, it was for his own good. He had a lot of responsibilities, and there was no need to trouble him with this.

Is that *why you never told him?* A small voice inside her head asked. *Is it really? It couldn't be because you think there might be some truth to those crazy stories, could it?* An image arose in her mind. A little boy, not much younger than her own son. He watched her mutely with unreadable black eyes.

She pressed a cold palm against her flushed face. Just a flashback—irrational and stupid. She had no need to feel guilty about the boy's death. He'd become lost in the cave, just like the rest of them. Could she help it if he'd wandered away from the rest of the group? Well, *could* she?

Something tugged at her memory—something that promised . . . sanity? She could do it if she wanted to. Drop her defenses and allow the memories to come back. It wasn't too late. Ben had told her the truth was driving him slowly crazy, and she could feel it herself. If she allowed them to, the memories would return. She could face them.

She could face them, but her family . . .

No. She snapped her head sharply left and right. No, there was no truth there at all—only lies. Lies designed to hurt her and her family. It would devastate them. And that was something she would *never* allow to happen.

She lifted her purse from the back of the couch and took out an amber prescription bottle—another thing her husband didn't need to know about. It held thirty capsules, obtained more or less legally. They helped her keep things inside—under control. Ordinarily she might not take any for a month or more. But over the past week, she'd nearly emptied the bottle.

She shook two of the capsules into her palm, considered for a moment, and added a third. As soon as she popped them into her mouth, dry-swallowing them all in a single smooth lump, she could feel her muscles beginning to relax. The drugs couldn't have taken effect that quickly, but just the thought of them doing their thing was enough to help her unwind.

She knew what she had to do. It wasn't really all that complicated when you came right down to where the wheels hit the pavement. She had to get back to the hospital and convince Ben Meyers—and his wife, if necessary—that it was in their own best interests to keep their fat mouths shut.

Over the last few days she'd been doing a little research of her own. Actually she'd hired a weaselly little private investigator with the unfortunate name of Kraphause to dig some dirt. He'd come up with several interesting little inconsistencies in a couple of the Meyers's tax returns and a woman in Ben's office who would be willing to invent some interesting peccadilloes for the right price. None of it was earth shattering on its own—but presented in the right light, it might be enough to shake up the Meyers's happy world.

If that failed, there was always money. Who hadn't dreamed of a fancy new car or a time-share in Vail? Cash often worked wonders, and it had the double-benefit of leaving behind a trail in case the partakers changed their minds down the road.

And if *that* didn't work?

Well, then she'd just have to do whatever it took.

"Theresa, are you in here?" Hugh Obrey, Theresa's husband, stepped into the entrance of the dim living room. As usual, he carried a thick sheaf of papers, one finger marking his place. Metal-rimmed spectacles hung perilously from the tip of his nose.

"Darling." Theresa moved away from the curtains, flashing a dazzling smile at her husband. She pushed his glasses up and gave him a solid, if passionless, smack on the lips. "All finished with your work?"

"Oh, uh, no . . . not yet," he said, holding out his papers as if to show how much heavy reading he still had left. "I was just wondering if dinner would be ready soon. I thought I smelled something in the oven."

"Yes, you did," she said, locking her smile in place. Just once she'd like to say, *If you're so terribly hungry, why don't you get your bony little butt into the kitchen and make it yourself?*

Instead, she patted his hand and said, "Why don't I have the kids set the table and get out the roast? I have to run a quick errand, so you all can start dinner without me, but I should be back in time to put whipped cream on the chocolate pie."

He frowned. "You're going to miss dinner?" She loved her husband, but right then it was all she could do to refrain from ramming his teeth down his throat. And she could do it too. After nine years studying under one of the best karate instructors in the state, she pitied the man who tried to sneak up on her in a dark alleyway.

"Yes, sweetheart," she said, forcing her jaw to unclench. "But I'll make it up to you when I get home. How does a good backrub sound?"

"That would be nice." He raised his narrow shoulders and grimaced. "I've spent the entire day bent over my desk."

"Poor baby." Tucking her purse under one arm, she gave him a quick hug and pecked his forehead. "I'll be back just as soon as I finish my . . . errand."

If Hugh Obrey had seen his wife's face as she turned away, he would have run screaming from the room, sure that his loving Theresa had been replaced by a demon.

CHAPTER 47

ONCE SHE WAS IN THE garage, Theresa began feeling better. She really needed to unwind. When this was over, she would take an art class or spend a couple of days at that great spa in Aspen—or maybe take up crossbow hunting. As she was stepping into her car, she slipped in a puddle of something on the floor of the garage. It had a nasty, metallic smell to it that burned her sinuses.

That was strange; she'd just had her car checked the week before. Scraping her shoe on the edge of the doorframe so she wouldn't track anything onto the carpet, she settled behind the wheel. Her mechanic was going to hear about this.

Pushing the button that raised the garage door, she checked the rear-view mirror to make sure there were no cars in sight. The street was clear, and, without turning on the headlights, she backed quickly out. As soon as she was through the door, she punched the garage door button again and pulled out onto a side street.

Now that she was moving and the drugs had kicked in, she was feeling no pain. She grinned, her teeth glimmering like those of sharks. This might prove to be kind of fun. It had been a while since she'd really chewed up someone and spit him out. And heaven help the nurse who got in her way.

Sure that no police were following her, she flicked on the lights and took the next turn without even slowing down, the tires of her luxury sedan squealing as she cornered. It was a steep drive down to the valley floor. In the winter it could be a bear if the roads hadn't been recently plowed, but now with the street dry and clear and the traffic light, she let the car pick up speed.

For most of the hill the stoplights were with her—a rarity at this time of day—and the speedometer nosed up past fifty. She knew she should keep her speed down; the last thing she needed was to get pulled over now, but she couldn't seem to help herself. It was as if some unseen power was urging her forward, drawing her ever more quickly toward her destination.

Three-quarters of the way down the hill, her luck with the lights ran out. The signal a hundred yards ahead changed from yellow to red. At the intersection, a young woman in yellow Lycra shorts and a bright pink halter-top started into the crosswalk, her backpack swinging from one shoulder.

Theresa pumped the brake, and it sank mushily before starting to engage. The car shivered, slowing only a little. She stomped hard on the pedal. This time it went all the way to the floor, and the brake light on the dashboard flashed red. In the crosswalk, the girl stopped halfway across the street, staring stupidly at the car that was barreling toward her.

Hitting the horn, Theresa cranked the wheel hard to the left. The car bucked violently under her grip, the tires leaving streaks of rubber on the asphalt behind her. At the last second, the doe-eyed girl jumped backward. Her backpack swung around, hooked on the car's passenger side mirror, and ripped so violently from her arm that the university doctors would treat her for a dislocated shoulder later that night.

Theresa barely had time to realize that she had somehow avoided hitting the woman before registering that her car was now headed toward a row of hundred-year-old maples. She wrenched the wheel back to the right, and the rear of her sedan began to fishtail.

With the car almost completely out of control, years of experience driving on slippery roads took over. Fighting against the urge to steer against the skid, she let momentum nose her back to the left. The sedan careened from one side of the road to the other, bouncing up against the curb, where it left a long black streak. Miraculously, it didn't roll. She might even have managed to get it straightened out if the child hadn't appeared from nowhere.

One second the road was empty, and the next second her headlights speared the moonlike face of a boy standing directly in front of her. With no time for thought, she twisted the steering wheel as hard as she could, sending the car into a tire-shrieking spin. Nose and tail switched places. For a brief second, as the car spun ever closer to the trees, she saw the boy's face again and thought, *I know him.* Then the tires lost all traction, and the sedan began to roll.

The accident report would state that the car flipped three and a half times before wrapping itself around a tree planted by one of the city's founders. All Theresa knew was that her body was caroming from window to floor to ceiling before catapulting through the windshield. She never bothered wearing a seat belt—they wrinkled her outfits. That wouldn't be a problem anymore.

Her body flew more than seventy feet through the air before bouncing twice off the sidewalk and landing in the front yard of a state senator with whom she and her husband dined regularly. The last thing she saw was the face of the boy, who had somehow managed to catch up with her, grinning in the moonlight.

She tried to speak, but nothing would come out. The mouth that had told television audiences how to cook, that had gotten her everything she ever wanted, that had ripped the hide from anyone who got in her way, coughed up a bubble of deep red blood and closed for good.

CHAPTER 48

CAL WAS IN A BOAT. He could hear water slapping against the sides of the small dinghy as it rocked back and forth. The dank smell of moisture filled the air and slipped into his nostrils with an almost dizzying power. He ran his fingers along the gunwale. Though he could feel the slick surface of polished wood beneath his fingers, he couldn't see it—couldn't see anything at all.

He tried to remember where he was and how he had gotten there, but for the moment his memories were as unfathomable as the darkness surrounding him. Was this a dream? It had the sense of unreality that dreams sometimes had, the feel of things just beyond his control.

Abruptly the boat jolted to the left, and he had to clutch the side to keep from falling. Now he could just make out a faint glow ahead of him. He seemed to be in some kind of tunnel. The light was growing stronger, and he thought he could make out the sound of . . . of singing.

He had a vague memory of being shot at—of pain. Was he dead, then? Was he hearing a choir of angels? Children's voices echoed off the walls that he could now faintly see to either side of the waterway. But it wasn't hymns they were singing. The tune was familiar, and for some reason it reminded him of Kat.

All at once he realized where he was. This was Disneyland. He was in one of the boats of the "It's a Small World" ride. It was Kat's favorite spot in the whole park. She said that no one could ever feel unhappy in "It's a Small World."

But what was he doing here? Kat was dead. She would never again watch the hundreds of dolls twirling in synchronized dance, their costumes forming brightly colored rainbows. She would never sing the "It's a Small World" theme song along with the children in each of their different languages as the boat passed from one country to the next.

Why was he here without her? Without Kat this ride was as pointless as everything else in his life. He buried his face in his hands.

Cool fingers touched the side of his face. "You don't want to miss the best part, do you?" He looked up, and Kat was sitting beside him, her eyes glowing as they always did when their little boat rounded the first bend.

The boat turned, and they entered the bright illumination of the ride. Their boat slipped past the signs reading *Welcome* in several languages.

"Kat, it's you . . . you're . . ." *Back* he wanted to say, but couldn't. Emotion blocked his throat. "Am I dead? Are we . . ."

"Shhh," she whispered, taking his hand and flashing him the smile that had won his heart the first time he saw it.

"I've missed you so much," he said, drinking in every line of her face. "I thought it would get easier. You know, that I would adjust. But everything I see reminds me of you, and it just keeps hitting me over and over that I'll never wake up next to you again. Only now . . . now you're here. Or am I *there*?"

Tears slipped down the sides of his face, and she reached across to brush them away. As her fingers touched his skin, he knew that he would give everything he had to be able to feel that touch forever.

She turned to look at the singing dolls, her eyes lighting up at the beautiful costumes. But he couldn't take his eyes off *her*. She was really here. Somehow she was back. He would never let her leave his side again.

Suddenly her smile faltered and her fingers tightened on his hand. "No," she whispered. "No, this isn't right."

He turned and followed her gaze.

For the first time, he noticed the dolls. There was something strange about their faces. They were smiling. Of course they were. Anyone who couldn't wear a dazzling toothpaste smile every minute they were in front of the public wasn't long for it in Walt's kingdom—even if they *were* robots. But the children's smiles seemed wrong somehow, almost sly. As if they were just waiting for him to turn away so they could stick out their tongues or make obscene gestures at him behind his back.

And the singing.

On the surface it was the same old, same old, about one moon, one sun, and friendship for everyone, sung in more languages than even a college professor could master. But the children's voices seemed to be placing a special emphasis on "a world of *fears*" and "a world of *tears*."

The tempo was off too. It was slower, more solemn—more like a funeral dirge. And just under their breaths, so low that he couldn't quite make out the words, were they singing something more sinister?

Cal turned to Kat. Her eyes were glassy with fear, her breath coming in quick, short gasps. He took her into his arms, pulling her toward him. "It's okay," he whispered. "Everything's going to be all right."

As the figures continued to whirl and spin, their shadows stretched out behind them like grotesque specters, parodying the joy of real children and turning it into something evil. Were they getting closer? He felt sure that the dolls should be moving in set patterns, up and down, around and around. But these children were gamboling, darting off their platforms and leaping down to stand near the edge of the water.

To his left a pair of Eskimo children crept stealthily up behind a cardboard polar bear. As he passed by them, Cal was suddenly sure that he had seen them somewhere before. They looked so familiar. If he had just another second, he knew that he'd be able to place them.

The boat left one land behind, rounding into another, and from the corner of his eye he saw a cowboy doll twirling a lasso above his head. The cowboy tossed the rope into the air, but instead of coming down on a cow or a horse, it looped around the neck of a cowgirl, and he pulled her screaming toward him.

Their faces. They weren't doll faces at all but the faces of children. His gut went ice cold as he realized why they were so familiar.

The cowboy pulling the screaming cowgirl into the darkness was Ezra Rucker, and the girl was Amanda Porter. And the Eskimo children—they had been Benjamin Meyers and Theresa Truman. What were the children from the mine doing in "It's a Small World"?

As if sensing his recognition, the children gave up any pretense of following the script and lined the sides of the waterway, jeering and laughing at him. Something launched into the air, and he turned, startled, in time to see an Indian that looked like a young Dickey Jordan throw a javelin. It glanced off Kat's head before sinking out of sight into the dark water.

"Kat!" he screamed.

"I'm okay." She tried to smile. "It's just a bump." But it wasn't a bump at all. Blood was gushing from the wound, dripping down the side of her face.

He ripped off his shirt and pressed it against the side of her head, trying to stanch the flow. "I've got to get you to a doctor," he said. He had to get her off this ride. This was a theme park; there would be plenty of emergency medical personnel on staff. He looked for one of the exit doors hidden behind the props, and froze.

They were no longer in "It's a Small World" at all but floating along a depthless black river running down the center of a long, dark mine. Pick axes and bits of rusted rail littered the ground to either side of them. Overhead an electrical sizzling was followed by a loud pop. The lights went out, leaving the shaft a sickly green.

The boat jerked to a stop, throwing him forward against the front of the boat. As he looked down into the water, a groan escaped his lips. Frankie Zoeller was floating just beneath the surface, his pale white face swimming behind dark glasses. Frankie's eyes opened, and his shriveled fingers reached up toward Cal.

Cal shook his head. "I can't help you," he shouted. "I have to save my wife. She's hurt."

Kat slumped against his shoulder and he turned, catching her in his arms as she fell forward. He had to get her out of here. They would get help. This time he'd make sure the doctors looked for a blood clot.

He began to lift her, only it wasn't Kat lying in his arms. It was Olivia. Her long blond hair was wet with blood, her eyes rolled back in her head like white hardboiled eggs.

"Do you like my new dress?" she asked, running her finger through her clotted hair. "The blue brings out my eyes, and the bloody flowers match my hair."

"Where's Kat?" he screamed at her. "Where is my wife?"

She smiled up at him, but it was the *rictus* grin of a corpse.

"You shouldn't have come here," she whispered, pointing to the water.

He turned back. Frankie was gone. Now Kat was the one drowning. Her eyes were red with blood. Bubbles exploded from her mouth as she tried to scream. From somewhere in the darkness, he heard the voice of Two Bears say, "There are underground springs in these caves that run hundreds of feet deep."

He dove for Kat's hand, lunging across the side of the boat. The ice-cold water closed over his arms and shoulders. He thought he had her— their hands were only inches apart. But just as his fingers began to close around her wrists, something snaked up from the depths, wrapped around her waist, and jerked her down into the darkness, where she disappeared.

"No," he screamed, trying to climb over the edge of the boat, meaning to dive after her. He wouldn't lose her this time. He wasn't going to let Kat spend eternity stuck in this rancid black pit.

Something pulled him back into the boat.

"*Grays Gahd.*" Olivia was gone, and Frankie was in her place tugging on Cal's arm.

"I have to save her," Cal screamed, trying to tear his arm from the boy's grasp. The air was thick and glowing. It tore at his lungs as he tried to breathe.

"*Grays Gahd.*" Frankie's grip was like iron.

"I don't know what that means."

Frankie pointed into the water, and for the last time, Cal looked down into its murky depths.

Now it was neither Frankie nor Kat but Olivia floating lifeless in the water. Only it wasn't Olivia—it only looked like her. Cal recognized the face from the portrait. It was her mother.

"*Grays Gahd.*"

Grace of God, Cal thought. *What did that mean?*

No, not God—Godwin. That's what the ghost had been trying to say.

"Grace Godwin," he whispered, "Grace Godwin."

CHAPTER 49

Waking up was like swimming through oatmeal. The first two times Cal tried, he slipped back down into darkness before he could make it all the way out. The third time he finally managed to reach the surface.

His first sensation was a tight burning running from the base of his neck to the top of his head, as if someone had doused his skull with kerosene. He reached up with one hand to explore the damage. Instantly, white-hot shards of pain shot across his head, and he jerked his fingers away.

"Looks like somebody scalped you while you was sleeping."

Cal opened his eyes a crack, wincing at the bright light. Someone was sitting in the corner of the room, holding a tattered paperback book.

"Two Bears?"

"Heard about your little accident. Thought you might want some cump'ny."

Cal reached back more gingerly this time. Most of his head had been shaved and was now covered in bandages. He tried to turn his neck, and again fire raced from his shoulders to the top of his scalp. "What happened?"

Two Bears shrugged. "Wasn't there myself. But the doctor tells me he pulled more'n thirty buckshot pellets from that hard head of yours."

Suddenly Cal remembered. "What about Greg. Is he all right?"

"He's fine. Went home a couple of hours ago."

"How long have I been here?" Cal asked, searching for the button that raised the top half of the bed. He felt helpless lying flat on his back.

"Nearly two years. You been in a coma."

"What?" Cal jerked forward, ignoring the pain.

"Take her easy," Two Bears chuckled, rising from his chair and helping Cal with the bed. "I'm only joking. It's been about fourteen hours."

"Geez," Cal groaned, rubbing his eyes. "Don't scare me like that." The events of the previous day were coming back to him.

"Where's Dickey?"

Two Bears stretched, his back popping audibly. He shook his head. "Detective Luke wrestled the gun away from him 'fore he could reload. Said the poor guy didn't seem all there. Guess they got him up to the jail."

"And his family?"

"They're upset, but okay."

How had this happened? Cal wondered. *If only he'd listened more closely to the man's complaints outside the church.* But it still didn't add up. Dickey had always been a little flakey, but never violent.

Something had set the farmer off—something other than a water dispute. What was it the man had shouted just before he started shooting? Something about a vision and seeing an angel. This couldn't have anything to do with the murders, and yet Olivia had warned him that he was in danger. Could this have been what she meant? How could she have known?

". . . to Greenwood."

Cal's thoughts were interrupted by the old Indian's words. "What did you say?"

"Imagine they'll send him up to Greenwood."

Greenwood—the mental hospital where Grace Godwin had been sent.

Grace Godwin . . . Grace of God. Images flashed through Cal's mind, and he remembered his dream. Kat had been there. He'd tried to dive into the water to rescue her, but Frankie Zoeller had stopped him. The boy had pointed down into the water at a drowning Grace Godwin.

Had Olivia Godwin been there too? He thought so, but for some reason when he tried to remember, he kept seeing yellow flowers on a blue dress. Why did that seem so familiar?

He reached for his recorder before realizing he was wearing only a hospital gown.

He looked at Two Bears. "I thought you left town."

The old Indian shrugged, his expression blank. "I came back."

"But why?" Without thinking, Cal started to rub the back of his head before pulling his hand away again with a wince of pain.

"Thought you might need my help."

"I see," Cal said, not sure that he did. "Where are you staying?"

"Got a motel out by the freeway."

"Why don't you stay at my place?" Cal suggested. "I've got a couple of spare rooms, and there's plenty of grub if you can stand TV dinners."

Two Bears grimaced.

"Okay, so maybe we'll have something delivered."

"Don't want to put you out."

"It'll be nice to have someone else around. It's been feeling pretty empty lately. We can talk more tonight."

Two Bears nodded. As Cal jotted down directions to his house and where to find the spare key, he thought of something else.

"How did you get the nurses to let you in here anyway?"

The old man smiled, raising both palms into the air. "Told 'em we were brothers."

CHAPTER 50

"Here you are, Mr. Hunt." Nurse Johnson, a petite woman with small hands and a beautiful chocolate complexion brought Cal his digital recorder and notebook. "Although I'm not really supposed to be doing this. Doctor Pender wants you to rest."

"I appreciate it," he said. "I don't imagine there's any chance you could bring me my gun?"

"Not in the slightest. Can I get you anything else, though? Juice, pain medication, bed pan . . . sponge bath?"

"What! No . . . I—" Cal faltered, his cheeks growing hot, before he noticed the gleam in the woman's dark eyes.

"Two Bears put you up to that, didn't he?"

She grinned an impish little smile. "He said you needed to work on your sense of humor."

Cal couldn't help chuckling. "I'm fine, thanks."

"All right, then," she sighed with mock disappointment. "I'll be back around with breakfast in about an hour. Just let me know if you change your mind."

Cal figured he'd find some way of getting back at Two Bears. Well, he had plenty of time to think on it while listening to the recordings. He'd nearly filled ten hours. He opened his notebook, pressed play, and settled back against the pillows.

Three hours later, the phone by the side of his bed rang. Probably someone else from the department—he'd received four sympathy calls already, and it was starting to get on his nerves. They all treated him like he was on his deathbed. He paused the recorder near the end of his interview with Esther Zoeller and picked up the phone.

"Chief Hunt, this is Dave Lyon." Cal remembered the name. It was the detective from the Denver PD. "Heard things have been getting a little dangerous down your way. Maybe you ought to come up here and take a breather."

"No thanks," Cal said. "I think I'll stay down here in the sticks."

"How are you feeling?"

"You know, if I have one more person ask me that, I think I'm going to explode."

"That bad, huh?" The detective laughed.

"My neck stings a little bit, but they tell me I should be able to check out this afternoon sometime. It won't be any too soon for me."

Detective Lyon's voice grew serious. "Have you heard?"

"Heard what?"

"About the Obrey woman—"

"What about her?" Cal had a terrible sick feeling in the pit of his stomach.

"I guess maybe you've been a little out of touch. She died last night, smashed her car into a tree. She was dead before anyone could reach her."

Cal's head spun. What did that mean? He'd been looking at her as a potential suspect—assuming that she was trying to cover up whatever secret Ben and the others had been hiding. But if she was dead, that left only . . . Olivia.

"You still there?"

"Yeah, I'm here." Cal tried to gather his thoughts. "Any idea how it happened?"

"Preliminary findings look like brake failure. The boys in the shop are going over it now." He paused for a moment before continuing. "You think this has something to do with your murders?"

Cal thought hard. "I don't know. But it's a possibility. Maybe a good one."

"You know, if it turns out that this was intentional, we're going to want everything you've got on the case," Lyon said. In some cities jurisdictional issues could be a nightmare.

"Don't worry, if this is the work of my guy, I'll take all the help I can get. I'll get somebody down at the station to make you a copy of everything."

"Appreciate that." The detective sounded relieved. "I'll let you know what we get back on the car."

Cal slowly hung up the phone. So now they were down to two—more like one and a half: Mandy, Ezra, and Theresa dead, and Ben lying in critical condition. Assuming the pattern continued, that put Olivia next in line.

He'd offered the Godwin family police protection—at least as much as he could provide with his limited resources. They'd turned him down. Although Olivia seemed relatively safe—locked behind the gates of the Godwin place—the others had thought they were safe too. Cal would do whatever it took to protect her.

But there was another alternative—one that he had to consider.

With Theresa alive, he'd assumed that the murderer might actually have been one of the survivors. With her dead, that left Olivia as the only suspect if he stuck to the theory. Cal mulled over the clues from each murder scene.

The stump in Ezra's backyard had been dragged across the grass to reach the light bulb—that and the size and location of the ax wound pointed to a short killer. Olivia was barely five feet tall.

And the rug burns on the backs of Mandy's legs suggested that her body had been dragged across the carpet. Her body couldn't have weighed more than a hundred and ten, which suggested that her killer had been unable to lift more than a hundred pounds. Could Olivia's hands have produced the bruises on Mandy's neck? As much as he wished otherwise, he had to admit that they could have.

That could also explain the warning she had given him. Was it possible that she had known about Dickey? Had she managed to convince the poor muddled farmer that the police were out to get him? It got Cal out of the way while the killer went after Theresa.

He remembered the way Olivia had scrubbed the clay from her knuckles as they talked. What if she was trying to wash away something else—something that wouldn't disappear with soap and water? The family did have a history of mental instability.

But if she'd wanted to kill him, why had she warned him? She talked about how she had to be clean to return to God. Maybe her warning was a way of justifying her actions in her own mind.

He hated even the idea of Olivia being the killer. He'd felt something around her that he'd felt only with Kat—a kinship, a protectiveness. If she were guilty, would he be able to put those feelings aside? He'd have to.

He found the recording of the first conversation they'd had.

"Maybe if you told me what you remember about that day. The day you and the other children went into the mine."

There was a long silence as the recording continued. He could just make out the sound of birds in the background, and then Olivia's voice came back into the recording. "Do you like my new dress?"

Her voice had changed— for one thing, the pitch was higher, a little girl's voice. He'd been too caught up in her words to notice that at the time. For another thing, it was more . . . carefree. More innocent?

"Mother bought it for me special. She said the blue brings out my eyes, and the yellow flower matches my hair.

"I was playing jump rope with Theresa, and I fell down in the grass. Father will be so angry when he sees the stain. He gets upset when we ruin the things Mother buys for us."

Cal stopped the recording. Hadn't Olivia said something like that in his dream? Something about her dress? He rewound the recording and listened again.

"Mother bought it for me special. She said the blue brings out my eyes, and the yellow flowers match my hair."

Mother bought it for me special. But that wasn't possible. Spencer said that—

He went to the recording he'd made with Spencer just the day before.

They'd been standing in front of the portraits. "Just noticing how much you and your sister look like your mother." The words were muffled faintly by the pocket of his uniform.

"Do you think so? Most people tell me I look like my father. Neither of us really remembers our mother very well. She left when we were rather young." Spencer's voice was calm, reflecting.

"Wasn't that shortly after Olivia disappeared into your grandfather's mine?"

He'd been trying to shake Spencer up, and it had worked. His tone had grown cautious.

"It was actually several months prior to that."

Cal stopped the tape. If Grace Godwin had been sent to Greenwood several months prior to the children disappearing into the mine, how had she picked out Olivia's dress? It was possible that she had purchased it months in advance, but if her condition had deteriorated so badly that she had to be institutionalized, it didn't seem likely.

He got out his phone and dialed the precinct. "Lindy, this is Cal. I have to go look into something. When Greg gets in, have him find everything he can get on Grace Godwin. And have somebody bring me my car."

Lindy took down the information and promised to pass it on to Greg. She asked him how he was feeling.

"All of a sudden, much better."

He disconnected the call and immediately called Two Bears. Just as the phone started to ring, Nurse Johnson stepped back through the door.

"Mr. Hunt, I have your—" Cal turned, belatedly realizing that he had nothing on beneath his gown, and it was untied in the back.

"You shouldn't be sitting up yet. You've lost a lot of blood."

"I need to leave now," Cal said. "Please get me my belongings."

"But Dr. Pender said—" she began to protest.

Cal cut her off. "Tell the doctor this may be a matter of life and death." He wasn't sure why yet, but his gut told him that finding out the truth about Grace Godwin was vital to his investigation.

On the other end of the phone line, the old Indian's voice mail picked up.

"Two Bears, this is Cal. Something's come up, and I'm checking out early. You can hang around the house until I get back tonight or you might want to head up to Boulder to see Ben Meyers. Maybe if you remind him you saved his bacon, he'll remember you and say something useful. Take one of my cards from the drawer next to the kitchen sink . . . they should let you into his room. See you tonight."

He ended the call and began to get dressed. He sensed that he was close to finding out something important, and any doctor who tried to get in his way was going to find himself on the wrong side of a bulldozer.

CHAPTER 51

TRYING TO NAVIGATE THE WINDING mountain road to Greenwood without turning his head was a physical impossibility, and by the time Cal reached the top of the pass, his neck was in agony. He tried not to think about the fact that he would have to follow the same twisting two-lane road back down into the valley in a couple of hours. The sample pack of pain meds Dr. Pender had reluctantly given him when he checked out were in his pocket, but he couldn't operate a car within four hours of taking them.

The only good thing about the drive was that, combined with the pain, it had acted to focus his thoughts. There was still far too much he didn't know, but some of the pieces were starting to come together.

Tomorrow would be thirty-four years to the day since Ezra Rucker, Amanda Porter, Ben Meyers, Theresa Truman, Olivia Godwin, and Frankie Zoeller disappeared into the Seven Stars mine. Sometime in days following the children's disappearance, Frankie Zoeller died. A jury might require a body, but Cal knew the boy was dead.

The real question was not whether Frankie had died, but how. For all these years the other five had protected that secret vigorously—three of them taking it to their graves. Had one or more of the other children murdered him? That would explain the secrecy. But could any of the five have possessed the kind of deep-seated depravity that would allow them to kill a schoolmate without showing any other signs of it since then? And unless all of the children were involved, what reason would the others have for protecting Frankie's killer?

That led him back to the current murders. If Frankie's death had been intentional, there were two obvious motives for someone to come after the people who knew the truth—fear of discovery on the part of one of the five or revenge by someone outside the group. The problem was that neither of those motives made any sense. In the first case, why would the killer risk drawing attention to a secret that showed no signs of ever being revealed? And in the second case, why wait more than thirty years to get revenge?

Cal sighed, touching the packet of pills in his pocket. If he could just get one break from this trip, it would be worth it—just one solid lead that he could use to start tying everything else together.

A sign on the right side of the road read *Greenwood Care Center and State Hospital—300 Yards*. Cal slowed and turned into the entrance. He followed a private driveway lined with tall hedges for nearly a quarter of a mile before stopping at a guard station. A man in a blue uniform leaned through the window of the booth.

"May I help you?"

Cal flashed his badge. "Twin Forks PD. I need to talk to someone about a patient."

"Can I see your driver's license?" Cal handed the guard his license and waited while he took down the information and spoke to someone on the phone.

"Okay," the guard said, handing him back his ID. "You can park in front of the first building. Just go inside and ask for Dr. Heinrick."

The traffic arm rose, and Cal pulled forward. As he rounded the hedges, he could see that there were actually two buildings. The one nearest looked like a posh resort, fronted by a long expanse of manicured lawn. Beautiful flower gardens surrounded the property, and off to one side swans glided across the surface of a small pond. The building beyond it looked more like a traditional boxy hospital—red brick interspersed with small windows.

He pulled into a parking spot marked *Guest* and entered the first building.

"Mr. Hunt?" A woman wearing a white lab coat over a blue designer dress met him at the door.

"Yes." He stepped through the door and was immediately struck by the decor of the small waiting room. Dark wood paneling lined the walls with several pieces of antique furniture artfully arranged around the plush carpeted floor. He was no interior decorator, but he estimated that he was looking at close to a hundred grand for the original artwork on the walls alone. The only sign that he was in a hospital at all was the intercom beside an electronically locked door.

"Quite a place you've got here."

"Thank you," she said. "We like it. I'm Dr. Heinrick. How may I help you today?"

"I need some information on a patient."

She led him to a wingback chair and took a seat across from him. "Would this be a patient here in the clinic or in the state hospital?"

"Is there a difference?"

"Oh yes," she said, waving one hand at the room around them. "This is our private clinic for our private pay guests. The hospital is a state institution."

"This would have been a guest," he said, amused by the word. It made the place sound like an elite weekend resort. On the other hand, he thought, looking around again, that might not be far off. It was certainly nicer than most of the hotels where he'd stayed.

"I'm sure you understand that the privacy of our guests is of the utmost importance." Her tone of voice was refined, but from the set of her jaw, he got the idea that getting information from this woman on a paying guest would be like trying to pull the teeth of a pit bull with his bare hands.

"This was some time ago," he said. "She's deceased now."

"I see." The doctor took out her iPad and began entering info into a database login. "That shouldn't be a problem. If you'll just give me her name and admission date, I'll see what information we have on the main computers."

"She would have arrived sometime in mid-1977," he said.

"Oh, I'm sorry," Dr. Heinrick said. "Our computer files only go back to 1982."

"What about paper records?"

She tapped her finger absently against the iPad screen. "Those would be in storage. It would take a few weeks to track them down if they haven't been destroyed."

"I don't have that kind of time," Cal said. For devices that were supposed to save time, computers seemed to do the opposite more often than not.

"You might try Francis Eccles."

"Who?"

"Francis Eccles. She was the admitting nurse from 1960 until 1983, I think."

"Does she live anywhere around here?" Cal asked, praying that she hadn't retired to Florida.

"I think she lives with her daughter," Dr. Heinrick said, standing. "I'll have someone get you the address."

CHAPTER 52

THE DIRECTIONS ON THE SHEET of paper led Cal to a white two-story house with a narrow screened-in front porch. As he mounted the sagging front steps, Cal could hear the sound of Tim McGraw crooning "Live Like You Were Dying." He rapped on the wooden screen door, and a few seconds later the music was turned down.

"Just a sec," a woman's voice carried from somewhere inside the house. The voice was soon followed by the woman herself. She was somewhere in her mid-fifties, Cal estimated. Her red face was beaded with perspiration, and a sweat-stained bandana held back curly shoulder-length salt-and-pepper hair.

"Sorry about that," she said, stepping out onto the porch. "I was just putting up some chowder."

Reaching the screen door, she took in Cal's uniform and wiped her hands on her apron. "You finally here about the Bentz's crazy dog?"

"I'm afraid not," Cal said, peering through the closed screen. "Cal Hunt. I'm with the Twin Forks Police Department. Would you be Abby Eccles?"

"Uh-huh." She eyed him suspiciously before opening the door a crack. "What can I do for you?"

"I was given your address by a woman at the Greenwood Clinic."

"The nut factory." Abby smirked. "Mom used to work up there. You should hear some of the stories she tells."

"That's actually why I'm here," Cal said. "I was hoping she might remember a particular patient."

"One of the whack jobs, huh?" She nodded. "Wouldn't be surprised. She saw 'em all. But it would have to have been a ways back. Mom's been retired for a while."

"This would have been in 1977," he said. "Would it be possible for me to speak with her?"

"She's out back in the garden." Abby stepped through the door and onto the porch, her light blue mules scuffing across the splintery wood. "Come on, I'll show you."

Cal followed her around the side of the house, past a towering lilac bush and rows of freshly planted petunias. They stopped in the backyard at the edge of a large vegetable garden.

A fragile-looking woman in an oversized straw hat was kneeling over what looked like tomato plants, hacking the ground around them with a clawed tool.

"Mom!" Abby shouted. The old woman continued to attack the weeds.

"She's a little hard of hearing." Abby shrugged. Moving a step closer, she shouted again. "Mom, someone here to see you!"

This time the woman looked up, her face wrinkling into a nearly toothless grin. "Oh, hello," she said, her lips smacking with each syllable. "I didn't hear you come out."

"Mom, this is Cal Hunt, with the police," Abby said, carefully enunciating each word.

Cal wondered if this was going to be another wild goose chase. The woman might not even remember her own name, much less a patient from so many years earlier. She approached Cal, brushing the dirt from her brown polyester pants.

"Twin Forks," she said studying his uniform. "That's down where they had those murders." If Francis Eccles's hearing was fading, her mind and eyesight seemed plenty sharp.

"Why, that's right," Abby said, her interest suddenly sparked. "Is that what this is all about? You think one of those fruitcakes from up to the cracker house got loose and started murdering people?" Her eyes glowed with anticipation.

"No. No relation to that case at all," Cal fudged. The last thing he needed was to start a rumor that might get back to the Godwins. "I'm just trying to track down a woman who would have entered the Greenwood facility sometime in the late seventies and stayed there until she passed away about five years later."

"You hear that, Mom?" Abby said, her interest fading quickly. "He says that—"

"I heard, I heard." Francis cut her off. "Why don't you just go back to your chowder?"

"Guess I will." Abby shot her mother a disgusted look before turning back to Cal. "After she gets done talking your ear off, why don't you come on up to the house, and I'll fix you something to eat. Sure would like to hear more about those murders."

"I just might do that," Cal said, knowing that he had absolutely no intention of doing any such thing.

"Seventy-seven, you say?" Francis took off her gloves and tucked them into her pockets where they formed round bulges against her bony hips.

"That's right," Cal said. "From Twin Forks."

"Doesn't sound familiar." Francis scratched at a long hair growing from the tip of her chin. "What did you say the name was?"

"Grace Godwin," he began. "She was—" But before he could say anything more, Francis burst into peals of high-pitched laughter.

"Grace Godwin, did you say? Howard Godwin's wife?"

"Yes," Cal wondered if the old woman was lucid, after all.

"No, no, no." She chortled. "Not in a hundred years would a Godwin have stayed at Greenwood."

"I don't understand."

She fixed him with a wry glare, wiping her lips with the back of her hand. "Don't know much about Greenwood, do you?"

"I was just there," he said, pointing in the general direction of the hospital. "What do I need to know?"

"Well that explains it, then. You're thinking of Greenwood the way it is now. All flowers and picture windows." She chuckled again, but this time the laughter turned into a coughing fit. She bent over for a moment, trying to catch her breath. Cal patted her on the back, hoping she wasn't going to pass out. At last she straightened up. "Don't get me laughing no more," she said.

"I'll try not to," Cal said. He could just see her dying out here in the garden before she could tell him whatever she knew. "But I'm confused. What do you mean I'm thinking of Greenwood the way it is now?"

Francis shook her head. "You couldn't know, of course. Not unless you were from around here. But up until seventy-five, right about the time I retired, Greenwood was a sanitarium for the mentally ill indigent. Folks with nowhere to go were sent there to get them out of sight. The government paid so much per day, and we'd get some donations from wealthy families like the Godwins.

"Then the state decided to put their hospital up there and the owners got a boatload of money and a contract to run the state facility. They rebuilt the old Greenwood like you see it now and put the new hospital back behind it. Then they sent all the indigent to the state hospital and turned the old place into a center for the rich."

"But there must have been some other location. Some private rooms. Why would a man like Howard Godwin send his wife to a mental hospital for the indigent?"

"No. No, I would have heard about that. I was the admitting nurse. I checked 'em all in when they came through the doors. Took their vitals, saw that they were deloused, set up their menus. No Godwin ever came through those doors."

"You're positive?" Cal asked. "There couldn't have been some kind of separate arrangement?"

Francis shook her head. "If you'd have seen the place back then, Mr. Hunt, you wouldn't even ask. I used to shower for forty-five minutes every night when I came home. The owners of that place were only interested in one thing—making a profit. They treated the patients like animals. We did the best we could—tried to make their lives a little easier—but it was a living nightmare. A woman like Grace Godwin wouldn't have lasted ten minutes in there."

CHAPTER 53

DARK THUNDERHEADS RACED ACROSS THE night sky, hurled by the stiff wind that had picked up over the last hour. Two Bears switched on his headlights and a moment later, as the clouds opened up, reached for the windshield wiper control as well. On the floor of the passenger side, Pepper curled into a ball and whined.

"What're you crying about? It's just a little rain," Two Bears said. But he felt uneasy too. Had ever since he'd returned to Twin Forks.

He thought that by taking Cal's advice, heading north to Boulder, he might shake off the gloom. But if anything, it had only gotten worse. All around him, cars raced past on the slick freeway. He edged as far to the right as he could without driving on the shoulder and let them go by. Where were they all in such a hurry to go that they were willing to risk their lives to get there a few minutes earlier?

"Had to come back, you know," he said as much to himself as to Pepper. "We got unfinished business here. Can't run away from it."

Pepper whined again but reached up to lick his hand.

A green highway sign appeared, glimmering in the beams of his headlights: *Boulder Community Hospital—Next Exit.* Two Bears turned on his blinker and began to brake.

CHAPTER 54

LYING IN HIS DARK HOSPITAL room, Ben Meyers had never felt more alone. He'd asked LuAnn to turn off the television set—specially mounted on the ceiling so that he could see it with his head clamped in place—before she went home to put the kids to bed. He couldn't concentrate on any of the shows. They all seemed like meaningless jumbles of picture and sound.

At least they'd kept his mind occupied. Now, with only the patterns of holes in the acoustic tile ceiling to look at as he listened to raindrops splatter against the window, his thoughts kept creeping back to the voice he'd heard on the side of the mountain.

He'd told the cop that the fall was an accident. He could blame the lie on Theresa and her pointed threats, but he'd already convinced himself that it *was* an accident before she ever showed up. It was funny how good you could get at deceiving yourself after thirty years of practice. Edit this, add that, and before you knew it, the things that were bothering you magically disappeared.

Only sometimes they came back—sometimes they came back with a vengeance.

Just look at Theresa. She'd been the master of self-deception. So good that she actually believed Frankie Zoeller had just wandered away sometime during that purgatory of eternal nights they'd spent lost in the mine. The same way she'd believed she was in love with her ice-water enema of a husband. The way she believed her life had turned out exactly how she'd planned it.

And look what it had gotten her. Yeah, baby. When the past catches up with you, it's doing sixty miles an hour, headlights flashing, radio blaring, and don't even bother your pretty little head about the brakes.

Outside the window, a bolt of lightning ripped through the night sky. Not that he could see it; he saw only the blue flash that briefly lit up his room like one of those strobes they used to have at all the dance clubs. His nose itched, but other than puffing out his lower lip and blowing stale breath up his nostrils, there wasn't much he could do about it.

He'd decided that when LuAnn came back later tonight, he was going to tell her everything. He'd have her call that cop too. Whatever the cost, it was time to stop the lies. The guilt would still be there, hanging around his neck like the proverbial millstone, but at least the lies would be over.

That was the fatal mistake they'd all made—assuming that guilt would eventually disappear if you just buried it deep enough. But all that really did was let it fester until it infected your body, your mind, and eventually your soul. Had the guilt left any of them unscathed? He'd been back home often enough, listened to the grapevine enough, to know the others' lives had all been just as screwed up as his.

The lightning flashed again, its forked tongue reflecting off the television screen. From the sound of it, the rain had changed to hail. Tiny pellets crackled against the outside of the glass like BBs.

He'd given up any hope of surviving Frankie's vengeful spirit or fate or the hand of God—whatever it was that had come to claim them all. It had missed him once, but he didn't expect that to happen again.

His fear now was that he would die without getting everything off his chest. Methodists don't have confessionals like the Catholics, though sometimes he wished they did. It would be easier to just go into a little closet and let it all out—do a hundred Hail Marys or whatever.

Of course there was repentance. But how could God forgive him for what he'd done? He couldn't give Frankie back his life. The best he could do was let the boy's mother and everyone else know what had really happened. Then if his life was taken in exchange for Frankie's, at least he could die knowing he'd done his best. He just hoped that LuAnn and the kids would try to understand.

To his left, he heard the sound of his door swinging open, and light from the hallway spilled across his bed. It was too soon for LuAnn to be back yet. It must be the nurse on duty. He thought her name was Suzie, Stephanie—something like that.

"Could you turn the lights on for me?" he asked. "It got dark all of a sudden."

There was no answer, no sound of footsteps coming into his room.

"Hello? Who's there? I'd get up to meet you, but I'm kind of tied up at the moment," he joked.

Maybe it had been someone looking for another room. That happened a lot. They'd swing the door partway open, realize that the person in the bed wasn't who they'd been looking for, and step back into the hall without saying anything.

He fumbled around the blankets, feeling for the call button. It really had turned dark quickly. He'd have the nurse, Stephanie—he was sure it was Stephanie—turn on the lights and the TV again too. Just until LuAnn got back.

As his fingers searched for the button—how far could it have gotten?—a shadow crossed the light from the doorway, and a quick chill ran across his body.

"Is that you, Stephanie?"

Still no answer, but there was definitely someone in his room. He heard the soft squeak-squeak of footsteps on the tile floor.

"Who's there?" He tried to turn toward the door, but the metal bars screwed into his skull held him fast. With the bandages on his face, his peripheral vision extended only a few inches to either side of his head.

Suddenly the door swung all the way shut, plunging the room into darkness. A child's soft laughter filled the air.

"Please, God, no," he whispered. "Not now. Not yet." His hand touched the hard plastic of the call box—somehow it had gotten turned around so that the button was up by his wrist instead of at his fingertips.

Palm damp with perspiration, he attempted to turn it around, but the smooth plastic surface kept slipping. A cold hand closed around his wrist, and the box was pulled effortlessly from his numb fingers.

"You won't need that." The voice that whispered softly in his ear came from less than a foot away.

"Help!" he screamed. "Nurse! Anybody, I—"

The hand left his wrist and clamped over his mouth, cutting off his screams.

"All the king's horses and all the king's men." It was the singsong voice from the mountain. "Couldn't put Benny together again."

Heart pounding, he tried to pull away from the hand pressing his lips against his teeth, but he had no leverage, nothing to push with. Thumb and forefinger pressed the sides of his nostrils together, cutting off his air.

He tried to scream again but could manage only a faint mew. Next to him, he could hear the monitor measuring his heart rate beeping out its alarm. But no one was coming to check on him. His chest burned, and the ceiling began to swim in front of his eyes.

CHAPTER 55

TWO BEARS LEANED THROUGH THE door of the empty waiting room looking for a nurse, but the desk was deserted.

"Anyone here?" he called out, taking a tentative step into the hallway. There was no answer, only a repetitive beeping coming from behind the nurses' station. The phone began to ring. Surely someone would show up to answer it. But after five rings, no one had arrived, and whoever was calling gave up.

Something was wrong. He could feel it in his bones. He took another couple of steps into the hallway, glancing past the rows of doors that extended out in both directions. He hadn't been to many hospitals, but he knew there had to be someone around—someone to keep an eye on things, monitor the patients.

A shiver ran up his arms, and he experienced a dread he had felt in only one other place. *Get out*, a voice in his head urged. *Get out while you still can.*

Instead, in what was probably the most insane action he'd ever made in his life, he stepped out into the hallway. *Room 913*, the nurse downstairs had said. That would be to his left. He began to walk past the other doors, 903, 904, 905. Although most of the doors were open at least a few inches, he couldn't hear any sounds coming from the rooms. No conversation, no television, not a cough or a moan. It was as if he was the only living thing on the floor.

The spit in his mouth dried up, and his tongue seem to swell to twice its normal size. Rubbing his fingers across sandpaper lips, he could feel his breath coming in short gasps. 909, 910, 911. There it was, 913. The door was closed, no light showing in the crack between door and tile.

Get out now. Run! The voice in his head was screaming—yammering with fear. He could actually see his heart beating through the thin cotton of his shirt. With trembling fingers he reached out to the knob and turned.

CHAPTER 56

GOD FORGIVE ME. GOD FORGIVE me, please, Ben repeated over and over in his head. The ceiling above him had turned crimson in his fading eyesight. He could feel his heart racing, trying to supply his body with oxygen that didn't exist. His lungs hitched. He couldn't last much longer.

Sudden light flooded across his eyes. The hand pressing against his mouth and nose pulled back, and for a moment he was too startled to breathe. Then his body took over, sucking air into his starved lungs.

As if from far away he heard a voice snarl, "Get out, old man. This is none of your business."

He didn't understand the reply. It seemed to be in another language. But instantly there was a hiss of pain, and something crashed into the side of his bed.

Light flashed, only this time it came from inside the room. Not the purple-white glow of lightning but a sickish green that made him think of radiation poisoning. Another cry of pain came, but this time from farther away—from whoever had just come into the room.

Ben gulped air, trying to make some kind of sound, but his vocal cords refused to work. His hand searched for the cord of the call button.

He heard footsteps and the sound of scuffling. A thud, ripping cloth, something slammed against the wall. The door banged closed, swung open, closed again, then exploded as though it had been ripped completely from its hinges.

There was a grunt—he couldn't tell who the sounds were coming from anymore—and more of the words spoken in the language he didn't understand. They sounded like some kind of chant.

The hair on his arms and head rose straight out as if the room had filled with static electricity. The words seemed to be creating their own energy. They echoed off the walls. He didn't comprehend their meaning, but he could feel their power coursing through his veins. Finally his fingers found the cord, and he began pulling the plastic control box back toward him.

There was a blood-curdling howl, and again something crashed against the wall. Another flash of green light—this one ten times brighter than before, a hundred, a thousand—stunned his eyes.

A body hurtled through the air, and he caught a brief glimpse of an old man's face, eyes glazed with shock. It crashed against the window, and he heard the sound of shattering glass.

It took Ben a second to realize he was holding the call box. He clamped the button down between numb fingers. He could hear voices shouting—the sound of running feet out in the hallway. Was that *thing* still in the room with him? He didn't think so. A nurse leaned over his bed.

"What happened—" she began, reaching for his monitor before noticing what was on the other side of the bed.

Her hand went to her mouth, and she started screaming.

CHAPTER 57

"I'LL GIVE YOU THREE MINUTES. But I'm warning you, Mr. Clapton has lost a lot of blood. If his vital signs begin to fluctuate at all, you're out of there."

"I understand." Cal took a deep breath. This was Kat all over again. He'd only known Two Bears for a couple of days, but he already felt like family—the only family Cal had left. He'd spent most of the night sitting in the waiting room as Two Bears was operated on. Seeing him would be worse.

Knowing what was waiting on the other side of the door, he almost couldn't force himself to go in. Only the knowledge that Two Bears needed him—that the old man had been asking for him—gave him the strength to open the door.

The cold sterility of the hospital room, the clear tubes and white bandages, nearly masked the damage that had been done to the man lying in the middle of the bed. Sixty seconds in Ben Meyers's hospital room had accomplished what more than eighty years of hard living had been unable to. Two Bears looked ancient—broken.

Trying not to look at the stump where the old Indian's left arm had been, Cal came around to the other side of the bed and took the cool, gray hand in his own. The bandaged head stirred and turned toward him. Cal knew that beneath the bandages, the old man's face was a mass of broken bones and torn flesh. The intelligent brown eyes would never see again.

"Cal?" The hoarse whisper was almost impossible to make out. Cal leaned closer.

"It's me."

The old man's thin chest rose and fell slowly beneath the sheet. Each raspy breath seemed to be pulled in with great effort as though it might be the last.

"Hurt."

"I know." Cal gave the old man's hand a gentle squeeze. "But you're going to be all right."

Two Bears took several more shaky breaths before regaining the energy to speak again. "Pepper?"

"She's okay," Cal said. "I'll take care of her for you until you come and get her yourself."

The old man's lips wrinkled into something that might have been a smile. Then his hand tightened around Cal's fingers, and the smile disappeared.

"Stop . . . it," he breathed.

"I will," Cal said, tears forming in the corners of his eyes. "I'm not going to let anyone else get hurt."

Two Bears lay back onto the pillow. His breathing eased, and for a moment Cal thought he'd gone to sleep. Then his head jerked forward as though he were trying to sit up. He gasped in pain, and Cal pushed him gently back onto the pillows. One of the monitors began going off, and the door opened.

"You have to leave now," the doctor said, coming into the room.

"I know." Cal tried to pull his hand away, but Two Bears would not release him. The old man's lips were moving as though he were trying to speak. Cal placed his ear to the old man's lips.

"Talisman."

Talisman? What was he talking about? Then Cal remembered the broken strand of rawhide leather they had found on the floor of Ben's room. What looked like bears claws hung from the end of it, surrounding a pounded silver and turquoise medallion. He fished the cord from his pocket and pressed it into the old Indian's hand.

"Here. It's right here."

With the last of his strength, Two Bears pushed the amulet back into Cal's hand.

"You . . . take," he whispered.

* * *

Outside the room, Cal leaned against the wall, trying to catch his breath. The smells of the hospital were cloying in his nostrils. Wiping the cold sweat from his forehead, he stood and walked back down the hallway to meet the two Boulder police officers who were waiting for him.

"Pretty bad, huh?" the younger of the two asked, earning a dirty look from his partner. Cal didn't bother to respond.

"Have you been able to talk with Meyers?" the older man asked.

"No. He's still pretty heavily sedated. You can talk to the nurse," he said, anticipating their next question, "but she's not much help. All she can remember is hearing movement behind her and then somebody clocked her on the back of the head."

"What about the other staff?"

"All on duty," Cal said.

"Guy must've had the devil's own luck to get in and out without being spotted," the younger cop said. *Luck*, Cal thought. Maybe it was luck, but he had come to believe it was something else, something darker.

"Any idea who the attacker might be?"

"Sure," Cal said, wanting only to get out of the building and back to Twin Forks. "Just look for a kid between four and five feet tall with the strength to rip a door off its hinges and throw a grown man across a room hard enough to break most of the bones in his body."

CHAPTER 58

CLARA BELL WAS JUST UNLOCKING the front doors of the library, opening up for the morning, when Cal pulled up next to the curb. Spotting him, she stepped quickly into the building, pulling the glass door closed behind her. Taking the stairs in three quick strides, Cal tugged at the door. It was locked.

"Clara, open up." Cal rattled the door in its frame. He pressed his hands to the tinted glass, trying to peer into the dark interior.

"I know you're in there," he shouted. There was no sign of movement inside.

He unsnapped the expandable baton from his belt and held it up in front of the window. "I'm counting to ten and then I'm going to break this glass, Clara."

"One, two . . ." he began to count, wondering whether he would actually have to use his baton. "Eight, nine . . . ten." He reached his arm back, shielding his face with his other hand.

"Stop!" Clara bawled, peering around the corner of the building. While he was counting she had sneaked out the back entrance. "Don't break the door. We don't have the budget to get it replaced."

"Then open it so I don't have to." Cal tucked his baton back in his belt as Clara fiddled with her keys.

"Would you really have broken it?" she asked, pulling the door open.

"Do I look like I'm in a joking mood?" he asked. Clara took one glance at his eyes and turned away.

"You know why I'm here, or you wouldn't be trying to hide from me," he said once they were inside.

Clara sorted through a stack of books on the counter without looking up.

"Why have you been lying to me?" he asked, putting a beefy hand on top of the books.

"I didn't lie." She sounded like a truculent child caught stealing cookies.

"You might as well have," he said, staring down at her. "You knew that I was looking for anyone who might have witnessed what happened at the Seven Stars that day, and you didn't even bother to tell me that your own daughter was right there."

"You don't understand." Her voice was so soft he almost couldn't hear it.

"Then make me understand. Help me out here, Clara. I'm trying to catch a murderer." He was shouting, but he couldn't help it. Because he didn't have all the facts, people's lives had been lost. And here was someone he considered a friend holding back information he needed.

"That's just it." She rubbed fiercely at her eyes with one hand. "I was trying to protect her. Can't you get that through your thick skull? You think I didn't want to tell you? But people were getting killed, and I didn't want her to be next.

"It was bad enough back when it happened. Paul Andreason tried to convince everyone that it was Sheila's fault. Can you imagine? A seventeen-year-old girl. It nearly killed her to hear what people were saying. My dear husband, God rest his soul, kept her name out of the papers. But people talked—they always do.

"We finally had to send her away to live with her aunt in Sacramento. Sent her away from home when she'd done nothing wrong. And she never came back." Clara picked up a book and slammed it down on the counter. It was the most uncharacteristic thing Cal could imagine.

"I'm sorry," he said. "I didn't know."

"Then this all started," she pulled a handkerchief from her pocket, wiping the tears from her wrinkled cheeks. "I didn't want her to get hurt all over again. I didn't want her to go through any more pain. And most of all, I didn't want to see her killed."

"You should have told me," Cal said, pulling out a chair and sitting down.

"I know, I know. It's no excuse." Clara collapsed into her chair. "I almost did. That night when I called. But then your voice mail picked up and I got scared."

"I need to talk to her," Cal laid his hand on the trembling shoulder of the old librarian. "Too many people have been hurt. This has to end."

"I'll have her call you," she said. "Right away."

"Thank you," he said. "And for what it's worth, I'll do my best to see that she doesn't get hurt again."

"I know you will," Clara said, trying to smile. "I know you will, dear."

CHAPTER 59

CAL WAS NEARLY BACK TO the car when his cell phone rang.

"Hello."

"Cal. Thank goodness I got you." It was Lindy, and she sounded frantic. "He's screaming like a crazy man. Said if I didn't get you on the line—"

"Stop," Cal commanded the young dispatcher. He'd never heard her so rattled. "Get hold of yourself."

Cal could hear Lindy take a deep breath. "I'm sorry," she said, sounding at least marginally better. "It's just that he said if I couldn't reach you, he'd do something drastic."

"*Who* said he'd do something drastic?" Cal felt a jolt cross his chest, his body involuntarily tightening as if preparing to take a blow.

"Spencer Godwin."

A hollow crash exploded in Cal's ears, and he had no idea whether it had originated from the darkening clouds outside or within his own head.

"Patch him through." He swung open the cruiser door and dropped behind the wheel.

There was a click, and Spencer's panicked voice shouted into the phone. "She's gone! She's gone!"

"Who's gone?" Cal forced himself to ask from between gritted teeth, although he already knew the answer. His entire body had gone ice cold as he twisted the key in the ignition and gunned the Crown Vic's big engine, leaving a patch of black rubber in the library parking lot.

"Who do you think?" Spencer screamed, his words drilling into Cal's brain like sharpened nails. "The killer's got my sister!"

Trusting his lights and siren to clear traffic, Cal increased his pressure on the gas pedal. The needle inched steadily farther to the right, but a voice in his head echoed darkly, *Too late, too late, you're too late.* He tried to shut it out. "Take it easy," he said, although his own heart was pounding as he raced recklessly past slower cars. "Tell me everything that's happened."

"Take it easy? How am I supposed to take it easy?"

Cal entered Highway 83 at a slide, narrowly avoiding an eighteen-wheeler loaded with gravel. *Keep it under control,* he told himself, as the truck driver hit his brakes and blared his horn. But it wasn't that easy. A hundred images raced through his mind. The purple handprints on Mandy's neck. The blood painted on Ezra's truck, and perhaps worst of all, the sight of Kat lying comatose in a hospital bed.

"I can't help her if you don't calm down," Cal said, as much to himself as to Spencer. Now that he was on open road heading toward the canyon, he let the speedometer slip up to the hundred mph mark. "How long has she been gone?"

"Richard called . . . this morning to say . . . she was missing." Spencer was sobbing, and Cal had trouble making out his words. "I thought she'd gone off for a walk or something, but we've looked everywhere."

"When was the last time you saw her?" Cal was forced to slow down beside a pair of side-by-side big rigs. He hit his horn in frustration, and the truck on the right slowed down to let the one on the left over.

"I dunno. About ten last night I guess. We had dinner together."

"Any chance she might have taken one of the cars?" As the truck in front of him began to move over, Cal pulled around it to the left, tires shooting gravel up into the undercarriage of the cruiser as he edged onto the median.

"She doesn't drive." Spencer sounded terrified. "I've got to find her."

"Stay there." The last thing Olivia needed was her brother going off racing through the city streets half-crazed with fear. Cal knuckled his forehead, trying to concentrate. Why hadn't he placed someone outside the gate? He should have demanded that the Godwins accept his security. Stupid, stupid, stupid.

"Did anyone hear anything unusual last night or this morning?" Cal's speed was back up to a hundred again, the patrol car's engine roaring in his ears as he raced up the winding canyon road. He was less than five minutes from the Godwins' house.

He could hear Spencer's muffled voice, as though he was holding the phone against his chest, and then he was back on the line. "Richard thinks he heard the dogs barking around six this morning."

"All right," Cal said. "I can have her description out statewide in ten minutes. Stay at the house until I get there."

"I've got to find her." Behind Spencer's voice, Cal thought he heard a door slam.

"Mr. Godwin, stay where you are!" He passed a Volkswagen Beetle like it was standing still.

"I have to save my sister. I've got to save her from that monster."

"Spencer!" Cal shouted. But the line was dead.

CHAPTER 60

HE COULDN'T HAVE MISSED HIM by any more than five minutes, tops. But when Cal screeched to a halt at the top of the Godwin's driveway and saw the butler standing on the front porch, he knew Spencer was gone.

"I told him to stay put." Cal was already shouting as he climbed from his car. His back and neck screamed as he stood and he thought he felt a trickle of blood run down his collar. One of the stitches must have pulled loose.

"He went to look for his sister. I couldn't stop him." Richard's tone was implacable, but to Cal, who had spent more than twenty years observing people, it was obvious that the butler was highly agitated. He flitted everywhere at once, while his hands folded and unfolded themselves like small creatures looking for a place to hide.

"Look where?" Cal climbed the stairs, standing chest to face with the smaller man.

"I'm sure I don't know." Richard looked up into Cal's eyes briefly before dropping his gaze. "He didn't tell me anything."

"Of course not," Cal said, his head pounding. "Tell me everything."

* * *

Ten minutes later, as Cal finished questioning the butler, Greg, Andy, and Sheldon showed up. "Greg, you and Sheldon take the perimeter. Look for any signs of forcible entry and check for prints. Andy, you stay down by the front gate. The media's going to be here any minute, and I don't want anyone trying to climb the wall."

As Cal watched the officers spread out, his cell phone rang.

"Yeah."

"Chief, Detective Lyon here. I've got some information on the Theresa Obrey case that I thought you might be interested in."

"Look, this isn't such a good time," Cal said. Theresa was dead, and right now his thoughts were focused on keeping Olivia Godwin from joining her. "We've got a situation here."

"Another murder?"

Cal grimaced, kneeling to examine a scratch on the front door lock. "Not if I can help it."

"No problem," Detective Lyon said. "I just thought you might like to know that someone tampered with the Obrey woman's brakes. Our techs found indications that the lines had been loosened and a pretty good-size puddle of brake fluid on the garage floor."

"The garage floor?" Cal stood. Brake fluid on the garage floor. Why did that ring a bell?

"They found traces of it on the soles of her shoes as well—like she'd stepped in the puddle before getting into the car."

"Sure, that would make sense," Cal muttered, trying to find the memory that floated tantalizingly close to the surface of his mind. On the other end of the line, he could hear another phone start to ring.

"Call me later," the detective said. "I'll let you go."

"Okay, thanks." Cal hung up the phone. Just then his radio crackled. "Cal, I think we might have found something," Greg said, and thoughts of brake fluid disappeared from Cal's head.

Cal found his two officers on the far side of the house. Greg was removing a small piece of blue fabric from the corner of a torn screen. Sheldon was examining a pair of boot prints on the ground outside the window.

Cal examined the edge of the tear. It was smooth. Someone had sliced through the window screen with a sharp knife. "What's this open into?" he asked, peering through the window.

"That would be the private dining room," said Richard, who had followed him around the house. "It's used primarily by the family."

"This is where they had dinner last night?" Cal pushed on the window, careful to avoid damaging any possible fingerprints. It slid smoothly open.

"That is correct."

"You always leave the windows unlocked?"

"No, sir." Richard tugged at his earlobe, thinking. "I believe they did have the windows open last night, though. There was a cool breeze blowing, and Olivia enjoys the smell of the roses."

"Where is her bedroom?" Cal asked, noticing the dirty footsteps leading across the dining room carpet.

"That would be upstairs, but I hardly think—"

"Let's take a look around inside," Cal said, shouldering past him.

"I don't believe that Mr. Godwin would approve of you traipsing through the private bedrooms without anyone here." The butler stepped in front of Cal, placing a hand on his chest as though he meant to hold the chief back.

"If you don't get out of my way right now," Cal growled, "you're going to be pulling rosebush thorns from your sorry hide for the next week."

Richard quickly stepped aside before following Cal into the house.

CHAPTER 61

OLIVIA'S ROOM LOOKED UNDISTURBED AS far as Cal could see. The bed was unmade and a white robe lay across its corner, but there were no signs of a struggle.

He glanced into a closet the size of his bedroom at home. "Any idea what she might have been wearing when she was abducted?"

"No, sir." Since their run-in by the rose bushes, Richard had proven far more subdued.

Cal stopped at one of the many sculptures that were placed throughout the room. "These are all her work?" he asked.

"Yes. She is quite talented."

That was an understatement. The work could have been in a gallery. Cal picked up a framed photograph. It showed Olivia standing next to the fish pond.

"I'll need to make copies of this to get out to other agencies."

As the two men left the room and walked down the hallway toward the stairs, Cal heard the sound of a television coming from behind one of the doors.

"Who's in there?" he asked, reaching for the knob.

"No, you mustn't—" Richard lunged forward, trying to grab Cal's hand, but he was too late.

The door swung open to reveal a white-haired man in a checked bathrobe. He was sitting in a high-backed chair, eating pretzels from a large blue bowl in his lap. On the big-screen television a crowd was cheering as a game show host called down the next contestant. When he saw Cal, his wizened face broke into a wide grin.

"Come to lock me up, have ya?" he called out, jubilantly popping another pretzel into his mouth. "Well, you'll never take me alive, Copper."

Howard Godwin—Cal recognized him from his portrait—reached into the pockets of his robe, and Cal dropped his hand to the butt of his pistol.

He'd unsnapped the holster and was drawing his pistol when he realized the old man had nothing in his closed fists. Holding out two gnarled pointer fingers, thumbs extended upward as if holding out pistols, Godwin began to shout, "Pow, pow, pow!" spraying pretzel crumbs from his mouth.

CHAPTER 62

"MR. GODWIN, I NEED TO ask you a few questions." Cal knelt next to the old man's chair. Howard Godwin had pulled his pale white legs up to his chest; his robe was ratty and covered with stains.

Godwin stared past Cal at a woman on television who was trying to guess the price of a toaster oven, a set of sterling silver, and an Alaskan cruise. "Door number two," Howard hooted and stuck a finger up his nose.

Cal turned to Richard, who looked away, embarrassed.

"Your daughter is missing," Cal tried again.

The old man turned toward Cal, squinting his eyes as if considering the question carefully. "Daughter, water, potter," he replied. He pulled his finger from his nose, examined its tip, and nodded at Cal with a sly wink. "Welcome back, Kotter."

"How long has he been like this?" Cal asked, a sick ache in the pit of his stomach.

"Nearly two years," Richard said. "He has his good days. But lately those have come farther and farther apart."

Cal stood, flexing his knees. Howard offered him a pretzel. Cal turned away, rubbing his forehead. "Why didn't anyone tell me?"

"It's not exactly the kind of thing you advertise, Chief Hunt. Howard Godwin has done a great deal for this community. He has been a pillar. There are many people who would love nothing more than to see that pillar crumble. They would kick him now that he's down—mock him. His children won't let that happen, and neither will I." The butler folded his narrow arms across his chest, a fierce loyalty in his eyes.

"Did it ever occur to you that by hiding information, you might have put Olivia in danger?" Cal's head was pounding. Every minute he wasted here was a minute closer to Olivia being dead. And yet, he didn't know where to go—what to do.

"I certainly don't think that Mr. Godwin's condition is any—"

Cal held a beefy palm up in front of the butler's face, cutting him off. "What about his wife?"

"Grace?" Richard asked, looking confused. But wasn't there something else hidden behind that look? Something . . . knowing?

"What happened to her?"

"She had a mental breakdown. Her husband sent her to Greenwood Mental Hospital for the best care money could—"

"The truth," Cal interrupted again. Listening to Richard speak was like listening to a child repeat the pledge of allegiance—rote memorization. "She never went to Greenwood, did she?"

"I don't know what you're talking about," Richard said.

Cal knew he was lying. It wasn't so much one particular sign—the way his fingers kept going to his left ear or his wide-eyed sincerity—but rather the internal lie detector that cops acquire over a period of time.

"I think you do, Richard." He walked across the room and took the butler by the arm. "I think it's time to tell the truth."

"I . . . I don't." Richard shook his head. "It's none of my business."

"You listen to me," Cal shouted, shaking the butler like a puppet on a string. "Olivia is in danger, and if you don't tell me what's going on now, I swear I'll beat it out of you."

Greg, hearing Cal's shouts, came down the hallway, started to enter the room, and froze. Cal closed both hands around Richard's arms, the veins in his neck bulging as he lifted the butler so that they were eye to eye. Richard's face had gone stone white; his eyes gleamed wet and wide. "Tell me the truth! What does this have to do with the mine?"

Behind them, Howard Godwin began to mutter again. "Mine, lyin', cryin'."

Cal whirled around, dropping the butler to the floor. "That's right, Mr. Godwin. Lying, crying."

He knelt in front of the old man. "What happened in the mine, Mr. Godwin? Why are they crying?"

"Crying, dying." The old man's lips began to tremble as his voice rose. "Lying, crying, trying, dying."

"Who?" Cal asked. "*Who is dying?*"

"Dying, dying, dying!" Howard Godwin began to scream. "All dying! All crying! All!" His voice cracked, spittle flying from his lips.

"Get out!" Richard shouted, wrapping his arms protectively around the old man. "Get out of here. You've upset him."

"All dead!" Howard screamed, pulling at his hair. "All dead!" he repeated before bursting into spasms of hysterical laughter.

CHAPTER 63

CAL WAS ON THE RADIO when his phone rang again. He didn't recognize the area code on the caller ID.

"Hello?" he said.

"Is this Chief Hunt?" The woman's voice sounded quiet and unsure.

"Who's this?" he asked impatiently.

"Sheila. Sheila Green." The name didn't mean anything to him. "I used to be Sheila Bell. Clara's daughter."

"Oh, right," he said, his voice softening.

"My mother said you wanted to talk to me about . . . about the mine." Sheila sounded as though it had taken some convincing. But unless she had some vital piece of information, now wasn't the time to conduct an interview.

"Thanks for getting back to me, but Olivia Godwin's gone missing and unless—"

Sheila gasped. "Little Olivia," she gasped. "What can I do to help?"

Sheldon's voice crackled over the radio. "We got more than twenty cars down here, Cal. I may need some backup."

Cal picked up the mic, shifting his cell phone to his shoulder. "I'll be right down, Sheldon."

He put the phone back to his ear. "I'm sorry to be abrupt, but unless you have any idea who might want to hurt Olivia . . ."

"I can't imagine," she said. "This is all so horrible. Poor Mrs. Zoeller."

"Mrs. Zoeller?" he asked. For some reason Esther's name reminded Cal of Detective Lyon's comments about the Obrey woman's death. What did Esther have to do with Theresa Obrey?

"Yes. She was so upset." Sheila sounded as though she might start crying. "Losing her only child like that. I think it nearly killed her. This must be bringing it all back again."

Cal tried to concentrate. An image was floating just outside his reach. "I didn't get the impression she was too upset about what's been going on here. She blames the others for her son's death."

"Can you fault her?" Sheila said. "It was surely the hand of the Lord that delivered her nephew into her care or she might very well have killed herself."

"Nephew?" The word hit Cal like a fist, driving the air from his lungs.

"Larry," Sheila said. "Her sister's boy. He came to live with Esther only a few months after Frankie died, when his mother passed."

"I never heard anything about a nephew," Cal said, a feeling of dread growing inside him. "Where does he live now?"

"Still with her, I suppose," Sheila said. "He was just a baby at the time, so he'd be in his mid-thirties now. But he's a little slow."

"In his thirties?"

Suddenly pieces were falling into place, and a cramp of fear ran through Cal's belly. Esther's freshly mowed lawn, the well-weeded flower beds. Hadn't he wondered at the time who was caring for her yard? The tools in the garage, the Cocoa Puffs he'd assumed were hers and . . . the puddle of oil. He had tracked oil from the garage onto her kitchen floor, but Esther didn't drive.

The look of anger she'd given him when she noticed the oil . . . might it have been fear, even guilt? When he told her about Ezra's and Mandy's murders, what had she said? Something like, "Those other kids are just as guilty."

"You've been a great help," he said. "But I have to go now."

CHAPTER 64

CAL HAD MADE MISTAKES BEFORE in the line of duty. If you said you hadn't, you were either a liar, a fool, or—in most cases—both. But this might have been the worst. How could he have overlooked something this obvious? He had taken at face value that Esther Zoeller lived alone. He hadn't thought to question her neighbors or even Clara, for that matter. She would have known that Esther had a nephew. But he'd never bothered to ask.

He blew through the intersection of Canyon and Pine Street without even slowing down. Greg's cruiser followed close behind.

As they screamed through the residential streets that led to the Zoeller house, he tried to fight off the gnawing certainty that they were too late—that Olivia was already dead. He'd been too late to do anything for Mandy, Ezra, and Theresa, and it was only pure luck and the intervention of Two Bears that had spared Ben's life. He couldn't fail Kat too—*Olivia*, he corrected himself. He couldn't make this personal. And yet hadn't he already?

The worst part of it was that Esther's bitterness had been staring him in the face the whole time. She was an angry old woman who'd lost the thing she loved most in the world. Had her hate infected the nephew she'd raised since he was a baby? You might as well ask whether the families living around Chernobyl had been affected by the radiation when the reactor melted down.

How long had she plotted her revenge? he wondered. Long enough to time the final act to the very anniversary of the last day she'd seen her son alive. Cal had always assumed there was only one perpetrator. Bonnie and Clyde teams were rare because serial killers tended to be loners. But knowing what he knew now, Cal could see how the clues all made sense.

Larry had probably turned off the power on Mandy's trailer. He'd been the one to punch her in the gut, and Esther would have finished off the job. Esther would have dressed Mandy and laid her body out on the bed. It must have given her great satisfaction to see the woman she viewed as her son's murderer lying dead at her hand.

Esther was a small woman, which matched most of the physical evidence left behind at the crime scenes. But she never would have been capable of incapacitating Two Bears or climbing the side of the mountain where Ben had been pushed. They'd worked hard to make it look like Frankie was exacting his revenge.

Maybe she even thought that her son's ghost was urging her on. It wouldn't be the first time a schizophrenic blamed a dead loved one for her actions. She'd even told Cal that Frankie visited her. But he'd overlooked that as well—written it off as an old woman's dreams.

All he could do now was hope that they still had Olivia at the house.

As they neared the house, both Cal and Greg cut their lights and sirens. There was a small chance they'd take Esther and Larry by surprise, but he wanted any edge he could get. They exited their patrol cars, and Cal waved Greg around to the back.

"What about a warrant?" Greg whispered.

Cal shook him off. "No time." Maybe no time at all.

He approached the front door, being careful not to cross in front of the big picture window. They would enter both front and back doors at the same time.

Cal gently tried the knob on the front door. It was locked, but the door was old. He was confident he could break it with one hard kick. The radio on his belt clicked, and Greg's voice came softly over the speaker. "Back door's unlocked."

"Okay," Cal radioed back, "on my count." In a situation like this where the victim was in danger of imminent physical harm, they would enter first and announce themselves later. They didn't want to give the killers any chance to prepare.

"Three, two." Cal stepped back from door and raised his right foot. "One!" His leg shot forward like a piston, and the thin wood collapsed beneath the force of his kick. The door flew open, bounced off the wall, and rebounded toward him. He caught it and, using the door as a shield, stepped into the entryway, gun drawn.

"Police!" he shouted. From the back of the house, he heard Greg's voice echoing the same warning. The hall was empty. Cal edged up to the doorway leading into the living room, remembering from his last visit that the curtains were pulled and lighting would be dim. Leading with his weapon, he crouched and spun around the corner.

"Freeze!" Cal tried to take in every corner with his eyes while training his gun on any potential targets. The room was empty.

On his radio, he heard Greg whisper, "Kitchen and bathroom clear. I'm heading into the garage."

"Be careful," he radioed back. "There's not much light in there."

Cal continued down the hallway, listening for any sound of movement. Past the kitchen, two more doors led off the hall, one to the right and another at the end. Both doors were closed.

Taking a deep breath, he reached out and grabbed the knob on the right. In one swift motion, he threw the door open, ducked, and stepped into the room. He quickly ascertained that this was Esther's bedroom and that it was unoccupied. Edging up to the half-open closet, he nudged the door the rest of the way open with the barrel of his gun. Dozens of talcum-smelling dresses hung from the clothes rod, but no one was hiding inside.

The bathroom door was open. By approaching it from an angle, he was able to use the mirror to see that the bathroom was empty, too.

"Garage is clear," Greg radioed.

"I've got one more room," Cal responded. "At the end of the hall. Back me up."

"On my way." The radio clicked off, and he could hear Greg walking through the kitchen. As Cal stepped back into the hall, Greg moved into place behind him.

Since the doorway took up the entire hall, they would have to enter this room straight on. Cal dropped to a crouching position, gun held forward in his right hand as he took the doorknob in his left. *Last chance,* he thought. *Please let her be here, and let her be alive.*

Behind him, Greg held his arms locked forward, gun at the ready and aimed over Cal's shoulder. Was that the smell of blood? It was just his imagination. It had to be, or else—

He pushed the door, slipping his gun through the opening as it swung wide. As the room came into view, he held his breath, his finger moving to apply light pressure on the trigger. What he saw inside the room stunned him momentarily. It was like a scene out of a movie.

He heard Greg gasp behind him. "It's some kind of shrine."

CHAPTER 65

CAL MOVED THROUGH THE BEDROOM like a man in a trance, unable to believe what he was seeing. On first glance, it could have been any boy's room. A twin bed with the bedspread hastily tucked over the pillow. A set of shelves filled with games and books, a partially finished model on the desk, a case of toy cars.

A perfectly ordinary room for a nine-year-old—if, that was, you could somehow convince yourself that you had magically been transported back to the mid-1970s. *A shrine*, Greg had called it, and rightfully so—a shrine to a boy dead for more than thirty years. But it was a lot more than that—it was literally a time capsule from the year Esther's son had disappeared.

He picked up an action figure. It was one of the motorcycle cops from the old CHiPs television series. Unopened beside it was a Bandai Godzilla model.

He flipped through the handful of comic books from the top of the dresser—*The Incredible Hulk, Billy the Kid, Captain America, Silver Surfer, Nick Fury*—none with an issue date of later than the mid-1970s. Without even looking, he knew that there wouldn't be any hybrids or Hummers inside the Rally Hot Wheels case.

The entire room was like a living memorial, a slice of the past that Cal remembered well. From the Fat Albert bedspread to the He-Man action figures, everything in the room could have come from his own boyhood.

That Esther had seemingly kept everything in her dead son's room intact was bad enough, but when he looked in the closet, Cal received an even greater shock. He pulled a shirt from its hanger and read the label. *Size 16 ½—34/35.*

"She made him live in this, this . . . mausoleum," he whispered, his heart ricocheting around in his chest. The pain in his neck had nearly disappeared beneath the adrenaline rush of the chase, but now it was coming back with a vengeance, and his head was pounding.

"Who?" Greg asked, putting down a KerPlunk game. "The kid?"

"Her nephew, Larry." Cal pointed to the neatly pressed shirts and pants that hung behind the sliding mirrored doors. They were men's sizes. The shoes lined up side by side looked to be at least men's size twelve or thirteen. "But he's not a kid anymore."

"It must have been like being raised in a museum," he muttered, shaking his head. Outside, he could hear the wind beginning to pick up and the splatter of raindrops against the windows. The storm that had slacked off this morning was picking up again.

"Hey, take a look at this." Greg had pulled a scrapbook from the half-open desk drawer. Cal leaned over his shoulder. The yellowing newspaper articles on the first few pages were familiar, even though he'd only viewed copies made from the microfilm reader. Esther had carefully clipped every newspaper article tracking her son's disappearance.

But she hadn't stopped there. As Greg flipped further into the book, the clippings became more recent. Here was a picture of the Twin Forks High graduating class of eighty-seven—that would have been Frankie's class. There was Amanda Porter's first wedding announcement and her second. Ben Meyers's acceptance into law school. A photograph of Theresa Obrey doing her cooking show.

Esther had been tracking them all—stalking them.

"Go to the end," Cal said. Greg turned to the last page of the book—it was empty—and began flipping back toward the front.

"Stop!" Cal stuck his finger on the last page that had anything attached to it. The newspaper article was so fresh he could still smell the ink as well as the glue that had been used to attach it to the page. It was from that morning's *Denver Post*.

The headline read, "Ute Mining Engineer Victim of Violent Hospital Attack."

CHAPTER 66

"I WANT YOU TO STAKE out the house in case they come back," Cal said. He and Greg were standing on the front porch of Esther's house, watching the rain come down in torrents. "I'm going to have Sheldon wait at the Godwins' for Spencer while Andy patrols the streets."

"Where are you going?" Greg asked.

Cal stared out at the black thunderheads hanging like a pall over the town. A knot of fear was forming in his gut. Esther had Olivia—the last of those she considered to be her son's murderers. She had gone to great pains to see that her son's death was revenged properly. Was there really any question where she would want it all to end?

"I'm going to follow a hunch."

"You're heading back up to the mine, aren't you?" Greg asked, searching Cal's eyes.

"Yeah, I am."

"Not alone. I'm coming with you."

"We don't even know where they are. We could both end up on a wild goose chase while the killers are right in our own backyard." Cal began to shake his head, and a bolt of pain shot up into his skull. He tried to hide his grimace, but Greg saw it anyway.

"You're in no condition to go anywhere, Cal. You're bleeding all over the back of your shirt, and you look like crap. You should be back in the hospital.

"If I see anything at all, I'll radio for backup."

Greg placed a hand on Cal's shoulder, his deep-set eyes dark and serious. "I don't like it. You could be walking into an ambush."

"I don't think so," Cal said. A blue flare of electricity hit somewhere nearby, and both men jumped at the deafening crack of thunder that followed immediately. "If they *are* at the mine, it's about one thing only—killing Olivia. I don't think either of them much cares what happens after that."

"Don't go in there alone."

"I'll call you the minute I see anything. You do the same."

"If I don't hear from you in an hour, we're coming up." Greg looked like he expected an argument, but Cal only nodded wearily, rubbing a hand across his bloodshot eyes.

"I just hope I'm wrong about this. You have no idea how much I hope I'm wrong."

CHAPTER 67

"COME ON, BABY, GIVE ME some traction." Cal eased off the brake with his left foot while feathering the gas with his right. The transmission growled as the car rocked forward on the slick, muddy surface. The road had deteriorated badly under the storm's onslaught, but he was only a mile or two from the mine.

"15-J-1," the radio crackled, "this is 15-J-2. Do you read?" It was Greg.

Cal grabbed the mic. "15-J-2, I copy. Go ahead."

"Everything's quiet down here, Cal. Do you want me to come up?" Greg's voice wavered in and out. The storm was playing havoc with transmissions.

"Negative," Cal answered. Above the car, the entire sky turned metallic purple as sheet lightning lit up the sky. "I'm still a good ten to fifteen minutes out. I'll call you when I know anything."

"Sorry, I . . . you . . . for a minute." The radio hissed and popped with static. "Can you repeat?"

"Stay where you are," Cal shouted, as though the volume of his voice could somehow overcome the electrical storm. "I'll call you."

"10-4," Greg's voice came through loud and clear this time. "I'll stand by."

Cal racked the mic, studying the road as best he could between the windshield wipers' feeble attempts to clear away the water. A hundred feet ahead, the road curved sharply to the left, following the contour of the mountainside. Winter runoffs had eroded a section of the dirt road, creating a dip that currently looked like a small river.

He gunned the engine a little as he approached the dip. For a moment the tires caught, and he could feel the Crown Victoria starting to pull up over the rise. But then—just as he thought he was going to make it—they broke loose, the tranny shrieking in protest as the rear axle spun freely.

Immediately he lifted his foot from the accelerator and let the car roll backward, mindful of the sheer drop-off to his right.

"Why now?" He pounded his fist on the dashboard. Only minutes from the parking lot and here he was, stopped cold by a six-inch bump in the road. Outside, the windshield wipers fought a losing battle with the rain that blew in blinding, nearly horizontal sheets over the car.

It was one of those situations where he was driving exactly the wrong vehicle for the conditions. The Ford's big, eight-cylinder engine had plenty of guts for the open road, but its weight was keeping the front of the car from clearing the hump while the drive train spun the back tires uselessly. A lighter car could probably have gotten through, and a four-wheel-drive—or even a front-wheel-drive, for that matter—would have had no problem at all. But the Crown Vic was all he had, and somehow he had to make it the rest of the way up.

It looked like the dip was a little shallower to the far right side of the road, but that would bring him perilously close to the edge, which didn't appear any too stable. Still, he had to get across—Olivia's life might be measured in minutes.

He dropped the car into reverse, backing up until he found a spot where the road seemed fairly solid. Dropping the car into low, he goosed the engine a little and was pleased to find that the tires didn't slip at all. With enough momentum, he should be able to clear the hump. At least he hoped so.

"Don't fail me now," he whispered as he pressed the gas pedal, and the big car lurched forward.

As his front tires cleared the dip, Cal breathed a sigh of relief. But his relief was premature. Hitting the lip of the rise, the front of the car veered hard to the right, and the back slewed around to the left. Suddenly there was nothing but empty air in front of the windshield. He cranked the steering wheel hard the other way and hit the accelerator, trying to bring the car back around.

Sliding in the loose mud, the rear end fishtailed sharply to the right. Cal hit the brakes, but it was already too late. He could feel the car slipping toward the edge of the cliff. Before he could do anything to stop it, the rear tire on the passenger side dropped over the edge, sending a shudder through the entire car. A second later, the ground beneath the front tire gave way too.

It was going. Cal could hear the frame of the cruiser groaning as it gouged divots through the muddy surface of the road. He had only a few seconds before the entire car went over the edge. He fumbled for the door. As the car took another big lurch to the right his fingers slipped on the chrome surface of the handle. Finally his fingers gained purchase, and he bulled his shoulder into the door. The car was tilted perilously over the edge, and it was all he could do to get the door open.

As he grabbed the frame, something rolled out from under the seat. It was his big eight-cell flashlight. His hand whipped out, snatching the barrel just before he dove through the door and into the mud.

With a screech of twisting metal, the car slipped, caught, and slipped again. Now the cruiser was tilted almost sideways. It slid over the edge like a ship taking on water. For a second Cal thought it might not go all the way over as the front axle caught on an outcropping of rock. Then the rock tore loose, taking nearly a foot of road with it, and his car was gone.

He crawled as near to the edge of the cliff as he dared, ignoring the pounding rain that stung the stitches in his neck and scalp, and watched his patrol car tumble end-over-end down the side of the mountain. When the car finally hit the bottom of the ravine with a crash of broken glass and metal, it was nothing but a shattered hulk.

Cal pulled the radio from his belt, increased the gain all the way, and keyed the mic. "15-J-1, to any unit. Do you read?" The only response was the high-pitched squawk of static. He tried again. "This is 15-J-1. I have an emergency. Is anyone out there?"

Nothing.

He was on his own.

CHAPTER 68

BY THE TIME CAL REACHED the parking lot, he was muddy, soaked, and cold. His emergency poncho had been shredded by the fierce mountain winds, and the bandages on the back of his neck were in tatters. He'd tried his cell phone and radio several times on the way up, but both proved to be useless. He'd just have to hope that Greg would come up when he couldn't get through on the radio.

Staggering through the icy downpour, he cupped his hands above his eyes and could just make out three cars in the lot. Closest to him was a black SUV, and beyond that a red sports car, but it was the last vehicle that drew his attention—a silver pickup with a rusty bed. He recognized it immediately as the truck he'd seen Esther in.

He was right, then. They were here. How much time had he lost? He ran across the parking lot, ignoring the thudding in his chest and the fire in the back of his head, and placed a hand on the hood of the truck. The engine was no longer ticking, but it was still warm. They'd probably been here for more than thirty minutes but less than two hours.

Using the butt of his flashlight, he smashed the driver's side window. Bright bits of safety glass covered the seat and floor. The inside of the cab smelled of sweat and old plastic upholstery. And just a lingering trace of something that smelled like Olivia's perfume. Cal opened the glove compartment. Inside were a roll of duct tape and a short length of rope. They'd tied and gagged her.

He pawed through the rest of the glove box and, using the bright beam of the flashlight, explored the floor of the cab and beneath the seats. Two things were conspicuously missing—a weapon and any sign of blood. Hoping that meant she was still alive, he turned and ran for the mine entrance.

CHAPTER 69

WALKING INTO THE CAVE WAS like sloughing off a heavy weight. As soon as Cal grabbed the rope Esther and her nephew had left behind and began to slip and slide down into the muddy opening, all the questions, all the doubts and recriminations of the last ten days disappeared.

Everything had come into focus. "Clear as the man in the moon," his mother had been fond of saying. He no longer had to worry about what he had or hadn't done to save his wife or how he'd failed to prevent the others' deaths. He had one job to do. Get in, get Olivia, and get out.

Not that he wasn't scared. His heart was pounding so hard he could feel it banging in his ears, and he knew his teeth weren't chattering from the cold alone.

Even more than the last time, entering the mine felt like being swallowed alive by some great dark beast. But one way or another, this was the end of the line. He would either climb back up this tunnel with the nightmare behind him or he wouldn't come out at all. That provided him a sense of calm, a sense of purpose.

Abruptly, Cal skidded to a halt, his mouth dropping in an *O* of dismay. Fewer than five feet ahead of him, the rope he'd been following disappeared into a mass of dirt and rubble. As quickly as it had come, his calm fled. He let the beam of his flashlight play across the rock, looking for some kind of opening, but the shaft was sealed completely. The passage was gone.

CHAPTER 70

"No. No, no, no!" Cal's shouts echoed off the walls around him, shattering and coming back in a thousand different fragments. He was too late again. He had no idea if there were other entrances, but even if there were, he didn't have the time to search for them. Olivia was going to die before he could get to her, and there wasn't a thing he could do about it.

He slammed his fist against the cave-in over and over, ripping his palm open on the jagged rock. But neither the blood nor the pain mattered. It was as if the Seven Stars was a living, breathing creature, determined to keep him out, to thwart him from—

Cal stopped pounding, pressing his wounded hand to his mouth. He turned slowly around, letting the beam of the flashlight play across the sides of the airshaft. Wasn't this where he had become trapped the last time down? Just ahead he'd thought he'd felt hands trying to hold him back. He'd been sure the shaft was collapsing around him.

Ever hear about the guy whose left side was crushed during a cave in? Cal turned, nearly expecting to see Two Bears standing behind him in the dark. This was where the old Indian had started telling jokes. Only Two Bears was back in the same hospital as Ben, busy dying. Maybe even dead already.

Go back, a voice whispered. He couldn't tell if it was coming from inside his own head or from the mine itself. *You've done everything you can. Now turn away before the whole place comes down on your head.* The earth seemed to tremble around him, and he was reminded of the dream where he'd tried to pull Kat from the side of the mountain—only the mountain had sucked him in instead.

He's all right now. It was the old Indian's voice again. What was the old man trying to tell him?

Leave! The walls shuddered, and he could actually see bits of dirt and rock trickle down the edge of the slide. *Go while you still can or be trapped in here forever.*

Trapped like Frankie. Like . . . Olivia.

Cal tucked the flashlight into his belt and bent his head, pressing against the cave with both hands as if somehow he could push his way through it. The flashlight cast crazy shadows off the walls, but he didn't see them. His eyes were pressed shut. He wouldn't leave her. As long as he had breath to draw, he wouldn't stop trying to save Olivia.

Go away! There was something in the voice. Frustration? Fear?

No, he opened his mouth to shout. But instead he found himself speaking words he hadn't heard in thirty years or more.

"What do you get when you cross a pig and a centipede? Bacon and legs." It was a stupid joke to be telling and an even stupider time to be telling it. But it felt right all the same.

Another one. He searched his mind for jokes. The only thing he could come up with was a dumb one he'd heard a sportscaster tell on the news a few weeks earlier.

"Why are the Dodgers like a possum? They both play dead at home and die on the road." He thought he felt something give beneath his hands. His eyes flew open and for a split second he saw . . . what? A railroad tie? He closed his eyes again, straining to remember any joke he'd ever heard.

"How much do pirates charge to put in earrings? A buck-an-ear."

"What did Snow White say when she took her film in to be developed? Some day my prints will come."

The walls began shaking again, but he kept his eyes screwed closed.

"How can you tell if an elephant's been in your refrigerator? There are footprints in the butter."

Get out! Go away! . . . It was the voice from his first visit to the mine.

"What did the cowboy say to his horse? Hey, partner, why the long face?"

Hurt you! Bite you! . . . It was the duplicitous voice he had heard in the Hall of Lost Souls.

He could feel his fingers starting to sink into the dirt and rock. *It isn't real. The cave-in isn't any more real than the hands were.* He tried to imagine the passage clear ahead of him.

Kill you! . . . The volume of the voice grew, clawing and grasping inside Cal's aching head until he could barely stand it.

Come on, think of something funny. Something that would make Two Bears laugh out loud. He tried to picture the old Indian's face as it had looked when Cal had tried tasting the dirt.

"What did the skeleton order when he went into the bar?" Cal imagined Two Bears grinning as he waited for the punch line—yellowed teeth shining behind leathery brown lips. *What?*

"A beer and a mop." He could actually hear the old man's laughter. Not inside his head, but echoing off the walls around him.

Not real, he whispered to himself, reaching for the rope with one hand while he kept pressing with the other.

Kill you. Kill you. KILL YOU! The voice grew frantic as he ducked his head, wrapped the rope around his arm, and, forcing all fear aside—*Nooooo!*—charged forward directly into and through the wall of collapsed stone and dirt.

CHAPTER 71

CAL PICKED HIMSELF UP OFF the ground. He'd tripped over something, barking his shin a good one as he fell. His neck felt like someone had replaced the tendons in it with barbed wire. He gently probed at the back of his scalp. His fingers came away wet and warm. He was bleeding again. But the voices were gone and with them the overwhelming feeling of despair.

Taking his flashlight from his belt, he saw that the cave-in was gone as well. It *had* been an illusion, an attempt by someone or something to keep him out. Aiming the beam of his flashlight downward, he could see that he had tripped over the iron rails. He was inside the mine again. He could also make out several sets of footprints leading away from the airshaft in the same direction he and Two Bears had gone the last time he was here.

Cal began to jog down the center of the tracks, alternating his light between the footprints he was following and the tunnel ahead. Several times he tripped over a discarded piece of equipment or a broken tie that had pushed up from the ground, and once he nearly knocked himself out on an especially low cross brace.

He was soon just as disoriented as the first time he'd come down. But as long as he had the fresh footprints to follow, he wouldn't get lost. Esther and her nephew had to be headed for the Hall of Lost Souls with Olivia. He didn't know what they planned to do there—something terrible, he guessed—but it was the only destination that made sense.

He wondered how long he had been down here. He checked the dial of his watch, but the rain had apparently gotten inside it, and now the hour hand jerked forward every few seconds while the minute hand had stopped completely. He had no idea how far he'd come or how far he still had to go. It was so easy to get confused when every passage looked the same.

Just ahead the tunnel dead-ended, with passages T-ing off to the right and left. As he followed the footprints to the right, he heard something in the tunnel ahead. A steady roar like the ocean or the sound of a big storm coming in, it seemed to be getting louder. He cocked his head, trying to determine what the sound was and where it was coming from.

Whatever it was, it was definitely getting closer. Now it sounded like a wall of white water boiling over rocks and trees. He held the flashlight out and above his head, trying to see what it was. The sound seemed to fill the mine, buzzing in his ears like a hive of angry hornets. Something shot through the beam of his light, brushing against his face.

Instinctively he jerked his arm back, and the beam of light bounced off the ceiling. Something else whizzed past him, its wings brushing against his forearm. Then another and another. It was the bats.

Without warning, thousands of tiny dark bodies packed the air around him, their pinprick eyes reflecting red in the beam of his light. They bounced off his body, sharp claws catching in his clothing, tearing at his face and hands. He tried to beat them off, but the entire tunnel was filled with them.

He gasped for air and one of them flew between his lips, its hot, bristly body pressing against his tongue and the roof of his mouth. Something sharp jabbed at the inside of his cheek and instinctively he bit down. Bits of bone and flesh crunched between his teeth, and something wet ran down the back of his throat, gagging him.

He spat out the furry body and tried to get his hands to his mouth, but it was like pushing his arms through wet cement. He could feel the hot pressing horde forcing him downward. The flashlight was knocked from his hands. He heard it crash to the ground, and its light went out. Tucking his head beneath his hands, he dropped face-first to the ground.

He didn't know how long he lay there, pressed against the ground, waiting for the bats to leave. But eventually he realized that the roar had diminished and he could no longer feel their wings and claws scratching against his back. Cautiously he raised he head. They were gone. He got to his knees and felt around the ground for the flashlight.

For one feverish moment he thought that the bats had somehow managed to carry it off with them. Then his fingers closed around its cold barrel. He found the button and pressed it.

Nothing happened. He pressed it again. There was a faint click, but no light. His heart began to race. He shook the flashlight and heard the faint tinkling of broken glass. The light bulb had broken in the fall, and he had no spare.

With mounting horror, he realized that not only would he not be able to find his way to the Hall of Lost Souls without any light, but he couldn't even find his way back to the entrance. He was lost in the Seven Stars.

CHAPTER 72

CAL STOOD IN THE DARKNESS, waiting for his eyes to adjust, before accepting that they weren't ever going to. He held his hands out in front of his face, waved them back and forth, and saw nothing—not even a hint of shape or movement.

"Okay, just stay calm," he told himself. But that was easier said than done.

The darkness seemed to take on weight and substance like a damp shroud wrapped skintight around him. Deprived of any visual stimuli, his optical nerves began firing random images into his brain. He thought he saw a yellow light swinging back and forth somewhere up ahead, but when he took several hesitant steps toward it, he walked into the wall.

There had to be some way out of this—there had to be. But every time he tried to concentrate, his mind kept slipping toward the edge of panic.

Don't move, a voice in his head warned. *You don't know what's out there. The next step could drop you down a hundred-foot shaft.*

Run. Run now! another voice demanded. *Get out while you still can. Get out before the whole place comes collapsing down on your head.*

He had to think. Grabbing the tender flesh of his upper lip between his thumb and forefinger, he squeezed until the pain brought water to his eyes—until it forced everything else from his head so he could focus.

Okay, that was better. At least now he could think, consider his options—what few of them he had. As he saw it, there were three alternatives. He could stay where he was, hoping that someone would find him. He could try to retrace his steps. Or he could continue on ahead, trusting what little he could remember of his trip with Two Bears, combined with dumb luck, to somehow get him through.

There really didn't seem to be much choice at all. He knew that he couldn't just wait—he had to *do* something. And his chances of finding his way back out weren't any better than going forward. But what it really came down to was the knowledge that if he gave up now, he would be as much as signing Olivia's death warrant. That thought got him going.

The first thing he had to do was make sure that he actually *was* moving forward. He'd gotten completely turned around when his light went out. Running one hand along the shaft wall, he began to take measured steps forward. With each step, his mind conjured up images of rusty shards of broken metal waiting to gash his legs or sudden drop-offs looming just ahead. But he forced himself to keep walking.

On his seventh step, the wall beneath his hand disappeared, and he nearly fell. That was what he'd been looking for. Just before the bats, he'd turned right at a T. He was back at that intersection now. He turned around, knowing that—for the moment at least—he was heading in the right direction, and he began to count off his steps.

He was up to two hundred and thirteen when, once again, the wall disappeared beneath his hand. Scuffing his feet slowly across the ground, Cal estimated there was about six feet of space before his hand touched the wall again. It was a fairly big opening. There didn't seem to be any rails running in that direction, but did that mean anything?

He racked his brain, trying to recall whether they had turned here or not, but it was futile. He'd been paying attention to the old Indian's words, not his direction.

As Cal tried to make up his mind, another disturbing thought occurred to him. He didn't even know if this was the first opening he'd passed. He'd only been running his hand along one wall. Who knew how many passages he might have passed on the other side? There was no way to check both walls at once—the shaft was too wide.

A mind-numbing chill settled over him. This must have been how it was for the children. With no way of knowing whether you were working your way out or deeper in, your mind quickly gave up trying to keep track of direction. He'd never had any real concept of how terrified they must have been.

He'd always pictured it as a kind of extended game of hide-and-seek—Tom Sawyer and Becky Thatcher hiding from Injun Joe. He'd thought he understood—comparing the children's ordeal to a time he'd become separated from his parents on a camping trip. Being lost in the woods was bad. He could remember the fear of believing that he'd never see his mother or father again—this was a hundred times worse.

"Don't freeze up." The words he spoke seemed obscenely loud in the absolute silence. But they helped him break the mental fugue he'd been stuck in. It was his way of whistling past the graveyard. "Just take it one step at a time. Right or straight, that's all you need to decide for now. We'll cross the next bridge when we reach it. Right or straight?"

Straight, his mind answered. "Good enough, then, straight it is," he said, and began counting again.

CHAPTER 73

CAL.

He didn't know how long he'd been shuffling forward—taking it one passage at a time—when he thought he heard someone call out to him from the darkness.

He stopped moving, straining to hear. It had probably been nothing. First his eyes had been playing tricks on him, and now it was his ears. And even if he had heard something, it was probably just the—

Cal.

There it was again. Only this time it sounded a little closer. He turned his head to the left, in the direction he thought the sound had come from and saw . . .

A light! It was dim and far away, but it was definitely a light

"Hello?" he called out. "Who's there?" Removing his right hand from the wall he'd been tracing for the last one hundred thirty-eight steps, he stumbled across the tracks and into a side tunnel he hadn't even known was there.

"Cal, it's me." The voice was clearer now, the light stronger. He could actually make out the ground beneath his feet and the walls. He began to run, his heart pounding. He was safe. He sprinted toward the light and found himself . . .

CHAPTER 74

. . . IN HIS LIVING ROOM.

"Cal, wake up, honey. Dinner's almost ready."

He sat up. He was on the couch in his living room.

"Are you awake yet, sleepy head?" Kat came into the room and kissed him on the forehead. "Don't think I'm going to let you sleep through my world-famous spaghetti."

"Spaghetti?" He rubbed a hand across his eyes. He could smell the sweet aroma of Kat's spaghetti sauce wafting in from the kitchen—oregano and basil—and the pungent smell of fresh garlic bread. "But how? I mean, you're dead."

He blinked. "I was in the mine, and Olivia needs my . . ."

"Quite the dream, huh?" Kat gave him a look of mock anger. "You've already planted me in the ground and found another woman? Well, you can tell me all about it over dinner, and then you can do penance by weeding my flower garden."

"A dream?"

"Of course." She reached down to give him a hand, and he let himself be pulled to his feet.

"Do I look dead to you?" Kat pressed her warm mouth to his, and as their lips touched he felt her body rise against him. She felt wonderful beneath his hands, that amazing combination of firm and soft that only a woman's body can achieve. She looked and felt anything but dead, and yet . . .

"I don't understand." It was like his head was filled with oil. His mind couldn't quite seem to get in gear.

"Hey, I thought I was the one with the bump on the head," Kat said, leading him into the kitchen. "Maybe we should take *you* to the doctor." Her laughter was so real, so *Kat*, that he couldn't help smiling himself.

The kitchen table was set with the good china, and a bouquet of African violets in the crystal vase he had given Kat on their first anniversary sat in the center. He leaned over the blooms to inhale their fragrance, but there was only the smell of the sauce. The flowers had no scent at all, as if they were plastic fakes. But they looked fresh from the garden.

"Is there a problem?" Kat stopped in the process of carrying the steaming pot of spaghetti sauce from the stove to the table and frowned, her eyes watchful.

"The flowers . . . don't have any smell," Cal said, beginning to shiver. It was a warm afternoon, so how could he be ice cold?

"Try again, dear," she said, her smile returning as she placed the sauce on a trivet.

Immediately the kitchen was suffused with the overwhelming perfume of flowers. The scents of begonias, roses, lilacs, and dozens of other flowers he couldn't name—everything but the African violets that were in the vase—filled the air with an overpowering kind of greenhouse stench.

"There, isn't that better?" Kat took a chair across from him. She scooped up a spoonful of pasta and dropped it onto his plate with a wet splat.

"Eat up," she said, covering the spaghetti with the thick red sauce. "You must be starving."

He *was* starving. It felt like it had been days since he'd eaten anything. Only now the sauce didn't smell quite so appetizing. Beneath the herbs and tomatoes was a sour, visceral stink, like spoiled meat.

"Stop that." Kat reached across the table and slapped his hand. Looking down, Cal realized that he'd been twisting his ring. It was a habit he'd gotten into since Kat's—

"You're dead." His voice sounded muted and far away, as if his mouth was filled with cotton.

"Eat your dinner." Kat's voice took on a shrill, demanding tone. Her eyes glowed feverishly.

Cal looked down at his plate. It no longer looked like spaghetti at all. The red sauce seemed to be clotting, and beneath it the noodles moved like living things.

"You're dead," he repeated dully. "How can you be here? How can *I* be here?"

"Do you want to kill me all over again?" Kat cried. Her fingers tangled in her hair, tearing at it. She began to pull it out in short dark clumps.

"No." Cal stood up from his chair, knocking it over behind him. "No, you're dead. I saw them bury you."

"It's all your fault!" Kat screamed. "You killed me!" She pushed the table aside, sending it flying across the room like a cardboard cutout. Cal's plate bounced onto the floor, and he caught a quick glimpse of corpulent maggots squirming through steaming blood. Kat's features were beginning to change now, dripping like hot wax. She came at Cal, her fingers growing and sharpening into black talons.

"No!" He stepped back from her, nearly tripping over the chair. His hand caught the corner of the wall, barely keeping him from falling. Somewhere he heard a cell phone ringing.

"You were too slow!" She'd become the graveyard corpse he imagined in his nightmares. Most of the skin had sloughed from her face, leaving behind a thick scum of black and green mold. Her eyes hung loosely in their fleshless sockets. "You did this to me. You let me die!"

"No. I tried to save you. I wanted to take you to the doctor. But you wouldn't go." They were back in the living room now. He backed past the couch. The ringing had become more persistent, and he vaguely wondered why no one was answering it.

"Look at me!" she screeched, gouging her talons across her face, leaving glittering white furrows in the bone. "You did this to me. *You* did this!" She was closing in on him. Two more steps, and he would be backed to the wall. He turned to run.

The phone continued to ring, its shrill tone drilling into his skull. Almost unconsciously, he plucked it from his belt. He could hear a voice calling his name. He put the phone to his ear.

"Get out!" the voice on the phone shouted. "Get out now!" It was Two Bears.

Suddenly he was back in the mine. He was holding his cell phone to his ear. He began to take another step and froze. The glow from the phone provided just enough illumination to see that he was in a small side tunnel. The rails ended abruptly. His right foot hung suspended over a vertical shaft so deep he couldn't see the bottom.

CHAPTER 75

IN A MOVE WORTHY OF a prima ballerina, Cal pivoted. He turned from the shaft, but his weight shifted. Hands pin-wheeling, he struggled for balance. For a second he thought he was going to make it; then he was falling backwards into the open pit. The cell phone flew from his fingers, and he watched it arch through the air, landing with a snap on the floor of the mine.

He just had time to think *That's the only sign they'll ever have of me* when his right hand caught hold of a crossbeam above his head. Fingers slipping on the oily wood, he nearly fell anyway. Then something that felt like a pair of small hands pressed against his back, and he was able to catch his balance

Lurching forward, he kept from stepping on the glowing phone and turned to pick it up. It had been another trap, and he'd been sucked into it like a fly to honey. Whatever entity was trying to keep him from the Hall of Lost Souls had known just where to hit him. It had picked his greatest love and his worst fear and used them both against him.

He kicked a small rock down into the shaft and counted to thirteen before it hit bottom. That's where he'd be right now if it hadn't been for the warning. Had it really been Two Bears communicating with him, or had it been just his own subconscious? And had something else saved him from what would have been a certain death?

If something or someone had been there, it was gone. And now that he had some light—minimal as it might be—he could find Olivia. He had a strong feeling that time was running short for her.

He had to crouch nearly to the ground to see by the light of the phone, every so often pressing a key on the dial pad to keep the small screen glowing. But it was enough. As he reached the end of the side tunnel, he could just make out footprints and the paw prints Pepper had left behind.

"I'm coming," he whispered, hoping that somehow his message might be communicated to Olivia. "Just hang on a little while longer."

Fifteen minutes later, he turned into a small passage. Instantly he smelled the ammonia-like odor of bat guano. This was the tunnel that led to the bat cave. He knew where he was now and began to pick up speed.

On the other side of the cavern, he ducked his head and entered the passage that led to the Hall of Lost Souls. It wouldn't be long now. As he crept forward, he listened attentively for any sound, trying to keep his own footsteps as quiet as possible. He didn't know what kind of weapons Esther and her nephew had, but Olivia's life might come down to who had the element of surprise.

As he squeezed through a narrow opening in the rock that seemed familiar, a light came into view. Instantly, he dropped to the ground. It was impossible to make anything out for sure from this distance, but it looked like a propane lantern. Someone stepped in front of the light, his silhouette briefly outlined by the yellow glow, and then moved past.

Cal crept closer. He thought he could hear Esther's voice. Although the words echoed and were indistinct, it was obvious that she was angry. Realizing that the darkness would hide him, he began to move forward more quickly.

At a rock outcropping near the cavern entrance, he crawled far enough to peer around the edge. Esther was standing just off to one side of the lantern. Beside her, a hulking figure who had to be her nephew lifted something from the ground. Cal recognized the shape immediately. It was one of the rusty pick heads that lay abandoned around the mine.

Larry raised it above his head with both hands, and for the first time Cal noticed the bundle at their feet. It moved, and he realized that it had to be Olivia. She was still alive.

Drawing his gun, he burst from his hiding place and drew on the man with the pick. "Police," he shouted, his voice echoing crazily inside the cavern. "Drop your weapon."

For a split second both Esther and her nephew froze. Larry continued to hold the pick above his head, and Cal's finger tightened on the trigger of his gun. At the first sign of movement he was prepared to fire. Then Esther spoke.

"Drop it, Larry." Her voice was weak, but her nephew obeyed her instantly. Cal tracked him in the sight of his pistol as he slowly turned and let the chunk of metal drop well clear of Olivia.

"Keep your hands where I can see them, and step away from her."

As Esther and Larry moved back, Cal stepped closer to the light. Approaching Olivia, he could see that her hands and feet were bound, and a strip of duct tape had been placed over her mouth. He dropped to one knee, keeping his gun trained on Esther and Larry, and reached out to pull off the tape.

With his hand halfway to her mouth, he froze. Something wasn't right. Olivia was shaking her head back and forth, her eyes opened wide—not with relief but with terror. He remembered the other cars in the parking lot. The red sports car. He'd seen it before.

He started to get up, body turning as he rose, his gun hand swinging around with incredible speed. But it wasn't fast enough. He was only halfway to his feet when something crashed against the back of his head, and his body collapsed to the ground like a sack of wheat.

CHAPTER 76

"MAKE SURE THEY'RE GOOD AND tight," a man called out.

Cal regained consciousness to the feel of cold metal being clamped around his wrists. He was lying face down on the dirt, and Esther was cuffing his wrists together with his own handcuffs.

He jerked backward and immediately heard the unmistakable sound of his pistol being fired somewhere off to his right. "Easy there, big boy, or the next round goes into your kneecap," the man said.

Dropping back to the ground, Cal allowed Esther to finish cuffing him.

"Okay, you can roll over now."

He turned slowly, trying to fight off waves of nausea that washed over him every time he moved his head. He glanced at Olivia. Her eyes were filled with terror, but she seemed to be unharmed.

"I wasn't expecting you quite so soon." The words were spoken by a figure standing in the shadows. He thought he recognized the voice, but he couldn't believe that's really who it was.

"You like to hide in the dark," Cal said. "Are you ashamed of being here?"

"Not in the least. In fact, I'm quite proud of what I'm doing." He stepped into the light. It was Spencer Godwin.

Cal's mind raced. What was Godwin doing here, and why was he standing by while his own sister was about to be murdered?

"You look a little confused, Chief." Spencer chuckled, waving the pistol in Cal's direction. "What's the matter? Doesn't this fit your nice little 'Columbo' mentality?" Spencer had another pistol tucked into his pants. Cal could see his utility belt lying about ten feet away, near Spencer's feet.

"Looks like I misjudged you," Cal said. He didn't know what was going on, but he knew that he needed to keep Spencer talking until he could figure out a way to get to his belt. The keys to his handcuffs were hanging from it. They would be the first step in getting out of this situation.

"In what way?" Spencer asked, a smirk on his narrow face.

"I pegged you as the kind of criminal who would steal an old lady's pension check or embezzle from your church. I never figured you for a cold-blooded murderer."

For a second Spencer's eyes narrowed and a dark wrinkle creased his forehead, but then he burst out laughing. "You really are confused. The murderer's lying bound and gagged next to you."

"I don't think so." Cal flexed his hands within the restraints of the metal bands. Most people underestimated how tightly you actually had to close a set of cuffs. He thought he might be able to get at least one hand free, even if he had to lose a little skin to do it.

"Let me tell you something, Chief." Spencer walked up to him and crouched close, waving the gun in his face. "You don't know half as much as you think you do. You drive around in your cop car and carry your big, bad gun. But the truth is you don't have a clue what really happened to this poor woman's son, do you?"

Esther, who had been standing quietly by her nephew up until this point, stepped forward. "She's the murderer." Esther pointed down at Olivia. "She killed my Frankie."

"Did *he* tell you that?" Cal asked. Esther looked uncertainly from Cal to Spencer and back again.

"You don't believe me, Chief?" Spencer grinned. "Well, you don't have to. Ask her yourself." This close, Cal could see his eyes clearly. They were the eyes of a lunatic. He knew that if he said the wrong thing, he'd be dead.

Spencer leaned across to his sister. Cal twisted his wrists. If he could just get one of his hands free, he'd take his gun back in an instant. As though reading his mind, Spencer pulled back, pointing the gun at Cal's forehead.

"Let me see your hands," he said.

Cal had no choice. He turned around and felt Spencer clamp the cuffs viciously tight on each of his wrists.

"I feel ever so much better now." Spencer laughed. "Don't you?"

Cal grimaced. There was no way he could slip loose of the restraints now.

"As I was saying . . ." Spencer reached out to Olivia and in one quick motion ripped the tape from her face. Olivia cried out in pain, and Cal could feel adrenaline pumping through his veins.

Ignoring her cry, Spencer crouched down to look into his sister's eyes. He held Cal's pistol loosely in his hand, resting his elbows on his knees and nodding to her. "Go ahead, little sister. You've been wanting to tell this story for a long time, haven't you?"

Olivia nodded dumbly, her eyes meeting Cal's before looking quickly away.

"Well, no time like the present, eh?"

Again Olivia looked to Cal. "I . . . I don't—"

Instantly Spencer was on top of her, smashing the barrel of the gun against her head hard enough to draw blood. "Tell them!" he screamed. "Tell them or I'll blow your brains out myself!"

Cal tensed. Handcuffed or not, he was sure he could drive this little punk's head into the ground hard enough to knock him out. He'd end up dead for his efforts, but it might be worth it.

Olivia turned toward Spencer, tears streaming from her eyes. "No, don't," she whimpered, tears streaming. Cal got the impression that although she was looking at Spencer, she was also speaking to him— warning him not to make a move. "I'll tell them. I'll tell them everything."

"Much better." Spencer moved back to sit by the lantern. "Take a seat," he said, waving to Esther and Larry. "The show's about to begin."

CHAPTER 77

"It . . . it all started out as . . . a game," Olivia began hesitantly. "At least most of us thought that's what it was—until we found out what Ezra and Amanda had planned."

She looked to Esther. "I liked Frankie. He was smart and sweet, and he could be really funny sometimes."

Esther said nothing, her fingers caressing the rusted iron of the pick head as she glared at Olivia.

"We were already in the mine entrance when Ezra told us what he was going to do."

(*So here's what's gonna happen.*)

Cal shook his head. For a minute he thought he'd heard the voice of a young boy, superimposed over Olivia's words like a bad dubbing job.

"There were boards across the entrance, and we could only see each other by the candles Ezra and Amanda were holding."

Amanda, gimme them matches.

There it was again. He craned his neck to see where the boy's voice was coming from, but, except for the five of them, the cavern was empty.

"Ezra took charge as soon as we were inside." Something was happening to Olivia's voice. Her words were growing softer—less *there*—while the boy's voice grew stronger.

You guys stay in here, and Amanda, you go get . . .

Cal glanced at Esther, wondering if he was alone in experiencing this phenomenon, but her eyes were tightly closed, her face drawn and unreadable. Spencer watched them all from beside the lantern smiling thinly, the pistol gripped in his right hand.

Cal turned to look at Olivia again and his stomach did a sickening flip-flop. Olivia was still there, but dimmer. The lantern's glow scarcely reached her face. And all around her, other images were beginning to appear. Like pictures seen through a wall of water, badly washed-out and unfocused, he could make out children's faces.

"What's—" He started to rise, his head spinning, but Spencer raised the gun to his lips in a shushing gesture.

"Ezra told Amanda to go get Frankie."

Olivia's voice disappeared completely, replaced by the voice of what could only be a young Ezra Rucker. "Tell 'im if he comes into the mine, you'll kiss 'im."

Cal's stomach hiccupped again, and he was reminded of taking off his red and blue glasses during a 3-D movie he'd watched as a kid. He could still see the here and now—the mine, the lantern, Spencer wearing a knowing grin—but it was rapidly fading out. Where Olivia had been sitting stood a young girl in a flowered dress—an Olivia Cal recognized only from her school picture.

Was this another illusion? Or was he actually seeing Olivia's memory somehow being projected in front of him? Either way, he found himself helpless to resist it.

"Kiss Frankie-Frog-Eyes?" A young Mandy Osgood—but back then it would have been Amanda Porter—grimaced. Like the other children gathered around her, she was illuminated only by the flickering of a long, white candle.

"Yuck!" she cried. "I'd rather eat a lemon." But Cal knew something. Although she would never in a million years admit it, Amanda secretly liked Frankie. The thought of kissing him was exciting in a way that only an eight-year-old girl could appreciate.

How could he possibly know Amanda's thoughts? Cal wondered.

"When he climbs through the opening, I'll grab him." Ezra was already showing the muscles of a farmer's son. He was a good twenty pounds heavier than any of the other children in the group. He liked being the bully. It made the other kids respect him.

"No, that's mean. Why do you want to hurt Frankie?" Olivia, who wouldn't have broken fifty-five pounds with her pockets full of rocks, was the only one in the group unafraid to stand up to Ezra. Her insecurities had apparently been acquired later in life.

"Ain't gonna hurt 'im. Just gonna give 'im a little scare." Ezra balled up his fists, daring anyone to disagree with him.

In another flash of insight, Cal realized that Ezra had been growing uneasy lately. He had always gotten by on his size and aggression. Now something new had come into play—brains. The kids who knew all the answers and scored well on the tests began taking some of the attention that had always been his. He was beginning to realize that he might be a little short in that department.

And did Ezra know that Amanda had a secret interest in Frankie? Cal knew he did.

Was he getting all this from Olivia's mind? The details were too precise to have come from a little girl's memories alone. And the thoughts had an adult quality to them that an eight-year-old could never have achieved. Besides, Olivia could possibly have remembered her *own* feelings. But how could she have known the innermost secrets of the *others*?

And if this wasn't coming from *her* memory, then whose memory *was* it coming from? The thought that the mine, or something in it, might be able to call up these images and communicate them directly into his head scared Cal to death. But what scared him worse was that something *in* the mine could read thoughts—might even be reading his right now.

"Nah, he's a 'fraidy cat. Let's just go without him." Ben, tall and rail thin, was trying to stick up for Olivia without directly crossing Ezra. He knew that Ezra could be maneuvered into changing his mind about things if you did it without him realizing it. This time, though, it wasn't going to work. Ezra had been planning this since he first heard about the picnic, and he wasn't about to back down.

"We're bringing that little Frog Eyes in here, and that's that." Ezra glared at the other faces in the circle. "Any of you don't wanna go along can just get out."

Although none of the children knew it, this was the point at which all of their futures hung in the balance. If even one of them backed out, the whole plan would fall apart. A network of invisible but very real connections held this group together. Cal could almost see the tiny cables running from Amanda to Ezra, across to Theresa, over to Ben, around to Olivia and back again to Amanda. If even one cable had been snipped, the fragile structure of the group would have collapsed. This time they held.

"All right, then." Ezra was still in power. "Amanda, you get Frankie. The rest of you guys go hide over by those rocks, and the first one who makes any noise gets punched in the nose."

Watching the rest of the scene was like sitting through a tragically predictable movie. Even at eight, Amanda exhibited the natural good looks that would have her married twice before she was twenty. Her full, auburn hair glowed like a halo in the bright June sun, and her too-short jumper revealed a pair of tanned coltish legs. Outside of the cave the images were no longer clear and crisp. Was that because the cavern was now relying on Olivia's memory alone? Was this scene taking place outside of its range?

"Hey, Frankie. C'mere."

From the moment Frankie Zoeller heard Amanda's voice, his decision to enter the mine was a forgone conclusion. Cal knew it as soon as he saw the deep-brown cow eyes behind Frankie's glasses and the goofy smile on his face.

Distantly beside him, Cal heard Esther moan, "My baby." So he wasn't the only one seeing this. Somehow the cave was communicating this vision to everyone. Was there any way he could use that to his advantage?

Amanda whispered into Frankie's ear. A look of distress crossed his face, and he shook his head. She whispered again, her lips brushing against his ear, and took his hand. At first he resisted her urgings, but in the end, he followed her past the picnic tables and up to the mine.

The scene now skipped, following Olivia's account, to back inside the Seven Stars, and the picture regained its earlier clarity. The group, packed together in a close line, followed a set of iron tracks. At the front, Ezra grasped Frankie's arm in his left hand and a half-burned candle in his right. Ben, standing toward the middle of the group, held the other candle. Based on how much of the wax had melted, the children had been in the mine for a while.

"Come on, lemme go. I wanna go back." Frankie, who had obviously been crying, pulled his arm loose from Ezra's grasp.

"Go ahead, bawl baby." Ezra sneered. He waved with one hand, holding the candle up out of Frankie's reach. "Have a good time. Don't get lost on the way out."

Frankie took a few steps into the darkness. The look on his face was one of abject terror, but the fact that he would even take those few steps away from the rest of the group bore testament to a greater fear that had been growing within him. He had begun to sense that they were not alone in the mine—that something malevolent was watching their every move.

The farther they went into the cave, the stronger the feeling had become, until finally even the threats of Ezra deserting him in the darkness or smashing his glasses lost its power. Frankie felt desperately sure that they all had to get out now.

And he was not the only one. Ben felt it too. For the last ten minutes or so, he'd kept glancing back over his shoulder, expecting to see something sneaking up behind him. In his mind, he could see a hulking figure slip from the darkness and grab him by the neck. It would look like one of the gorillas from *Planet of the Apes*—the movie that had given him nightmares for two weeks after he saw it—only it would have glowing red eyes.

"Come on," he said, "let's just go back. Mister Andreason will give us holy heck if we're late for the bus."

"Don't wimp out on me, Oscar Meyers," Ezra said. "My brother said that if you keep following these tracks, you get to a big pool with fish that have no eyes." He didn't know if he really believed what his brothers said or not. They usually lied to him. But no one was going back until he said so. And if Meyers thought differently, he was in for a big surprise.

"I want to go back too," Theresa said. The cables had finally begun to snap, but now it was too late. They had come too far, and the events that would follow had more to do with the Seven Stars than they did with any of the children.

"Come on." Ben started to turn back, but Ezra grabbed his arm and spun him around.

"That's my candle, and you ain't going anywhere with it." The same power that had made Ben uneasy was having the opposite effect on Ezra. He'd begun to feel a kind of electric energy singing through his body and mind. Just a little farther, he kept thinking, and we're going to find something amazing. Maybe the fish his brother had talked about, or maybe something even better—maybe there was still gold in here.

Ben shook off Ezra's hand. Normally an even-tempered boy, he tried to stay out of arguments and playground scuffles, but something about this place set his nerves on edge. Ezra might be able to push kids like Frankie around, but Ezra would be sorry if he messed with Ben.

"Stay here as long as you want," Ben growled, "but we're leaving."

"Gimme that." Ezra lunged for the candle. Even as his arm knocked Ben back, Ezra wondered what in the world he was doing. Why didn't he just go out with them, see if he could swipe a couple of extra slices of pie? But if his actions had ever been completely under his control, they no longer were.

Ben had his arm in the air, trying to hold the candle out of reach, when Ezra's elbow caught him in the chest. He stepped backward, trying to catch his balance, and his foot caught on a section of track. As he began to fall, he snatched at Ezra's hand, and they both collapsed to the ground. Both candles extinguished as the boys fell.

For a moment there was complete chaos. In the dark, everyone seemed to be screaming. Somebody tripped over somebody else and went down hard. Someone ran into a wall and cried out in pain.

Finally Ezra's shouts overcame the others. "Amanda, give me the danged matches so I can light the candles again!"

"Okay. Hang on." There was a long pause, during which the only sound was Amanda muttering to herself as she searched her pockets. Finally she made a small hitching noise, as if she was trying to hold back a sob. "I . . . I think I left them back . . . back at the entrance."

From that point on, the rest of the images came in erratic snatches of sound and movement. Trying to follow the rails out. Realizing they had somehow taken a wrong turn. Clinging to one another in complete terror. In turn, each of them arguing, screaming, blaming, weeping. Wandering ever deeper into the mine—until inevitably, they ended up in the Hall of Lost Souls.

"Oh-h-h-h," a girl's voice cried from the darkness. "Something touched my head." It sounded like Amanda. This was followed by more screams and general confusion until Olivia managed to calm them.

"It's all right. It's just those rock things, stalag-somethings. Reach up," she said, "you can feel them." Cal noted that the hall wasn't glowing for the children as it had done for him.

Someone began to weep, "I want my Mom." It was Frankie.

"Shut up!" Ezra screamed. "I can't take any more of your bawling. Just shut up, why don't you? It's your fault we're lost anyway, you freaky frog-eyed puke."

"It's not my fault!" Frankie cried back. "I never wanted to come in here. Amanda tricked me."

"You leave her out of it. If it hadn't been for you crying to go back, the candles wouldn't 'a gone out." There was a sound of fist hitting flesh and something that sounded like water splashing. Frankie began to scream.

"What's wrong with . . ." Ezra's words died out as Frankie's cries continued.

"Help . . . I can't—" Frankie's voice cut out with a wet burble sound then started up again. "Help, you guys! Can't swim!" More sounds of splashing, and then he began to shriek.

"What did you *do* to him?" Theresa shouted.

"Somebody help him!" Olivia's voice echoed. There was a sound of shuffling movement beneath Frankie's panicked cries.

"There's some kind of hole or something," Ben called out. "It's slippery. I can't get to him."

"You have to do something!" Olivia called back.

"Drowning!" Frankie's voice was getting weaker. "Help m—" Again his voice disappeared in a watery gurgle.

"I can't stand this," Amanda cried. "I have to get out of here. I can't listen to him anymore."

"There's nothing we can do." Ezra's voice wavered. "We'd better go before another one of us falls in too."

"No!" The sound of Frankie's splashing was growing quieter, but his voice was desperate. "Please . . ." *gurgle*, "I can't—" his words ended in a bout of coughing.

"We can't just leave him." Olivia was weeping. But she was also moving away from Frankie's cries. They all were.

"Help!" The sound of Frankie's voice was growing dimmer now. None of them said a thing. Clinging to each other—moving steadily farther away—they tried to close their ears to his pleas. But it was impossible not to hear him.

"H-e-e-e-l-l-l-l-l-l-l-p-p-p-p!" Frankie's last cry echoed off the cavern walls.

It would echo in their memories until they day they died.

CHAPTER 78

"I AM SO SORRY." OLIVIA was weeping, tear lines streaking the dirt from her face and soaking the collar of her nightgown. "We . . . we let him drown. We just left him there. We were so young and so scared, but we just left him there . . . alone in the dark."

She gulped, her voice catching as she sobbed. "I could never forgive myself for what we did. None of us could." She turned to Esther Zoeller. "It's our fault," she wailed. "It's our fault your son is dead."

Through his own tears, Cal could see that Esther and her nephew were weeping as well. But one person wasn't weeping. Spencer's grin widened with a fiery brilliance. His eyes glowed.

"You see," he cried out with glee. "They're murderers, every one of them."

He pointed a long, thin finger at Esther. "They killed your boy," he screeched. "They killed your boy, and he's taken his revenge upon them from the grave. Now it's your turn to finish it. Deliver the final judgment down upon their heads.

"Kill her, Esther. Kill her now!"

CHAPTER 79

"KILL HER!" SPENCER SCREAMED.

"No!" Cal struggled to get to his feet.

"Sit down and shut up or you die." Spencer swung the pistol and centered it on Cal's chest, his finger on the trigger. Cal remained standing. If this was it, he was ready to take a bullet.

Esther turned from Spencer to Olivia, her face a palette of conflicting emotions. She seemed locked in some inner turmoil, her mouth twisted with alternating anger and grief.

Larry lifted the pick head, his thin arms shaking. Though the tool was old and rusted, its point was still deadly.

"Now," Spencer commanded. "Do it!"

Larry turned to his aunt for confirmation.

Cal looked to Olivia, whose eyes were closed. Tears dripped down her cheeks as her lips silently moved. He thought she was praying.

"Esther, don't—"

"One more word, cop. Just one more word, and you die too." Spencer's right finger trembled on the pistol's trigger.

Larry hoisted the tool above his head, point down. He looked to Esther again, but her eyes were locked on Olivia's, her pale face unreadable. Closing his eyes, he took a deep breath and mouthed something that might have been, "Sorry."

Cal prepared to lunge between Olivia and the pick. It would only delay the inevitable, and he would probably be dead from Spencer's gunshot before the pick ever hit him, but it was the only option he had left.

"Wait." Esther reached out to take her nephew's arm. "Put it down."

He looked at her, questioning. She nodded. "Yes, throw it away."

"What are you doing?" Spencer's gun swung halfway between Cal and Esther. Larry tossed the pick off to one side and stepped between Spencer and his aunt.

Esther knelt at Olivia's side. She ran a wrinkled hand over Olivia's hair, grimy now with dirt. "I'm . . . I'm . . ." Her thin lips trembled as she clasped a blue-veined hand to her mouth, shaking her head slowly back and forth. "I'm sorry."

"What are you talking about?" Spencer's face turned a livid red. "She murdered your son! You heard her say so yourself."

"No." Esther shook her head. "I didn't understand. Not until now. They was so little, so scared."

Olivia looked up, eyes wide, her head shaking back and forth as if she was disagreeing, but Esther continued. "No, dear. 'Twas an accident. Not your fault."

She looked up at Spencer. "I thought . . . you told me that they murdered him."

"Your son came to you. He told you that. *He* told you!" Spencer's face was red with rage. Spit flew from his lips.

Esther blinked back tears. "My boy is dead. I know he suffered. But your sister's suffered too. I'm not going to make her suffer any more."

"You have to." Sweat dripped from Spencer's temples; the gun shook in his hand. "Frankie killed the rest, but it's up to you to kill the last one—to prove your love for your son."

"No," Esther whispered, staring down into Olivia's wide, blue eyes as she continued to stroke her hair.

"Fine!" Spencer screeched. "Then I'll kill her myself." He pointed the gun at Olivia and began to squeeze the trigger.

"Why?" Cal's voice was low yet commanding.

Spencer turned to stare at him. He didn't lessen his pressure on the gun's trigger, but he didn't finish squeezing either. "Why *what?*"

"Why is it so important to you that your sister die?" Spencer was teetering on the edge. In a minute he would start firing randomly, spraying them all with bullets if Cal couldn't find a way to back him off. Cal dropped back to the ground to keep Spencer from simply exploding, but his eyes locked with Spencer's, holding them in his stare.

"You claim that Frankie Zoeller killed the others. So why do you need to kill your sister?"

"You think you're so smart, don't you? Why don't I kill you first? Then maybe you'll finally stop asking questions." Spencer's lips rose into a thin icy smile but it looked forced—as if invisible wires attached to the corners of his mouth had just been pulled.

Cal's eyes never wavered. "What are you hiding, Spencer?"

"Hiding?" Spencer giggled, his eyes rolling wildly. It was like watching a spooked horse, Cal thought. He had the impression that things were quickly slipping out of Spencer's control—if they ever had been in his control in the first place.

But if Spencer wasn't running things, who or *what* was? "I think you have a story to tell," he said. "Your sister's told hers, now why don't you tell us yours? We're not going anywhere."

"You're not going anywhere but *there*." Spencer waved the gun toward the spring where Frankie had drowned. His eyes lingered a moment on the dark pool with what looked like fear, and suddenly Cal understood.

"Who *else* is in there, Spencer? Who else is in the spring?"

"I don't . . . don't know what you're talking about." Spencer giggled again, crossing his legs like a little boy who's been holding it for too long. He rubbed his palm across his mouth and it came away bloody, as if he'd been biting the insides of his cheeks. His gun hand was shaking badly.

More than ever, Cal had the impression that Spencer was only a marionette—the face on something that had stayed hidden until now. But he was beginning to break down; a few more minutes of shaking and jiving like this and he would be completely useless. Then maybe the real puppeteer would have to show its face.

"Olivia wanted to tell what really happened to Frankie, didn't she?" Cal asked. "And you couldn't have that. Is that why you killed Mandy and the others? Was it because you were afraid they might talk? Why didn't you want anyone poking around the spring? What were you afraid they'd find?" Hot sweat rolled into Cal's eyes. How had it suddenly grown so warm in here?

"Find?" The grin was still painted on Spencer's face, but his eyes were physically bulging from their sockets as if a scream was trying to force its way through any orifice it could find. A shock seemed to run through him, and his body stiffened. "They'd find everyone."

"Everyone?" Cal asked, his stomach churning.

"Sheehy. The boys who worked the mine. They're all down there."

"Are you saying your grandfather . . ."

"Killed them? Yes. He killed them all, and then it was everyone into the pool." In the shadows cast by the lantern, the sweat pouring from Spencer's face looked like blood dripping down his cheeks.

Cal was stunned. Caleb Godwin, the millionaire, had murdered his own workers—his own partner? "Why?"

"Gold, of course." Spencer wiped his forehead with the back of one trembling hand. "Sheehy wanted to close the mine. He thought it was haunted. *Haunted*," Spencer tittered. "Little did he know. But my grandfather was a great man. He couldn't shut down the Seven Stars. He needed the money to build his empire—to build *our* empire."

"So he killed him and dumped his body in the spring?"

"It's really quite deep." The way Spencer's arms and legs jittered and shook reminded Cal of a robot falling apart. He could practically hear the springs and gears inside shrieking in protest. "My grandfather found this cavern shortly after they opened the mine. It was his secret."

"And the boys?" Cal asked. "Was that about the gold too?" In a way, Spencer's story made perfect sense. He wanted to protect his family's reputation. But it still felt wrong. If he'd wanted to hide the bodies, why kill the others? Why not just come in with a couple sticks of dynamite and blow the whole place up?

"Those thieving redskins were trying to steal the gold. Oh, they were tricky little devils. They tried to hide it in their mouths, between their toes—other places." Spencer's laughter was maniacal, his eyes burning. "They might have been able to fool Sheehy, but they couldn't fool my father."

Cal stiffened. "You mean *grandfather,* don't you?" Cal asked. Spencer's right eye began to twitch. Cal considered making a move, but although Spencer's hands were shaking wildly, his finger was still on the pistol's trigger.

"That's what I said. My grandfather."

"If you say so. But your father worked the mines too, didn't he?"

Cal had an idea that whatever had amplified Olivia's memories was also pulling Spencer's strings. Was it possible that whatever inhabited the Hall of Lost Souls liked the killings—wanted to brag about them? Could he force it to pull out whatever Spencer was hiding?

Carefully, as if handling hot coals, he asked, "Do you think maybe your father killed some of those boys too? That your grandfather showed him how?"

Spencer's face tightened. His breath was coming in hot, hard gasps. "You shut up about my father." Beside him, Cal heard Olivia moan, but he didn't dare shift his gaze from Spencer.

"What else did your father do?"

"Shut up!" Spencer clapped a hand to his mouth. Blood leaked between his fingers. But it was too late. Cal could feel his head starting to spin again. Could feel the same sense of vertigo pulling at his stomach—like a rollercoaster going through a series of corkscrews—that he had felt when Olivia began to tell her story.

"It's okay, Spencer." His hunch had been right. He could already begin to see Spencer's memories—hear the voices. "It's time to let it go."

"No!" Spencer wailed, but the images were starting up again—the cavern tapping deep into his subconscious.

CHAPTER 80

ALTHOUGH IT WAS STILL EARLY in the morning, the June sun was already beating down with a vengeance. It looked to be even hotter than the day before, when Olivia and her friends had disappeared. The parking lot was filled with dozens of vehicles—mostly big pickup trucks with dented beds and well-worn suspensions. Howard Godwin was forced to park his red '68 Cadillac off to the side in a grassy meadow.

As Howard and Spencer got out of their car, a hush fell across the crowd of people gathered around the picnic tables. Many of them had been there through the night, taking part in the search. Spencer could hear snatches of hushed conversation. *Olivia . . . his only daughter . . . must be devastated.*

They passed a group of men drinking handfuls of cold water from the creek and splashing it over their heads. The men looked exhausted, with dark circles around their eyes and stubble covering their cheeks. One of them glanced up and nodded.

"We'll find her, Mr. Godwin."

Howard nodded but didn't stop to talk. He was walking quickly, and Spencer was having a difficult time keeping up with his father's long, purposeful strides.

At the entrance to the Seven Stars, town constable Harvey Atkins was looking over a clipboard with three other men. All of them wore yellow hard hats with strap-on lamps. They looked up as the Godwins approached.

"Good to see you, Howard," Harvey said, his broad red face dripping with sweat.

Howard shook his hand. "I was out of town, but I came as soon as I received word." If anyone heard the tremor in his voice or noticed the way his hands shook, they surely wrote it off to the disappearance of his daughter.

"I was getting ready to send in another group. Why don't you grab yourselves a couple of hard hats and lamps?"

Spencer stopped to pick up a yellow helmet from the pile near the entrance, but his father jerked him by the arm. "No need," he said, waving a battered metal flashlight. "I think we'll head in on our own. I know where to look."

"Well, at least take a couple of other men with—" Harvey began, but Howard brushed past him.

Spencer had seen the outside of the Seven Stars once or twice on hunting trips with his father but had never actually been inside. Solid planks had been bolted across the entrance. That was fine with him—the place had always seemed a little creepy anyway.

Now the boards lay off to one side, like the scattered teeth of a deep black mouth. As they left the bright sunlight behind and stepped into the darkness, his father switched on the flashlight, its beam looking small and insubstantial to Spencer.

Behind them he heard one man mutter something like, "Strange one." One of the others said, "If your daughter was in there, you'd probably—" But the rest of his sentence was cut off as they headed into the main shaft of the mine.

Once inside the mine, Spencer stuck close to his father's back to avoid tripping over the uneven cross ties. He wished his father had allowed him to take a lamp. Unlike being outside at night, when there were at least the stars and moon to provide some light, the darkness in here was total. If he let his father get even a few feet ahead, he couldn't see the ground beneath his feet at all.

As they left the entrance behind, he could hear the occasional shouts of other searchers, calling out to the children or to each other. Chalk marks on the support beams seemed to indicate which areas had already been searched. But his father paid no attention to the other searchers or the chalk markings, moving from one tunnel to the next with an assurance that both impressed and unnerved Spencer. He would never be able to find his way back if anything happened to his father.

"Don't you think we should wait for some of the other men?" he asked, eyeing the complete darkness around him.

"No need to," his father barked, not bothering to look back.

The deeper into the mine they went, the more uneasy Spencer was becoming. Even at the age of eleven he recognized that his father's actions were strange. They weren't stopping to look for footprints or searching side tunnels. It was as if his father had a particular destination already in mind. They weren't even shouting. What if Olivia was somewhere nearby but couldn't see their light?

Cupping his hands to his mouth, Spencer called out at the top of his lungs, "Olivia, where are you?"

Instantly his father came to a stop, whirling around so that Spencer ran into his chest and nearly fell.

"Be quiet," he growled, his face hidden by the blinding beam of his flashlight.

"But I was just—" Spencer's words were cut off by his father's hand, which appeared from the darkness like magic, slapping him across the face.

"One more word from you," Howard said, his voice quivering in a way that Spencer had never heard before, "and I'll leave you here—alone." Without another word, his father spun around.

Cal instantly knew two things. Spencer was terrified—both of the mine and of his father's increasingly odd behavior—and the boy was too scared to admit the extent of his fears to anyone, even himself.

Spencer knew that something was wrong with his father. He'd known it for at least a month. He didn't think Olivia had noticed yet; she was too young. Still, more than once over the past few weeks he'd caught her studying their father with an expression of watchful distrust. So maybe she wasn't too young to have at least an inkling, after all.

His mother had noticed—of that he was sure. He'd overheard her talking on the phone to Dr. Galovich just last week. Dr. Galovich was the man who'd treated Grandpa Godwin when he had started acting funny. Not funny in a joking way, but funny in a scary way. "Crazy as a bedbug," his father had said when Grandpa wasn't around.

When Mother got off the phone, she was crying. Spencer had tried to sneak from the room without her notice but she'd spotted him as he edged toward the door. He'd expected her to be angry at his spying, but instead of punishing him she'd swept him into her arms, patting his hair and whispering, "My poor baby, my poor, poor baby," over and over again.

Dr. Galovich had arrived the next day in his dark suit and tie. But Howard had sent him away, screaming that if he ever came back, he'd shoot him dead. Two days later, a nanny had arrived, and their father told them that Mother was very sick. He'd sent her up to Greenwood, where she could get better. Olivia didn't know what Greenwood was, but Spencer did—and he also knew who *should* have been sent there.

These thoughts weighed heavily on Spencer's mind as he followed his father's dark figure deep into the side of the mountain. As they slipped into an especially tight passageway, so low that his father had to actually duck his head to enter it, a powerful stench assaulted their nostrils.

"What—" Spencer began to whisper, but his father shot him a dark glare that instantly silenced his question.

Now his father began to move more carefully, pausing at each bend in the passage to listen before continuing on. Unexpectedly the passage opened out into a cavern that smelled to Spencer like years' worth of dirty diapers had been stored there. It sounded like something was moving around near the ceiling, but his father took no notice.

They were halfway across the cavern, their feet kicking up small white clouds of some powdery substance that coated the ground, when, without warning, Howard froze. He cocked his head to one side. Behind him, Spencer froze as well.

What were they listening for? Spencer wondered. And then suddenly, he heard it too. It sounded like a little girl crying. Spencer's heart leaped in his chest. His father had done it. As if guided by an internal compass, he'd found the lost children! Spencer drew in a breath to shout. But before he could make a sound, his father slapped a rock-hard palm across his mouth and dragged him from the cavern.

CHAPTER 81

"HOLD ON TO MY BELT," Howard said, and without turning to see if his son obeyed, he began to run through the dark passage.

Spencer—half running, half dragged—clung for dear life to the black leather strap that his father had used to whip him with more than once. A thousand questions flooded his mind. *Where were they going? Why had they left Olivia and the others? Why did his father seem so afraid?* But he dared not ask any of them. His father had threatened to leave him, like the woodcutter in the Hansel and Gretel fairy tale, and he was coming to believe that it had not been an idle threat.

Sometime over the last few minutes they had left the mineshafts with their squared walls and supporting timbers behind and turned off into a series of smaller passages. Ahead of him, he could hear his father muttering to himself. Although the words were unclear, the tone terrified Spencer. It was the same tone his grandfather had used when he'd begun to go mad.

They squeezed their way past a tight opening, and immediately the walls fell away. Spencer gasped. They were standing in some kind of huge cavern. Rock formations rose from the ground and stretched up toward the ceiling. But most surprising, after all that time in the dark, was how everything glowed.

"Yes. Yes," his father cackled, scurrying past the glowing rock. "Safe, I'm still safe."

Spencer clung to the back of his father's belt, his eyes growing wide. This place . . . there was something so wrong about it. Didn't his father notice how the rocks seemed to have faces? Couldn't he hear the voice in the air? Something brushed against the back of his neck, and he shrank away from its ice-cold touch.

"Yes, I'm—No!" his father screeched, skidding to a stop. Spencer stumbled past him and nearly rolled down a steep embankment. In the glow of his father's light, he could see a little boy sitting on an outcropping of rock behind a pool of water. The boy's face was deathly pale, his dark eyes like bright round coals against the white flesh. His hair was plastered to his head like a helmet. But it was his mouth that Spencer noticed.

The boy's lips moved, but no sound came out. Finally a mew like a newborn kitten escaped his lips. "He-lp . . . me," he squeaked. It was Frankie Zoeller. He was shivering, and his clothing looked soaked. He pointed down into the water.

Howard lowered the beam of his flashlight to the pool, and for a moment Spencer couldn't understand what he was seeing. Something was floating on the surface. Something that looked like a pile of old rags. As if unseen hands had grasped it from beneath the inky depths, it rolled over, and Spencer's mind snapped. He wouldn't accept it—couldn't accept it.

He would not allow himself to believe that staring up at him like the underbelly of some rotting, bloated fish were the dead, clouded eyes of his own mother.

CHAPTER 82

HEATHER CORSON WAS JUST COMPLETING her final round of the afternoon—already planning an evening of *Buffy the Vampire Slayer* reruns and white chocolate macadamia cookies—when she stopped by the old man's room.

"Two Bears," she murmured, glancing at his chart. What an interesting name. It sounded kind of like an ally Buffy might meet. *Buffy and Two Bears team up to save Sunnydale from a demon Willow accidentally summons from a malevolent microwave.* That was actually pretty good. She should be writing scripts instead of taking temperatures and checking bedpans.

Then she remembered that there weren't any new Buffy episodes. Why was it that all the really good shows were pulled off the air, while the garbage seemed to run forever? Like those reality shows her husband liked so much, where the contestants all seemed like such scum. Well at least there was still *Supernatural.* Those Winchester brothers were smoking hot.

Anyway, it didn't look like Two Bears had any demon fighting in his near future. In fact, if you wanted her opinion—which no one ever seemed to—Mr. Two Bears didn't have much of *anything* in his future. According to his chart, he'd been going downhill pretty quickly since this morning. At a little after eleven his breathing had become erratic and they'd put him on a ventilator. His vitals didn't look any too good either.

It was a shame. Even with the bandages across much of his face, he was a handsome man—rugged in a Clint Eastwood kind of way. Old, she thought, but probably tougher than most guys half his age. She didn't know what he'd done for a living, but she was willing to bet he wasn't an accountant—or a fat TV executive who took away all the best shows.

She clipped his chart to the foot of his bed and was just walking back out the door when she thought she heard a voice. She turned around to check the television, wondering if someone had left it on with the volume turned way down low, but the green power light was off.

It must have been the storm, she decided. It had been a really nasty day, and of course she had taken her car through the Scrub and Shine just the day before. That was her kind of luck, all right. Glancing out the window at the blowing curtains of rain, she was hoping for a clearing just long enough to let her run out to her car without getting soaked, when she heard it again.

It sounded like someone whispering. But there was no one else in the room, except for the old man. And it couldn't have been him. He was out cold—looked like he might even be in a coma—and had a tube running down his throat. No way he was whispering secrets to anyone. And yet—

She stepped closer to his bedside, and sure enough his lips were moving. She leaned her head close to his mouth but couldn't make out what he was saying. It sounded like mumbo jumbo—the kind of stuff they always said on *Buffy* to send demons back to their infernal lairs. And it was giving her the willies.

Suddenly she remembered the stories the other nurses had been telling this morning about what had put this guy here in the first place, and she backed away from his bed. The hair on the back of her arms was standing straight up like little antennas, and the fillings in her teeth were actually beginning to buzz.

Afraid to let him out of her sight for even a minute, Heather backpedaled toward the door. It wasn't until she was completely into the hallway that she turned and ran, her shoes squeaking on the tile floor.

"Doctor," she shouted. "Doctor, come quick!"

CHAPTER 83

THE FIRST THING CAL BECAME aware of was someone screaming. For one fearful moment, he thought he himself was screaming. The sight of those eyes—those blank, dead eyes—staring up at him from the black pool had been so bad. It had been so much like his nightmares of Kat that, given any more time, he would have screamed. But someone had beaten him to it.

"What's happening?" It was Olivia. Her voice bounced off the ceiling of the cavern, shattering into a million echoes. "What's happening to him?"

Cal followed the direction of her terrified eyes, and all the blood in his body seemed to piston up into his brain with so much force that he was surprised the top of his head didn't simply explode.

It was Spencer. He was writhing on the ground, his body bucking and flopping like a fish on dry land. Only it didn't look like Spencer anymore. In fact, it scarcely looked human at all. His contorted face reminded Cal of a rubber mask twisted by the unseen hands of a cruel child. The surface of his skin bubbled and rippled with hundreds of black thumb-sized lumps.

"Do something!" Olivia screamed again. She was struggling to get free, but her hands and feet were tied too well.

Cal was no longer listening to her, though. He had spotted his pistol lying on the ground only a few feet away. "My gun! Get my gun," he shouted, looking to Esther and her nephew. Neither of them seemed to hear him. Their eyes, filled with equal parts fear and revulsion, were locked on Spencer.

Cal tried to get to his feet, but after sitting with his legs twisted awkwardly beneath him for so long, he'd lost all feeling from his thighs down. Instead he scooted himself backward across the cavern floor, until his fingers touched the cold metal of the pistol. Lowering his body, he managed to grab the barrel of the gun. Now if he could just get to his keys.

His eyes searched the shadowy floor for his belt. It had been right there just a few minutes before. How could it have disappeared? Then he saw it, several feet away, hung up on the edge of a small stalagmite. Spencer must have kicked it during his struggles.

"Cal, look out!" At Olivia's warning, Cal looked up just in time to see Spencer coming toward him. Although Spencer's flesh still roiled with what looked like swarms of black spiders crawling just beneath the skin, he was on his feet and coming fast. His hands rose up above his head, and Cal saw that he was holding a rock nearly the size of a loaf of bread.

Cal twisted around, trying to reach the trigger of his gun, while at the same time opening a line of fire with his wrists still cuffed behind his back. His hands were damp with sweat, and even as his finger touched the trigger he felt the pistol's grip beginning to slide from his palm. He tried to squeeze off a shot, but the gun slipped through his fingers before he could get enough pressure.

He just managed to catch the gun before it hit the ground, but it was too late. Spencer was already on top of him, swinging the rock down with deadly force.

CHAPTER 84

"When did this begin?" Dr. Simmons read the old Indian's chart, checking the monitors with a worried expression on his face.

"I don't know for sure. I was just finishing my rounds a few minutes ago when he started—" But she didn't need to go any farther. They could both hear him now, even without leaning over his bed. He was saying the same unintelligible words over and over. It sounded like he was repeating some kind of chant. She didn't know how he could manage to talk with a tube shoved down his throat—but he was, and it was scaring the wits out of her.

"His blood pressure's up, and I don't like the look of his heart rate. Get Nurse Beecher in here and bring me—" Dr. Simmons stopped speaking as the old man's legs began to jerk up and down on the bed. His right arm flailed, ripping the tubes from his wrist, and his head slammed up and down against the pillow.

"He's convulsing," the doctor shouted, grabbing the IV stand before it could fall onto the bed.

Heather reached for the old man's arm, trying to keep him from injuring himself, but it was like trying to hold on to a jackhammer. She was thrown back against the wall.

"Get security," Dr. Simmons hollered, trying to hold the old man down and not succeeding any better than she had. "And bring me ten milligrams of Diazepam STAT!"

CHAPTER 85

TOO LATE. As CAL DROPPED his shoulder and began to roll, he knew that there was no way to avoid Spencer's crushing blow. He heard the sound of screaming somewhere in the distance, but it seemed far away and unimportant. He had seen the rock coming down on him, instinctively calculated the time it would take to avoid it, and knew that he would never make it. After nearly thirty years living as a cop, he was going to die as a cop.

These thoughts raced through Cal's mind in the fraction of a second it took to duck his head. And yet as he hit the ground, the concussion that should have killed him—*would* have killed him—never came. He somersaulted across the floor of the cavern, trying desperately to maintain his hold on the gun, and came up staring at Spencer.

For a moment he couldn't understand what he was seeing. As if he had suddenly been frozen in time, Spencer was standing rigid. His arms were still outstretched only inches above where Cal's head had been. The boulder was still in his grip. But he wasn't moving. The only sign of movement in his entire body was the barely discernible quivering of his arms.

Then, with grinding slowness, as if his neck were made of concrete instead of bone and sinew, he turned his head and looked at Cal. His eyes bulged like a bodybuilder hoisting a great weight, the lantern's glow reflecting off the beads of sweat that coated his forehead.

Distantly Cal felt something in his pants pocket growing warm against his leg, but he paid it no attention. He was too mesmerized by what he was witnessing.

One by one, Spencer's fingers released the rock. As it dropped to the ground, he took his head in his hands and began to squeeze.

"No, Daddy," Spencer moaned. "No, please don't make me kill Frankie. Please, I don't . . ." His body shook as though he was struggling against some incredible force. His eyes looked up to meet Cal's.

What Cal saw there took his breath away. The eyes that met his were no longer those of a crazed man. They were not the eyes of an adult at all. Instead, staring out at him from the ravaged face were the wide, desperate eyes of a frightened little boy. They were the eyes of the eleven-year-old Spencer who had stared down at his dead mother. The child who had been forced by his own father to kill another child.

"Please . . ." he whispered to Cal, his voice barely audible. A tremor rattled through his body, and for a moment it looked like he would simply shake apart. Then he seemed to pull himself back together. A single tear rolled from his right eye and, drawing each word from some inner reserve of strength, he whispered again, "Please . . . kill . . . me."

CHAPTER 86

THE DEMON CONTROLLING SPENCER GODWIN was not used to being resisted. At least not after it had taken full possession of a body. It had been thousands of years since the dark power had faced any real opposition— so long that it had nearly forgotten how to deal with resistance. And yet now—during what should have been a moment of glory—this pitiful, weak-minded man was fighting back.

How could this have happened? When the boy had been brought here at a tender age and in a moment of weakness by his father, the demon had slipped into him so easily he might not even have known it was there. He had been so pliable, so easy to manipulate, that the demon had let down its defenses. Then, almost without warning, Spencer had turned. It could feel him breaking free.

A shudder of fear ran through the darkness. It had been tricked— tricked by the tiresome lawman and by its own ego into stretching its human host too far. It had pushed the human until he not only broke—which was to be expected—but actually rebelled, which was unthinkable.

This cavern was its seat of power. For more than two millennia the demon had called it home, seducing the weak with power, the greedy with riches. It had inhabited the bodies of Indians until they refused to come near. It had bided its time, living in the bodies of the bats and any other mammals unwary enough to enter into its trap.

Until, as it knew would eventually happen, the white man arrived. Caleb Godwin had come searching for gold. His desperate desire for wealth had provided the door the darkness used to enter him. It had simply been a matter of playing on that need, cankering his soul with fear and envy, until he began to bring the others.

He had fed the demon's bloodlust for years, bringing his partner and the sweet Indian boys whose fear it drank in so readily. When Caleb's mind had begun to fail, he passed the darkness on to his son. Howard Godwin had been just as greedy, just as hungry for power as his father. But then his mind had snapped. The demon convinced him that his wife had betrayed him, knowing that it would be the ideal way to move on to his son.

What it hadn't expected was his daughter. Howard had left the mine entrance open after bringing his wife, and like little mice the children had come traipsing in. It had been a simple matter of finding the one who craved power and using him to lure all the others here to the cavern.

But with Frankie something had gone wrong. For some reason the boy had been beyond the dark power's reach. Despite his fears, the dark power had been unable to get to the boy—and because of Frankie's pure presence, the demon had been unable to fully reach the others. Even after Howard had forced Spencer to kill the boy, Frankie had remained apart. It could feel him, could sense his presence, but it couldn't touch him—until Spencer provided the link it needed.

If the darkness couldn't break Frankie, it would break his mother's spirit and body while he watched. It had been so easy to play on her hate, to trick her into thinking she was seeing her son. What made it even sweeter was that even as the darkness used Spencer to kill the others one by one—despite Frankie's warnings—the boy's mother continued to think it was her own son taking his revenge.

Its plan had gone perfectly. The demon had lured Esther and her dimwitted nephew here into its lair, knowing instinctively that if the boy saw his mother murder Olivia, it would finally break him. When Spencer then killed Esther and her nephew in turn, it would only be that much better.

It had come so close. Even with the lawman's interference it might have succeeded—except, without any warning, Spencer had rebelled. He was slipping through the demon's grasp, and there was nothing the demon could do about it.

Now its anger was kindled. The dark power's fury had been awakened, and its wrath would spare no one. It would escape the body of this weakling. There were others here. The sister would be amusing . . . it hadn't inhabited a woman for a while. Or the feeble one—he would do until it could find another more capable host.

But the lawman would suffer worst. It would make him feel pain as he had never imagined pain could feel. It would flay his agonized flesh over burning coals. And when his physical being finally collapsed, it would trap his soul here with all the others. He had so many fears to prey on. Here in the dark, he would be the demon's to do with as it pleased forever.

CHAPTER 87

"Please . . . kill . . . me."

Even as his heart screamed *no*, Cal's finger found the trigger of his gun. Having given up any hope of understanding what was going on, he was relying solely on his cop's instincts. And his instincts told him that not to shoot would be to condemn them all to something worse than just death.

Spencer had reopened the cuts on the back of Cal's head when he'd knocked him out, and now as Cal tried to aim the gun with his hands still locked behind his back, he could feel the room starting to swim. Squinting his eyes, he tried to steady his vision. "Let it be quick," he whispered.

As he squeezed the trigger, something that looked like an inky black cloak uncoiled itself from Spencer's body. For the briefest instant, he saw what looked like relief cross the man's face, and then the pistol kicked in his hand. Spencer's body spun around before dropping to the floor.

"Leave her alone!" Esther cried.

Cal turned just in time to see a dark human-like shape drifting toward Olivia. He shot at it, but the bullet passed harmlessly through the figure as if Cal had fired at a plume of smoke.

The rock formations had begun to glow again around the cavern as the shrieks of the black specter filled the room. The air was glowing too, thickening like some radioactive broth. Ignoring the pins and needles that stung his legs and feet and the way the floor spun beneath him, Cal got to his feet and began to run toward Olivia.

Before he could take two steps, he was lifted from the ground and thrown across the cavern. The pistol flew from his hands. Lights flashed in front of his eyes as his body hit the wall and slid to the floor. Esther and Olivia were both screaming now as Larry swung his fists at the black cloud. Larry's blows didn't appear to have any effect. Cal tried to sit up.

Kill you . . .

Something brushed against Cal's back.

Bite you . . .

An invisible hand pushed against his chest, knocking him onto his back.

Eat you . . .

A cold wind blew across his ear.

Cal turned and saw his belt only a few feet away. If he could just get his hands free, he could carry Olivia from the cavern before that thing could hurt her.

He started to crawl to his belt, but something held him back. Dozens of unseen hands pulled at his legs and arms. The raw stench of putrid flesh filled his nostrils.

Across the room Olivia was screaming. Cal could hardly see her through the cloud of darkness that surrounded her head and body.

"Leave . . . her . . . alone," a voice echoed across the chamber.

Cal stopped reaching for his keys and froze. It was Frankie. Standing at the edge of the pool, he was barely visible, but the glowing haze burned away where he stood.

"Frankie?" Esther stood wide-eyed.

"Go away!" The specter's voice split the air, sounding like rocks being crushed into dust. "The woman is *mine*."

"Go back to where you came from." Frankie's ghost stepped toward Olivia and his mother, his voice high but strong. With each step he took he became more real, more there. It was like watching a Polaroid picture develop.

"No! I *need* her," the dark presence howled.

Frankie held one small hand out toward his mother; a flare of light shot out from the crown of her head to his fingertips. Now he was actually brighter than the lantern. The glow surrounding him extended to Olivia and then to Esther and Larry, forcing the dark cloud back in front of it. Cal found that he could barely stand to look directly at the boy's shining figure.

"You can't have her," Frankie called. His voice filled the room.

The ground began to tremble violently beneath Cal's feet, and the whole cavern started shaking. He heard what sounded like a city bus being ripped in two as half a dozen sharp spears fell from the ceiling. As he watched, the walls began to crack and shatter around him.

Hurricane-force wind blew through the cave, knocking Cal flat to the ground. He saw Olivia picked up and tossed across the room. Larry reached out to take his aunt's hand, but they were both thrown to the floor.

"If I can't have her," the voice screeched, "no one will."

Cal rolled to one side. Something on his right leg burned like fire.

And at that moment a voice exploded in his head.

CHAPTER 88

"I CAN'T HOLD HIM!" Two orderlies, a doctor, and a nurse were trying to keep the old man down. He shouldn't have had the strength to sneeze, and yet hanging on to him was like wrapping your arms around the neck of a Brahma bull.

Dr. Simmons had hit him with 120 milligrams of Diazepam, yet the old man had managed to jerk every wire and tube loose from his body.

Without warning, Two Bears sat straight up, sending the doctor flying over the foot of the bed. His right hand pushed the 200-pound orderly holding him aside as if he was a child, and he yanked the breathing tube from his throat.

In a voice that woke every patient on the floor, he screamed, "Now!" And every piece of equipment in the room exploded.

CHAPTER 89

"Now!" The voice was like a thunderclap inside Cal's head.

"Two Bears," he whispered, and his hand went to his pocket. Up until this point he'd forgotten all about the talisman the old Indian had given him. Twisting his arms around to one side, he was able to reach into his right pocket. As soon as his fingers closed around the necklace, the hands holding his arms and legs disappeared.

"The pool!" Frankie screamed. The black cloud cycloned around him. "Hurry," he cried out. "I can't hold onto it much longer."

Getting to his feet, Cal stumbled to the edge of the water. Rocks were falling everywhere around him, and so much dust filled the air it was almost impossible to see. Turning his back, hands still cuffed, he flicked the necklace toward the pool. His throw was short, and for a minute he didn't think the talisman was going to go in. Then it caught the incline and slid down into the water.

Instantly water began to geyser out of the pool. A white plume of steam rose into the air. As Cal watched, the plume formed itself into the image of a huge silver grizzly bear. Frankie dropped his hands, and the black cloud around him shot straight up into the air. In a flash, the silver bear was on it. With a furious roar, it wrapped its powerful paws around the demon.

"Let go!" The frenzied screech seemed to come from the very earth itself, and for a moment Cal thought he could see the cloud twist into a horrible face, contorted with anger and desire. It tried to pull itself free, darting toward Larry, but the bear's grip was too powerful.

"Stop!" the black nightmare howled. The bear was drawing back toward the pool now, the straining mass in its hold squirming and writhing to get away.

"No. No. *Nooooooo*!" Hot bolts of bright green lightning shot through the air. A ball of green fire rolled only inches away from Cal, leaving a trail of scorched earth behind it.

But the bear was at the pool now, the water roiling and churning around it. It held the dark shape above its head in both paws. The demon gave one last tug, screaming in fury, and then both it and the bear disappeared beneath the water. As soon as the dark mass hit the surface of the water, the pool erupted in a great green wall of flame, and the entire ceiling above collapsed into it.

"Get out!" Frankie screamed. Cal could scarcely see him through the floating dust and falling rock, and he couldn't see Olivia at all. With a thundering crash, one wall of the cavern collapsed, washing a wave of rocks and debris all around them.

Stumbling back through the rubble, he searched frantically for his belt. He was afraid that it had been buried in the falling rubble, but then he saw a flash of silver. It was the key ring. Dropping to his knees, he found the key to his cuffs and socked it into place. First the left and then the right cuff clicked open, and his hands were free.

He raced back to Frankie's light, which was fading just as quickly as it had appeared, and found Olivia lying on the ground. She was bleeding from a cut over her eye, and her pale white face was covered with dust. *She's dead,* he thought, his heart plummeting. Then she opened her eyes.

"Help me," she called weakly to him.

She was alive! After everything they'd been through, the sound of her voice brought back that fact. They were *all* alive. Despite his pain and weariness, the thought made him almost giddy.

"Count on it, little lady," he shouted, his hoarse voice just audible above the roar around them. He lifted Olivia into his arms and turned to run.

"Come on." Larry was pulling on his aunt's hand. But her eyes were locked onto her son. Tears dripped down the craggy topography of her wrinkled face.

"We have to go," Cal shouted. "This whole place is coming down."

Frankie reached out to his mother. The fading glow from his fingers lit Esther's face. He leaned forward, kissed her cheek, and whispered something into her ear.

Esther's eyes lit up, and for the first time that Cal could remember, a smile crossed her face.

"Let's go!" Larry screamed, pulling at her arm. She nodded, wiping a dusty hand across her eyes. She waved a last good-bye to her son, and together the four of them raced from the cavern.

EPILOGUE

"CAN WE PLAY WITH HIM?" The little girl with the long, dark eyelashes asked. Her younger brother peeked out from behind her.

Cal looked to Ben and LuAnn Meyers. LuAnn nodded her assent, and Ben, who was still in a wheelchair, nodded as well.

"Sure," Cal said to the kids. "But *he's* a she."

"Oh." The little girl looked slightly skeptical. "What's *her* name?"

Cal glanced at Olivia. They'd arranged a kind of a joint custody of the old Indian's dog.

"Well," she said, "it used to be Pepper. But she seems to like Little Bear better."

"Little Bear," Ben murmured. "I think he would have liked that."

Another car pulled up a few yards away from the picnic table where they were all sitting. Tamara Rucker got out with two her sons. "Cool dog," the oldest one said, tossing a black and gold plastic disk through the air. "Does she play Frisbee?" Instantly Little Bear gave chase.

"Well, she'll catch it," Cal laughed. "But I can't promise that she'll give it back."

Cal waved to Sam and pointed toward the car they had arrived in. "That thing got an alterbator?" he asked.

"Alter-*na*-tor," the boy carefully enunciated, looking up to his mother.

"He's been working on that," Tamara smiled. She turned and watched her sons as they joined the Meyers children in chasing after Little Bear, who had run off with their Frisbee, then took a seat next to LuAnn as introductions were made.

Tamara nodded her approval at the park. It was nice, with a big duck pond and lots of shady benches. "I'm glad you decided to have this get-together here instead of . . ."

She didn't complete the thought, almost as if saying the name would bring everything back all over again. But she didn't need to. They all knew what she meant.

"No, I won't ever go there again." Olivia crossed her arms and shivered. It was early October, and the air had started to get a bite to it, but her shiver had nothing to do with the weather.

"I hear they've fixed up the place now that it's become something of a *tourist attraction*." Cal gave the last two words the same tone of voice he might have given the word *cesspool*. "But I've got no interest in checking it out."

There was a moment of silence as they all sat quietly sipping their drinks and remembering.

"Did anyone, you know . . . ever try to go back in?" Ben was the first to ask the question, but Cal suspected that LuAnn and Tamara had both been wondering the same thing.

"No. The cavern was just the beginning. Most of the mine ended up collapsing as well," Cal said. "We were lucky to get out at all."

"Did they ever find . . . ?" Ben asked, looking at Olivia.

She shook her head.

"I'm sorry," he said softly.

"Don't be." Olivia looked over the pond at a pair of swans that swam gracefully across its surface. Her thoughts seemed far away. "Spencer died along with Frankie. What's buried back in that cave isn't my brother. It only looked like him."

There was another drawn-out silence in which the children's laughter and Little Bear's barks carried on the still autumn air. Finally, Olivia brushed back a lock of hair from her face and gave Cal an appraising look.

"The charcoal's probably about ready. You think you can manage to cook those steaks without incinerating them?" she asked.

"Hey, lady, just because you like your meat still mooing and grazing doesn't mean you can bad-talk my cooking prowess." He reached down to twist his ring before remembering that it was home in a jewelry box. Olivia noticed and gave him a small grin, biting her lower lip to keep from laughing.

"All right, big guy. Why don't you wheel Ben over there, and you men can show us womenfolk your *prowess*."

"How'd I get suckered into inhaling charcoal fumes?" Ben asked mournfully. But he didn't complain when Cal wheeled his chair over to the barbecue. Cal knew that Olivia was giving him a chance to speak with Ben privately, while she did the same with LuAnn and Tamara.

The steaks were perfectly marbled New York strips Cal had picked up from a local butcher who gave police officers a special deal. As he laid them on the grill, they spit and sizzled nicely.

Ben glanced back over his shoulder toward Olivia.

"She seems to be doing better."

"Yeah," Cal nodded, evening out the coals. "She had a rough go of it for a while. Finding that kind of thing out about your family would be tough on anyone, and her brother had her doped up on so much medication that it was a wonder she could think at all. It's been hard, but she's been drug free for nearly two months now."

"What about her father?"

"He's taken up permanent residence at Greenwood. In the state-funded wing," Cal said with a trace of a smile. What he didn't say was that Dickey Jordan was recovering in the private side of Greenwood, courtesy of the Godwin estate.

Ben rubbed at the cast that still covered most of his right leg, his head lowered. When he looked up again, Cal could see the deep pain that hovered just beneath the surface of this afternoon's activities. That was part of the reason Olivia had suggested they all get together. The wounds from what had happened to them were slowly healing, but the infection needed to be aired out—needed to be *talked* out.

"So it was Spencer all along?" Ben's words came slowly, like pulling an especially stubborn splinter. "He killed everyone?"

Cal studied the glowing coals before nodding. "I imagine that from the day he saw his mother dead—the day his father forced him to kill Frankie—Spencer was never really himself again. He became a puppet of the . . . *demon.*" The word still came to his lips with difficulty, but he didn't know what else to call the evil he'd seen with his own eyes.

"Spencer's body was the vehicle it used to kill Mandy, Ezra, Theresa, and Two Bears," he continued. "By then Spencer was completely under the demon's control. I don't think he knew until right at the very end that he still had the power to stand against its will."

"But the voice I heard on the mountain was a child's," Ben argued, shaking his head. "And what about in the hospital? Spencer didn't have the strength to throw Two Bears five feet, let alone across the room."

Cal shrugged his shoulders. "I'm the wrong person to ask. Up until all this happened, I'd have bet my pension that ghosts were no more real than the Loch Ness Monster, and the only monsters I believed in were the kind I could throw in jail."

"All I can tell you is that whatever was inside that cave—inside Spencer—had powers I can't even begin to imagine. If it could make me think I was seeing and talking to my wife, it stands to reason that it could have made you think you were hearing a child's voice."

Cal flipped the steaks and poured his secret marinade over the tops of them, watching the fames lick at the dripping sauce. The smell of seared beef rose off the grill in waves. Over at the table the women were deep in their own conversation as they spread out paper plates and cups.

Ben scratched his leg inside the cast with a long piece of coat hanger he kept for just that purpose. "Then Frankie's ghost, and the clues, were all to make us think Frankie was committing the murders?"

"Yes and no," Cal said. "Based on what you've told me and the conversations I've had with the surviving spouses, I believe that Frankie appeared to each of you. My guess is that he was trying to warn you. He appeared to me as well to point me in the right direction.

"When the demon realized what Frankie was up to, it decided to use your guilt and fear against you. But the clues were also designed to throw our investigation off track. It wanted me to believe that Esther and her nephew were the murderers. It worked."

"But why now?" Ben asked "Why after all these years?"

"I'm not sure I can give you a nice, tidy answer," Cal said. He and Olivia had spent countless hours discussing that very subject, and the best they'd been able to come up with was a theory.

"Part of it was that after years of repressing what happened to Frankie, Olivia finally remembered. She wanted to go to the authorities and tell them the truth. Spencer found a doctor to convince her that it was a false memory. For the right price, the psychiatrist was more than willing to put her on enough medications to keep her in a permanent daze."

Ben laughed ruefully. "I think we've all seen our share of shrinks." Then his smile disappeared as he ran his fingers through his hair. "She was the only one with enough guts to come forward. If the rest of us—no, strike that—if *I* had come forward with the truth about Frankie, this never would have happened."

"I wouldn't be so sure." Cal laid down the tongs he'd been using to turn the steaks and fixed his gaze firmly on Ben's. "That's the second part of my theory. It's not much more than a seat-of-the-pants hunch, but it feels right. What if this wasn't really about covering up the death of Frankie and the others at all? What if that was just an excuse to get Spencer and Esther together?"

Ben shook his head, rubbing his leg with a grimace. "I don't follow you."

Cal turned his eyes toward the canyon, toward the ruins of the mine. "After all those years trapped in the mine with that evil, Frankie's spirit never became corrupted the way so many of the others did. His was the only soul that *didn't* get lost. Maybe there was something about him—an innocence, a lack of guile, I guess you might say, that insulated him from the demon's power. He would have been a constant bee in the demon's bonnet, a reminder that it was not all-powerful."

Ben scratched with the hanger, considering what Cal had just said. From up in the canyon came the deep whistle of a train. "You think this was really all about getting to Frankie, then?"

Cal shrugged. "Spencer kept track of Esther over the years. He knew how strong her hate still was. Maybe the demon saw a chance to use that hate against her own son."

"So the demon used Spencer to convince Esther that Frankie was the one killing the others—for revenge."

Cal nodded. "And it convinced Spencer that killing Mandy, Ezra, you, and the others was the only way to keep the Godwin name unblemished. Spencer planned on having Esther and her nephew kill Olivia in the mine. After she was dead, he could have killed them both and laid the blame of all the other murders at their feet. If it hadn't been for Frankie, it probably would have worked."

"Why did the demon need to give Spencer a reason at all? I mean, couldn't the demon just make him kill the others?" Ben asked, shaking his head.

Cal chuckled. "Like I said, you're asking the wrong guy." He looked back at Olivia, who, along with the other women, was unpacking salads from an ice chest. He tilted his head in her direction and looked back at Ben. "She doesn't think evil works that way. She says it can find your weak spots—tempt you—but that ultimately you have to go along with it for it to have power over you. Maybe that's why it had to offer her brother a reason, weak as it was."

Olivia looked up, noticed them watching her, and called out, "You'd better not be burning my steak."

"The steaks!" Cal yelped, nearly scalding his hand trying to get them onto a plate.

Ben grinned at the way Cal hopped to Olivia's orders. "You two seeing each other?"

Cal's face dropped, and he reached again for the wedding band that was no longer there. "I'd like to. And I'm pretty sure she would too, although what she sees in a guy like me is something I'll never understand. But . . . I just don't know . . ." He started to take the plate to the table, and Ben placed a hand on his elbow.

"That thing," he said, "the demon. Is it gone?"

Cal's eyes steeled, his fingers tightening on the edge of the plate. "I never believed in an afterlife until all this, and now . . . I guess I really don't have any choice. I still don't understand it all. But after twenty-some years as a cop, I can tell you one thing for sure. Evil never goes away completely."

* * *

"Good-bye, Chief." Tamara Rucker reached out to shake Cal's hand. Ben Meyers and his family had left earlier. As the sun began to set, the five of them and Little Bear were the only ones left in the park.

"Please, call me Cal," he said, taking her hand. "And you two," he looked down at Joshua and Sam, "feel free to come by the station sometime and I'll take you for a ride in my patrol car."

Joshua and his mother started toward the car, but Sam motioned for Cal to lean down. Standing on his tiptoes, he whispered into Cal's ear, "That guy who kilt my dad. You put him away. He won't hurt no one else ever again?"

"Yeah," Cal whispered back, hoping that what he said was the truth.

"Good." Sam turned to follow his mother back to the car and then stopped, his eyes deep and serious. "My mommy says that your wife is dead, too. Like my dad."

Cal nodded. "Yes, she is."

"Maybe she could say hi to him. You know, keep him company in heaven so he won't be lonely until I get there?"

"Yeah, maybe." Cal felt his eyes watering and quickly reached up with one hand to wipe them. "Maybe she can."

Sam bobbed his head and, without another word, ran to join his mother and brother. As they stood beneath the pink evening sky, watching the Rucker car drive away, Olivia slipped her hand into Cal's.

It was a strange sensation, holding the hand of a woman who wasn't Kat. It felt odd but also a little exciting. Still, there was a part of him that couldn't help wondering—couldn't help feeling guilty at feeling pleasure. Olivia squeezed his fingers and looked up at him, dark blue eyes reflecting the sunset.

"She's okay, you know," she said softly.

"I just wish I knew for sure," he said, staring out over the glassy water of the pond. "If she really is out there somewhere, I want to know that she's happy."

While Little Bear chased flying insects, they stood together, enjoying the cool breeze. Another few weeks and the last of the colored leaves would have dropped from the trees. Fall would give up its last hold to winter, and the snows would come. But for now, everything seemed still and perfect.

From the busy road beyond the parking lot, a vehicle turned into the park's entrance, its headlights two glowing eyes in the twilight's dusk. Cal recognized it instantly, and he and Olivia glanced toward each other. Although they'd both agreed to invite Esther and Larry to the picnic—knowing that the two of them had been duped as much as everyone else—neither Cal nor Olivia had really expected them to show up.

Larry pulled the truck up next to the edge of the grass but left the engine running. As he rolled down the window, Olivia called out to them, "Come on over. We've got more steaks, and the coals are still warm."

"No, we can't stay," Esther said, her face drawn. "I just . . ." She put one hand to her mouth, leaning on her nephew for support. "I just wanted to say thank you for what you done. For me and Larry . . . and for Frankie."

Cal and Olivia walked up to the truck, Little Bear at their heels. Cal put a hand on the window. "Come out, Esther, and sit with us. There really is plenty of food left, and we'd love to have you."

She shook her head. "Maybe some other time," she said, looking tired and embarrassed. "I need to give you something. Should have done it months ago, but my memory's not all it used to be."

She leaned across her nephew and handed Cal a scrap of paper.

"What's this?" he asked.

Sitting back, she pulled out a handkerchief and dabbed at her eyes. "When we were in the cavern, and everything was coming down, I . . . I didn't think I could leave my Frankie again. Not there in the dark all by himself. But then he kissed my cheek, and he whispered to me.

"He told me that he loved me and that he was all right now. He said him and the others was leaving that place." Esther cleared her throat, wiping at her tears as though they were some kind of annoying insects.

Now the tears were rolling down her wrinkled old cheeks. Cal swiped at his own eyes, not surprised to see that Olivia's cheeks were wet with tears as well.

"Then he told me one other thing. He said he had a message to pass on to you. Said you'd know who it was from. In all the excitement I forgot to tell you. But once I got home, I wrote it down." She glanced at the paper in his hands, and Cal unfolded it with trembling fingers.

He read it slowly, rereading it twice before handing it to Olivia. Esther's spidery handwriting was hard to see in the fading light, but the message was short. As Olivia read it, her face lit up with the same wonder that filled Cal's.

Tell him there are gardens here. Beautiful gardens.

"Does it mean anything to you?" Esther asked, her voice trembling.

"Yes." He nodded, his own voice husky with emotion. "It means everything."

ABOUT THE AUTHOR

Jeffrey S. Savage is the author of eight published novels, including the Shandra Covington mystery series, the Farworld fantasy series (writing as J Scott Savage), and the Case File 13 series from Harper. He lives in Utah and has a brilliant and beautiful wife, four delightful children, and a faithful border collie. He loves to hear from readers at jsavage@jeffreysavage.com.